Praise for Lorelei James's
Redneck Romeo

"Once again Lorelei James has given us a story that will resonate with so many people...she always manages to surprise, overwhelm, and give us a story like no other."

~ *Guilty Pleasures Book Reviews*

"I love this family and with *Redneck Romeo*, Ms. James tackles the last McKay left unmarried. It was guaranteed to be just as exciting as the others and I wasn't wrong. There's always something unexpected happening with this wild and crazy bunch..."

~ *Literary Nymphs Reviews*

"This book is beautifully written, the storylines flow seamlessly to weave the perfect picture of the McKay family we come to love and care about. [...] Haven't read the series yet? You are MISSING OUT!"

~ *Under the Covers*

"All in all, I enjoyed *Redneck Romeo* and the chance to get to know Dalton on a more intimate level. He was definitely not what I had expected and I was impressed with the depth of his character."

~ *Smexy Books*

"Whether they're pissed off at one another, teasing each other, or coming together in grief, Ms. James keeps the relationships real and emotional."

~ *The Good, The Bad and The Unread*

"Lorelei James makes it look so easy. Her books are beautifully written, her characters so charmingly developed, and her stories are just intense, with no gaps or mistakes."

~ *Mrs. Condit Reads Books*

"Lorelei writes their story in such a way that you can't help but root for them to make it."

~ *The Book Reading Gals*

Look for these titles by
Lorelei James

Now Available:

Redneck Romeo

Lorelei James

SAMHAIN PUBLISHING

Samhain Publishing, Ltd.
11821 Mason Montgomery Road, 4B
Cincinnati, OH 45249
www.samhainpublishing.com

Editing by Lindsey Faber
Cover by Scott Carpenter

First Samhain Publishing, Ltd. electronic publication: June 2013
First Samhain Publishing, Ltd. print publication: May 2014

Prologue

"Do you, Dalton Patrick McKay, take Addie Maureen Voorhees to be your lawfully wedded wife? To have and to hold, for better or for worse, for richer, for poorer, in sickness and in health, to love and to cherish, from this day forward, until death do you part?"

Dalton froze.

This was it. The minister's final words would pronounce them husband and wife and he would be tied to this woman permanently.

Dalton McKay, husband.

Jesus. That sounded all wrong. Really fucking wrong.

It's just momentary cold feet. Breathe. It'll pass.

But it didn't.

Sweat beaded on his brow, dampening the collar of the white tuxedo shirt choking him like a noose.

The flutter beneath his breastbone wasn't from nerves, but the gut instinct that'd never failed to warn him to cut his losses in playing cards.

The stakes were much, much higher now.

When that debilitating panic set in, his brain split into two warring camps. One side screamed at him to just say *I do* and be done with it. The other side, the side breaking out in hives at the very idea of forever, yelled at him to flee.

Say I do.

Run the fuck away.

He had been gazing at Addie's face, but at some point...his unfocused gaze had landed on the Bible digging into his forearm like a painful burr.

Dalton heard the whisper of fabric as members of the wedding party shifted nervously. The cloying scent of lilies caused his throat to swell, cutting off his air supply. The sunlight shining through the church's stained glass window threw fragmented strobe-light effects across the far wall.

And Addie's soft hand remained in his, awaiting the placement of the wedding band.

Wedding band. Married. To this woman. Forever.

Was he having a crazy booze dream after a night spent drinking too many Irish car bombs?

Or was he really standing before a minister, in front of a church packed with his and her family members, about to pledge his life and eternal love to Addie Voorhees? The town sweetheart whom everybody loved?

Yes.

No.

Dalton tried to track the source of that phantom voice. He lifted his head and looked across the altar.

In that moment he knew; he fucking *knew* he couldn't do this. This was all wrong. This marriage wasn't meant to be.

Please God, forgive me, for what I'm about to do.

His brother Tell cleared his throat behind him.

Addie squeezed his hand and whispered, "Dalton? Here's where you're supposed to say *I do*."

He finally met Addie's eyes. Loving brown eyes that would soon lose the look of adoration and fill with disbelief or hatred. Or both.

Dalton released her hand and whispered, "I can't."

"What?"

"I'm sorry, Addie. But this..."

"Stop it, Dalton, you're scaring me."

"I'm scaring myself."

"Why?"

"Because you're so great, in so many ways, but I can't marry you. I just...can't. I'm sorry."

Dalton gave in to his flight instinct, shouldering his brothers aside as he left the altar and slipped out the side door of the church.

Chapter One

Three years and four months later...

Bang bang bang. "Dalton! Come on man, open up. I know you're in there."

Dalton cracked one eyelid and cast a bleary eye at the alarm clock. Seven a.m. He yanked the quilt over his head and mumbled "fuck off" to Boden Hicks, the idiot beating on his door.

"McKay. I'm not fucking around. This is an emergency."

That hauled Dalton's ass out of bed. He unlatched the old-fashioned bolt and opened the door. "What's the emergency?"

Boden hustled inside but a gust of snow followed before he slammed the heavy oak door shut. He stamped his feet. "Damn snowstorm came from out of nowhere."

"You better not have tricked me out of bed to complain about the goddamned weather."

Boden shuffled over to the woodstove to warm himself, but it'd been a good ten hours since Dalton had loaded it up. "It's like a damn freezer in here."

"That's because I was sleeping. In my own bed, after roughing it on an elk hunt, remember?"

"Yeah, I remember. I'm just glad the hunting party made it out before this storm hit." Boden unzipped his parka and pulled out Dalton's cell phone, still attached to the wall charger. "Normally I could give a crap if you stay in bed a week after a hunt, but you left your phone charging at the lodge last night. The thing's been buzzing like crazy. When I unplugged it, I noticed you've got twenty-seven missed calls. So it's gotta be something important."

Dalton's stomach knotted. Since he had little to no cell service in the mountains, he forgot he even had a cell phone most of the time. Few people had his number—just his brothers, his mother, his cousin Sierra McKay, his accountant, his banker and his investment guys.

"Gimme that." Dalton scrolled through the missed calls. Twelve from Brandt, twelve from Tell, three from Sierra.

Had to be bad news if his family had reached out to him.

The family he hadn't seen in three years.

"What's going on?"

He glanced up at Boden. "No clue. I haven't bothered to set up my voice mail on this phone so I'll have to call to find out."

Boden sighed. "Speaking of...I wanted to make sure your two-way is charged. Since you have an issue with technology that allows people to get in touch with you."

"It's charged. I laid in a store of food before the huntin' trip so I can ride out the storm."

"Good. We're supposed to get a foot of snow today and maybe more tonight." Boden crouched in front of the woodstove and chucked kindling in the cold embers before setting the torch to the pile. "Might be a couple days before you can get out, if you need to go home."

Home. It didn't have the same connotation it once did. When it was all he'd known. "I'll let you know what's goin' on as soon as I know."

Boden piled several small logs in the black box before he stood. "You worried?"

Dalton shrugged.

But Boden didn't buy his act; he never had, which was why they'd become such good friends. "You want me to stick around?"

"Nah. I'll put on a pot of coffee before I call my brother." He smirked. "Get on back to the lodge. Bree would jam my nuts in a vise if you got snowed in with me instead of with her."

"Your nuts ain't ever gonna be anywhere near my wife's hands, McKay."

He laughed. "I know your kink doesn't extend to sharing."

"Damn straight." Boden zipped up his parka and slipped on his gloves. "You need anything, buzz us. If we don't answer right away—"

"I'll assume you're tied up. Or rather, you're tying Bree up."

As soon as Boden left, Dalton started coffee. Then he stripped off his long johns and took a cold shower. That ensured he'd be fully awake.

The main room of the three-room cabin had warmed up by the time he'd dressed. After downing two cups of coffee, Dalton stood by the window in the kitchen and called Brandt.

His oldest brother answered on the fourth ring. "'Bout damn time, Dalton. Where the hell have you been that you can't return a phone call?"

No doubt Brandt thought he was fucking off someplace. Little did he know how tiring it was leading a ten-day hunting party into the mountains. But Dalton no longer explained his life choices to anyone. "What's goin' on? I had twenty-four missed calls in the last twelve hours." No one knew Sierra had his number. His brothers would be pissed if they knew Dalton kept in better contact with Sierra than with them.

"Dad had a stroke."

Silence. Finally Dalton asked, "Is he okay?"

"He's alive, if that's what you mean. He's havin' difficulties talkin'. They're not sure if it's permanent. They're not too sure of anything at this point. So we—me'n Tell—are asking you to come home."

Dalton closed his eyes. He didn't want to play nursemaid to the man who'd made his life hell. Especially not after the last conversation they'd had, which was the biggest reason Dalton had left Sundance for good—not that he'd told his brothers or anyone else about what'd gone down. "I don't know if I can."

"Can't? Or won't?" Brandt demanded.

"Why do you want me there?"

"Hey, bro. Brandt put you on speaker phone," Tell said. "Look, we need you to help us make some decisions about Dad's care."

Dalton let his forehead rest against the frosted windowpane.

"We haven't seen you in over three years. It sucks that something like this had to happen for you to even consider comin' home. But we do need you here."

He pictured his brothers, Tell leaning against the window in the cab of Brandt's truck, his restless fingers tapping on his leg. Brandt seated behind the steering wheel, his posture stiff, arms crossed over his chest.

"When did this happen?" Dalton asked.

"Brandt got a call from the hospital in Spearfish yesterday morning. They wouldn't let us see him until late afternoon. Soon as we had some information, we tried calling you." Tell paused. "You ain't gotten any better at returning calls."

"But I did return it. Not fast enough for you?" he asked sharply. Jesus. Within two minutes of talking to his brothers he'd reverted to the defensive guy he'd left behind. He exhaled slowly. "Sorry. Cell service here is spotty."

"Where are you?"

Don't feel guilty they don't know. "Alder, Montana. We're in the midst of a blizzard so it might be a couple days before I can make it out of the mountains."

Silence.

"Has the doctor given you a time frame on how long he'll be in the hospital?"

"No," Brandt said. "But when Dad is discharged, it'll be to the rehab wing in a nursing home."

That oughta make Casper even more the patient from hell. "Sounds like it won't matter then if I'm not there for a couple of days. I'll let you know when I'm on my way."

"Sure. Will you be staying with one of us?" Tell asked.

"Nah. I've got it covered. Thanks though."

Neither of his brothers asked where he'd be bunking down, although he sensed they wanted to.

"Okay, then. I guess we'll see you when we see you."

"Yep. Later." Dalton hung up.

He stared out the window for the longest time, even though he couldn't see shit through the swirling snow.

But this storm wasn't anything compared to the one he faced in Sundance.

The blizzard lasted two days. On the morning of the third day Dalton packed up his stuff, closed up his cabin and headed down the mountain.

Once he had a clear cell signal, he gave Brandt a heads up he was on his way. Brandt said they'd moved Casper to the rehab wing and to meet them there.

Then he placed a call to Sierra.

She answered with, "I swear every time I call you and I don't hear back I live in mortal fear that you've disconnected from the world completely and you're out in the forest running naked with woodchucks and shit."

"Not hardly. I returned the calls in order of importance."

"So you've talked to your brothers?"

"Yeah. I'm on my way to Wyoming right now."

"They giving you grief about...well, everything?"

"They both knew it wouldn't take much for me to refuse to come back." He flipped on the defroster. "How'd you find out about Casper's stroke?"

"Keely. I knew your brothers would get a hold of you first, so my call isn't about your father."

"Then why did you call?" Dalton heard her take a deep breath and he went on full alert.

In a rush, Sierra said, "You've got to promise me that you won't get mad at me for what I'm about to tell you."

"No conversation ever ends well that starts that way."

"True, but I want you to remember I was only following your parameters. And I kinda hoped someone else would tell you about this, so I didn't have to. But then, you'd have to actually *talk* to someone who lives there, and we both know that's a rarity, so I guess it falls to me."

"You been drinkin'? 'Cause you ain't making a lick of sense. Quit dancing around the subject, college girl, and spill it."

"Rory is back in Sundance and working for Wyoming Natural Resource Council."

Everything switched into slow motion. Dalton couldn't breathe. Couldn't think. He had to pull onto the shoulder so he didn't wreck his truck.

"Dalton?"

"You said Rory is livin' in Sundance."

"Yes."

"With her fiancé?"

"No. She, ah, broke off the engagement."

"When?"

"Six months ago."

This was not happening. Sierra had *not* kept this information from him about Rory for half a goddamned year.

"Dalton. I know your head is about to explode—"

"Jesus, Sierra, do you fucking *think*? Why are you just telling me this now?" he roared. "Do you have any fucking idea—"

"That you've been holed up in the middle of freakin' nowhere moping because Rory got engaged to someone else? Why yes, I was completely aware of that little factoid, cuz."

Silence.

"Besides, you were doing your lumberjack gig and completely off the grid when Rory ended the engagement. I'll remind you of your zero tolerance policy—me not talking about Rory or sharing information about Rory's life was your *edict*, Dalton. I was just following your parameters. And now the parameters have changed."

"Seriously not fucking amused. Will you just get to the point?"

"I really have to point out that you and Rory will actually be in the same place for the first time in over three years?"

"Three years? Try *ten* years since she's lived there. I'da been in Sundance six months ago if I'd known she was there without some other asshole's ring on her finger," he snarled.

"Whoa. Take a step back, wolverine. I'm telling you now because maybe you're smart enough to handle it the right way this time."

"This time?" Dalton repeated sharply. "Don't make this out to be my fault. I offered her—"

"Don't snap at me or interrupt me again or I will hang up, understand?"

"Yeah, yeah, keep talkin'."

"Rory is my sister. You're my business partner and one of the few people I trust. I hate that I'm pulled between you two. It's time you manned up, Dalton. And don't remind me that you did that once three years ago after you walked out on your own wedding. Even you can admit it was piss poor timing on your part."

"But that bad timing didn't stop *her* from giving me an edict, did it?"

"Like I've told you ten thousand times, that wasn't an edict. Two years was a time line for Rory to finish grad school and a frame of reference for you to understand how important that was to her. You shouldn't have taken it as gospel."

"Then she shouldn't have given me false hope."

"Then you shouldn't have turned tail and run again," Sierra retorted. "Especially after you gave her false hope that things might finally change between you two."

Like he needed that reminder. "Does she know about Casper?"

"Doubtful. She's been out of town and she stays out of McKay gossip completely."

Then Rory wouldn't suspect Dalton was on his way back to Sundance. The element of surprise might work in his favor. "What's the best way to approach her?"

"She bartends at the Twin Pines on the side. She's working tonight. Anything else I can do for you besides making your day with this news?" Sierra asked sweetly.

Making his day? Hell, she'd made his life, because now he had a shot at getting the life he wanted. "Where are the keys for the house in town?"

A pause. Then, "Why?"

"I need a place to stay."

Sierra heaved a put-upon sigh. "They're under the back deck on a key hook. But there are two conditions before I'll let you stay there. First, you don't tell anyone I own it. No one."

"Deal. And FYI, that's why we have a silent partnership." He'd supplied Sierra with some capital to start her own business last year and he also wanted it kept on the down low. "What's the second condition?"

"I need a handyman to do some things. Okay, a lot of things.

You're handy, you're there and voila—you're selected. I'll FedEx my repair list today but anything else you see that needs fixed just go ahead."

"I'll do it but I want to be reimbursed once a week for whatever I buy. You don't get to pull that sixty day wait for payment bull crap like you money people usually do."

She laughed. "That's how we become money people. We hold on to money as long as possible. Be warned, some of what needs done will be major costs."

"I ain't a carpet installer," he warned. "Nor will I put in windows."

Sierra sighed again. "You *are* a handy handyman, right?"

"Guess you'll have to trust me, huh?"

"I'll be keeping tabs on you." Another pause. "I'm sorry about your dad. If you need to talk about anything—except for Rory—call me."

By the time Dalton crossed into Crook County hours later, he had a plan in place.

Patience. Perseverance. He would not blow this chance.

Rory Wetzler was his. *His.* She always had been, she always would be.

And he'd do whatever it took to prove it.

Chapter Two

"Rory, can I get two Bud Light drafts and a cherry Coke?"

"Coming right up." She pulled the tap and dumped cherry juice over ice, aiming a stream of cola at the glass and swapping the full beer mug for an empty one. She lined the order on the bar top, then wandered to help a new customer.

Ten minutes later, she poured herself a Coke and leaned against the counter. Old man Duffy grinned at her.

"You're scaring me, Duff. What's that look for?"

"Missed you last week. Where were you?"

"At a two-day conference in Rock Springs."

"Huh. I thought you mighta bailed on us. Can't for the life of me understand why you're still slinging drinks at the Twin Pines."

"My job with the state is part-time. So while I'm waiting for a fulltime position to open up or a decent job in my field to magically become available, I'm working here to make ends meet." Rory chomped on a piece of ice.

"It's a waste. A gorgeous blonde amazon woman like you oughta be home every night, bein' spoiled rotten by a man who appreciates and worships you."

She laughed. "Now there's a fantasy."

"If I was fifty years younger…"

"I'd take you up on it." And she would, no lie. Her love life—for lack of a better term—was a joke. She'd had one date in the last six months since she'd returned to Sundance. A pity date from the plumber who installed a new toilet at the Wyoming Natural Resources Council office where she worked.

She'd jumped out of the dating pool for almost a year when she'd been with Dillon. While she had no regrets about breaking off their engagement, she was lonely. She missed the companionship, even when that companionship was what had driven her away.

Rory kept telling herself that it was better to be dateless and alone than married to the wrong man. Some days it empowered her. Other days it depressed her.

Her love life wasn't the only source of melancholy. Twenty-eight years old, with a bachelor's and a master's degree, and she was still slinging drinks for tips. She was still living in the same small hometown in the same small cabin she'd grown up in.

The more things changed the more they stayed the same.

But she'd had a full, exciting life in college, which made it worse, living in Dullsville, USA again. She'd joined several exchange programs during grad school, which had added almost two years to the time it took to earn her degree. But it'd been worth it, seeing the world outside of Wyoming. She'd spent half a year in South America studying tropical land conservation practices. She'd lived on a large cattle ranch on the big island of Hawaii. She'd mapped wildlife habitats and migration patterns in Alaska and Canada.

After graduation she'd interned for a year with the Wyoming State Parks Department. But the hiring freeze meant she didn't land a permanent job after the internship ended. Her relationship with Dillon, her boss in the WSPD office in Cheyenne, had hit the skids at the same time, so taking a part-time position with the WNRC in Moorcroft had been a no brainer. Her living expenses were next to nothing. Working part-time gave her time to apply for jobs all over the country, with every agency under the sun.

Pity she hadn't bothered sending off any applications in the past month—she could only take so much rejection. Maybe that was another sign of depression? Or boredom? She knew it wasn't a sign of contentment.

At least her mom seemed happy to have her around, although she and her husband, Gavin, were joined at the hip and lips when they weren't traveling across the country. Most of her friends in the area were married or in a steady relationship. Even her stepsister Sierra was all grown up and living in Arizona while she attended ASU. Rory got a little misty-eyed thinking about when Sierra had shown up at the Twin Pines with her dad and Rory's mom on her twenty-first birthday so Rory could make her first legal drink. She missed that sweet little brat.

"Rory? You are a sight for my tired old eyes today."

She looked up at a new customer and grinned. "If it isn't Donald, my favorite bald man. What's up?"

"The wind for one thing. Getting cold out there." He rubbed his hands together.

"You want the usual?"

"Nope. I'm feeling daring tonight. How about you add an extra kick to my red beer? A couple slices of jalapeños, some of them peppers and a handful of olives."

"You got it." Just like that her mood brightened. Hard to pity

17

yourself when faced with a cancer survivor who'd been through chemotherapy hell. But Donald was always upbeat. Her favorite part of bartending was talking to customers. If she was totally honest, she hadn't taken the bartending gig because she needed money, but to stave off loneliness. Hard to believe she could be lonely in her hometown, but she did spend many of her nonworking hours by herself. At least slinging drinks gave her some social interactions.

Rory slid the drink in front of Donald. "Taste it. If it's too spicy I'll dump it out and start fresh."

He sipped. Smacked his lips and grinned. "Perfect. Your talent is wasted here, Rory girl. You oughta be in New York City, making killer tips as head mixologist or whatever fancy name they're calling bartenders these days."

"I'll take the compliment, but I'm too much of a bumpkin to ever work with sophisticated clientele and booze."

"How're things going at the day job? You been out massaging black-footed ferrets' poor tired feet and polishing the horns on the horn-billed prairie grouse?"

She laughed. Like most lifelong Ag men, Donald poked fun at state wildlife and conservation agencies' policies. But unlike other men she'd run across, he meant it tongue-in-cheek. "I can always hope that's on my to-do list at the office tomorrow."

"If you catch one, let me know. My wife's got a killer recipe for poached grouse."

Rory groaned at his pun.

An hour later the crowd had dwindled. She asked Naomi, the manager, to watch the bar so she could take a break.

As she left the bathroom, a hulking guy barreled toward her. His hair was as unkempt as his scraggly beard. She flattened herself against the wall to let him pass, but he boxed her in. At six foot one, she was used to towering over most men. But this ZZ Top impersonator topped her by two inches.

Then he was in her face.

"Look, buddy, I don't know what you want, but I don't have any cash on me and if you don't back off, I'll—"

"Rory."

She froze. That deep voice. The way he said her name reminded her of... No. Couldn't be him. He'd just up and disappeared from her life three years ago without a word and as far as she knew, no one knew where he'd gone.

"Sweet Jesus. You're even prettier than I remembered." He ran his knuckles down her jawline.

"Stop it." Rory jerked her head away. "I don't know who you think you are—"

"You really don't know who I am, do you?"

She had a split second of recognition right before he said, "It's me. Dalton."

And then he kissed her.

When Dalton tried to deepen the kiss, Rory shifted. He automatically twisted his pelvis to protect his crotch—the crazy woman had kneed him in the 'nads before—so the swift punch to the gut caught him unprepared. He stumbled back a step and managed to duck when he saw Rory's fist headed for his head.

Out of reflex he grabbed both her wrists in one hand, trapping her hands between them as he pinned her against the wall. "The gut punch and haymaker might lead me to believe you're not as happy to see me as I am to see you."

Rory's breathing was choppy. Her pulse jumped erratically beneath his fingers. And her eyes, those stunning green eyes stared back at him with suspicion and just a little hatred.

Great.

What did you expect? That she'd fall into your arms?

"You're stronger and quicker than you used to be," Rory said.

"Got tired of getting my ass kicked."

"You deserved it most of the time."

He grinned. "No doubt."

"Let me go."

"You gonna take another swing at me?"

"Not unless you try to kiss me again."

"Might be worth a black eye."

"Don't."

Now her eyes held panic. Awesome. "Rory—"

"Dalton," she said sharply, cutting him off. "What do you want?"

"To talk to you."

"Then let me go and come up to the bar and I'll make you a drink."

"I won't turn you into a pariah for associating with me, jungle girl."

Her lips formed a sneer. "You reminding me of the times when we were kids and I didn't hate you isn't helping your case, McKay."

"But it ain't hurting it, either." He released her.

"Did you go to law school since I last saw you? Because that was a lawyer's tactic."

"That's why I cornered you. I wanted to plead my case without interruptions. Or without anyone recognizing me."

Rory gave him the wide smile that made his heart skip a beat. "I doubt your mother would recognize you."

"Guess we'll see if that holds true later this week." Dalton slumped against the wall next to her.

"FYI, no one is gunning for you anymore about jilting Addie."

"I heard that she married Truman. I'm happy for them."

A few beats later, she said, "Enough with the bullshit small talk and you trying to maul me, Grizzly Adams. Why are you here?"

He snorted. Grizzly Adams. "In Sundance? Or at the Twin Pines?"

"Both."

"I'm in Sundance because Casper had a stroke."

The hard glint to her eyes softened. "I'm sorry. Is he okay?"

"He can't talk. And without coming across like a dick, that ain't all bad. Weather was shitty in Montana and I just got here mid-afternoon. Saw Casper, took a rash of shit from my brothers and I figured what the hell. Why not add your scorn to the crap I've dealt with today. Facing my demons and all that."

Rory cocked her head. "I'm a demon for you?"

Dalton couldn't stop himself from touching her beautiful face. "You're my biggest demon. I wish things had happened differently. But at the time...I didn't have a choice."

"And now?"

"You tell me. I had no idea you were livin' in Sundance."

"How'd you find out?"

"Sierra."

Rory muttered, "I'm gonna kick her ass. You're back in Sundance for...how long?"

"No idea. So can we get together and talk?"

"About?"

"You know what about," he said softly.

"Don't do that," she snapped. "Act like everything was just a misunderstanding and give me those goddamned puppy dog eyes, Dalton. You know what you did to me."

"And you think it was easy for me?"

"Yes. Because you left the next day. The *very* next day, after you told me—"

"Don't you think I at least deserve a chance to explain?"

Rory laughed bitterly. "Fat chance, McKay."

Then he was done being a nice guy. Dalton blocked her body with his. "You'll give me a chance or I'll seize the chance when it arises and I won't give a damn about whether it's convenient for you."

"Like right now?" she demanded. "When I'm working?"

His mouth brushed her ear. "So I'd pick a time and pick a place for us to meet if I were you, or make no mistake, it *will* be on my terms."

"Pushy bastard. Fine. I'll meet you. Now get your scruff outta my face, Chewbacca. I can't breathe."

Dalton laughed and eased back. "Tell me where and tell me when we're meeting."

"I have to work at the WNRC tomorrow. I'm on call for the happy hour shift here tomorrow night. So how about if I call you?"

Nice try. "Sure. But since you don't have my number..." Dalton grabbed her left arm and pressed her body against the wall. He removed the Sharpie from his pocket and quickly scrawled his digits down her forearm.

"Omigod, you are such a pain in my ass," Rory snapped. "You couldn't have just written it on a scrap of paper?"

"Nope." Keeping hold of her arm, and locking his gaze on hers, he kissed her wrist. "Because you'd conveniently lose it. I want you seeing that number and thinkin' of me."

"Fair is fair. Gimme that." She snatched the Sharpie, pushed up the sleeve of his thermal shirt and printed her digits much larger.

He bit back a laugh when she realized what she'd done—now even if she didn't call him, he could call her. "Thanks. But you forgot to kiss it."

"No, I didn't. And for the record? I hate the beard."

"So noted."

She turned and stormed off.

Dalton let her get to the end of the hallway before he said, "Rory."

She whirled around. "What?"

"I'm really happy to see you again. And this time I'm not goin' anywhere."

Then he slipped out the side exit.

After Rory got home, she paced, a glass of bourbon in her hand.

I'm really happy to see you again.

Hah. What was she supposed to do with that? Believe him?

Wrong.

21

Everything about this was so wrong and had the potential to fuck up her head again. Dalton being in Sundance, showing up at her job. Acting so un-Dalton-like, sweet and contrite.

Bull. He acted like that all the time when he wanted something from you, and it worked every time with you.

No. She wasn't falling for this again. She'd been down this road with him before.

Three times as a matter of fact.

Rory drained her drink and flopped in the big Papasan chair, pulling her knees up to her chest. She closed her eyes. Maybe she'd drift off before the memories crushed her.

No such luck.

For days after the unexpected and abrupt halt to the wedding, Rory had remained by Addie's side. Listening to her cry. Being the supportive best friend. Running interference with Addie's family members who were out for Dalton's head on a spike. Or a bloodletting. Or both.

But Rory hadn't chimed in about Dalton McKay's status as douchebag supreme. Yes, it hurt to see Addie's misery, but a part of her—a very large part—wasn't surprised. Rory had been a victim of Dalton's douchebag ways—not that she'd ever shared those moments with Addie. Some things were just too embarrassing to share with anyone.

So when Dalton had fled the ceremony, Rory had been relieved. He was intuitive enough to know the marriage wouldn't work, wouldn't last, and he'd done the right thing in stopping it before it started. Maybe he could've come to that determination before he was literally ready to say *I do* but she'd secretly given him props for doing the right thing for once in his life.

After several of Addie's relatives bragged to her that they'd dished out the beating Dalton deserved, and no one had seen the man since— she'd gone looking for him.

Maybe it was luck, maybe it was karma, maybe it was fate that Rory had found Dalton in the wooded area by the creek where they'd played as kids.

Dalton had been shocked to see her. The way he'd cringed against the rock, he'd expected to feel her wrath too.

In that moment, the June day became so clear she could feel the cool breeze flowing from the river. She could smell the dank, half-decayed leaves on the sun-warmed dirt. She could see the dappled light streaming through the treetops.

She remembered the bruises, cuts and swelling on Dalton

McKay's face.

He'd looked at her and sighed. "I'm hoping you're unarmed."

"I am. Although I'll point out I could make a killing selling your location to the rest of Addie's relatives who haven't taken a shot at you."

"Wouldn't be much of a contest. I'd lie down like the dog I am and let them kick the crap outta me."

Rory sat next to him on the rock and tilted her face toward the cloudless, vibrant blue sky.

Neither said anything for a while.

Dalton spoke first. "How'd you find me?"

Instinct. "I figured since no one could find you it was worth checking here."

His gaze turned suspicious. "Has my family been lookin' for me?"

"Yes." Rory's eyes took in every bruise, scrape and bump on his face. "I assume everyone you've run across has been hard on you."

Dalton rubbed the bruise on his jaw. "A couple of Addie's cousins caught me outside the convenience store in Moorcroft. Mean little fuckers."

"They responsible for the shiner?"

"Nope. Two of her uncles and her aunt cornered me in Hulett. Got a knot on the side of my head where the woman hit me with a marble cheeseboard. Guess she decided not to take back the wedding gift she'd bought us and repurposed it as a weapon instead."

"That's not even funny."

Dalton sighed. "No, it's not. Especially not when I consider the worst beating came from Truman. Guess Addie's tears turned him into a superhero revenge seeker for jilted brides. The asshole popped me in the mouth hard enough to loosen a tooth, kicked me in the ribs and punched me in the fucking kidney. I pissed blood for two goddamned days. Thing of it is...I deserved it."

Silence settled between them again.

Now when she finally had the chance to ask him the question that'd kept her up at night for months, her lips seemed glued shut.

"Come on, Rory. I know you've got something to say to me."

"Why?" she asked him quietly.

"Why what? Why did I walk away from her?"

"No. Why did you ask her to marry you in the first place?"

He picked up a rock and chucked it into the water. "Wasn't that what I was supposed to do? Time to settle down, they said. Time to grow up, they said. So half of my family was lookin' at me like I was a

23

defective human because no woman would stay with me longer than a couple of weeks. The other half of my family was lookin' at my single status as an affront to their family values. Like I was clinging too hard to the wild McKay reputations they'd built over the years. Since they were all done with it, I should be too. Bear in mind many of *them* didn't get married and settle down until they were well into their thirties."

"Were either of the McKay camps right?"

Dalton shrugged. "No. I'm not...some smooth operator like most of them." He shot her a sheepish look. "As you know firsthand. After Tell and Georgia got together, I was the odd man out everywhere. Spending time alone...never really been my thing. I always had my brothers or my cousins around. And without sounding like this is a fucking pity party, I may as well have been a ghost. So I spent a lot of time on the road, learning to be by myself, doin' what I wanted to do. Then last summer after you went to South America, Addie and I ended up shooting pool at the Golden Boot. Shocked the shit outta me that she didn't hate me."

"Why? Addie doesn't hate anyone."

He raised a dark eyebrow. "I assumed you'd told her about us?"

Rory shook her head.

"I never mentioned those, ah, incidents either when she and I started hanging out. She's a sweet woman, nice to the core, everyone in town loves her and after three months of dating, she told me that she loved me."

Rory clenched her jaw to keep it shut.

"You know what's pathetic? I was so desperate at that point in my life for someone to profess their love for me that I proposed to her. She said yes and I figured we'd make a good life together."

"Did you ever love her?"

"Thought I did, until..."

"Until what?"

He opened his mouth. Closed it. Picked up another rock and threw it.

Pushing was her way, but this time, she didn't push. Part of her was afraid to hear him voice her suspicions out loud.

"So we set the wedding date. Everyone was happy."

Were you happy?

"Addie focused her worries on the flavor of the cake and the color and monogramming on the napkins. I kept a lid on my worries. I convinced myself it was nerves. All men get screwed up thinkin' about becoming a husband, and a provider, and only bein' with one woman for the rest of his life."

"You didn't talk to your brothers, your cousins, your friends—anybody—about this since they'd gone through it?"

"No." Then he went quiet.

"That's it? That's all I get about how you decided to leave my best friend standing alone in front of a church full of people?"

"I can't..."

"You can't? You *won't* is more like it," she spat.

"You wanna know why? I'll tell you. But you answer this first. How did you react when you found out Addie and I were getting married?"

Sick to my stomach. Jealous. Mad. She tossed out a cool, "I was all right with it."

Dalton met her gaze head on. "Bullshit. I'm bein' honest with you, at least have the goddamn balls to be the same with me."

"Fine. I was upset, okay? You and Addie aren't a good match. But how could I say that to her? How could I be negative, without giving our stupid past history as the reason for my negativity? Especially when she immediately asked me to be her maid of honor? I had to suck it up, McKay. Act like I was happy for her."

Those blue eyes turned shrewd. "But you weren't happy. Addie and I weren't a good match...why? Because she's too good for me?"

"Fuck that. You two only ended up together because you were both lonely and wanted to end that loneliness. She'd felt that way a lot longer than you. She wanted to be a wife and a mother more than anything in the world. You offered it to her so she took it." Immediately Rory regretted blurting that out. "Sorry."

"Sorry because it's true?"

"Maybe." Rory exhaled. "Look, you should've been honest with her when you started having doubts."

Dalton laughed. A little hysterically.

"What?"

"Nothin'."

"You insisted on this honesty thing, you damn well better stick to it."

His blue eyes were fierce when he got in her face. "I had worries, not doubts, certainly not flat-out *what the fuck am I doin'* thoughts prior to putting on my tuxedo last Saturday morning. I didn't feel that doubt, that absolute wrongness of standing in front of a minister, about to promise my devotion and my life to the wrong woman until..."

Rory didn't back down and she wouldn't let him either. "Until...?"

"Until I looked across the altar and saw you."

Every molecule of air left her body.

"In that moment I knew marrying her would be the biggest mistake of my life. Don't insult me and pretend you didn't feel it when I looked at you, Rory."

She'd felt it. Everything she'd ever wanted from him had been right there in his eyes...as he was about to marry her best friend.

"Since I've had several days to do nothin' but think about this fucking mess, I realized if you'd been here instead of in South America, I never would've proposed to her."

"Omigod. You are not seriously blaming this on me, Dalton McKay."

"I'm saying if you'd been around I would've been reminded."

"Of what? Of all the great times we've had together in the last six years? Let's not forget all the shitty things that you've done to me—"

Dalton grabbed her upper arms and yanked her closer. "Shitty things we've done to each other. You're not completely blameless in this, Rory."

She hated the truth in that statement. He'd acted; she'd reacted. She closed her eyes. "Stop. Let go of me, Dalton."

"I can't."

"Why do we keep doing this to each other? You should've just married her and we'd be done with this."

"No."

"Yes."

"*No*, goddammit, look at me."

Rory lifted her chin and met his gaze.

"I've got no idea on how to make this right. It's all too...raw right now." His eyes were filled with anguish. "I won't compound the problem and ruin a friendship between you and Addie by asking you to be with me here. Even when that's what I want." He reached for her ponytail, sifting the long strands through his fingers. "It's what I've always wanted."

"Don't do this to me."

"I can't help it."

"I can't be with you anyway. My life is in Laramie, not here. I've got two years left before I get my master's degree. I've busted my ass my entire academic life to get to this point."

"What then?"

"I don't know where I'll be when I'm done with school. But I know exactly where you'll be."

"Where?"

"Right here."

"Don't be so sure of that."

Now Rory knew he was bullshitting her. His McKay roots were sunk deep in ranching, his family and Wyoming. He'd never leave.

Except...last time they'd crossed paths, he'd mentioned feeling untethered. She thought he'd found an anchor in Addie. But now he made it sound like she—Aurora Rose Wetzler—was the missing piece in his life.

Don't get your hopes up.

Confused by his mixed signals and the stupid girlish hope that things would work out between them like they were supposed to, she scooted off the rock.

"Rory. Don't go."

"I can't stay here with you, Dalton. I need...time."

"I get that. When can we talk again?"

"I leave for Laramie on Sunday."

She started up the path toward her house.

"Don't leave things like this. Please."

When had Dalton McKay ever said please? She found herself stopping and facing him. "When do you want to talk?"

"Come by my house tomorrow night. We'll figure it out this time. I swear."

But she'd showed up to find him gone. No note. No text. No nothing. Just...gone.

And he'd stayed gone for over three years.

She'd been right not to trust him, not to pin her hopes on that one perfect moment they'd shared—because maybe it hadn't been as perfect as she'd remembered.

Question was: what did he want from her now?

Chapter Three

Dalton had agreed to meet his brothers at Brandt and Jessie's place. Things had been strained between them at the rehab hospital the previous afternoon. They hadn't recognized him at first, and then they'd given him a rash of crap about turning into a Montana mountain man. There'd been a thread of unease in all their conversations, so it'd be interesting to see if they'd hide their hostility when they weren't in public or whether they'd toss it down like a gauntlet.

A few things had changed at Brandt and Jessie's house. A jungle gym, a tree house and a swing set were situated behind a new two car garage. A line of trees had been planted on the left side of the house. The expanded garden was enclosed by a five-foot-high fence. The improvements over the years allowed Dalton to forget he'd been raised here. Much happier memories were being made in the house these days.

Tell's truck was parked next to Brandt's. An SUV, probably Georgia's, was lined up behind it.

For some reason Dalton's gut knotted climbing the steps.

Jessie opened the door and threw herself into his arms. "Dalton McKay, I was beginning to wonder if you'd ever come home." She squeezed him tightly—as if she really was happy to see him. When she pulled back, she hastily wiped her tears.

His stomach dropped. "Jess—"

"He missed you, okay?" she whispered. "We all did. It's been harder on him than he'll ever admit. Yes, we have our own family now, but that doesn't mean you aren't..." She stopped. Inhaled. Smiled. "Sorry. Too soon for this." She reached up and ruffled his beard. "Brandt warned me, but it in no way prepared me for how different you look."

"Grizzly Adams is one of the least offensive comparisons that've been made," he said dryly.

"Come in. We're all bustin' our buttons for you to meet the newest McKays."

Dalton wiped off his boots and shrugged out of his Carhartt

jacket. When he looked up, he saw Tell with a black-haired boy cocked on his hip.

"Jackson, that's your Uncle Dalton. You wanna go say hi?"

Jackson yelled, "No!"

"Our two-year-old's favorite word," Georgia said behind him.

He turned and grinned at his pregnant sister-in-law. "Is it my brother's goal to keep you knocked up?"

Georgia hugged him. "It's a McKay plot, since Jess has another bun in the oven too."

"Holy sh...shoot." He glanced over at his brother and sis-in-law. "Congrats."

Then two boys raced into the room and Jackson squealed to be let down. They skidded to a stop in front of Dalton. Hard to believe the last time he'd seen Tucker the kid had just started walking. He'd never met Wyatt, Brandt and Jessie's two-and-a-half-year-old son. Tucker looked like Brandt, dark-haired and stocky. Wyatt had lighter hair and Jessie's hazel eyes. They didn't look like brothers.

That thought sliced him to the bone because everyone used to say that about him and his brothers.

Not the time nor the place to think about this.

He crouched down. "Hey, guys."

Jackson joined his cousins in staring at Dalton.

"Why you got that long beard?" Tucker asked. "You hidin' scars on your face or something?"

Dalton tried not to laugh when he heard Jessie's sharp, "Tucker McKay, you will apologize to your uncle right now."

"Sorry." But Tucker's narrowed gaze took in every inch of Dalton's face like he was checking for evidence.

"I don't s'pose you remember me," Dalton asked. "I used to babysit you sometimes."

Tucker shook his head.

"Uncle Dalton sent you the rhinoceros horn, the maracas and the stuffed toy elk," Jessie prompted.

"Really? That was you?"

"Yep."

"Where'd you get all that stuff?"

"Picked it up in my travels."

"Cool. Did you give Wyatt that stuffed grizzly bear?"

"Yes sir. And I gave you—" he poked Jackson in the belly, "—the stuffed buffalo."

Jackson blinked at him. Up close the kid was a perfect mix of Tell and Georgia. Black hair, icy blue eyes.

"Why're you here?" Tucker asked.

"Because Grandpa is in the hospital," Brandt said.

"Are you really my dad's brother?"

"I really am. I'm Uncle Tell's brother too."

"Not the one who died. That's Landon's dad, Luke." He frowned. "How come I don't remember you?"

"I've been gone a while."

"Why?"

Jesus. Did this kid ever stop asking questions?

"Why don't you boys go play? You can grill Uncle Dalton later."

Tucker raced off, Wyatt and Jackson right behind him.

Dalton stood and looked at Brandt and Jessie. "How many questions do you answer a day?"

"Seems like a million. Let's sit in the dining room."

Jessie sliced up coffee cake and poured coffee. No one was talking so he looked around the room. How many meals had he eaten in here growing up? How many times had he tiptoed past Casper's captain's chair at the head of the table, hoping not to be noticed?

"Dalton?"

He glanced up at Jessie. "The place looks good. This house finally has a happy vibe."

"We need to talk about Dad," Tell said, "but I wanna hear what you've been up to and why the fuck we haven't seen you for over three years."

Georgia whapped his biceps. "That is not a good way to start a conversation, Tell, and you know it."

Tell was giving Dalton the steely-eyed stare that reminded him a little too much of Casper.

"Sorry, Georgia, but I'm with Tell on this." Brandt pointed with his fork. "You're here, so start talkin'."

"I don't know where to start."

"The last time we saw you in person was a week after you pulled your runaway groom routine," Tell reminded him.

"But the last time we actually saw your face was on TV a few months later when you were in the celebrity poker match with Chase," Brandt added.

Dalton sipped his coffee. "So you, along with the rest of the country, watched me lose the million dollar pot?"

"Made me sick to my stomach just thinkin' about gambling with that much cash," Brandt said.

"The buy-in was a hundred grand, right?" Tell asked.

"Yep. Winner-takes-all tournament. Half the buy-in was my money. Chase's sponsors put the other half up. I'm assuming everyone in the McKay family believed Chase lent me the money and I lost it?"

His brothers and their wives looked at each other.

Just another reason he'd gotten a cool reception from his uncles yesterday. "Due to confidentiality contracts, Chase couldn't confirm or deny to anyone where the buy-in cash came from. My gag order expired two years after the event. So now I can tell you that I was paid to lose."

"What? That was all faked?"

Dalton shook his head. "No, they're real poker games with real stakes. But world championship poker is big business, lots of fans, turning players into celebrities. The operators specialize in holding tournaments in small casinos. Which means advertising dollars pay for most the revenue. A regular Joe can see how the pros do it."

"How'd you get roped in?" Tell asked.

"Chase had been asked to play a trio of celebrity couple tournaments and the sponsors were expecting Ava, but she had to back out because she was scouting movie locations. I'd hung out with Chase at the poker tables in Vegas after the PBR World Finals. He'd seen me play and knew I had the cash for buy-in, knew I was traveling around, so he asked me to fill in." Dalton grinned. "We thought it'd be hilarious if I showed up in drag—blond wig, evening dress, the whole nine yards—trying to look like Ava, but Ava nixed that idea."

Georgia and Jessie laughed.

"Chase got knocked out early on. I kept playing the angle that I was his rube cousin from Wyoming. The crowds ate it up. Hell, I even had folks askin' for my autograph, which was weird. An hour before the final round started, the TV producers and sponsors called a meeting with me. Said they wanted me to throw the game because my opponent, JT Judson, was riding the comeback wave and it'd make for better drama if he won."

"Did you tell them to stick it?" Tell demanded.

"Nope. Luckily Chase was with me. He's used to dealing with them TV types. He said I'd go all in if I got my seed money back and if they put me on the tour for at least a dozen stops. So basically I got to play in a million-dollar poker tournament for free. For the next eight months I ran the circuit. Then I'd had enough."

"You disappeared."

Dalton nodded. "I'd had my fifteen minutes of fame and that was fourteen minutes too many."

"Is that why you grew the beard? So you weren't recognizable?" Tell asked innocently.

"Fuck. Off."

Tell laughed.

Brandt said, "What did you do after that?"

"Yeah, the *I'm fine* texts once a month and the occasional package from some weird place overseas really doesn't tell us what you'd been doin'."

"After I had extra cash I made a list of all the places across the world I wanted to go and I went there."

"By yourself?"

"Yep."

"Bro, ever since you were a little kid you never liked doin' stuff by yourself."

"Because I never had to. I always had you guys or our McKay cousins." Or Rory. "When I got older, I had girls—" he flashed Tell a sly grin, "—not as many girls as I'd claimed."

Tell gave him an odd look—as if surprised that Dalton had admitted that.

"I met a few people in my travels, so I wasn't always alone, but the majority of the time, yeah, I was and I preferred it."

His brothers wouldn't understand why he'd chosen to redefine himself without his family's influence. It'd been scary shit, being forced to do things on his own. No one telling him to feed cattle or move cattle or mow the hayfield. No one telling him to fix fence, or demanding explanations for how he conducted his social life. He'd been one hundred percent in charge of every decision he made every day. It'd been overwhelming at first, especially in countries where he didn't speak the language—he'd almost turned tail and run home. But he'd stuck it out.

So he'd learned a few things about himself: he was adaptable. He was a self-starter—he could count the number of times he'd lazed in bed on one hand. It'd been easy to get up and start his day when he hadn't a clue what the day had in store for him.

"Didja take pictures, play tourist, what?"

"Not really. I mostly wandered here and there. The reason I haven't tried to explain it to you guys before now is because I can't. Not over the phone, not in person. Alls I can say is I had to go and I don't regret a minute of bein' gone."

"So now you're livin' in Montana? What do you do up there?"

"Been a logger in the summer. I've been leading elk-hunting parties in the autumn during bow hunting season for the past two years."

"So you really have become some kind of Montana mountain man? Hunting, logging, and livin' off the land?"

"You say it like it's a bad thing," he answered Brandt a little testily.

"Just don't seem like your kinda thing. Your social life was almost as busy as Tell's. And now you're just happily holed up in the middle of nowhere Montana?"

Tell leaned forward. "Ya ain't on the run 'cause you killed somebody?"

"No. Enough with the questions about me. I'm here to talk about Casper, remember? I understood about half of what the doctor said yesterday."

"Dad refuses to speak. But he won't get better without therapy. So the doctor wonders if there's anyone Dad will listen to about resuming therapy," Tell said.

"What about the uncles?" Dalton had seen them briefly yesterday.

"He fakes sleep whenever they show up. They'd be the hardest ones for him to face with his stroke-altered speech issues."

"Was the woman I saw darting in and out of the room a nurse or something?"

"No. That was Dad's girlfriend. Barbara Jean."

Dalton laughed. "Good one, Tell."

"I'm serious. Barbara Jean and Dad have been together for over a year."

"They met at church," Georgia said. "She's really sweet. She takes good care of him."

"Casper has a girlfriend," he repeated. "Is she deaf so she doesn't care if he yells his head off at her?"

"Jesus, Dalton, that's not funny."

He looked between his brothers. Then his brother's wives. "Am I missing something? Or did I stumble into an alternate reality where Casper isn't a flaming asshole?"

"No, but—"

"But what? He made some kind of amends with you guys, given how horrible he's always been?"

"It's not like that," Tell said.

"Then maybe you oughta tell me what it *is* like."

"It's gotten easier."

"Like you're havin' him over for supper kind of easy?"

Brandt shook his head. "He asks to see the boys and we meet.

During that time he doesn't give us ranch advice, or try to convince us to join his church. He ain't allowed to run down Mom, or say nasty shit to our wives."

"So the meetings last...under four minutes? Because that's about as long as he can go without bein' insulting."

"Guess you wouldn't know, huh? Since you ain't been around him for three goddamned years?" Tell shot back.

Thank God for that. Dalton changed the subject. "Can he stay in the rehab wing indefinitely?"

"Guess that's a week by week thing and we're back to it bein' dependent on how his therapy is goin'."

"There's no reason for them to keep him if he isn't making progress," Tell said. "So they'll turn him out and make it someone else's problem."

"Meaning our problem," Brandt said.

"Whoa." Dalton's gaze winged between his brothers. "Are you actually considering moving him into one of your houses?"

Uncomfortable silence.

How in the hell could either of them even consider that?

"Brandt. Do you need me to remind you that after Luke died he kicked Jessie out? Off the ranch? Out of our lives? He didn't give a shit if she was homeless. What goes around comes around."

"Don't you think I know that?"

Dalton looked at Tell. "You're willing to have that man in your house, around your kids day after day even knowing what he's capable of? For who knows how fuckin' long because we all know the man is too goddamned mean to die?"

"Dalton. That's not helping," Jessie said quietly.

"Well, it needed to be said because it doesn't seem like any of you are lookin' at this from any angle besides guilt."

"Fine. How would you handle it?" Tell asked.

Their skeptical looks didn't deter him. "Casper still gets financial compensation from the ranch although he's retired. If he gets kicked outta the rehab place then he'll need to be set up in a long-term care facility where he's not paying for expensive therapy he has no intention of doin'. The place might eat up every bit of his ranch income and anything he might've saved up, but it's the most logical choice."

"Finally the voice of reason," Georgia said and reached over to squeeze Dalton's hand.

Jessie nodded. "It'd be a different situation if Casper was a guy everyone loved. Heck, I'd be fine havin' him live with us. But he's not that man. And he's not gonna change now. Like Dalton said, I suspect

Casper will act a whole lot worse."

"He can suck it up and start doin' rehab, or he can live in a nursing home." Dalton looked between his brothers. "So which one of you is gonna tell him?"

"Why you pushing this all off on us?" Tell demanded.

"Because I'm the youngest and he'd discount anything I said." His phone vibrated. The caller ID read *Rory*. "Sorry, I hafta take this call." He excused himself from the table.

Chapter Four

Rory swore she wasn't going to call Dalton. That'd teach Mr. I-Can-Kiss-You-Anytime-I-Want a lesson.

So why was her phone in her hand?

Because you're a freakin' marshmallow when it comes to Dalton McKay.

No, she wasn't. Not anymore. But after the flashback, she'd wondered where he'd been the past three years. The jerk owed her an explanation. So she'd hear his excuses and move on.

She hit dial before another voice popped into her head with advice.

He answered with, "I knew you'd call me."

"And there's the reason I shouldn't have."

Dalton laughed. "Don't hang up on me. Just a sec."

Rory heard muffled voices in the background.

"Sorry about that."

"Where are you?"

"At Brandt's. And you timed this call perfectly because things had started to get a little heated. Anyway, are you working at the Twin Pines tonight?"

"No."

"Can I see you?"

She fiddled with the straw in her to-go cup. "What do you have in mind?"

"Dinner. Conversation. Friends catching up." He paused. "Don't deny there's unfinished business between us."

"I don't. But I'd really like to keep the Sundance and McKay gossip mongers out of our...unfinished business or whatever it is."

"Which is why I'll cook for you. I'm renting a house on Royal Street. It's baby blue with red shutters. Can't miss it."

"Aren't you staying with your brothers or in your old trailer?"

"I gave the trailer up when I left. I've been on my own too long to try and follow someone else's rules. So do you wanna come over right after work? Or do you need to go home first?"

Wearing her less-than-flattering work uniform would reiterate the friendship line. But part of her wanted to saunter in wearing a sexy outfit, even when that'd give Dalton the wrong idea.

"Rory?"

"Sorry, yeah, I'll need to go home, change and let the dog out."

"You still have Jingle?"

"Yep. She's getting up there in years though. Anything you want me to bring?"

"Just yourself. I'm really looking forward to spending time with you, Rory."

When she almost admitted she felt the same, the angry girl who'd been taken for granted and taken for a ride by this man reared her ugly head and barked out: *don't fall for this because it's an act; always has been, always will be.*

So she said, "See you later," and hung up.

The rest of the workday dragged ass. Rory wondered if she'd ever get out into the field and utilize what she'd learned earning her degrees. Given she hated this job, it'd be easy to spiral into the my-degrees-are-worthless-what-the-fuck-was-I-thinking school of thought.

After she got home, she poured herself a drink. Standing in front of her tiny closet, she pondered clothing choices. A dress? Trying too hard. Jeans, hiking boots and a flannel shirt? Not trying at all. Rory slipped on her favorite khaki pants, a soft-hued angora sweater in heather brown, and drove into town.

She parked behind his pickup at the seen-better-days house and entered the yard through a chain link fence. She held her hand up to knock only to have the door opened immediately.

Dalton grinned so widely his beard moved. "Hey, gorgeous. Come in."

Rory started to take her coat off, and Dalton was right there, helping her. "Thanks."

"No problem. The kitchen is this way."

The living area didn't have a stick of furniture. At least the eat-in dining room had a table and chairs.

"After I invited you I realized I hadn't been to the store. Since I spent most of the day at the rehab place in Spearfish, I picked up pizza, fried chicken and hot wings." He headed to the fridge. "Want a beer?"

"Ah, no."

"That's right. You've never been a beer drinker. Sorry, but alls I've got is Coke."

"Coke is fine. But the food—"

Dalton got right in her face. "Please tell me you haven't turned vegetarian in the last three years?"

Tempting to lie to test his reaction, but she shook her head. "I'm not a vegetarian. I tried it for six months but couldn't stand a life without bacon."

"That's no kinda life. Let's get this stuff moved to the table."

"It'll be easier to dish up here."

"Good plan." Dalton didn't back off. He remained in that too-close-for-comfort zone.

"What?"

"I thought about you a lot over the years. More than was healthy, that's for damn sure. But those snapshots of you in my head didn't do you justice. Here I am, standing in front of you. And honest to God, you are so beautiful I can't think straight."

Her stupid belly swooped. "Still the same bullshit charmer, I see."

"No ma'am. I've told you that you're beautiful before this."

"I didn't believe you then, either."

Dalton followed her, step for step as she tried to retreat. "Don't run from me, Rory. It's long past time we both stopped running."

His eyes were the bottomless blue that pulled at her like an ocean current.

He'll suck you in, spin you around and spit you out.

That broke whatever weird hold Dalton had on her. She reached up and tugged hard on his beard. "Back off, Jeremiah Johnson."

He laughed. "For now. But first, this." He pressed his lips to hers in a gentle kiss that should've been chaste—but wasn't. Not at all. He murmured, "I'm glad you're here."

This was the Dalton she remembered prior to the night everything had changed between them. As much as that comforted her—because she hadn't seen this side of him in a long time—it also scared her; she'd never been able to resist this Dalton.

He backed off. "I'll bet you're starved after workin' all day. Help yourself."

"There's a ton of food here." She dished up KFC mashed potatoes and gravy, coleslaw, green beans and macaroni salad.

Dalton poured her a Coke. "It'll tide me over for a couple of days. Livin' where I do, there's no fast food. I don't miss it, except for fried chicken. The frozen kind from the store never tastes as good."

Rory added a slice of pizza to her plate and a breadstick. "When I went to college I lived on the fast food I'd been denied in my youth. I packed on the freshman fifteen in no time. I lost it all after I returned to healthy eating." Why had she blathered that? And why was she acting nervous and jittery like this was a first date?

"It's good to indulge sometimes." Dalton sat across from her, his plate piled high.

"So what's going on with your dad?"

He gave her the basic rundown, finishing with, "Freaked me out to see him like that."

"Do you have any idea how long you're staying?"

"There are things I've been putting off that I'll deal with while I'm here."

That wasn't an answer. "How'd you end up living in Montana?"

"When I returned to the States after my European jaunt, I intended to settle wherever..." He paused and looked away. "Those plans fell through, so I spent the summer workin' as a logger. Then a buddy who owns a hunting lodge in Alder needed a guide for elk season. I stayed on through the winter and did odd jobs to earn my keep. Went back to logging in the spring and throughout the summer. Then autumn rolled around again and I was back on guide duty."

They ate in silence for a while. But she couldn't stop thinking about how things had played out between them. The lies. The lust. The moment when all of that had come to a head and altered their friendship beyond repair.

"Rory?"

Startled, she glanced up at Dalton. "What?"

He gestured with his spork. "You're pulverizing them poor green beans."

She glanced down to see a smashed pile of green goo on her plate.

"What were you thinkin' about that put you in a murderous mood?"

Do you really want to talk about this?

Yes. They'd avoided this subject for far too long.

Rory pinned him with a hard stare. "I was thinking about the summer after my senior year. Specifically that night you sweet-talked me into the cab of your pickup. The night you punched my V-card?"

Dalton choked on his beer.

"You didn't even call me the next day. Then I left for college two weeks later. Is that night ringing any bells for you? Or as a McKay male have you popped so many cherries that you don't even fucking remember?"

"Of course I remember." He took another long swallow of beer. "I was an ass, okay? I was also twenty, with big plans to get laid at every opportunity."

"I was just another opportunity to get your rocks off?" she demanded.

"I was a horny twenty-year-old," he repeated. "Getting my fair share of ass is all I cared about. Do I wish I could erase the shitty things I've done? Especially to you? Absolutely. You want me to apologize? Fine. I'm sorry. I should've called you. But if I had, I probably would've asked if you wanted to hook up again and fucked you *against* the pickup, just to mix it up."

"That is not an apology, Dalton McKay."

Dalton stared at her thoughtfully.

"What?"

"Maybe you're not lookin' for an apology from me. Maybe you oughta forgive yourself for bein' a starry-eyed eighteen-year-old girl who let a punk-ass cowboy you trusted sweet-talk you out of your virginity."

Had that really been her issue? Was it still her issue?

"If I could go back and do it over, I'd give you more than some fevered groping in the cab of a truck."

He traced her hairline from her forehead to her ear.

Hey, when had he moved so close? And why wasn't she pulling away?

"I'd romance you underneath the starry sky. I'd take my time with every inch of you and try not to set the world speed record for how fast I could get off. You deserved better and I knew it. I knew how lucky I was to even get with you."

His smoky eyes and deep rumbling voice hypnotized her. She found herself leaning closer. "Why?"

"You had this way of scaring most of the boys off."

"Except for you."

"Except for me."

"Why?" she asked again.

"I knew you. I'd seen your sweet side beneath that in-your-face persona you'd adopted the year you grew from a shrimp into a pinup dream."

Rory bit back a groan. In ten months she'd shot up eight inches, a complete transformation from a waifish girl into a clumsy amazon. She'd gone on the offensive to stave off anyone verbally attacking her and calling her a freak.

"Your height, your brain, your body—" big shocker that Dalton didn't offer her a lascivious grin, "—were intimidating, even for me, and we were friends. I dreaded the day when you finally realized how gorgeous you were. So you were taking off for college and I wanted a

40

piece of you for myself—a piece that no other guy would ever have."

He'd always been calculating; she hadn't expected him to admit it. She didn't know how to respond.

"But I promise you that's not me anymore."

She snorted. "So you've changed?"

"Yep."

"How?"

"In all the ways I needed to. Getting away from here was the smartest thing I ever did. I got a chance to see the world outside of Crook County and the McKay ranch. I got to see who I was outside of bein' part of the McKay family."

"Why are you telling me this?"

Dalton took her hand. "Because in order for you to trust me I have to prove to you I've changed. And I intend to do whatever it takes to do that."

Keep it light. "Whatever. I don't suppose you bought dessert."

"As a matter of fact, I did. Two of those fancy pudding cups from KFC with the whipped cream and chocolate shavings on the top."

Rory smiled. "I remember how jealous we were of the kids who got pudding cups in their lunches because we never did. Now I can buy them anytime I want and I never do."

Dalton said, "I buy 'em. Or I did when I lived here."

The way he kept saying that made her think he wouldn't be here permanently.

Rory cracked the foil on her cup and scooped out a tiny bite. And another.

"You still eat pudding like it's a rare delicacy. It's cute."

She stuck out her tongue. "How'd you end up renting this house on such short notice?"

"I know the owner. She's been meaning to install updates before she decides to rent or sell. Since I'm not doin' anything else, we're swapping rent for my handyman skills."

Rory wanted to ask who owned the house. If the woman was a former lover he'd kept in touch with.

Dalton kept talking. "But she's getting the better end of the deal. A FedEx package was on the steps when I got here with a list of changes five pages long. I also have a packet of paint chips color-coordinated to each room."

"So what are you doing first?"

"Be easier to show you." She followed him out of the kitchen. He led her past the empty living room and cut down a hallway with five closed doors. He paused outside the last one. "Too bad you don't have sunglasses on 'cause you'll need them.

He opened the door and Rory winced.

"Holy shit that's hideous." The room was neon yellow. Not a pretty yellow, but a cross between yellow and green so it looked like someone had pissed all over the walls. "How many coats will it take to cover this?"

"About ten thousand." He flattened his palm against the wall. "Fortunately I'm texturing this room first, so that'll cut some of the glare."

Since she was by nature such a helpful person, it was on the tip of her tongue to offer to help him paint.

Don't do it.

"It's a small house so it'll be a short tour."

"This place isn't as small as my cabin. Sometimes it makes me claustrophobic."

Dalton turned around so fast she ran into him. "Your cabin is great."

"Great in that I don't have to pay rent, but that's about it."

He brushed a hair from her cheek. "And?"

"And living there makes it seem like I never left here." Somehow the man had backed her against the wall. "Dalton, what are you doing?"

"You have chocolate pudding on your lip and I'm gonna lick it off. And then I'm gonna kiss you. Really kiss you like I've been dyin' to since you showed up today."

Since when did he... Oh God. A warm, wet tongue slid across her lower lip. He tugged her bottom lip between his teeth and sucked. He slowly released it and crushed his lips to hers.

Dalton's mouth demanded. Controlled. Teased. He clasped her hands in his, letting the kiss ebb and then building it back up. No body parts were touching beyond the clasp of their hands and their locked mouths.

Rory never remembered him kissing her like this—with such single-minded absorption.

That's because he's had lots and lots of practice.

He ended the kiss before she pulled away. He murmured, "I had to do that out here. Because if I did it in my bedroom we might never come out." He placed a kiss below her ear.

She ignored how her body tingled just from his soft mouth on her skin. Annoyed, she gave him a tiny head-butt. "Wishful thinking, McKay."

He chuckled. "Guess we'll see."

Smug man. "And I hate the beard anyway."

He stepped back and opened the door.

Rory looked at the sleeping bag on the floor, then at him and poked him in the chest. "I'm beyond the age that doing it in a sleeping bag holds any appeal for me."

"Oh, I don't know. Two sleeping bags hooked together out in the middle of nowhere, beneath a big starry sky, will always hold appeal for me."

"Who are you?" She poked him again. "It's this damn beard that's turned you into a mountain man, isn't it?"

"No." He kissed her. "I've changed. But with you, proof is in the pudding—ha ha—so that's what you'll get."

"More pudding?"

Dalton looked at her—more like he looked through her. His blue eyes held something warm and dark that she'd never seen and her belly cartwheeled.

That's when she knew he'd honed that boyish charm into a sharper instrument. A much more dangerous tool.

Then the look vanished and he smiled. "Maybe we oughta go finish our pudding."

They returned to the kitchen. Dalton's eyes were glued to her mouth as she licked every bite of chocolate from her spork.

"Besides handyman stuff, what are you doing to fill your days?"

"I'll put in an appearance at the rehab hospital. Then at some point this week I gotta get furniture for this place and a TV. I need something else to fill the void while I'm stuck here."

Fill the void? Was that why he was being so cute and flirty with her? Because she was the void he intended to fill...in more ways than one?

Enough. You got what you needed, he explained why he left so walk away. Now.

"Well, good luck with that." She tossed her empty pudding cup on her paper plate and stood to gather the trash.

"Rory. What's wrong?"

"Nothing. I have to go."

"Already? Stay."

She whirled around. "Why? So you can fill a void? I'm just another way to kill time while you're stuck here?"

Dalton took the garbage from her and flung it on the counter. Then he grabbed her upper arms. "Spend every waking hour that you're not workin' with me."

"What? No. That's ridiculous. I—"

He cut off her retort with a steamy kiss that made her wonder why she didn't mouth off to him all the time.

After he thoroughly scrambled her brain, Dalton rested his forehead to hers. "If you would've said yes, then I wouldn't need to buy a damn TV."

"You are going to drive me crazy with this need to prove you've changed, aren't you?"

"Something worth doin' is worth doin' well. And make no mistake, I'm doin' it right with you this time." He touched her face with the back of his hand. "Question is: will you let me?"

"Knock yourself out."

"So flip," he murmured. "You scared it might work?"

"So confident," she shot back. "You scared you can't convince me?"

He laughed.

Rory held up her hands. "Enough for one night. Please. I need to go home."

Dalton helped her with her coat.

When she spun around to say something, he put his finger across her lips.

"Give me a chance. That's all I'm asking."

Chapter Five

Day two in the rehab hospital sucked ass.

Dalton didn't know why he and his brothers were sitting in an overheated bedroom with a bitter man who didn't want them there. The one time when he'd made eye contact with Casper, he'd seen that mean gleam—as if the asshole was remembering the last conversation they'd had three years ago that'd resulted in Dalton leaving.

The TV blared behind him as Casper flipped between twenty-four hour news channels. At least the noise cut the tension in the room.

How long did they have to stay?

The respiratory therapist came in and Casper made that frantic motion that he wanted them out.

The three of them wound up in the reception area. Listening to the constant *ding ding* that indicated a resident needed assistance. The phone at the receptionist's desk rang constantly. A couple of people in wheelchairs parked outside the reception area stared at them with vacant eyes. One guy waited by the door, intent on making a break for it.

The sights, sounds and smells overwhelmed him, but didn't seem to bother his brothers at all.

Tell flipped through a newspaper. He read interesting tidbits out loud. Then he said, "Whoa, check this out."

"What?" Brandt said.

"Remember last year when the legislature revised that law about elk farms?" Tell asked.

"Elk farms aren't allowed in Wyoming," Dalton said.

"True, but they passed a bill that allowed for privatization of a few elk farms on a trial basis. That last brucellosis outbreak with the Yellowstone herd fucked up the brucellosis-free status for cattleman too. Which pissed off the Wyoming Stockgrowers Association. They demanded policy changes with the state's wildlife management plan, but I know this ain't what they had in mind. There'd been talk of privatization, but no one really believed it'd happen. No one wanted it to happen, but now it has happened. They're takin' applications. Only four permits will be issued."

"What areas are included on the list?"

"Everywhere in Wyoming with the exception of the two areas where the state is already feeding wildlife—in Yellowstone and the Tetons."

Years ago when he and Tell had discussed putting in a livestock feedlot adjacent to the land Gavin Daniels owned, Dalton had researched the wildlife end of it as an alternative, mostly thinking they could get into the buffalo business if the feedlot idea didn't pan out.

When the feedlot hadn't looked feasible, he'd gone so far as to check out privatized wildlife farms in Colorado and South Dakota to check the topography and containment and find out what type of acreage was needed for how many head.

Dalton hadn't bothered checking the regulations for elk farms because they weren't allowed in Wyoming. But now...this changed everything.

He needed something to do and a way to prove to Rory he intended to stick around. The section of land he owned might be a perfect fit for the program. Chances were slim his brothers had done improvements. After he checked the regulations and determined whether his land fit the criteria, he'd send in an application. No one would have to know until the applicant's names were made public. Then he could offer Rory proof that he'd applied right away so she knew he was serious about staying in Sundance since she'd chosen to settle back here. He'd deal with any fallout with his family after the fact.

"Dalton? You okay?" Tell asked.

He glanced up. "I'm fine. Why?"

"You're wearing an evil smile."

"Because I'm planning ways to escape this hell." He rested his elbows on his knees. "How long we stayin' here?"

"Why? You got someplace else to be?" Brandt asked.

Anyplace besides here. "Casper don't want us around. And I've grown past sticking around someplace where I'm not wanted."

Tell and Brandt exchanged a look.

"What?"

"Do you really need us to point out how selfish and unsupportive that statement is?" Tell asked and tossed the newspaper on the table.

"But you didn't dispute the truth of it. Look, maybe you guys have had reconciliation time with him. I haven't. I haven't seen the man in three years and I sure as fuck didn't miss him."

Brandt's gaze sharpened. "Why're you bein' so hostile about this?"

Two fucking days back here and Dalton was slipping into old

patterns. Be enough to make him roar with outrage if he hadn't gotten a handle on that former tendency too. "I'm not hostile. I'd like to know why it was so all-fired important for me to be here when it's obvious he doesn't want me here."

"You wondering why he don't want you here?"

No. I already know.

Brandt blew out a frustrated breath. "Look, he's mentioned over the years he don't think it's right that you just up and left your ranch responsibilities to us."

Dalton shoved his anger down, way down deep. After the mean bastard had all but chased him out of town, he had the fucking balls to talk smack about him to Brandt and Tell?

You're surprised? He always tried to get you and your brothers to turn on each other.

Pointless. All of it. And he wouldn't get sucked into an unproductive fight with his brothers because Casper had orchestrated it. He stood and gathered up the newspaper. "You're right. My hostility, veiled as it may be, is causing problems. So I'll go. I wouldn't want to impede Casper's recovery process."

Maybe a small part of him was disappointed when his brothers didn't try and stop him from leaving.

Tell stared at the door that'd banged shut after Dalton's abrupt departure. "What the fuck is goin' on with him?"

"Hell if I know," Brandt said.

"I hate this." Tell forced himself to flex his fingers, which had balled into fists. "Why won't he talk to us?"

"I wish I knew." Brandt got up and started pacing. "I never understood why he took off like he did after the thing with Addie. Something else happened. Something he didn't tell us then and he ain't tellin' us now."

Tell agreed. He'd gone over that last conversation between Dalton, Brandt and himself a million times. Still made his chest tighten when he remembered how fast it'd happened and everything in their lives had changed.

He and Brandt had shown up at their little brother's trailer five days after the wedding fiasco at Dalton's request. He'd taken his lumps for being a runaway groom and the three of them exchanging the good-natured barbs they always did. Then he'd tossed them the keys to his trailer and announced, "Thanks for coming by. Just a heads up that I'm leavin'."

"What? Why?" Brandt had demanded.

"I don't fit this place anymore."

"Bullshit. It's just a kneejerk reaction," Tell said.

"I assure you it's not." Dalton pointed to his pickup. "I'm packed." He pointed to the house. "It's cleared out. Propane is shut off. They're coming to cut the electricity Monday. The water is turned off. I wanted to say goodbye before I take off."

"To where?"

Tell had watched as Dalton's gaze swept the land he'd worked on, cursed at and been part of his entire life. "Anywhere but here."

"No need to do nothin' rash because of the Addie situation," Brandt said. "It will blow over. We'll help you figure something out that makes more sense than you running off."

"Look, I appreciate the offer but my mind is made up."

"Just like that? You didn't come to us about any of this?" Tell demanded. "You just handled it on your own, like you do everything else? Fuck that, Dalton. You don't get to leave."

"Tell, that ain't helpin'," Brandt warned.

"I don't care. This has been building for a while and we all know it. I thought if you settled down with Addie, things would go back to normal between us."

"Normal...how?" Dalton asked.

"Don't be a smart ass."

"I'm not. I'm dead-ass serious," Dalton said, trying to keep his tone even. "Things haven't been normal around here since Mom and Casper split up and he got hit by the Jesus stick. We lost our family unit—shitty as it was. We've lost out on land. We've bought land. We've made plans to do something different in agriculture to expand our income base beyond what we're makin' as part of the McKay ranch. But I realized it's all talk." Dalton held up his hand when Tell started to protest. "Not laying blame. Just stating facts. The feedlot ain't gonna happen. We've got extra acreage but we're not running more cattle. Haying it does save us feed costs, but I didn't charm Charlene Fox to become a damn hay farmer." He paused. "And I get it, all right? You guys have wives and families of your own and you're settled in. Those plans don't mean as much to you now as they used to. But I sure as hell can't implement any of those plans on my own, so I'm gonna take my cue from you two, let it go and move on."

"So we didn't do things your way, on your time frame, so you're showing us how pissed off you are by leavin' town? That's pretty freakin' childish, bro," Tell said. "Plus, you are part of this ranch. It is your job to hay. Just because you ain't happy with the work we're doin', or the way we're doin' it, don't mean there ain't work to be done."

"My job, huh? When was the last time I helped either of you with chores?" Dalton asked, looking between them. "You don't know, do you? I do. It's been over a month. Five weeks and four days. The fact that neither of you noticed I wasn't around at all during that time just proves you don't need me around."

Dumbfounded, Tell said, "Dalton, that ain't—"

"Let me finish. Jessie helps out. Georgia helps out. Not because they have to; because they want to. That's what both of you wanted in a wife—a partner who understands ranch life and is a daily part of it. Problem is, there's nothin' left for me to do." Dalton's jaw tightened. "I'm already known as the youngest McKay. I'm already known as the last single McKay. I sure as fuck won't be known as the worthless McKay. Which is why I'm leavin'."

"Tell?" Brandt prompted.

Jerked out of the memory, he opened his eyes and looked at his older brother. "Sorry. What?"

"We have to figure out a way to get Dalton to talk to us," Brandt said softly. "It's on us as much as it's on him that this has gone on so long."

"I know. Got any ideas on how to get him to open up?"

"Nope. He's changed. So I don't think the usual *insult him until he fights back* way we used to deal with him will work."

Tell couldn't even laugh at that. This situation with Dalton was no laughing matter.

Brandt sighed. "Dalton is right about one thing. Sitting here is a waste of time. Let's go home."

Rory's office phone buzzed right before lunch. She checked the line and saw the call was coming from Director Tibke's office. "This is Rory Wetzler."

"Rory? Could I see you in my office, please?"

Her stomach did a slow, sick roll. She'd never been called into Director Tibke's office before. Had she done something wrong? Was she about to get fired?

Relax. Alice in HR does the hiring and firing.

But that didn't mean Alice couldn't be lying in wait in Director Tibke's office.

Answer the man. "Yes, Director Tibke. Right now?"

"Give me ten minutes."

"Yes, sir."

Rory hung up and somehow stopped herself from hyperventilating. She focused on the projects she'd accomplished, her interpersonal relationships with other agents. She didn't think she'd had negative evaluations, either from her boss or any of the constituents she'd helped.

They had to be letting her go.

And her ambivalent feeling about that scared her. She didn't love this job—okay, she sort of hated it, but that didn't change the fact she needed it.

Rory checked her appearance in the bathroom. She'd made extra effort today on the off chance she'd see Dalton. Sort of pathetic that she dolled herself for a man but not for her job.

Stop finding negativity in everything. You are a professional.

Not much of a pep talk, but she'd take it.

She paused outside of Director Tibke's door and inhaled a deep breath before she knocked.

"Come in."

Whew. No sign of Alice inside the room. "You asked to see me, sir?"

"Yes, I did. Thanks for making time for me. Have a seat."

Rory wondered if the visitor's chairs facing the desk were purposely uncomfortable so employees squirmed.

Director Tibke was in his early sixties and had been at the helm of this office since its inception in the 1990s. He'd dealt with a myriad of ecological issues that affected the Wyoming environment—coal mining, methane gas extraction, toxic waste cleanup "super sites" from WWII ammo and chemical dumps. Not to mention dealing with national wildlife endangerment groups who affected state policy as much as the Wyoming Stockgrower's Association that strong-armed the state on Ag management policies. Rory respected Director Tibke because he'd always done what was best for the environment—no matter which group disapproved.

"Rory. Relax. You're making me nervous in my own office."

"Sorry, sir."

"To put your mind at ease, I'm not about to fire you, lay you off or reprimand you." He sighed. "But after you hear what I've got to say, you might wish I'd fired you."

Startled, she said, "Excuse me?"

"I'll get right to the point. Last year the legislature approved a measure that will allow limited private elk farms to operate in our state. It isn't really a pilot program, but rather a test program on whether a permanent change in governing laws might be applicable. As you know, this has been a hot topic in all the affected state agencies."

"Yes, sir. I studied both sides of the issue extensively since my master's thesis dealt with wildlife survival rates in natural habitats versus supplemental assistance either from private citizens or government agencies."

He nodded. "I'm aware of that, which is why you've been selected for this special project."

"Really?" Jesus. Had that high-pitched squeal of glee really come from her?

"Let me explain before you get too excited. The state has already decided on the criteria and I'll be the first to admit that criteria is very loose, which leaves us in a helluva position in choosing qualified recipients."

"How so?"

"Basically any landowner in our district can apply."

Rory frowned. "But since we're in the middle of cattle country, and most ranchers are dead set against any type of elk farm abutting their grazing land, wouldn't that mean we'll have fewer applicants because they'll want the test program to fail?"

"I'd thought of that angle. But the truth is they'll probably all apply for the permit to have some measure of control about the placement of the elk farms. If they're awarded the permit, then they can sabotage it at will and the program will be deemed a failure, thereby getting the Wyoming Stockgrowers Association exactly what they want: no change in the status quo as far as wildlife management policies."

"The application process is that lenient?"

The director laughed. "Of course, because the state requires a nonrefundable application fee. They want the money and they don't have to do much work beyond kicking the applications to the WNRC. We're tasked with choosing the recipients of the temporary permits. We—meaning you. This is your project if you choose to accept it."

"Permission to speak honestly, sir?"

"Of course."

Rory weighed her words before she spoke. "Can I ask if you chose me to run this special project because I'm part-time and you suspect I won't complain about the extra hours without the extra financial compensation?"

"Very astute. I'll admit I like coming in right at my budget every year, so that would've been my second consideration in assigning you. But the WNRC has been allocated money specifically for this project.

51

As special project manager, you'd be upgraded to a fulltime employee for the three-month duration. At a pay rate higher than your current pay level."

That was very good news, but Rory focused on what he hadn't said. "Additional income is always welcome. If my part-time status is your second consideration in assigning me, what is your first consideration?"

"You don't have a horse in this race." He leaned forward. "Half the people who work in this office are dependent upon ranching in some way for their livelihood. You don't have that conflict, and more importantly, neither does anyone in your immediate family. You've lived here your whole life and have a better insight about which ranching families would be feeding you a line of bullshit as far as the genuineness of their application."

Very true. During her high school years she'd earned a reputation for her environmentalist bent. It'd been exaggerated; she'd been called everything from a tree-hugger to a PETA-loving tool. All because she'd tried to raise awareness that everyone involved in agriculture had a responsibility to keep a balance between long-term and short-term land sustainability. She believed in it so strongly she'd made it the focus of her college studies.

"Rory?"

She glanced up at him. "Sorry. Just trying to process this."

"I imagine it's a surprise. The other reason I'm asking you to fill this position is I read your thesis. You've delved into environmental impact studies and shown you're impartial. I need someone running this project who doesn't have an axe to grind with the ranchers but won't choose the recipient because their ideologies are the same."

"I understand."

"So what do you say? Are you willing to take on this project?"

Rory didn't hesitate. "Yes, sir. It would be an honor."

He thrust his hand across the desk and grinned. "This is great. You are perfect for this job. Just a quick reminder that you're not allowed to speak specifics about this special project to anyone outside the office—without my prior approval, at least until the permit application deadline has passed. So, if you have any questions just ask, as I will be your direct supervisor."

No more answering to Horrific Hannah? Sweet. "When do I start?"

"Monday. You'll need a couple days to read over the information." He hefted two six-inch binders onto his desk.

"All of that?"

He shoved the binders across the desk. "You've been here six months. Reading between the lines in governmental doublespeak is second nature to you now."

His phone rang and she slipped out.

Might make her a dork, but she did a little happy dance in her office. A fulltime position. She could quit working at the Twin Pines. After all the years she'd bartended in college and grad school, she'd now have her weekends free.

She probably wouldn't know what to do with herself.

Now you at least have the option of spending time with Dalton.

Dalton.

She'd managed to shove last night's conversation to the back burner. Okay, after she'd stayed up half the night replaying it in her head.

What was his end game? What did he have to prove? And was he proving it to her? Or to himself?

But the part of her that'd always been crazy about him wanted to believe he'd pined for her these past few years. Okay, he hadn't exactly said he'd pined. But he had said he'd thought about her a lot.

Why had he been so vague about the business he needed to tie up while he was here? Did he consider her unfinished business he needed to handle?

God. Why was she obsessing over this stuff like a teenage girl when she had work to do?

Rory turned one more happy circle before she settled behind her desk.

Yes, it was a good day.

Chapter Six

On his way back to Sundance, Dalton's mom called. "Hey, Ma."

"Dalton! I'm so happy you're finally in our neck of the woods."

"What's up?"

"What are you doing tonight?"

He'd hoped to spend it with Rory, but then he remembered she worked at the Twin Pines after her regular job. "Nothing. Why?"

"Come spend the night with me. I'll whip up a batch of chicken and dumplings. And I'll make your favorite sour cream strudel cake."

He groaned. "You win. I'll swing by my place and pack a bag."

"I can't wait to see you, son. I really missed you. Drive safe."

He texted Rory his plans to visit his mom; wouldn't want her to think he was out catting around the night after he swore he'd prove to her he'd changed.

Dalton pulled up to his mom's condo a little after five. He'd barely gotten out of his truck when she threw herself at him. He hugged her back just as strongly.

When she released him, she scrutinized his beard and whapped him on the chest. "If I hadn't known your truck I would've believed some thug from a motorcycle gang was in my driveway."

"You've been watching too many episodes of *Sons of Anarchy*." He held her at arm's length. Her hair was styled short, in a trendy cut, blond and brown mixed in with the gray. With no Casper stress in her life, a good portion of her worry lines were gone. She looked a decade younger now than she had a decade ago. Dalton kissed her cheek and caught a whiff of the perfume she wore on special occasions. Made him feel guilty his visit was considered a special occasion. "You look great. I might not've recognized you either."

She looped her arm through his. "Come inside. I've got beer or coffee."

"Coffee would be great." He shot her a grin. "To go with the cake."

"Which is for dessert," she reminded him.

"My new motto is dessert first."

"Then it's a good thing I already cut you a slice, isn't it?"

While his mother futzed around in the kitchen, he wandered through the living room of her condo. He'd never thought much about decorating styles growing up—the stuff in their house was just the stuff that'd always been there.

Her furniture—a couch, loveseat and recliner in vivid red—reflected the bold changes in her life. The end tables were simple and clutter-free except for the photos of her sons as boys, as teens and as young men. Now pictures of her grandsons were interspersed with those snapshots. Pictures of Brandt and Jessie. Tell and Georgia. He squinted at the last one on the shelf. How had she gotten a picture of him at the world poker tournament? And a rare one of him smiling during a poker game?

"I got that by watching the video of you online and freezing it. I made a print off the computer. I didn't have any recent pics of you."

Dalton faced her. "Are you gonna chew me out for—"

"No." She placed her hand on his biceps and squeezed. "You needed to go, Dalton. I'm glad you did. And we don't have to talk about this two minutes after you've walked in the door."

"Thanks."

"Dump your bag in the spare bedroom. You get to bunk in the room with the toys I keep around for my grandsons. Then wash up and come to the kitchen."

He took his time checking out the remaining pictures in the hallway, surprised to see his parents' wedding photo in the mix. Why would she keep that? But as he looked around, he didn't see another picture of Casper McKay anywhere. Dalton wandered to the kitchen. "Smells good in here."

"I sort of went overboard. Get tired of cooking for one so be warned. I hope you're hungry."

"Always."

"So the last time I talked to you, you were getting ready to lead your last hunting party of the season. How'd that go?"

"Great. Hunters are always happy when they get an elk. All three guys did. They were lucky they got to see the rugged beauty of Montana and not the rugged weather."

His mother poured him a cup of coffee and sat across from him. "I promise I will get up there sometime." She shot him a look. "Unless you're moving back to Sundance permanently?"

He hedged. "So you didn't let Brandt and Tell know we'd kept in contact the last three years?"

"No. If they suspected I knew where you were they never pushed me to tell them."

"I appreciate that."

"I appreciate that you did keep in touch with me, Dalton. You're a grown man, but I still worry. I'm thrilled you got out of Wyoming and saw the world. Even if you're still trying to find your place in it."

"You ever encourage Luke or Brandt or Tell to take off?"

She wiped her mouth with a napkin. "Luke? No. Brandt? No. Wait, I take that back. Maybe after Luke started stepping out on Jessie. Brandt wanted to be anywhere besides on the ranch where he had to watch his brother act like a fool and destroy the woman Brandt loved. But Brandt was loyal to both of them even when it ripped him apart. And Tell? If you remember, I did push him to go out on the road rodeoin' that one summer. But he had it in his head he'd never be good enough to make a living on the rodeo circuit, so he came back home."

"Casper tellin' him he sucked all the time might've played a part in that," Dalton said dryly.

"Not that I disagree, but bein' the cousin of Chase McKay had a lot more to do with it."

Dalton cut a dumpling in half and popped it in his mouth. The taste took him back to his teen years. Mealtimes were some of his favorite memories growing up. His brothers laughing and teasing each other. Casper had behaved for the most part, rarely picking fights with his sons at the dinner table, lest his wife stop cooking. She'd insisted they'd enjoy at least one civilized meal each day.

"Dalton, sweetheart, are you okay?"

He glanced up at her and smiled. "Yeah. Just thinkin'. This food takes me back. To, you know, growing up." He paused. "It wasn't all bad, was it?"

"No son, it wasn't. When you boys were little, for a few years, it was decent. I'd hoped Casper..." She shook her head. "Like so many things with him, it didn't stick."

"Why did you stick around?" Dalton couldn't think of any woman who'd put up with what Joan McKay had.

"Because I thought I loved him. I wanted to believe that Casper was capable of being a good father. I thought if I didn't micromanage every second he spent with you boys, he'd grow into his role in your lives." She reached for his hand. "It was the hardest thing I've ever done, besides burying Luke, letting you boys work with him every day." Her eyes filled with tears. "Look how that turned out with you. I had no idea what he was doing and you paid the price for my trust and hope. I've gone over this dozens of times with my counselor—"

"You're still seeing a counselor?"

"I stopped for a while. Then Tell and I had that big blowup and I realized not all the changes I'd made in my life since the divorce were good. I'm more...settled when I have an unbiased person to unload on." She squeezed his hand. "Which still makes me wonder if you resent me."

Dalton wasn't sure how to answer. Wasn't sure if he should answer.

His mother retreated. "You know what? Scratch that question."

"No. It's okay. There's no way you could've protected us from him twenty-four/seven—especially not in the family ranch environment. Luke told me he'd figured out when he was fourteen that if he didn't learn how to do everything on the ranch and teach us how to do it, there wouldn't be anything for us to inherit. He also explained that Casper failing on his section of land didn't reflect poorly on him, but all the McKays. That's what Casper wanted—to be a burden to his brothers so they couldn't ignore him.

"He's that guy, Mom. An expert at verbal abuse and manipulation. Takin' out his bitterness on everyone around him. He showed us that ugly side and it wasn't like you were safe from his mean mouth. I'd resent you if you'd hid in the house so we bore the brunt of whatever fucking anger was eating him, rather than you. But you've never been that type of mother."

"I appreciate you understanding that." She sniffled. "I did leave Casper once."

A sick feeling formed in the pit of his stomach. "When?"

"Tell was just out of diapers. I don't remember what Casper had done, wasn't anything like he did in later years, but I'd had enough. I left for five days, maybe a week." A faraway look entered her eyes. Then she caught herself. "Didn't mean to ruin your appetite with this conversation. Eat up."

"Yes, ma'am." But he couldn't. He wanted to know where she'd gone and what she'd done when she'd walked out. Who she was with. But the words stuck in his throat.

"So Casper is in a rehab unit?"

Dalton nodded. He'd wondered if she'd ask. "He can't speak and refuses to work with the speech therapist. Which is why I don't understand...never mind. My opinion won't matter."

"It does matter. Tell me."

"Why are Brandt and Tell wasting time with him when it's obvious he don't want them there? They got pissed off at me today, like I was some callous—hell, they even called me selfish—asshole for not wantin' to sit in his room for hours on end watching him glare at the TV."

"They're there out of guilt."

"But why? It ain't like he's gonna have a change of heart and become a completely different person."

"It's been known to happen with strokes. There's part of your brothers that have always held hope for reconciliation."

Dalton raised his eyebrows. "Meaning that Casper will wake up one day and have such remorse that he'll try to make things right with his sons?"

She nodded. "They'll never admit it out loud, but there's still that boyish hope." Her gaze encompassed his face. "You don't have that same hope. And before you get defensive, the way you feel doesn't make you callous. It makes you a realist. You're different from your brothers, Dalton."

It was on the tip of his tongue to ask how different.

"I know Casper has given you years of grief about that. Calling you...well, I won't repeat it. Takes a stronger man to walk away from constant conflict. You did that."

"According to some, that makes me a coward."

"Bullshit."

His gaze snapped back to hers.

"I'm a coward, for staying as long as I did after you boys were out of the house. I shoulda left him after you turned eighteen and moved out. I shoulda left him after Luke died when it became apparent we wouldn't grieve our son together. The only reason I found the guts to do it at all was because of Brandt and Jessie. They deserved the happiness and love they found in each other." She looked away. "I'll admit I'm a big part of your dad's bitterness. I felt staying with him was my penance for the way I trapped him into a marriage he didn't want."

They'd never talked about how or when his parents had met. "Have you talked to your counselor about how you're still takin' the blame?"

"Son, I willingly admit my part. Not all, but I'm not blameless."

"I'm glad you've got your own life now."

"There are times I miss the ranch." She took a sip of water. "Did you miss it when you were traveling?"

"The people more than the place. Did I miss the work? No. Not because I'm lazy, but even the work dynamic changed when Jess and Georgia became involved. I did my own thing. Still got grief for it. Probably always will."

"So how long will you be in Sundance?"

"No set time frame. A couple of things came up I need to handle. Truth is, I wasn't looking forward to spending the entire winter in

Montana. I hate the feeling of bein' stuck. When it snows two feet at a time in the mountains, it's unavoidable."

"Would Rory Wetzler bein' back in the area have anything to do with that decision?"

Dalton pushed his plate away. "Yep."

She laughed. "That's all I'm gonna get outta you?"

"Not much to tell." He grinned. "Yet."

"I see you haven't lost the McKay charm in your world travels."

His grin vanished. But his mother didn't notice; she'd started picking up plates.

"So what would you like to do tonight?" she asked.

He shrugged. "I'm good hanging out."

"What about going out? To a honky-tonk just up the road. Do a little dancin'. There's a great band playing this week. You up for that?"

Dalton kept his shock in check. His mom wanted to go out dancing? Didn't seem like her thing. Then again, she had a different life now and this was his chance to see her in action. Since he intended on taking Rory dancing soon, it'd do him good to brush up on his two-step skills. "I could be. Is your boyfriend gonna be there? 'Cause I don't want you to ditch me in some strange bar so you two can suck face in the corner."

"Dalton Patrick McKay! I would never do such a thing!"

He laughed. "Kiddin', Ma. But I will need your help with something before I leave in the morning."

Chapter Seven

Two knocks sounded on Rory's office door.

She highlighted the section of proposed state regulations—easy to get lost in repetitive government double-speak—and said, "Come in."

Glennis, the receptionist, poked her head in. "Rory? There's a man out front who'd like to speak with you."

She frowned. "Why didn't you just send him back?"

"Well, ah...I wasn't sure..." Glennis's cheeks grew flushed.

Why was the receptionist blushing? Then Rory knew.

Dalton.

"The man in question looks like Charles Manson? Don't let the crazy beard fool you. He's harmless."

Glennis appeared startled. "This guy doesn't have a beard. And he insisted you come out to the reception area."

Not Dalton after all. Not an unusual request, either. Some men she dealt with believed their questions about certain programs would be less official if they weren't asked in her office. Made no sense, but mindsets around here were off center anyway.

Rory pushed back from her desk. "Thanks, Glennis. I'll handle him."

"I wouldn't mind handling him," Glennis muttered.

She headed down the hallway, her brain still mired in processing the morning's paperwork. She glanced at the man standing in front of the windows with his broad back to her. Not that she minded; his rear view was excellent. Dark Cinch jeans—which she preferred to Wranglers—a black wool vest worn over a crisp white shirt and a black hat.

"Sir? You wished to see me?"

He turned around and Rory froze. Good thing she'd locked her knees or she might've ended up falling to them.

It was Dalton. Without a beard.

Holy, holy, holy crap.

She'd always considered him a level beyond cute in that baby-faced way, with his dimpled smile, big blue eyes and full lips. This

Dalton...goddamn. He defined hot and rugged man—all man.

"Rory?" he asked softly.

She managed to eke out, "You got rid of the beard."

Dalton rubbed his fingertips over his face. "Yeah, well, it feels weird." He laughed self-consciously. "Probably looks weird too."

"God, no. It looks..." Fucking fantastic.

Why don't you just blurt out what a hottie he is?

He raised an eyebrow, waiting for her to finish.

Flustered, she dropped her gaze and noticed he held flowers. She met his eyes again. "For me?"

"Yes."

"Why?"

He took a step closer. "To prove to you that I've changed." His mouth brushed her ear. "So prepare yourself, darlin'. I'm gonna romance the hell out of you."

"Here?" she whispered.

"Here, there and everywhere," he murmured in that deliciously deep voice.

"Rory?" Glennis said somewhere behind her. "I've got an extra vase for those flowers if you need one."

Rory had to stop herself from jumping away from Dalton like a guilty teen. "That would be great, Glennis."

"If you wanna take Mr...?"

"McKay," Rory inserted.

"Mr. McKay to your office, I'll bring the vase to you."

"Thanks." Her gaze hooked Dalton's. "If you'll follow me." She turned down the hallway. A few of her female coworkers poked their heads out as they passed by. Word spread fast in this office.

Dalton probably did that whole cowboy hat tip-nod thing that made women swoon.

I've changed.

Yeah, right. Rory whipped around to try and catch him in his charm-the-pants-off-every-woman-within-range act, but Dalton's gaze was firmly on her ass. Nowhere else.

That shouldn't have made her feel better, but it did.

Those big blue eyes met hers. "You caught me lookin'."

No apology. No surprise. "Because you can't keep your eyes off this sexy uniform?"

"It's not clothes that make a woman sexy, Rory."

She spun back around and cut through the copy center to reach her office. She'd intended to sit behind her desk, putting some space

61

between them, but Glennis followed them in.

Talk about speedy.

Glennis set a vase already half-filled with water on the desk and handily plucked the flowers from Dalton.

Rory gave her an arch look at her uber-efficiency.

"I saw him with those and figured someone in this office was getting flowers. It's my job to be prepared." She left and shut the door.

She started to open the door, but Dalton intercepted her. "Leave it closed."

"Why?"

"Because I want to talk to you in private."

Before she could ask what he wanted to discuss, the *ooh pretty!* side of her brain focused on the hunky man flesh within touching distance. Almost without thinking, she placed her hands on his face. His skin was so warm and smooth. And he smelled amazing.

"Damn you, McKay. You should've kept this good-looking mug of yours covered up under that ugly fur."

"What? I shaved it because you said you didn't like it."

He'd shaved it off for her? Her fingers traced the edge of his strong jaw. His cheekbones. The dimple in his right cheek.

Dalton made a growling noise and Rory found herself pressed against the door by two hundred pounds of cowboy. "Deal is, you touch me, I get to touch you."

"Hey. I didn't agree to that deal."

"It's unspoken." Dalton angled his head and placed a kiss on the side of her neck.

She should've demanded he stop after that first soft kiss. Or the second, placed on her neck below the first. She really shouldn't have let him string hot kisses down one side of her throat and up the other side. She probably should've moved away instead of leaning closer when he started rubbing his smooth face against hers.

But it felt so good.

"Rory," he murmured in her ear. "Have me for lunch."

That snapped her out of it. "What?"

"Have lunch with me."

Jesus. This man muddled her brain to the point he could make her hear things she wanted to hear. "Dalton. I can't."

"Too short of notice, huh?"

"It's not that."

Dalton eased back but his hands remained braced beside her head on the door. "Then what?"

"This is going way too fast for me. You show up at the Twin Pines and bully-kiss me into giving you my phone number."

"Bully-kiss? Never heard that one before."

"The night before last when we had supper at your place you used that bully-kiss tactic on me then too."

"I didn't use the bully-kiss tactic yesterday," he pointed out.

"Only because you went to visit your mom and we didn't see each other," she retorted.

"I haven't used the bully-kiss tactic today." He grinned at her. "Not yet anyway."

Her eyes searched his. "I'm serious. You just blow into town after three years and I'm supposed to take it on faith that you want to be with me? Especially after we hadn't been on the best terms for several years before that? It's only been three days."

A fierce look entered his eyes. "If I'd known you were back after breaking your engagement I'd been here six months ago."

Rory stilled. Dalton hadn't brought up her broken engagement the other night so she wasn't sure he'd known about it. "How'd you find out?"

"That you kicked that douche-fucker—who wasn't good enough to date you, let alone marry you—to the curb? Sierra told me four hours after I left Montana. And I let her have it for keeping such a big fucking secret from me."

Rory ducked under his arm and put distance between them. "I didn't know you were so tight with Sierra."

"I keep in touch with her because she's the only McKay who never knew me during my growing up years, so she doesn't hold a fixed opinion about me."

"So you could keep in touch with her, but not me?" Crap. Why had she said that? "Did Sierra blab all about me?"

Dalton crowded her again. "Only if I asked. So I knew about your engagement. You were seriously gonna marry a guy named Dillon Doland?"

"He goes by Dil. Besides, it's not the person's name you fall in love with, but the person."

He grabbed her upper arms and pulled her closer. "Were you in love with him?"

Given the jealous fire flashing in Dalton's eyes, she was surprised how easily she manipulated the truth. "We had a lot in common."

"Did. You. Love. Him."

"Why does it matter now?"

"Dammit Rory, I can't stand the thought..." Then Dalton's hands slid up, framing her face as his mouth took possession of hers.

The kiss started out red-hot and spiraled higher from there. Every slide of his tongue against hers, every tiny suck, every nibble, every time he pulled back he made a low groan and dove into the kiss again. He read her reactions and adjusted accordingly with the perfect combination of passion and temptation. Making her crave more body-to-body contact, more...everything.

He slowed the kiss and backed off. "Didn't mean to do that here, but I just wanted you to know."

She rested her backside against the desk because her legs were jelly. "You wanted me to know that you intend to romance the hell out of me?"

"No."

"Know what then?"

Before he could respond, the door swung open and Hannah walked right in.

Rory was relieved Hannah hadn't showed up two minutes earlier and caught her and Dalton in a hardcore lip lock.

"Oh, hello," Hannah said to Dalton's chest, "I didn't realize you had a visitor, Rory."

Like hell you didn't.

Dalton said, "I'll leave and let you get back to work."

The hungry way Hannah was eyeing Dalton annoyed the piss out of her. Rory set her hand on Dalton's arm. "We're still on for lunch, right?"

He didn't miss a beat. "Of course. Is the Mexican joint still in business?"

"Yes. I'll meet you there in...fifteen minutes?"

"Works for me." He gave Hannah the cowboy nod before he walked out.

And lecherous Hannah cranked her head around—much like that chick in *The Exorcist*—to watch his backside as he ambled out.

"Was there something you needed, Hannah?"

"Just checking to see if you ordered additional office supplies for your new temporary position."

Right. Hannah just wanted to let Rory know she could barge in any time she liked—regardless if she technically wasn't Rory's boss for the next few months. "No. I'm covered."

After Hannah exited the office, Rory spent five minutes brightening her makeup before she drove the mile into town.

Dalton stood when he saw her and kissed her cheek. But he

frowned when Rory sat across from him and not next to him.

"Did you get in trouble with your boss lady?"

"No. She's just a snoopy bitch."

"I figured as much. I didn't order you a margarita because I wasn't sure if you could have a drink at lunch."

"Better not. Hannah will probably do a breath check on me when I get back." She scrolled down the menu choices. "I'm so glad I don't have to answer to her for the next three months while I'm in charge of a special project."

"What's the project?"

Rory looked up at him and grinned. "It's a fulltime project, that's what matters at this point."

"Is this project a stepping stone to getting a fulltime position at the WNRC?"

God she hoped not. If anything it'd add interest to her resume so she could escape this job from hell. She hedged. "We'll see. I gave notice at the Twin Pines. I have to work Saturday night but after that I'm done. One job."

"Will you know what to do with yourself with only one job?" he teased.

"Probably not."

"Luckily I've got some great ideas on how to keep you entertained."

I'll just bet you do. As Rory was about to point out that she wasn't a source of entertainment while he killed time in Sundance, the waitress came by.

Rory ordered a pulled pork burrito and Dalton ordered a salad with spicy grilled chicken. "A salad in a Mexican restaurant? Really?"

"I'm not used to eating this much. Between the junk food feast the other night and my mom cooking a triple helping of my favorite meal, which included cake, I've gotta watch it."

"You look more...buff since I saw you last."

"Logging will bulk you up in a helluva hurry."

"How is your mom?"

"Really good. She dragged me to a hole-in-the-wall bar last night, where apparently she's a regular. I got a huge kick outta seeing that side of her."

"My mom is different since she and Gavin hooked up. Not in a bad way. She's got that best friend, confidant, lover thing with Gavin. I'm happy for her because she deserves it."

Dalton took her hand. "But?"

"But nothing. Although there is the teeniest part of me that is jealous."

"Is that why you decided to settle for Dildo?"

"Dildo?" she repeated.

"Dillon Doland, your ex-fiancé. Dildo for short, from here on out."

She laughed. Hard. "I forgot how funny you are."

"I didn't forget how beautiful you are when you laugh."

"Dalton. Don't."

"Don't what?" His thumb swept over her knuckles as his gaze roamed her face. "Tell you when Sierra told me you planned to marry someone else that I drowned my sorrows in a fifth of scotch?"

"You did?"

"Yep. For three nights in a row. You might find this hard to believe, but my fightin' days ended after I left Wyoming. So it'd been a while since I'd picked a fight. But I found the biggest, meanest logger in the bar. You know how the rest of this goes—he beat the fuck outta me."

Rory's gut clenched. Not only at the mental image of him being bruised and bloody, but that he'd actually told her the engagement caused him to snap.

Don't fall for it. He's playing you.

"Don't you believe me?"

"I just don't get why you're telling me this now."

"So you know that the supposed fast pace between us and the way I feel about you...ain't something that just happened in the last three days."

Talk about being steamrolled. Before she could ask how he felt about her, the waitress delivered chips and salsa.

"Got plans for tonight?"

"Yes, I do."

His eyes narrowed when she fidgeted. "With who?"

Rory glanced down.

Strong fingers lifted her chin. "With who?" he repeated.

"A couple of girls I met at the community center. We're all single so we call it our Friday night date."

Dalton continued to stare at her. "Then you'll just have to invite me as your date next Friday night. Because, sweetheart, you're no longer single."

Her jaw dropped. "You're kidding, right?"

"Nope." He angled forward and flashed his teeth. "I want to make it very clear to everyone that you and I are together."

"What if I'm not ready for that?" Rory demanded.

"Then get ready. I've waited long enough."

"FYI: I don't like the pushy bastard McKay side of you."

Dalton got nose to nose with her. "FYI: Tough shit. I'm not hiding our relationship from anyone."

"We don't have a relationship. One lunch date, one dinner date and a bunch of stolen kisses do not a relationship make, Dalton."

"Fine. Rory, will you go steady with me?"

She scowled at him. "Not funny."

"You have a set number of dates in mind before we can call this what it really is?"

"What this is, is you having delusions about what we—"

His very loud, very male growl of displeasure stopped the flow of bullshit from her brain to her mouth.

"Don't pretend this is one-sided."

She said nothing.

Which seemed to further annoy him. "If you don't want me in your life at all, say the word. I'll walk away right now and you won't see me again."

Her mouth opened. Closed. She tried to open it again but she'd contracted a case of lockjaw in the past five seconds. She couldn't force the denial out of her tightly closed lips.

That's because you can't deny it.

Christ. She had to be the most masochistic woman on the planet, jumping in the mosh pit with Dalton McKay again.

But Dalton didn't gloat. He seemed relieved. "Answer the question. How many dates?"

Somehow, Rory tossed out, "Five dates. Real dates."

"What constitutes a real date?"

"The usual. We meet. We talk." *Too easy. Add another stipulation.* "And we kiss."

"I'll agree with that definition."

Wait a second. Why was he being so agreeable? And why did she feel she'd stumbled into another trap?

"Our first date was down by the creek the time you asked if we could touch tongues because you didn't get how French kissing could be fun and not gross."

"That was not a date! We were ten and twelve years old."

"Hey, I'm following your criteria." His voice dropped to a husky murmur. "And we kissed that day, jungle girl. I still remember the taste of your lip gloss. Something sweet and fruity. The flavor was sugar...something."

"Sugarplum."

"You still use it?"

"My tastes are a little more refined than a ten-year-old girl's these days."

"Pity. Our second date was the night I so charmingly rid you of that pesky virginity. I kissed you then."

"You're insane."

"Our third date was the night in Laramie when I drove you home from the bar and we ended up in bed. I kissed you then too." His gaze dipped to her chest. "More than just your mouth, if I recall."

Her face heated from his purely sexual look. "If I recall, I was drunk, so it shouldn't count."

"You sobered up damn fast after you threw up all the alcohol. You knew exactly what you were doin' when you invited me into your bed."

Why didn't he have selective memory like most men?

"Then the night I caught up with you at the Twin Pines? Date four."

Rory shook her head. "No way. That one is reaching."

"How about the second time we were together in Laramie?"

She remained stoic. "I don't even want to think about that time, Mr. How-fast-can-I-put-my-pants-on-and-run-out?"

"Not fast enough if I recall correctly. Didn't you kick me in the balls?"

Rory smirked.

"I'll disqualify that one. How about two nights ago when you came to my place? That was very date-like and we kissed. So by my count? We've reached that magical dating number today. Right now as a matter of fact." He smiled with utter confidence and charm. "Face it, sugarplum. We are officially in a relationship. Feel free to tell your girlfriends you'll have a plus one next Friday night for date night."

The food arrived, cutting off her retort.

While she shoved bites of burrito in her mouth, Dalton kept sneaking looks at her and smiling, a little too...pleased with himself.

She set her fork on her plate. "You're gonna make me ask about that smirk, aren't you?"

"Nope. It's not a smirk; it's a smile. This is what I look like when I'm happy." He picked up her hand and kissed her knuckles. "You have no idea how happy I am."

Oh, how sweet.

Are you out of your fucking mind? He's not sweet. This man has an agenda, he's working an angle. And you're falling for it.

"What's wrong?"

You. Me. This. But mostly me because I cannot believe I'm getting sucked in by you again. "I, ah, think I ate too fast."

His eyes showed concern. "Do you have antacids? If not I've probably got some in my truck."

See? Sweet. Genuinely sweet. Like the time when you were kids and you jabbed a piece of wood in the bottom of your foot and he carried you to the cabin.

She'd forgotten that. What other good things had she forgotten about Dalton McKay? A lot.

What's goin' on between us ain't really so sudden.

That freaked her the fuck out. She stood abruptly. "Thanks for lunch, I gotta go or I'm gonna be late getting back to work."

That marked the first time she ran away from Dalton McKay.

Chapter Eight

For the past two days, Rory's concerns, accusations, whatever they were, kept popping up while Dalton was alone working on the house. He admitted they had a tumultuous past, but it hadn't started out that way.

Dalton remembered the first time he'd met Rory when he'd been nine years old. Most kids didn't recall specific days from their childhood with such clarity, but meeting her had been a life-changing event for him.

Had he ever told her that?

Probably not. And if he told her that now she wouldn't believe him. The woman was so damn suspicious of him. Not that he blamed her, given their history.

That afternoon he'd raced away from home as fast as his legs could carry him to the secret spot he'd discovered—a mini oasis compared to the dry, flat land around his house. The creek zigzagged, leaving one section accessible through the fence line. He'd been warned to stay out of the area, but the sound of water soothed him. The icy coldness of it numbed the pain from the strap marks on his backside. He could lie on the flat rock beside the creek and gaze at the sky, lazing in the sun like an old barn cat. Lazing in a way that'd get him whupped again at home. He'd hidden himself away there more than a dozen times, always alone.

Until that day.

A shout of, "Hey!" had jolted him out of the peaceful place.

Dalton had turned around so fast he'd tumbled off the rock. He'd been on his hands and knees, when a pair of red cowboy boots had stopped right in front of him. He looked up into the scowling face of a pigtailed blonde.

"What are you doing on my rock?" she demanded.

Before he could answer, she hit him with another accusation.

"You're not supposed to be on our land."

He'd picked himself up off the dirt and loomed over her. "Yeah, what are you gonna do about it, short stuff? Tattle?"

"Maybe."

"Hey, I know you. You're in first grade."

"I'm going into second grade," she corrected him.

He eyed her suspiciously. "If this is your land, how come you don't ride the bus with me'n my brothers?"

"Because my mom works in town and she picks me up after school."

"What about your dad?"

"I don't got a dad."

"Why? Did he die or something?"

"No. It's just me'n my mom." She scowled. "How'd you sneak in here?"

"Didn't sneak. I walked." He pointed. "From that way."

Her mouth formed an "O".

"What?"

"You're one of them."

Even at age nine Dalton hadn't needed an explanation on what she'd meant. But he'd immediately shot back, "And you're one of them hippies."

"Am not!"

"Are too!"

"Am not!" Then the blonde sprite had charged him, knocking him on his butt in the dirt. He'd cried out, not only because a girl had tackled him—a girl!—but by pouncing on him, he'd hit the ground hard.

"You take that back," she'd shouted in his face.

She'd sat on him and kept his arms pinned down. Man, she was really strong. "Lemme go."

"Not until you take it back."

"All right, all right, you're not a hippie."

Not three seconds later she'd grinned at him and let him go before she stood.

Indignant, Dalton heaved himself to his feet. "I wasn't really tryin', you know. I could've gotten away from you at any time."

"Then why didn't you, huh?"

"Because I ain't supposed to hit girls."

"Oh."

"What's your name anyway?"

"Aurora Rose Wetzler. But everyone calls me Rory."

"Aurora Rose? Ain't that the name of one of them Disney princesses?"

She lifted her chin. "No. The princess in *Sleeping Beauty* was named Briar Rose when she was in hiding with the fairies. I'm Aurora Rose. Not the same at all."

"Huh. I'm Dalton—"

"McKay," she finished with him. "You're in third grade."

"Goin' into fourth grade," he corrected.

Rory walked around him and scrambled on top of the rock. "This is my rock."

"Says who?"

"Says me."

"Bet I can knock you off and make it *my* rock."

"But you ain't supposed to hit girls, remember?"

That'd put him in a dilemma. He'd scrambled onto the rock beside her. "Not the same thing. It's like a contest. Or a game. Like playing king of the mountain."

"That's a stupid game."

"We could play something else." Might be fun to play with a girl for a change. He used to play with his cousin Keely but she bossed him around as much as his brothers did. Not that his brothers wanted to play anymore. And since he was older than Rory, he'd get to be in charge. "We could play pirates! The rock could be our ship." Dalton struck a pose. "I could be the pirate king. You could be the princess I rescued from another ship."

"No way," Rory said. "I don't wanna be some dumb princess. I wanna be the pirate king."

"You're a girl, you can't be a king," he scoffed.

"Then I'll be the queen of the jungle." She'd pushed him off the rock.

Rather than getting mad, he laughed at her audacity.

Surprised by his laughter, she laughed. And they'd become fast friends. Secret friends, running through the woods, splashing in the creek, making forts. The friendship parameters had changed during their teen years, but they'd been a constant in each other's lives.

Dalton needed to remind her there was more than just bad history between them.

So on a whim Sunday morning he'd texted Rory, telling her he'd swing by her place at noon. But Rory's dog, Jingle, was a lot happier to see him than Rory was—and Jingle growled at him.

Only not as much as Rory did. "You cannot just show up at my house whenever you feel like it, Dalton McKay."

"I texted you."

Arms crossed over her chest, she blocked the entrance to her cabin. "You didn't *ask* if you could come over. You just said you *were* coming over. Big difference."

Man, her hackles were up as much as Jingle's—not that he'd voice that comparison. "So you're not interested in the glazed donuts and raspberry-filled bismarcks I brought?"

Her gaze moved to the grocery bag dangling from his fingertips. "That is cheating. Plying me with my favorite donuts so I forgive your breach of etiquette."

"Then why don't you go ahead and add this onto my list of broken rules." He pressed his mouth to hers, intending to share a sweet kiss. But the instant her lips parted, he couldn't help but sneak his tongue inside for a tiny taste of her, which wasn't enough. So by the time he forced himself to back off, his cock was as hard as his breathing.

Good thing he wore a long coat.

"Not fair," she murmured against his cheek.

"I warned you I ain't gonna play fair." He kissed her temple. "I haven't seen you for two days. Which is two days too long. So you gonna let me in? Or will I be sharing these donuts with Jingle?"

"Come in."

Dalton kicked off his boots and headed for the small kitchen.

"Sit and I'll get plates. Would you like coffee?"

"Sure."

Neither spoke until they were both settled at the table with food and drink. "How late did you work last night?" Dalton asked.

"Till it closed at two. The bar side was hopping so I helped out." She ran a hand over the top of her head. "That's why I'm a mess. I slept in."

"You don't look a mess to me. You look perfectly beautiful, as always."

Rory's green eyes turned shrewd. "Yeah, I'm some stunner today. No makeup, my hair pulled into a ponytail and I'm wearing sweats."

Dalton shrugged. "I stick by what I said. Ain't the clothes that make a woman sexy."

Not sure what to say, Rory focused on demolishing her donut. "So why are you here?"

"To bully-kiss you, 'cause I know you missed it."

She snorted.

"I thought I'd see what your plans were for today."

"Not much. Laundry. Catching up on some reading for work. Why?"

"Because I need furniture. You've got great taste so I'd like your help."

"That's it? You're falling down in the charming and cajoling department. Try again."

Fishing for compliments? He could oblige her. "Rory, my stunningly gorgeous, sinfully sexy, surprisingly sweet, whip-smart and all-around perfect dream woman. If you don't help me choose decent furnishings, I'll buy mismatched bean bag chairs and TV trays and call it good." Dalton leaned forward, the picture of earnestness. "Please, goddess of all that requires a shrewd eye and a deft hand, save me from myself."

She laughed. "That's much better. We going into Rapid City?"

"I thought we'd start in Spearfish."

"Why? You interested in antiques? Secondhand stores?"

"No and no."

"That narrows your shopping choices in Spearfish."

Jingle put her paws on Dalton's knee and he ruffled the dog's ears. "Then let's head into Rapid. I don't want anything that has to be special ordered. The furniture has to be in stock so they can deliver it next week. I'm sick of sitting on the damn floor and sleeping on the floor."

Rory drained her coffee and stood. "I'll go get ready."

Dalton was pleasantly surprised when Rory walked out of her bedroom about five minutes later. In his past experience with women, "getting ready" took anywhere from twenty minutes to an hour. "That was fast."

"No need to fuss when you've already seen me *au natural.*"

He tugged her against his body. "I haven't seen you *au natural* for a long damn time and I'm makin' it a priority to change that."

Rory twined her arms around his neck. "I half-expected your reason for showing up today was to convince me to take a tumble or ten with you, since I actually have a bed we could tumble into."

"Tempting." He kissed her. "Make no mistake that I want you like fucking crazy, but I won't rush it."

"So if I said I *wanted* you to drag me to my bed and ravish me right now...?"

Dalton clamped his hands on her ass and started pushing her toward the bedroom.

She laughed. "Just checking."

He'd always hated shopping until he'd gone with Rory.

She refused to let him settle for bachelor-bland furnishings. But the couch, loveseat and recliner she picked were comfortable and not too girly. He chose a king-sized mattress and she convinced him he needed a nightstand and a chest of drawers.

However, she wasn't invested in his home entertainment choices at the electronics store. Dalton picked the most basic setup, including a dish for satellite TV and the internet, a DVR and a DVD player and it still set him back more than he expected.

On the way back to Wyoming, he joked, "I intended to take you someplace nice for helping me out today, but I'm thinking DQ is the extent of my budget." Might make him pathetic, but he was testing the waters—see if Rory had an issue being seen in public with him in Sundance. "I'm sure Dewey's has a decent Sunday special. If you're all right eating there."

"Cool."

Dewey's Delish Dish was nearly empty. The hostess seated them in the back row of booths.

Rory ordered hot tea. Dalton ordered iced tea. They both chose the same open-faced hot turkey sandwich and a dinner salad.

"See? We have things in common."

"Food? That's hardly an endorsement for our compatibility."

Their easy companionship from the day had vanished.

"Dalton, I need to ask you something." When she struggled to speak he knew he wouldn't like her question. "Why do you think a relationship will work between us?"

"It just will."

The waitress dropped off their salads.

"Why are you supposedly so crazy about me?"

It appeared Rory wasn't letting him off the hook. "You're talkin' like this is something that just came up."

"But it *did* just come up when you returned to Sundance."

"So the fact I've known you since you were a bratty, pig-tailed six-year-old doesn't hold any weight with you?"

Rory stabbed her salad. "I'm no more the bratty six-year-old than I am the virginal eighteen-year-old, or the big-mouthed twenty-two-year-old that you used to know. You're trying to convince me that you've changed?" She looked at him. "So have I."

"I realize that."

"Oh yeah? Maybe that's what you oughta be proving to me. Not that you've changed, but in the few times we've seen each other you've noticed the changes in *me*."

Dalton gestured for her to bring-it-on while he forked a chunk of iceberg lettuce into his mouth.

"Name three things about me that are different from three years ago. And any cosmetic changes aren't an acceptable answer," she warned.

Dalton sipped his tea. "If I do this are you willing to do the same for me? And admit I've changed?"

"Sure. But only if I agree your three guesses are accurate."

"I ain't gonna be guessing, 'cause sugarplum, I know that's what scares you." He paused with his fork midair. "There's a melancholy in you that's never been visible before. Maybe it's always been there and you've been good at hiding it, but now I see it." He said, "How'd I do?" before he shoveled in a bite of cucumber.

"Better than I expected." She sliced a cherry tomato in half. "Are you waiting for an explanation for my supposed melancholy?"

"Nope. The more time we spend together, the better my chance to figure it out myself. Besides, I've got two chances left to wow you with my insight into you."

"Bring it."

"You're not as quick to anger as you used to be."

"What makes you say that?"

Funny how she'd snapped that question at him. "You only punched me once when I ambushed you at the Twin Pines." He smirked. "Before? You'd've gotten at least another shot in."

"That doesn't count because I was shocked to see you and off my game."

Dalton lifted an eyebrow.

Rory fidgeted. "I'll admit I have mellowed some."

"Got you down cold, don't I?"

"Don't get cocky, McKay. You still have one answer to go."

"You marked an occasion in your life with a tattoo."

Her mouth fell open. "How did you know that?"

"I didn't. But I suspected." Dalton leaned forward. "What is it? A heart? A flower? A butterfly? An Asian symbol?"

"I'm not telling you. And since that is a cosmetic change, it doesn't count. Try again."

"I noticed you stopped biting your nails."

He watched as she automatically curled her fingers into her palms. "You've always had ripped cuticles and short nails. Now you don't."

The waitress delivered their main course and conversation ceased.

It wasn't uncomfortable silence, just contemplative.

They must've been hungry because the food disappeared fast.

"Now before you start in on the changes in me, I want you to tell me three things about you that I don't know. Big. Small. Funny." He flashed her a grin. "Sexy."

"Oh, I can do sexy." She lowered her voice to a throaty purr. "I like to wear matching lingerie. Doesn't have to be the high-end stuff, but my bra and my panties have to match." She took a quick look around the restaurant before she started to undo the buttons on her blouse. "Today I wanted to feel feminine so I chose this red number." Watching his avid eyes, she let her finger trace the satin piping of the bra cup across the mound of her breast.

Dalton made a low sound in the back of his throat.

"In spite of the pretty packaging, this one offers a lot of support. Which makes the girls beg to be noticed." Rory kept gliding her finger up and down over the swell.

"I'm likin' this bolder side of you, Rory." He gazed into her eyes. "Is it just a tease or is it real?"

"What do you mean?"

"What would you do if I sat beside you and ran my tongue along that line? Would you push me away? Or would you arch your back and offer me more?" Dalton leaned forward. "Would you let me slip my hand into your pants so I could see for myself that your panties matched your bra?"

Flustered, Rory buttoned up her blouse. "I'll save you the trouble. It's a red thong."

Not so bold after all, are you, sweetheart? But you wanna be and I can work with that.

They stared at each other, both of them breathing hard. There'd never been this intensity between them before. Not even the times they'd been naked together.

"What are you thinkin' about, jungle girl?"

"Underwear," she blurted. "Whether you wear boxers or briefs."

"Boxers. Tell me something else about you I don't know."

She paused. "I teach a yoga class at the community center on Monday nights."

"Yoga, huh? Did you learn that from your mom?"

Rory rolled her eyes. "She can't stand still long enough. I enrolled in a class in college, loved it and I've been doing it ever since. Got my teacher's certificate just for fun. There weren't any classes available here so I started one."

"So technically you're not down to one job if you're still teaching yoga."

"Teaching yoga isn't a job. It saves my sanity."

"Anyone can come to your class?"

"Yeah. Why?"

Dalton shrugged. "Never tried it. Might be interesting."

"Challenging," she corrected.

He shoved his plate aside. "Tell me something you haven't told anyone."

"Why are we still playing twenty questions?"

"You claimed we don't know each other. I'm aiming to learn everything I can about you. So quit stalling. Answer the question."

"Some days I feel like a prisoner to my college degrees and wish I would've done another field of study." She froze. "Shit. Sorry. I didn't mean to say that. Forget it."

"Hey." Dalton picked up her hand. "You don't have to apologize or pretend with me. I won't tell anyone what we've talked about."

Her defiant gaze burned into him. "Like you kept the secret about my mom's financial troubles when she ran the B&B? Oh, right, you went running to Tell with that information as soon as possible. And you also told your cousin Ben. So I'd really rather you forgot what I just said because I don't need my boss getting wind of my feelings because of your loose lips."

Dalton had clenched his teeth so hard the muscle on the left side of his jaw rippled.

He collected himself and while he did that, he ran the ragged edge of his thumb over her knuckles in a soothing manner. Was he calming her down? Or himself?

Keep focused. She's baiting you to see if you lose your cool like you used to.

"How about I ignore that outburst and tell you three differences about me. I can claim I've changed until I'm blue in the face and you still won't believe me, which is why I'm gonna prove it.

"First off, I don't blab all to my family. I hadn't done that for a while even before I left here. And yes, that is one claim I *can* prove. My brothers didn't know I'd been livin' in Montana."

"Were you mad at them or something?"

"No. I just liked havin' my own thing, my own space. Far as they knew I was a wanderer. Second—"

"You're a deliberate thinker," Rory interjected. "You used to say the first thing that popped into your head. Now you factor other things into your response instead of just blurting out whatever you want."

Dalton grinned. Then he kissed her hand. "You noticed. Awesome."

"How long did it take you to change that about yourself?"

"Still an ongoing process. I got tired of bein' known as a loudmouth. It's amazing how much more I've learned when I shut my mouth and listen."

"Lastly..." Rory tapped her fingers on the table and studied his face. "You don't need to be surrounded by people. You're not afraid to be by yourself. You can't deny that you never liked your own company. I always knew when your brothers or cousins didn't want to hang out with you because you came looking for me."

"While you're right about me learning to like bein' by myself and letting go of the circus of fools that surrounded me all the time, you're wrong about the last thing. You never were my last choice, Rory. Then or now."

That flustered her.

Good.

"Would either of you care for dessert?" the waitress asked.

"What are the choices?"

"Pumpkin cheesecake, apple strudel pie, lemon honey cake, peanut butter pie, chocolate caramel brownie. Or we've got ice cream."

Rory's eyes took on a devious gleam. "Sugar pie, honey bun, doll face, knowing my tastes *so well*, which dessert would you pick for me?"

A challenge. "Depends on if you're planning on sharing or if this is just strictly your treat."

"No sharing."

"Ah, there pops out the *mine* demand of an only child. So I'll say...the peanut butter pie."

Her look of surprise was classic.

Dalton smiled at the waitress. "But go ahead and bring us two forks."

"How did you know?" she demanded. "Was it just a lucky guess?"

He kissed the inside of her wrist. "Nope."

"Let go of my hand."

That demand only made him slide his lips farther up to nibble on the soft inner flesh of her forearm.

"You are trying to fluster me, aren't you?"

"Yep." But she didn't remove her hand from his. "So I believe it was my turn to tell you three things about me that you don't know. Big. Small. Funny." He sank his teeth into the base of her thumb. "Sexy."

Rory made a soft noise.

"Here's a small thing. I keep a hundred dollar bill in my truck and another one folded up in my wallet. I've never used them but they're there if I need them."

"Is that because you didn't have enough money for something at one time and it embarrassed you?"

"I can't trace it to a specific incident, but probably."

"Interesting." She pulled their joined hands closer and rubbed her lips across his knuckles. The entire side of his body broke out in goose bumps. "Tell me something sexy, McKay."

"How sexy we talkin'?"

"As explicit as you wanna get."

"When I was in Amsterdam, I hired a lesbian prostitute. For twenty-four hours she taught me everything about sexually satisfying a woman. And I mean everything."

Her eyes widened. Her mouth opened and closed. Then she said, "Are you serious?"

"Nope."

She dropped his hand. "That was..."

"Funny, actually."

"No, it was not!"

"Come on, Rory. Admit it's a little funny."

Her lips quirked. "Okay. It was a tiny bit funny."

The waitress dropped off the pie.

Rory immediately snatched both forks. "For that lesbian hooker story, you lost pie. If you behave yourself, I might give you a little taste." She sliced off a forkful and popped it in her mouth. "Mmm."

He growled, "You're gonna torture me. Makin' sex noises while you're eating that pie."

"Sex noises?" she asked innocently.

"Sex noises like you'll make when my mouth is buried in your pussy. When I'm licking up every bit of your sweet cream and then when I go back for another bite. And another because I'm positive I won't be able to get enough of the slice of heaven between your thighs."

Rory sliced off a huge piece of pie and held it up to his lips. "I'm gonna love hearing that deep growly voice whispering sexy things in my ear when you're making me moan those sex noises. But for now, how about if we stop teasing each other because it's bound to get us into all sorts of trouble in a public place."

He grinned. That was Rory's way of telling him he'd passed her *I've changed* test. "I agree." He let her feed him the pie.

"So were you really in Amsterdam?"

"Yep. Wasn't my favorite place, but I had a good time."

"Where was your favorite place?"

"Lloret de Mar in Spain." Dalton started talking about his travels. Then Rory told him about her experiences overseas and they completely lost track of time.

The waitress pointed out the lights were off in Dewey's, and she showed them the door.

"First time we've closed down a restaurant."

"Far more fun than closing down a bar." He took her hand as they walked to his truck.

"I'll definitely have a clear memory of tonight."

At her house he left his truck running so he wouldn't be tempted to stay, but he walked her to the gate. "Thank you for today. For all your help and hanging out. I had a great time."

"Me too. Do you, ah, want to come in?"

"Yes." Dalton twisted a strand of her hair around his finger. "More than anything. But I'm gonna turn around, get in my truck and go home instead."

"Okay."

He pressed his lips to hers. "I'm goin'."

"Uh-huh."

Another kiss. "Seriously."

"I believe you."

The sweet kisses ended and he damn near inhaled her.

Jingle raced out the doggie door and barked at them.

Dalton broke the kiss. "Helluva guard dog, Rory."

She laughed.

"I'll see you this week."

Chapter Nine

Rory couldn't believe it when Dalton waltzed into her yoga class at the community center.

She just about swallowed her tongue seeing him in a black tank top and baggy athletic shorts, his feet bare, his hair just a little too shaggy, dark stubble on his face, those damn dimples and a gleam in his ridiculously blue eyes. The man looked like a rogue pirate. A hot pirate, with thickly muscled arms and a broad chest. When he stretched his arms above his head and his shirt rode up, she noticed that sexy cut of muscle on either side of his hips. She envisioned herself dropping to her knees and following that deep line with her tongue.

And yep, she caught a glimpse of his abs. Whoa. Did he have a six-pack, an eight-pack, or my god...was that a *twelve*-pack of abs?

No. Fucking. Way. Now she really wanted a closer look.

The other ladies in the class were taking a serious gander at the delicious Dalton. It'd be all over town tomorrow that a macho McKay male had attended a women's yoga class. Then again, a McKay being surrounded by swooning women wasn't exactly news.

That thought annoyed her. Rory marched up to him and completely invaded his space. "What are you doing here?"

"Takin' your advice. You said if I wanted to get to know you, I'd show interest in what matters to you. So I'm here ready to be bent to your will, Teach."

"Do you have any idea what goes on in a yoga class?"

"Nope. That's why I'm counting on you to show me all your moves." Dalton's gaze dropped to her mouth. "With your lips this close I'm tempted to give you one of them bully-kisses you're so fond of."

Rory took a step back. "Not happening. There are yoga mats in the corner. Grab one so we can get started."

"Yes, ma'am."

She whirled around and walked to the front of the gym. When she faced the group, Dalton flashed her a very male grin. Then she watched as Lou-Ann handed him her pink yoga mat and trotted to the back of the room to get another one for herself.

Unreal.

"Welcome, everyone. Since we have a new member in our midst tonight, I feel it's important to go over the rules. First rule. No talking. This isn't a social activity. Second rule. If your muscles become fatigued during a pose, drop into downward-facing dog or child's pose. Please don't pack up your belongings and interrupt class by leaving. Third rule. Remember to breathe." Rory smiled at the sixteen regular class attendees. "Let's get started."

Tempting not to explain any of the warm-up exercises, or demonstrate the resting poses, but her class motto had always been "all who enter are welcome".

Including the man who's only here so he can get into your yoga pants?

Yes.

Maybe she ought to modify that motto on the flyer.

Rory sat cross-legged at the top of her mat, hands resting palms up on her thighs. She demonstrated the *uji* breathing technique before she segued into basic stretches.

Then they were on their feet performing sun salutations. Four sets of each series got the blood pumping and the sweat rolling. She talked them through standard standing poses. While she started the second set, her advanced students worked through backbends.

"Now we'll move to basic triangle and work on all triangle poses before we switch to hip openers." Rory shot a look at Dalton.

His face was bright red. Sweat coated his arms and damp rings darkened his tank top. He looked like he was in pain. But he also wore the determined look she recognized.

So she hid her smirk and kept going.

During the last round, she wandered through the class, making adjustments to individuals' postures.

Dalton struggled—like so many did in the beginning—with the basic downward-facing dog pose.

She stopped in front of him.

He immediately dropped to his knees, breath choppy. He sent her a questioning look from beneath those thick black eyelashes.

"Watch how I get into proper position." Rory placed her palms flat on the floor and hiked her hips up, while rolling her shoulders down and back as she dropped her heels to the floor. She spoke in a low tone. "Now breathe in for three counts and exhale for three counts." As soon as she finished, she said, "Your turn."

His upper body strength was impressive but he had little flexibility in those massive shoulders.

"Elongating the spine is key to flexibility in yoga. Since you can't get your heels on the mat it's all right to keep your knees bent. Drop your head between your arms. No, not that far. Ears by your biceps. That's it. Now stay like that. I'll adjust your hips." Rory widened her stance, setting her feet beside Dalton's hands. She flattened her palms on his lower back and pushed.

Dalton grunted.

"Feel the difference in that stretch?"

"Uh. Yeah." His arms shook and stopped supporting his body, so when he dropped to his knees, Rory's hands slid over his butt.

His perfectly round cowboy butt. She wanted to dig her fingernails into that hard, tight flesh. When he flexed his butt cheeks like he'd read her intentions, her hands fell away.

Dalton lifted his head and her crotch was in his face. Right at his mouth level. So close she could feel his rapid exhalations between her thighs. So close it would only take a slight tilt of her pelvis...

Their eyes met.

The hunger in his sizzling blue gaze had her retreating.

Rory strolled to her spot, trying not to imagine the rough stubble on Dalton's face abrading the inside of her thighs. Or how she'd direct that smirking mouth exactly where she wanted it and put that sassy tongue of his to good use.

Her gaze met Dalton's and he licked his lips. Had the man been reading her mind?

Probably. Because face it, Rory, you're pretty damn transparent.

She shook herself out of it and worked through the final stretching exercises before instructing her students to grab their straps for cool down.

Normally *savasana* was her favorite part of class. Stretched out on her mat, eyes closed, remaining motionless as her mind drifted into blissful nothingness after a hard yoga workout.

But tonight, her thoughts were focused on a hunky man five mats away. A man who'd taken her suggestion about getting to know her seriously. A man it was getting harder and harder to shake off. She wrestled with the truth that she didn't want to shake him off. She liked his attention.

People around her began to get restless—her sign *savasana* was over. She coaxed everyone out of the relaxation state and finished the practice in lotus position with *Namaste.*

The yoga group didn't stick around to chitchat after class. Vanessa pointed to Dalton, waggled her eyebrows and mimed *call me* before she scooted out the door.

Leaving Rory and Dalton alone.

She wandered over. He remained in *savasana* on his mat. "Dalton? You all right?"

"No," he groaned. "You wrecked me. I can't move. I think all the muscles in my body have seized up and you'll need to take me to the ER." He groaned again.

"So you're admitting yoga is hard?"

"Hell yes." Dalton cracked an eye open. "Wasn't there supposed to be chanting? Sitting around doin' deep thinkin' about life and shit?"

Rory laughed. "In some yoga disciplines there's meditation and chanting. Not in this one."

"I'm a pretty fit guy. And this class kicked my ass."

"I've heard that a lot. Come on. I'll help you up."

"No. I'm good. The padding on the floor ain't all bad. I'll just sleep here tonight. Or I'll be dead come morning."

"Dramatic much? Since you're the last one here, by default you're selected to help me put away the equipment."

"Mmm-hmm. Give me a day or two to get back to normal."

"Dalton."

"But if I die...dyin' was worth it."

"Excuse me?"

"Seeing your ass in yoga pants? Definitely worth havin' this post-yoga paralysis."

Rory leaned over and thumped him on the chest. She shrieked when Dalton's hands circled her biceps and he tugged her to the mat, rolling to pin her body beneath his.

"Omigod, you pervert. Get off me."

He grinned. "Say please."

"I'm so gonna kick your ass, McKay."

"Bring it, but I'm pretty sure I've got you locked down, yogi."

She studied him. God. She could get lost in the masculine planes and angles of his face. The man was just too damn good-looking. Her gaze dropped to his full lips. Lips that could be hard and yet soft. Lips that could coax and tease. Full lips that showcased his panty-dropping smile. Lips that were curled into a very cocky smirk. "Were you faking?"

"Nope. My body aches like a motherfucker right now." He bent to nuzzle her neck. "I wanna taste you, Aurora. Lick the salt off your skin."

Why was this turning her on?

Then Dalton's tongue snaked out and swept down the side of her throat. His deep, male groan vibrated right down the center of her. "I'm dying to learn every inch of you with my mouth."

Rory's body arched when his lips connected with the skin below her ear.

He murmured, "Want you, need you, have to have you. Goddamn, woman, the way you respond to me is such a fucking turn-on."

Somehow her brain came back online. "I figured you were turned on with the way your cock is digging into my belly."

His lips brushed her temple. "I've got a better idea of where I could put my cock so it'd be out of the way."

"It'd still be in my way and hard for me to talk since I'm pretty sure you'd like to shove it in my mouth."

"Mmm-hmm. But that's not my first choice of where I'd like to put it." His lips moved down the side of her face, his teeth nipping at her jawline. Her chin. He eased back and looked into her eyes, their mouths a breath apart. "You gonna let me kiss you?"

"Wow. You're asking? That's a first."

"And that right there, smart ass, is why I don't ask." Dalton pinned her arms above her head and captured her lips.

No sweet start to this kiss. His mouth assaulted hers with pure hunger. A wet, hot clash of tongues, of gliding lips and shared breath.

So much passion. The kiss would've knocked her to her knees if she hadn't already been lying down. Her body reacted to this man—a blood-pumping, dizzy, wet-between-her-thighs reaction. Just when she'd begun to wonder why they hadn't stripped, why his mouth wasn't on her nipples as his cock rammed into her, Dalton ripped his mouth from hers.

He buried his face in her neck and a full body shudder rolled through him. Then he sighed—his breath a hot wash on her damp skin. "I want you like fuckin' air, Aurora, but not here. Not like this." He placed a soft kiss below her ear and pushed upright.

That show of control was not how the old Dalton would've acted. He would've sweet-talked her into believing no one would catch them fucking around.

Proof right there that he had changed.

Sad to think she hadn't changed when it came to him. With his hard body on hers and those intense kisses clouding her brain, she would've gladly ditched her clothes and fucked him right there on the pink yoga mat.

Show some restraint.

Problem was, she didn't want to.

But somehow she did. She rolled to her feet. "You are dangerous,

McKay."

"Me? Why do you say that?"

"You know why. I don't care if you're sore, you will help me return the equipment to storage."

"Yes, ma'am."

After she'd shoved everything in the closet and locked it, she slipped on her jacket and gloves. "So you think you'll become a regular at yoga class?"

"We'll see if I'm alive tomorrow." He buttoned up his black duster. "Speaking of tomorrow...what are we doin'?"

Rory eyed his ensemble. Black gunslinger duster, neon orange hat with fuzzy earflaps. His bare calves stuck out from beneath the duster and he wore white athletic shoes and black socks. He was a prime example of what not to wear—so why was she thinking that he looked so damn cute?

Because you're a fucking sap and this man can't wait to tap you.

"Since when do we spend every evening together?"

Dalton leaned over and kissed her nose. "Since you'n me are a couple."

Her argument dried on her tongue when she realized he'd said that almost with...pride. "That may be problematic tomorrow night since I'm having supper with Addie and Truman."

"Great. I'll come along. I need to clear the air with them anyway."

"So you don't think it might, oh, *bother* my best friend that I'm coupling with the guy who dumped her?"

"Oh, you and me ain't even started coupling yet."

"You know what I mean."

"Of course I do. But you have my promise I wouldn't hurt Addie again for the world. She never has to know the real reason that I walked out on her was because of you." He stroked her cheek with a gloved finger. "No one besides us ever needs to know that, Aurora."

Such a sweet man.

Stop that. Right now. He is not sweet. He's a manipulative heartbreaker.

Despite the warnings, she found herself saying, "I'll talk to Addie tonight." Rory poked him in the chest. "But if she or Truman don't want you there, you don't get to whine about it."

He scowled. "When the fuck do I ever whine?"

"You used to—"

"I used to do a lot of shit that I don't do anymore. Proving to you I've changed, remember?" He poked her chest right back. "If Addie and

Truman won't welcome me into their home I'll suck it up and act like a big boy. I'll probably write a poem about hurt feelings, broken friendships and the rocky path to true love."

Rory's eyebrows rose. "A poem? Really?"

He laughed. "Fuck no. But I did have you worried there for a sec, huh?"

She whapped him on the arm and exited the building.

No surprise that Dalton walked her to her Jeep. No surprise, either, that he laid a big, wet steamy kiss on her before whispering good-night.

But it wasn't a good night. Rory tossed and turned in her bed because she couldn't get the man out of her mind. This thing with Dalton was driving her batshit crazy.

She mentally corrected the word *thing* and inserted his preferred term: relationship.

Goddammit. How had the man invaded her life and her thoughts so completely that her word choices weren't even her own? The fact she then heard his confident little male chuckle in her head was just another example of why she was so completely screwed up by all of this. In her book, and in her experiences with one Dalton McKay, screwed up equaled screwed over.

Now the man was acting like he was in love with her, for Christssake.

In love.

With her.

As if he'd always been in love with her.

Yeah, right.

He'd been in lust with her, but that wasn't exactly news since the man-whore had been in lust with any number of women over the years.

She'd replayed their conversations from the past week on the drive home. More questions bounced around in her brain than answers.

If it'd been a one-time thing between her and Dalton—like the night she'd given him her virginity—she could blame him. But she'd slept with him two other times.

The night she'd spilled her guts to him about her mom's financial woes. They'd both been slightly drunk and had no business climbing between the sheets, but they had. From what she remembered...the sex hadn't been that good, just sloppy, quick and regrettable.

And yes, Dalton had been gone when she'd woken up hung-over as hell the next morning. And yes, he'd used the information she'd shared in a drunken rant to try and screw over her mom. Typical fucking McKay. So it'd been a double betrayal.

But had Rory learned her lesson?

Of course not.

When Dalton had shown up out of the blue at her place in Laramie two years later, a dejected man, admitting he'd been second-guessing everything about himself and his life, she'd taken him in. She'd listened to him. Offered him reassurance. She'd shoved aside the bad parts of their shared past and reminded him he'd always been able to confide in her.

But Dalton hadn't wanted his old friend Rory. He'd wanted the woman, not the girl.

And she'd been so mesmerized by his intensity and by his desire for her that she'd been powerless to resist when he kissed her like her mouth existed strictly for his pleasure. When he'd touched her body as if it was solely his to worship. When he'd whispered such sweet and hot promises she'd wanted so desperately to believe.

The sex that night? Whoo-boy. Dalton had seemed equally blown away that it'd taken them two times to get it right. She'd naively hoped they'd started a new chapter in their lives.

But Dalton had reverted to his love-her-and-leave-her persona, except that time, she'd *caught* him trying to sneak out in the middle of the night.

Infuriated, Rory had knocked him on his ass as he'd been putting on his jeans. Then she'd morphed into crazy—shouting threats at him, while he was prone on the floor covering his junk with one hand and his head with the other.

Not her finest hour.

Especially not when she'd locked herself in the bathroom because she couldn't stand to see him walk out on her again. After her crying fit, she'd stared at her red-rimmed eyes and blotchy face in the mirror, then she'd scrutinized the suck marks on her neck and repeated, "Never again, Douchebag McKay," until her hatred overtook her hurt.

So things had turned ugly between them every time they'd crossed paths after that incident. Dalton had too much McKay pride to apologize for who he was and Rory had too much anger to let it slide.

Once Sierra had stepped in, keeping Rory from taking a swing at Dalton's pretty face—even when he'd sworn he'd only been trying to apologize.

But she had no choice except to be civil when Addie and Dalton became engaged. For all intents and purposes the groom and the maid of honor had avoided each other—not that anyone noticed.

So Dalton's confession of why he'd ditched Addie at the altar had knocked her sideways. Even when that time, she knew he hadn't been feeding her a line. Remembering the look in his eyes at that moment still gave her chills.

Now here he was acting like nothing had changed. Like he'd just been waiting for *her* to get her shit together.

Wrong.

Dalton had run out on her too many times for her to take his insistence he'd changed at face value. He'd leave when it suited him—like he always did, regardless of who it hurt.

But this time it could be different—because she was different. Rory wasn't some starry-eyed eighteen-year-old with visions of forever. She had goals and dreams and no man would ever get in the way of them again. Living in Sundance, working at the WNRC wasn't anything more than a temporary pit stop on her way to something better.

So Dalton wanted her—no surprise. She wasn't immune to Dalton's charms—a fact he was perfectly aware of. As much as he'd use it to his advantage, she'd use it to hers too. Let him try and convince her he'd changed. Let him prove to her sex between them would be off the charts fantastic.

After all the shit he'd put her through over the years, she deserved every bit of his sexual attention and expertise. She had no delusions about what she wanted from him; hot sex, companionship on her terms that didn't interfere with her career goals. She could reap all the benefits and take none of the risks.

Because she'd be the one walking away from him this time with her heart and her pride intact.

Chapter Ten

Stay cool.

Dalton tried to pretend he was calm about seeing Addie as he parked in front of the house she shared with Truman.

After all, three years had passed since he'd left her and left town. She'd married one of his best buddies and according to Rory, was perfectly happy with her life. He knew she'd never forget what he'd done, but had she forgiven him?

He'd opted to show up early to clear the air. He rang the doorbell. Dang. Should he have brought flowers?

Too late now, he thought as the door opened. "Hey, Addie."

Addie squinted through the screen. "Dalton? What're you doin' here? Supper isn't for another hour."

"I figured maybe you and me oughta talk beforehand."

It appeared she might slam the door in his face, but she grudgingly said, "You're probably right."

"Thanks." He stepped inside. As in most ranch houses, the door opened into the living room. He paused and wiped his boots.

"I'm in the kitchen putting everything together for tonight," she tossed over her shoulder and disappeared around the corner.

Once he'd settled at the kitchen table, he got his first solid look at Addie. She didn't look much different except for her pregnancy. He smiled. "Smells wonderful in here."

"Nothin' fancy, I assure you. I'm too tired lately to do more than throw food together."

"You look great, Addie. When's the baby due?"

"Two months. We're having a little boy." She rubbed her belly, as so many pregnant women did. "Would you like something to drink?"

"A glass of water would be great."

Addie filled a glass and sat across from him.

"Thanks." He wet his dry throat.

An uncomfortable pause lingered.

There was no way to ease into this, so he jumped in. "I'm truly sorry for the crap you had to deal with after I didn't go through with the wedding."

She folded her arms over her chest, her brown eyes unreadable. "I had no choice but to deal with it since you skipped town."

"Skipped town, chased out of town...big difference. Although I was a brawler back then, my body couldn't take any more punishment from people who beat the shit outta me on your behalf."

Her face paled. "What happened?"

"Your family, your coworkers, your current husband," he said dryly, "all took turns whaling on me."

"Dalton. Are you serious?"

He gave her a suspicious look. "No one bragged about it? No one told you they had your back and they'd taken care of me?"

"No! My god. I had no idea."

"I admit I didn't fight back because I probably deserved it. Except for the scuffle with Truman. I hobbled around for two days after he finished with me."

"Is that why you left Sundance?"

"Partially. I knew it'd be a while before I wasn't the object of scorn. But there was other stuff goin' on that pushed me that direction." He slid his glass back and forth on the quilted placemat. "There was a lot of stuff that we never discussed, Addie."

"I know that now. At the time, I didn't wanna sweat those small details. I thought we'd deal with them after the wedding. For about two months after you left, my mind kept going back to those months we were engaged. Trying to find warning signs I missed."

Dalton met her gaze. "What did you think you missed? Because I had every intention of marrying you that day. Up until the..." *Moment I looked across the altar and really saw Rory.*

"Moment you realized you were about to say vows that were a lie," she said softly.

He nodded.

"The signs were there. You had no interest in wedding planning—I chalked it up to being a guy thing. You hadn't moved a single item from your trailer into my house. In fact, you never brought up the difficulties of living in town when all your family members live and work on the ranch."

His brothers hadn't brought it up either, another reminder how out of touch they'd all been.

"Why were we both eager to pledge ourselves to each other?" Addie shifted in her seat. "When I think back to our engagement? I didn't know you at all."

"I had a moment of doubt at our rehearsal dinner when the

minister started askin' me that list of your favorites. I got one right, your favorite movie, only because we spent a lot of time watching TV."

"I was equally shocked when I got so many of your favorites wrong."

Dalton would never admit Addie had gotten most of his favorite things right, but because he'd sucked at naming her favorites, he'd lied just so she looked as clueless as him.

You were some prize.

"It's not like we had any excuses not to know each other better. We dated for three months and were engaged for six." She fiddled with the ruffled placement edging. "What I can't figure out? Why did you propose to me in the first place?"

"Because you said you loved me."

Her mouth dropped open.

"And you were sincere. You were too good for me, Addie." That had appealed to him. Marrying Addie might make him a better man. He'd known for months prior to their engagement things in his life needed to change. He believed Addie was the catalyst. And she had been—just not in the way either of them expected.

"Is that why you suggested we wait until our wedding night to have sex?"

Dalton blushed. "Most likely. Although I'd convinced myself that's what you wanted. In hindsight, I attributed a lot of feelings and ideas to you that weren't there."

"You got that right." She leaned forward. "A little secret between you and me? I didn't tell Truman that you and I never had sex. In fact..." She laughed. "Exactly the opposite. I told him you were an animal in bed and no man could ever compare."

Now his jaw nearly hit the table. "Addie! Why in the hell would you do that?"

"What? You owed me that lie, given your reputation as a McKay stud that I didn't get to experience." She smirked. "Besides, Truman got it in his head that he needed to be a lover to me that'd make me forget all others and *whoo-ee.* It's worked. I'm always walking around with a big ol' smile on my face." She shook her finger at him. "So don't you ruin my sweet gig and offer some kind of confession to my husband tonight, got it?"

"Got it."

"That said, I cursed your name for months after you left, Dalton McKay. But as time marched on, I realized you were right to call off the wedding. I wish you'd done it before the ceremony. Getting left at the altar ranks as one of the worst things that's happened to me, yet it also led to the best thing that's ever happened to me." She smiled. "Truman."

"I'm glad that you're so happy, Addie. I really am. Although, I gotta admit I never would've put you and Truman together."

"He's no McKay bad boy, that's for sure. Then again, neither were you when we were together."

"Was that why you agreed to date me? Because I was the last supposedly wild McKay?"

"That was part of it. I wasn't the type guys panted over. Not like Rory."

Like Dalton needed the reminder that guys had lusted after Rory. She'd been sort of sweetly clueless about it. Or hostile about it, depending on the day.

"It was fun being the one who hooked the last McKay man. Might sound stupid, but people around here looked at me differently."

"Did they look at you differently after I bailed?"

She shrugged. "Not with pity, if that's what you mean. More like the, *we all should've known he wouldn't follow through with it* kind of looks."

"I'm sorry. Jesus. I can't seem to say that enough."

Addie patted his arm. "I'm over it. I won't ever forget it, but the fact I'm fine with you in my kitchen talking about it says a lot."

"Thank you."

"So I feel entitled to ask you something."

His stomach tightened, but he said, "All right."

"What's goin' on between you and Rory?"

Should he toss off a breezy, *I'm trying to convince her that I'm a great guy, a changed guy and she oughta spend the rest of her life with me?* Nah. Addie would see it as him being flip, and he wasn't joking. "We're spending time together."

"While you're in town visiting your father? Or are you back for good?"

"There are a few factors that'll determine where I end up, so it's a day by day thing."

"Well, as long as you don't mind bein' the rebound guy."

Dalton frowned.

"You knew she was engaged, right?"

He nodded.

"Rory's been hiding here since she broke it off with him. She won't talk about what happened, but I suspect she was pretty broken up about it since she hasn't dated at all." Addie pushed up from the table and offered him a sad smile. "Until you. But face it, Dalton, she knows you're not the settling-down type. Which is why this will be fun for both of you for the short term. Just don't expect too much from her."

Addie was wrong about him. She was wrong about Rory, too. Wasn't she?

"I need to do a few things so why don't you head into the living room. Truman will be home soon. I'm sure you've got things to say to him too."

Dalton stood. "I hope we can talk with our mouths instead of our fists this time." He wandered through the room, looking at pictures and knickknacks. Wondering why he didn't see a TV. He'd bent down to check out the sheet music on the piano when the front door opened.

Truman stared at him for a second from the entryway before he removed his outerwear. Then he said, "McKay. Want a beer?"

"Sure."

"Gotta check on my wife and then I'll be back." Emphasis on *my wife*. "The beer's in the den. Room at the end of the hallway. Can't miss it."

It was a guys' room—no windows, no frilly curtains or throw pillows. Just a big-ass TV, and reclining furniture.

Truman arrived and reached into the bar fridge, handing Dalton a can of Coors Light. "Have a seat."

It'd never been awkward between them. They'd been friends since sixth grade. Since Truman's brother Thurman and Tell were best pals, they'd pulled pranks on their older brothers. They'd double dated. They'd gone to strip clubs and concerts and rodeos together. They'd gone fishing and hunting and talked about cars, girls, sex, guns and sex nonstop.

And right now, Dalton couldn't think of a damn thing to say. A younger version of him wouldn't have been comfortable with the silence. He would've blurted out something inappropriate to break the ice. He sipped his beer and waited.

"I heard about your dad. How's he doin'?"

"Casper is Casper."

"Thurman said that Tell wasn't sure if you'd come back."

"About didn't."

"How long you here for?"

Dalton shrugged. "I'm at the wait-and-see point for a lot of things." He took another drink. "Addie looks good. Congrats on…everything."

Truman sighed. "I'm sorry. I probably shouldn't have beaten the crap outta you that day. But Jesus, Dalton. I had no idea what the fuck was wrong with you and why you'd do that to Addie. Just walk away from her. Seein' her cry...I wanted to put the hurt on anyone who made her cry."

"You certainly put the hurt on me that day."

"Yeah, well. You deserved it. At the time. Now I can't thank you enough for walking away. 'Cause Addie is it for me."

"Did you feel that way about her when me'n Addie were engaged?"

"I was jealous as hell. I knew you didn't appreciate what you had in her."

"You're right. I didn't deserve her. I think I knew that all along."

Truman smiled. "I ain't gonna argue with you."

"So we good?"

"Just as long as you ain't here to try and get back whatcha lost."

I am, but Addie isn't what I lost. "You have my word."

"Good. So tell me what you've been up to the last few years."

Dalton hit the high points and the low points, but he steered the conversation back to Truman. And he seemed eager to prove he could more than take care of Addie and they were blissfully happy.

They'd just cracked open their second beer when the den door opened. Addie stood in the doorway, but Dalton barely spared her a glance. His focus was entirely on the blonde bombshell behind her.

"Rory is here so if you guys wanna come into the kitchen, we can eat."

Truman hopped up. "I'll help you set the table."

The instant Addie and Truman were out of view Dalton yanked Rory into the room, pressed her against the wall and kissed the holy hell out of her. His hand wrapped in the golden silk of her hair. His mouth on hers, owning hers. When he ended the kiss, Rory's eyes were glazed with lust. Her mouth so full and ripe he had to kiss her again.

This time she twisted her head away. "I'm happy to see you too, but will you please quit mauling me?"

"Huh-uh. I knew you'd be pissy if I didn't give you at least one of them bully-kisses when I first saw you. And for the rest of the night, I gotta act like this is casual between us."

Those green eyes blinked at him slowly. "It is casual."

"The fuck it is. And the fuck I'm your rebound guy from Dildo either."

"Rebound guy? That's what Addie said you were?"

"Yes." He paused. "Am I?"

Rory didn't deny it. She suddenly became very interested in the carpet.

His stomach roiled. "Rory?"

Addie yelled, "Come and get it!" before Rory had a chance to respond.

During dinner Dalton had fun reminiscing with Truman and hearing some of the things Addie and Rory had done over the years.

They left after dessert—the separate cars thing sucked, but Rory didn't balk when Dalton suggested he stop by her place for a little while.

Her dog Jingle met him at the gate. "Hey there. Remember me?"

Jingle sniffed and licked. Then her tail started to wag. "You're a good guard dog."

"She thinks she's a guard dog but she's scared of squirrels."

"Well, we've all got fears."

"Even you?"

Especially me, especially when it comes to you.

Seemed more of a rhetorical question as Rory held the door open for him.

Dalton stole a kiss as he brushed past her. He took a look around her place as he shed his outerwear. Such a contrast between Rory's home and Addie's. Nothing matched in Rory's space. The furniture, the pictures hanging on the wall, even the objects decorating the room were colorful, funky and decidedly bohemian. He loved this place that was so perfectly Rory.

"Would you like a drink?"

"I'd love it, but I gotta drive home, so I'll pass."

"Sit down. Take a load off."

He waited to see where she sat and then parked himself right next to her.

"So it seemed like you and Addie were all right," Rory said.

"I'm happy for her and Truman too. He apologized for beating me, but swore he'd do it again if I got it in my head to try and win Addie back."

"That's just ridiculous. You'd never do that. And Addie is madly in love with Truman, so she wouldn't throw him over for you anyway." She sighed. "Guys. It's three things with you. My dick is bigger than yours, I make more money than you and I can beat the fuck outta you."

"Pretty much." He stretched his arm across the back of the couch so he could toy with her hair. "Add in I can outdrink you, outdrive you and whip your ass at cards and that's the brain of a man."

"You forgot the 'and I can fuck any woman I see' too."

"Nope. That falls into fantasy territory for most guys."

"But not for you, or any of the McKays," she retorted. "Alls you gotta do is crook your little finger and women drop to their knees in front of you."

Dalton tugged her closer by her hair. "Alls you gotta do is say the word, sugarplum, and I'll be on my knees before you."

That shocked her.

Good.

She squirmed away. "So was it weird? Seeing Addie?"

"I guess. But to be honest, when I saw her, I felt nothing except an almost giddy sense of relief." Instead of meeting Rory's eyes, he focused on a metal candleholder on the table across the room. "I walked into that house and thought, this would've been my life if I'd married her. Sensible couches, floral curtains, shelves of knickknacks. An ordered life."

"That's not what you want?"

"No. I would've suffocated. I'm relieved she found a man like Truman who thrives on it."

Rory's fingers touched his jaw. "I'm glad you didn't tell her that you dodged a bullet by not marrying her."

"I do have some tact," he said testily. "A lot more than I used to have."

"Oh yeah? Prove it."

He locked his gaze to hers. "For instance, I'm imagining all the ways and all the places I want to put my mouth on you."

Heat flared in her eyes before she banked it. "What does that have to do with tact?"

"I'm keeping the explicit details to myself. Isn't that the definition of tact? Stating the truth in an inoffensive manner."

"Having tact means you shouldn't have said that at all."

"That right?" He twined a hank of her hair around his finger and stared at her. "Guess I don't have as much tact as I thought. Because I'd like nothin' better than to strip off your jeans and spend an entire day with my face between your thighs. Maybe saying that makes me tacky, but I won't lie or pretend that I haven't been thinking about it nonstop." He changed the subject. "How's the special project goin'?"

"Too early to tell only two days into it. I'm still setting up databases."

"Do you like that part of the job?"

"It's part of it whether or not I like it, so it's easier to suck it up and just do it rather than complain. I knew what I'd signed on for when I went to work for a governmental entity. But if I'd known my freshman year in college what I know now? I would've chosen a different field of study."

"Why'd you choose Ag management?"

"I had visions of saving the herds of wild horses. Creating sustainable wildlife habitats. Protecting species from extinction. But with the emphasis on Ag in my degree, I'm dealing with an entirely different area. I should've gone into wildlife biology with a minor in Ag management." She sighed. "Getting a master's degree was a no brainer when UWYO offered to pay for it."

He continued to play with her hair. "From the time we were kids I always thought you'd be a crusader for a cause. But something more rebellious and outside the norm. Becoming a pirate to stop whaling and the clubbing of baby seals."

She smirked. "Like fighting against man's need to conquer the animal kingdom by destroying habitats?"

"Yep."

"You disappointed in my more practical choice of being a nine to five government lackey with health benefits and a dental plan?"

"Not on your life, jungle girl." Dalton leaned over and kissed her.

Rory shifted to sit on his lap; her hands cradled his head as she took control of the kiss. Sweetly seductive, a little hungry, a little fierce, completely captivating.

It took every bit of restraint to act passive when he had visions of kicking the coffee table over, pinning her to the carpet and fucking her until she came at least twice.

Her lips skated across his cheek with butterfly kisses that caused the left side of his body to tingle. "Show me, with your hands," she whispered huskily. "Where you want to put your mouth on me."

Dalton pushed her shoulders back so he could touch her. He followed her jawbone from below her ear to the tip of her chin, then down the long line of her neck to the start of her cleavage. The V-neck sweater, the same earthy tone as her eyes, hugged her curves but also emphasized the flat plane of her belly. His finger traced the edge of the sweater, from collarbone to collarbone, stopping to linger at the midpoint.

Rory's breath hitched when his hands closed over her tits.

He bent his head and kissed the hollow of her throat. "In my version of playing *show me*, you're nekkid."

"Poor baby. Work with what you've got."

"That I can do." He slid his hands down. Palming her ribcage. He stroked the section of skin between her hipbones. The fact he was touching her over her clothes didn't seem to matter; Rory became really squirmy.

Instead of sliding his fingers between her thighs, he placed his hands on her lower back, letting his thumbs follow her spine up to her nape. "I'd spend a lot of time on this side. My lips learning every muscle and curve." He drew a line from the outside of her wrists to the cups of her shoulders.

Then his palms drifted down to her ass. He squeezed a butt cheek in each hand. "Don't get me started on how long I'd spend worshiping this ass. Bet these soft, sweet cheeks would love to feel the rasp of razor stubble against them."

She groaned and let her head fall back in surrender.

"You've got a pair of legs that goes on forever, so I'd give them their proper due." Dalton watched her face as his hands slid up from her knees. Resting the heels of his hands on her inner thighs, his thumbs stroked her pussy. "But this spot right here? I'd save for last. I'd spread you wide and kiss every inch. Then I'd let my tongue come out and play. Maybe my teeth." He knew he hit the right spot beneath the fly of her jeans when she gasped. He pressed his thumb in and rubbed side to side. "I've all sorts of plans for you, Aurora. But not until you give me the green light."

"Umm...it's bright fucking green right now."

Dalton laughed. He leaned forward and kissed her as he removed his hands from temptation. "We'll test that response another time, when my hands aren't on you, okay?"

"You're serious."

"Yep. I want you, I'm dyin' for you to be honest, but you're not ready."

"Ready for what?"

He brushed his thumb over her bottom lip. "Ready for me. For how I'll be when you're completely mine."

A strange look came into her eyes and vanished. "Dalton."

"Aurora." He kissed her and lightly tapped her ass. "I need to git."

When she didn't budge, he rolled to his feet, his hands on her ass, lifting her with him.

Rory shrieked. "What are you doing? I'm too damn heavy for you to cart around like a log, McKay."

He ignored her protests and carried her to the front door. His lips moved to tease his favorite spot at the base of her throat before he set her down. As Dalton slipped on his jacket, he asked, "Will I see you before Friday night?"

"You're serious about crashing my girls' night out?"

"Yep. They can have you for a while. Then you're mine."

Rory traced the edge of his jaw. "There's some caveman showing, McKay."

He shrugged. "I ignored my natural instinct to drag you into the bedroom by your hair."

"I probably wouldn't have resisted much."

"You're getting very close to the limit of my control."

"Sorry." She smooched his mouth. His dimples. The tip of his chin. "I'm glad you came with me tonight."

"Me too."

"Drive safe. I'll text you or call you tomorrow, okay?"

"Sure."

Halfway back to Sundance, Dalton saw a pickup parked on the shoulder with the hood up. He automatically pulled in behind it and got out.

The windows on the inside of the pickup were all fogged up. Maybe that's why the driver hadn't known Dalton had stopped to help. He rapped on the window.

A girl shrieked and a deeper voiced shushed her.

Not good.

The door opened. No interior light came on. "You okay in there? Havin' car trouble?"

A lanky dark-haired teenage boy jumped out. "Yes, sir, the battery..." The kid stopped speaking. "Dalton?"

He peered at the kid's face. Blue eyes, dark hair, rugged, yet boyish looks. No doubt. This kid was the spitting image of his father. "Jesus. Kyler, is that you? All grown up and shit?"

Kyler threw a look over his shoulder and slammed the pickup door. "Yeah, it's me."

When his eyes narrowed, he looked so much like Cord that Dalton had to laugh. "Fancy running into you out here. What're you doin' at ten on a school night?" He couldn't believe Ky was old enough to drive.

"I was takin' Jocelyn home and the battery, ah, just died."

Dalton lifted a brow. "The truck just crapped out in the middle of the road while you were driving it? 'Cause that sounds more serious than just a battery issue." He paused. "Is your dad on his way to get you?"

Pure panic spread across Ky's face and he shook his head. "I haven't called him."

"All right. No bullshit. Why haven't you called him?"

"Because I told him I was at Ryland's house studying and..."

"You were out here sucking face with Jocelyn instead? And you got so involved with sucking face that you forgot you'd what? Turned the radio on for a little mood music and drained the battery?"

Kyler hung his head. "Yeah. Dumb, huh?"

"Yep." Dalton had done the same thing once and still remembered the nasty shit Casper had said to him for months afterward. He doubted Cord would do that to his son, but Dalton wanted to save the kid from punishment and embarrassment. "What did you plan to do?"

"I was waiting for Ryland to call me back. He was looking for his dad's jumper cables so he could drive out here and give me a jump. If that didn't happen, then I was gonna call my dad."

"He'll be more pissed that you lied than anything."

"I know. I never do this, I swear." He looked over his shoulder again. "But it's *Jocelyn Mears*," he said her name reverently. "She's like the hottest girl in the senior class and when she said we oughta do something tonight...dude. It's my chance with her so I had to take it."

Dalton sighed.

"You're gonna call my dad, huh?"

"Nope."

Kyler's head snapped up. "What?"

"I'll give you a jump and send you on your merry way, but there are a couple of conditions."

"Name 'em. I swear I'll do anything."

"First, no more lyin' to your folks about this kind of stuff. You wanna spend time with a girl, talk to your dad and tell him it's important. Tell him it's *Jocelyn Mears*. I'm sure he'll understand."

Kyler looked as if he didn't believe him.

"Second, I could use a gopher on the house I'm fixing up. I'd expect you to help me out after school, let's say once a week."

He nodded vigorously. "Sure, no problem. I can do that."

The driver's side door opened and a girl jumped out. "Ky? What's going on?"

Jocelyn was a very pretty girl—dark hair, dark eyes, a dark hickey on the side of her neck.

Kyler said, "This is my cousin Dalton. He's gonna give us a jump."

"Oh. Okay." She rubbed her arms. "It's getting cold in there."

Kyler immediately took off his jacket. "Here. This'll keep you warm."

Smooth, kid, real smooth.

Jocelyn offered Kyler a dazzling smile. "Thanks." Then she crawled back in the cab.

Yeah. Dalton had been thrown for a loop by a smile like that a time or ten in his life. Poor Kyler hadn't stood a chance.

He clapped him on the shoulder. "Come on. Let's get that beast running so your girlfriend doesn't freeze and your dad doesn't send your Uncle Cam out lookin' for ya."

Chapter Eleven

Friday night in the Golden Boot with Rory wasn't going as well as Dalton had hoped.

She sighed. "We've been sitting here alone together for ten minutes and no one has wandered up to chat."

"Don't you mean to ask us questions that ain't none of their business?" Dalton countered.

"It's Sundance, Dalton. You gotta expect we're being gawked at and gossiped about."

"We can leave and go someplace else if you'd rather."

Rory shook her head.

The stiff way she held herself and the way her eyes darted around the room gave him the impression she didn't want to be here at all.

"I didn't mean to chase your friends off."

She raised an eyebrow. "Yes you did."

"Was it that obvious I wanted you all to myself?"

"Only to me. And it was sort of pissing me off, the way Vanessa drooled over you."

"Drooled," he scoffed. "Right."

"You are looking particularly drool-worthy tonight, McKay. Nothing sexier than a cowboy in a crisp white shirt, a black hat and a pair of Cinch jeans."

"How much had you been drinkin' before I got here?"

"Not nearly enough after the week I had at work." She drained her drink.

"Special project turning out to be not so special?"

"Frustrating. It'd be easier if all the paperwork came directly to me, but of course it's gotta be officially stamped in Cheyenne and then forwarded to me so I can log it in which is a gigantic pain in my ass."

"So that's what you and your friends discuss on Friday nights? Your crappy work week?"

"No. We're usually trolling for..." Her mouth snapped shut. "Never mind."

Dalton swigged his beer, trying really hard not to scour the bar and check out his competition.

"What have you been doing the last couple days?" she asked.

"I worked on the house. They delivered the furniture on Thursday. Planned to do a couple other things but the week got away from me."

"I know how that goes."

"Have you eaten?"

"Yeah. Ordering bar food is a habit since I've worked in so many bars over the years."

He sighed. "There goes my chance to wine and dine you on our date."

"I don't expect that from you."

"But you deserve it. And I want to give it to you. How about if we dance?"

"Let's go."

He slid out of the booth and took her hand.

She led them to the middle of the dance floor. "None of that fancy two-stepping stuff or western swing you cowboys are fond of."

"So we'll just sway together?"

"For a little while. Is that okay?"

"Very okay."

They didn't speak through three songs, just moved together in near perfect synch. Their physical closeness and the lack of conversation attuned his senses just to her. The gradual softening of her body against his. The increased tempo of her heart. The quicker intake of her breath.

He brushed his lips over her ear. "I like havin' you in my arms. Have I mentioned I love that you're tall?"

She laughed softly. "No."

"Well, I do. We're a perfect fit. In every way."

"Tell me what you're really thinking," she said dryly.

"I'm thinkin' the scent of you so close to me is driving me insane." Dalton ran his nose along her neck. "Sweet and musky. And goddamn do I want the scent of you all over me." He wondered if she'd stiffen after that confession, but she melted into him.

"Dalton."

"Aurora."

"Nobody calls me that but you."

"I can call you that all the time, if you'd prefer."

The soft warmth of her breath on his neck sent a tingle down the right side of his body. "I like that you call me that when we're alone and you're being romantic."

Although the band picked up the pace with a faster song, they continued dancing slow.

He murmured, "Will you come home with me tonight?"

Rory tensed but didn't answer.

So he continued dancing with her, like it wasn't killing him to have her curvy body plastered to his. His cock behaved as long as he didn't bury his face in her sweet smelling hair, or fill his lungs with the addicting scent of her skin.

When the song ended, he released her hand and stepped back. "I'm ready for a drink, how about you?"

Rory blinked those beautiful green eyes, confused he wasn't pressing her on tonight's sleeping arrangements. "Sure."

Dalton led her off the dance floor to their booth. He slid across from her rather than next to her.

Since it wasn't busy, Cindy, the waitress who'd worked there since Dalton could remember, stopped by immediately. "Another round?"

"I'll switch to Coors Light. Rory, you want another whiskey sour?"

"No. Tell Lettie to make a tall half 7UP, half sour mix with a splash of orange juice."

"Got it."

"You're done drinking for tonight?"

Rory lifted a shoulder. "Wasn't feeling it right now."

"What are you feeling?"

"Like I need a clear head before I decide whether or not to go home with you." She closed her eyes briefly and inhaled a deep breath. "Between you and the booze..."

He fought a frown. "What about me?"

"Being close to you packs a powerful punch, Dalton. The way you move, the way your deep voice seems to burrow into me and sets off these little electric charges under my skin."

Now Dalton fought a huge-ass grin. "I'm liking the direction this is goin', sugarplum."

She slapped her hand on the table, startling him. "And then there's that."

"What?"

"That sexy way you tease me. Sometimes it's blatant; sometimes it's sweet. You keep me off balance."

He reached for her hand, bringing it up to kiss her knuckles. "What would tip you the right way into spending the night in my bed?"

Rory laughed. "See? There it is again."

"And yet I'm not hearing an answer from you." He kissed the

inside of her wrist and lightly nipped the base of her thumb. "You really haven't made up your mind yet? After the time we've spent together?" He placed a kiss in the center of her palm. "Or maybe I should point out all the time we've spent apart. You haven't imagined how it would be between us now?"

"Of course I have," she said a little too quickly, which seemed to annoy her.

Cindy dropped off their drinks. "Sorry to bug you, Dalton, but there's a woman at the bar who says she knows you."

"Is she a relative of mine?"

"No. She's a blonde with big..." She paused and amended, "She's blonde."

Dalton never looked away from Rory. "What's she want?"

"To buy you a drink."

"Tell her I'm not interested."

"Will do."

Rory let go of his hand to pick up her drink. "Aren't you the least bit curious about who it is?"

"Nope."

"Not even to look over there and see if you recognize her?"

"Nope. Now that's settled, can I please have your hand back?"

She frowned. "What?"

"You have two hands. I'd like to hold one of them."

"Why?"

"Because I like touching you, Rory. Even if it's just holding hands."

Rory exhaled a put-upon sigh that was totally bogus before she slid her arm across the table. "Happy now?"

"Been happy since the moment this date started." Dalton threaded their fingers together. "How's your virgin drink?"

"Good. I noticed you haven't touched your beer."

"Sorta sorry I ordered it, if you wanna know the truth."

"I'll share mine." She nudged it to the center of the table.

"Thanks." He slid the straw between his lips and sucked. "Not bad. So what's your favorite drink to make?"

"Martinis. There are so many variations with all the different flavors of vodka. There's this bar in Ft. Collins that has one hundred and seventy-five flavors of infused vodka. I had an amazing Skittles martini with such cool presentation—a rainbow-colored sugared rim, a swizzle stick speared with candy and bright blue liquid."

"How'd it taste?"

"Like candy. I could've gotten totally shitfaced on them."

Dalton grinned. "I felt the same way the first time I tried expensive scotch. I wanted to steal the whole damn bottle and drink it down. But I figured it wouldn't taste so good coming back up."

"I remember you had to deal with that issue with me that night in Laramie."

He stroked the back of her hand with his thumb. "Over and done with. Goin' forward, not back, remember?"

Rory brought their joined hands to her face and rubbed his wrist against her cheek. Then she dragged an openmouthed kiss up his forearm. "Funny you should mention wanting to hold my hand. Seems I have a thing for your hands too. So big. So strong. I'd like to feel these rough-skinned hands all over me."

Outwardly he went still. Inwardly he was so revved up he had to speak slowly so his voice didn't waver. "What are you sayin'?"

"That I'll spend the night with you."

Dalton immediately dug out his wallet and threw a twenty on the table. "Let's go."

"But you haven't even touched your beer."

He wrapped his hand around the back of her neck and brought her close enough to kiss. "I'd rather be touching you. We're leavin'. Now."

Somehow he managed a leisurely pace out of the bar when his legs wanted to sprint.

He stopped beside his truck.

"Dalton. Wait."

He ignored the sinking feeling in his gut and faced her. "What?"

"We met here, remember?"

He'd forgotten that. "Do you want to leave your car here or drive it to my place?"

"I'll drive it. I'll follow you."

Dalton crowded her against the door. With his hands curled around her face, he could stroke her stubborn jawline. "I want you. I've wanted you for years, especially after the number of ways I've always fucked things up over the years..." He inhaled a silent breath as his eyes searched hers. "I'm goin' home. You know where I live. Show up or don't. But I ain't gonna pressure you."

Rory's hands inched up his chest. "Wanna know a secret?"

"What?"

"I'd intended to decline the invite into your bed."

That sucked. "What changed your mind?"

"For once your actions spoke louder than words."

He waited. It fucking killed him, but he waited for her explanation.

"When that mystery blonde wanted your attention, you didn't give it to her. Your eyes never wandered that direction. Not even one time. You didn't make a charming excuse about needing to use the bathroom just so you could see who the heck she was. The Dalton I used to know? He would've drained his beer within two minutes and said, 'Hang tight a minute, sweet thang, I need another beer. I'll go up and get it.' Then you would've left."

His face flushed. "Do you know how much I hate that I used to be that guy?"

Rory mimicked his pose, placing her hands on his cheeks. "But you weren't that guy. You stayed one hundred percent focused on me. Like I was the only thing that mattered to you."

"You are the only *person* that matters to me," he corrected softly. Then he kissed her—going beyond the lazy seductive kisses, straight to the I-wanna-fuck-you-right-here-right-now passion that'd been waiting to erupt.

She clung to him, returning the passion without hesitation.

"I gotta stop while I still can," he murmured against her lips after he found the strength to stop devouring her mouth. Dalton eased back to look at her. Eyes glazed with passion. Mouth damp from his. Breathing choppy. She seemed a little out of it. "Rory, you okay to drive?"

"Yeah. You just..."

"Come on, I'll walk you to your car."

"Dalton. This is Sundance."

"Don't care. Bad shit can happen here too." He pushed away from her and reached for her hand. "Lead the way."

Rory took a couple of steps and stopped. She looked at him with a hint of frustration. "That kiss flustered me to the point I don't remember where the hell I parked, McKay." Her eyes narrowed. "And no, that comment doesn't entitle you to a cocky little smirk."

No, but he'd definitely give her one when she was writhing beneath him later.

"I don't want to know what that gleam in your eyes is about either."

"That's probably best."

Dalton beat her to his house—but not by much. Not by enough so he had time to do what he needed.

As soon as she entered the house, he kissed her. Then he towed her to the dining room. "I wasn't planning on this, so can you give me some time? Say ten minutes?"

"Time to do what? Wax your balls?"

He laughed. "I spent my monthly manscaping allotment on getting my back waxed. So, sorry, you'll have to put up with my hairy balls."

"That's something I never thought I'd hear you say." She touched his face. She did that a lot, which he hoped meant she liked his face.

He pecked her on the lips. "You want something to drink? Soda?"

"I'll pour myself a soda while you're...jacking off so you last longer or whatever you're doing."

The flip, semi-mean comment meant Rory was nervous.

That made two of them.

Dalton really hoped she wouldn't laugh when she saw what he'd worked up. He headed to the bedroom and shut the door behind him.

He finished in eight minutes and allowed himself a minute to breathe. He kicked off his boots, ditched his socks and whipped off his shirt.

Rory stood in front of the living room window. Those rhinestone-encrusted jeans immediately drew his gaze to her ass. He couldn't wait to have it in his hands.

"You do realize that growling sound you just made isn't helping ease my state of mind?"

Dalton glanced up to see her looking over her shoulder at him. He moved toward her. "Where's your mind right now?"

"Focused on what's behind door number one."

He set his hands on her shoulders. "So come take a look."

"I almost left," she blurted.

His hands gripped her shoulders as if that'd keep her from fleeing. "Why would you have left?"

"Because this is weird. I thought you'd meet me at the door, blow my mind with another kiss. Then clothes would fly, we'd go at it right on your couch in a fit of passion."

"It's been like that between us before. I didn't want that again."

"Didn't want what? Passion?"

He kissed the section of skin below her ear. "You're testy, sugarplum. If you've changed your mind, say so."

Rory whirled around to face him. "Why did you need time to prepare? I wondered if you were just sitting in there, seeing how long it'd take me to bust in."

"When I said no games, Rory, I meant it."

"But—"

Dalton got right in her face. "Stop. Talkin'." He shook his head when she opened her mouth to protest. He kissed her forehead. "Trust me. Now close your eyes."

As soon as she complied he pressed a gentle kiss on each eyelid.

Then he caught her peeking as he kissed her mouth. The little sneak. So he spun her, herding her back toward the bedroom, putting an end to her peeking.

Once they were through the doorway, he said, "Turn around."

She spun so fast she almost lost her balance.

Dalton stayed behind her and let her look her fill.

He'd transformed his plain bedroom into a romantic space. Clean white cotton sheets on the bed. A dozen red candles scattered about, filling the room with a subtle scent and a soft light. He'd draped a bronze neckerchief over the bedside lamp, creating a golden glow.

Rory didn't say a word.

Did she think it was tacky? Too bachelor pad? Too over the top? Was she holding back her laughter? That would be the worst—hearing her make fun of his attempt to recreate a first time for them.

"Rory?"

She'd wrapped her arms around herself. "Yeah?"

"You're quiet."

"Why?"

His first response was to answer, *how would I know why you're quiet?* But as he took a second to find the right words, she blurted, "Why did you go to all this trouble?"

"To make up for the fact I took your virginity in the front seat of my pickup with little care and thought besides getting myself off." He ran his fingers down her hair. "This is how it should've been for you. I tried to make this special tonight in a way I was too stupid to do the first time. Or the other times."

Rory turned and twined herself around him. "You are such an idiot, Dalton McKay. You didn't have to do this. I was a sure thing tonight."

Dalton trapped her face in his hands, forcing her to look at him. "The only sure thing is that I've screwed it up every single time I've been nekkid—or partially nekkid—with you. Hell, that first time I don't think I even took my jeans off all the way."

"You didn't. I had the imprint from your belt buckle on my left calf from where you'd pressed my leg into the back of the seat."

He groaned and rested his forehead to hers, not even sure what to say.

"So are we gonna stand here all night? Or are you gonna give me a peek at your hairy balls on that big bed as we're surrounded by candlelight?"

Was it any wonder he was so crazy about this woman? "Maybe later. Right now, I want you to let me undress you."

Rory retreated to squint at him. "What do you mean *let you* undress me? Why don't we just rip our clothes—"

"And that, right there, is what I meant." He drew a line from the tip of her chin to the start of her cleavage. "My pace tonight, jungle girl. And I'll warn you upfront. That pace is gonna be slow."

She seemed torn for a minute before she smirked. "Guess we'll see how long you'll keep that slow mindset, won't we?"

"I live for a challenge." Dalton jerked her against his body and kissed her.

Her mouth opened fully but he denied her the immediate tangling of tongues in a hot soul kiss. Not for any reason besides he intended to take his time with her tonight—even kissing her. He rubbed his lips against hers as their breath mingled. He tracked the soft inside of her upper and lower lip with the inner rim of his, trying to memorize the shape of her mouth.

The strands of her hair slipped through his fingers like silk. He wanted to feel her hair trailing over every inch of his body. His cock pulsed behind his zipper, totally onboard with the idea.

Rory's head fell back when he moved his lips to plant soft kisses down her throat. He paused briefly at the base to feel the rapid beat of her pulse.

When his mouth connected with the fabric of her shirt, it needed to go. Dalton released her hair, smoothing his hands up her sides and over the curve of her breasts, to the top of her blouse. Snap buttons, thank god. After he popped the first one, he placed a kiss on each new bit of exposed flesh as he undressed her. He pushed the shirt down her arms, letting it flutter to the floor.

She wore a girlie yellow bra covered in pink and turquoise polka dots. Lace edged the cups, highlighting her cleavage.

"I like this," he murmured, bending down to run his tongue along the lace.

"I'd like it if you'd tear it off. Preferably with your teeth."

"I'll take it off."

"Ah, now?"

"Nope." Dalton dipped his tongue inside the cup.

Rory tried to pull him closer, her hands gripping his hair, mashing his face into her almost bare chest.

He stepped back. "Huh-uh. Hands by your sides."

"But Dalton."

"My pace," he reminded her, pulling her arms down. "And believe it or not, I can go slower."

Dalton captured her snappish response with his mouth and set his hands on her waist. For being so tall, there wasn't a bulky thing about her. Rory's torso was long and lean, flaring into curvy hips and thighs. His fingertips traced the skin above the waistband of her low-cut jeans.

She kissed him harder, her eagerness obvious.

He unhooked the button on her jeans and lowered the zipper. He moved his mouth to her ear. "Lose the jeans, Aurora."

A delicate shiver rolled through her and she shimmied the denim down her legs.

"I can get it from here." Dropping to his knees, he kissed her belly as his fingers tugged the denim to her feet.

She kicked them away impatiently.

Dalton stroked the outside of her legs from her anklebone to the lacy edge of her panties. He tipped his head back to look at her. "Damn, woman, you've got a set of legs on you."

"It's part of why I'm so tall," she deadpanned.

"Get on the bed."

He saw the wheels spinning, taking in the inequality situation. Him in jeans, her in a bra and panties.

But whatever had caused that frown line disappeared. She grinned and threw herself back on the bed. Then she spread her legs and crooked her finger at him. "Come and get me, cowboy."

Chapter Twelve

Rory could get used to seeing that lustful glimmer in Dalton's eyes.

But she'd really, really like to get his pants off.

"What are you waiting for?" she asked.

"Just soaking in the moment. Convincing myself that you're really here and this isn't another damn dream."

Would he be soft and sweet and loving tonight? Instead of showing that dangerous edge she'd seen in him?

Then he crawled across the mattress toward her—all sinuous movement and animal hunger. Definitely dangerous.

Rory reached for the button on his jeans only to have him circle her wrists and pin her arms above her head.

"I don't think you realize how serious I am about taking this slow," he said softly.

"I don't think you realize how serious I am about us getting naked first."

"Are you gonna counter everything I say?"

"Are you willing to compromise on the pace?"

"Maybe." Dalton lowered into a pushup position and slowly rolled his hips. The jean material rubbed the inside of her thighs as he dragged the hard bulge beneath his zipper across the rise of her mound. Over and over. With perfect precision.

She hadn't realized he'd released her wrists until she arched up, wanting skin-on-skin contact.

He placed a kiss on the top of each breast. As his mouth followed the edge of her bra, Rory clamped her legs around his hips and propelled her body forward, forcing him to roll to his knees.

"Whoa. Neat trick." Dalton grabbed her ass and hoisted her more securely onto his lap. "All right. Since it's obvious you ain't gonna do it entirely my way, lose the bra so I can put my mouth on you."

Rory ditched her bra in two seconds flat.

"Put your hands on my shoulders and press your tits together so I can get to both those sweet nipples."

The instant she moved, his lips encircled one rigid tip. He suckled forcefully, then softly, switching back and forth between her nipples. He tortured her with his sinfully talented mouth. Scoring her delicate skin with his teeth. Rubbing his cheek and his chin across the tips of her breasts, nuzzling and then returning to tiny licks.

Dalton sucked and tongued her nipples until they were wet and tight. His hot, ragged breath on her damp skin had her vibrating from head to toe. Wanting more. Wanting everything.

He nibbled on her throat as his hands slid up to the middle of her back. He slowly angled forward, returning her to the mattress with him on top.

A subtle scent of apples and cinnamon wafted over them as the heater kicked on, stirring the candle-scented air. Rory turned her head until her face connected with his warm neck. She breathed him in, needing something familiar in this unfamiliar situation in which she had no control.

Dalton was in charge. And he intended to prove it.

His lips traveled from her temple down to the edge of her jaw and to the tip of her chin. Nipping kisses followed the arch of her throat back to her breasts.

This time he ignored her nipples.

His soft mouth on just the outside curve of her breast drove her out of her mind. The butterfly light touches of his fingertips were beyond a fleeting tease, but a sensual stroke that electrified her as if he'd run his fingers across the nerve endings on the inside of her body.

Energy crackled between them. He didn't tell her how beautiful she was. Or how much he wanted her. His hands on her and his mouth on her conveyed far more heat and need than any words ever could. Dalton's silence was more arousing than a play by play.

Finally those deft fingers slipped beneath the lace waistband of her panties and he tugged them off. When she grabbed his forearm, he brought that arm above her head and commanded, "Leave. It. There."

"I want—"

Her words were cut off by the brutal possession of his mouth.

Dalton curled his big hand over her mound. His middle finger stroked the outer rim of flesh beside her clitoris. Almost touching it, but not quite. Teasing it until she swore her clit swelled just to reach that stroking finger. Then he'd sweep his finger across that hot spot a few times and return to teasing.

"Dalton. Please."

Maybe please was the magic word because he pushed back and shucked his jeans. Then his boxers. Picking up the new box of condoms on the dresser, he opened it, pulling out a strip of six. Ripping off one, he tossed the rest on the dresser, tore open the packet and suited up. His palms slid up her legs, over hipbones, ribcage and breasts.

Her breath caught at the sexy, slinky way he'd covered her body, letting the heat and the roughness of his skin skim hers.

Planting his hands by her head, he stared into her eyes.

So fiercely male. Yet in the glow of the flickering candles, so utterly sensual.

Rory reached between them and circled her hand around his cock. She rubbed the head through the slickness at her opening. "You make me wet. Your hands on me and the way you kiss me gets me so hot and ready—"

"Aurora. Stop."

Gave her the good kind of chills when he said her name in that deep raspy murmur.

He kissed the slope of her shoulder. "I never thought I'd get the chance to be with you like this again." He continued to drag openmouthed kisses across the same section of skin. The eroticism of it had her head spinning. "That's why I want to take it slow. Savor it. Savor every inch of you."

In the past she would've discounted his flattery. But cocky Dalton McKay almost sounded...humbled. Since she didn't know what to say, she didn't say anything.

Dalton pushed up and moved, gently rolling her onto her stomach. He kissed her spine above the dimples of her ass. "I found your tattoo." He dragged his lips across it. "A rose. I'm not surprised."

His heated breath and soft lips sent chills dancing across her body.

"I want you like this." His muscular body covered hers. His hard chest on her back, his hips digging into her ass, his legs outside of hers. His mouth—that warm, hungry mouth—worked the back of her neck until she writhed beneath him.

He threaded his fingers through hers and slipped their joined hands between her thighs. "Touch yourself, baby."

Rory blushed. She'd never masturbated in front of anyone.

Sensing her tension, he angled his hand to stroke her slit. "Can you do that for me?"

"I'll...try."

Rough-skinned hands landed on her shoulders and slid down her back to her waist. Then he hiked her hips up and spread her knees apart with his. "I don't see your hand moving."

"Because I...I've never..."

"I'm gonna have some fun getting you over that bit of shyness." His fingers followed the cleft of her butt down to where her fingers rested. "Wet, but not wet enough. Push up onto all fours." Dalton scooted back.

The next thing she knew, his head was between her legs and his mouth was on her pussy. "Omigod."

He licked and ate at her until she became slick and shaky. Then he moved back over her and his voice was in her ear. "Next time I put my mouth on your pussy I'm gonna be there a while." He gently pushed her shoulders to the mattress. His fingers gripped her hips and he slowly fed his cock into her.

Dalton stayed buried in her for several long breaths. Building the anticipation, making Rory wetter, hotter, crazy to have his hard flesh pounding into her.

She could feel his body shaking. Feel the burning heat where they were joined. Hear the breath sawing in and out of his lungs at the same ragged tempo as her own.

What was he waiting for?

"Touch yourself," he demanded gruffly.

Oh. *That's* what he was waiting for.

Rory shifted her balance, slipping her right hand beneath her. She followed her slit from the top down her swollen folds to where Dalton's cock filled her. She traced around his girth, teasing the small strip of his shaft that wasn't stuffed inside her.

He hissed in a breath.

Then she fondled his balls. They weren't drawn up tight, but hung low.

Dalton didn't move. Didn't start fucking her like a madman. He waited for her to touch herself. And she knew he wouldn't move until she did what he asked.

The instant her finger swirled around her clit he pulled out oh-so-slowly. A brief pause and then all that thick hardness glided back in to the hilt.

She fingered her clit in the way that would get her off quickly. No reason to drag it out. She expected that Dalton would pick up the pace once her body was stretched and ready. So the sooner she came the sooner she'd get that body-pounding fury. But he didn't waver in the slow and steady. Slow and steady.

And she sort of wanted to scream at him *to hurry the fuck up.*

Then he rammed in deep and stayed there. He leaned across her body and whispered, "Problem?" directly in her ear.

God. That voice. The heat and weight of his body. The scent of his skin. The man could screw up her senses just by existing.

"Aurora?" he murmured.

"Why are you going so slow?"

He nuzzled the side of her neck. "Because it's fuckin' hot watching my cock driving in and out of you. Seeing it covered in your sweet juices, knowing what I'm doin' to you is makin' you hot. Makin' you wet."

"Dalton—"

"When it's you and me together like this? Baby, you come first. Always."

"So if I make myself come?"

His mouth brushed her ear. "Then I'll fuck you like a goddamned jackhammer until you come again."

"You are so bossy. Lucky for you I like this sexual beast side of you."

His growl reverberated from her ear straight to her clit.

"Stay like this. With your body on mine and your mouth doing—" she wailed when his teeth nipped the arc of her shoulder, "—that. Yes."

"Touch yourself."

With her body caged beneath his, impaled by his, her pleasure points throbbed from the wicked things that mouth of his was doing and the rapid stroking of her finger on her clit. Didn't take much for Rory to come. She gasped as the pulses started, scrambling her brain, leaving her breathless.

Then Dalton was making good on his promise to fuck her with hard, grinding thrusts. His hips hammering. His cock relentless. A hot steel rod as he drove them both to the edge of oblivion.

He grunted and his body tightened above hers.

Rory felt his cock jerking inside her. She bore down on it, milking him so strongly that another orgasm rolled through her.

Dalton stopped moving. He pressed a lingering kiss to the back of her head. Then he pulled out before he turned her over.

Their eyes met. He said, "Fuck, woman, you own me," and kissed her. And kept kissing her. And touching her.

Lost in the sensual haze, Rory buried her face in his neck and sighed.

"You tired?" he asked.

"Mmm-hmm. You wore me out."

He seemed content with that. He continued to mess with her hair. Brushing it from her face. Running his fingers through the long strands. Wrapping it around his palm. While his mouth teased her skin and the heat from his body warmed her.

"Every part of you is so perfect." He nuzzled the back of her head. "Perfect," he repeated. "I can't get enough of you. And jungle girl, I need to know if that's gonna be a problem for you."

"I'm not sure I understand what you mean."

"Now that we've started this—" his warm breath floated across her nape,"—there's no goin' back. I won't be able to keep my hands off you, now that you're finally mine."

Mine? "Dalton—"

"I ain't gonna lie. I was obsessed with you before this. And now..." He placed a soft kiss below her ear. "I want you again. And again. And again. Maybe you should rest while you can."

She laughed. But part of her knew Dalton wasn't joking.

Chapter Thirteen

Dalton awoke to feel Rory's instep sliding up and down the inside of his calf. Her skin was so smooth. His was so rough. She must've liked the sensation because she kept doing it.

No sunshine peeked through the blinds. The world beyond this bed would be cold and bleak. Filled with that colorless wintery gray light.

But in here...he had the warmth of Rory's body against his. He saw the creamy color of her flesh against the white sheets. Her silken hair teased his skin. Her scent both stirred and soothed him.

Yes, in this bed, he had everything he'd ever wanted.

So he'd be happy to lie here with her all day.

Rory raised her arm above her head and arched her body into a long stretch. "I like this snuggly side of you, Dalton."

"That right?"

"Uh-huh. It's unexpected." Her fingernails dug into the back of his neck. "But I really liked the fuck-me-until-I-screamed side of you too."

He chuckled. "Good to know."

She wiggled her backside into his groin. "Is that for me, or just morning wood?"

"Only one way to find out."

"Ooh. A challenge. Let's see if you're up for it." Rory rolled her hips and ground her ass into his cock. All the while running her foot up and down his leg and keeping her hand on the back of his neck.

Goddamn she was sexy as fuck first thing in the morning.

"Aurora," he murmured beside her ear. "If you don't wanna start this day out with a bang, you'd better stop givin' me a horizontal lap dance."

"Lap dance?" She let loose an evil little chuckle. "Another time. But I do want you to bang me like a drum, McKay. Right now."

"Bend forward for a sec."

Dalton reached behind him until his fingers connected with the strip of condoms on the nightstand. He tore one off and managed to roll it on with one hand.

She started to back into him.

He stilled her movement. His mouth connected with the sweep of her neck. "I fucking love your nails digging into me. Stay like that and grab the headboard with your other hand."

"Is that your way of warning me to hold on?"

"It's my way of telling you to do what I ask." He slipped his left arm under her as she reached up.

Spooned against him, with both her arms above her head, Rory was completely accessible to whatever he wanted to do to her. He ran the tips of his fingers from the inside of her elbow down to the outside of her knee.

She shivered.

He kept the caresses lazy, but thorough. He loved the softness of her body and how, as he heated her up, that supple skin released its own sweet musk. On the next pass he tasted the long line of her neck from behind her ear to the ball of her shoulder.

Rory angled her head, giving him complete access.

That tiny sign of surrender made him growl with pure male satisfaction.

"You're acting so patient and then you make that noise..." She shivered. "It's hot."

Dalton cupped her breast with his other hand and gently rolled her nipple the same time his mouth found her ear. His lips followed the outline to the lobe where his teeth took over.

"How can you do so many things at once?" she asked breathlessly. "Feels like you have two sets of hands on me... Oh, yeah, I like that."

He blew in her ear again. The next pass he pinched her nipple hard the same time he sucked on her earlobe.

"Dalton!"

Not a protest. More like a plea.

"How hard would you come if I pinched your clit like that?"

She moaned.

"Answer me."

"I-I don't know. I've never tried it."

"Mmm," was all he said as he returned his focus back to her. Completely on her. Stroking her belly. Her collarbones. The impressive valley of her cleavage.

Rory writhed with every caress.

By the time Dalton finally slid his hand down her belly to toy with her clit, she was panting. Thrashing. Begging.

"Please. Touch me."

"Baby, I *have* been touchin' you. That's what I want you to understand." He nuzzled her cheek. "It won't ever just be insert dick into hole between you and me. I've waited too goddamned long for you."

"Then I'd think you'd be more eager to fuck me."

He chuckled. "I have more patience than you know. Goading me won't test it."

"What will test it?" Rory turned her head and pressed her mouth to his jaw, running her tongue across the stubble. "Your cock in my mouth?"

"Sugarplum, I'm so lookin' forward to you takin' that test." He snared her mouth in a brutal kiss even as his hands remained gentle.

Then he lifted her leg up and over his, prodding her pussy with the head of his cock. But he didn't push it in. His middle finger dipped into the wetness and he stroked her clit. He broke the kiss to say, "Come for me."

"Gotta do that faster."

"No. Like this."

Rory's nails bit into the back of his neck. "Faster. Please."

"Let it pull you in." His mouth drifted from one spot on her body to the next. "Don't force it."

"I want to force it."

"Focus on how good it feels. How wet you are."

"You make me wet. Never feels this good when I touch myself."

Dalton started pinching the fleshy folds of skin surrounding her clit. Then he'd rub. Grind his finger down and return to that subtle rubbing. The next pinch was a little more forceful. Lasted a little longer.

Rory moaned louder, bumping her pelvis into his hand. She turned her head until their lips met in an openmouthed kiss.

He rubbed the slippery skin together. Then in the moment when her body went rigid, he pinched her clit hard.

She started coming immediately. He had to break the kiss and watch her because she was so fucking hot when she came.

Stroking that pouting piece of flesh in time to the pulses caused her to shudder. He continued to slide his thumb back and forth to keep her primed.

Then Dalton impaled her with one deep stroke.

Rory's cunt clamped down on his shaft, threatening to pull him under and turn him into a two-pump chump. But he held on, held off, not pushing in fully on every snap of his hips.

"Dalton," she panted against his neck. "Don't hold back with me. I came first." She rubbed her lips in the morning stubble on his cheeks. "Let go."

He lifted her leg higher and pounded into her wet heat. Over and over until that moment when he needed more. That extra something...

Rory's fingers dug into his neck as she pulled his head down. She whispered, "Now come for me," in his ear and tightened her pussy around his shaft.

That was it. Dalton came so fucking hard he saw stars. He came so fucking hard he might've shouted. He came so fucking hard he might've sworn his love for her. But then again...he might've come in silence; he couldn't hear shit over the roaring in his ears and the blood pounding in his head.

Soft fingers sifted through his hair. He opened his eyes.

His beautiful Aurora was smiling at him. A little shyly, yet with that smug female tilt to her lips.

He pecked her on the mouth. "Damn good way to start the morning."

"I agree."

Dalton kissed her again, this time on her knee before he lowered it to the bed. "Be right back." He headed to the bathroom and ditched the condom. When he returned to the bedroom Rory was getting dressed. "Are we doin' something today? Or are you goin' home?"

"I have to go check on my dog. What are you doing?"

"Probably oughta start painting the yellow submarine room."

She fastened her bra. "Do you want help?"

"Really? You'd help me? On your day off?"

"Sounds like more fun than sitting on the couch studying government regulations for hours on end, wondering what the cool kids are doing."

"You should know since you were one of the cool kids."

"In what universe? I was considered the prickly kid because of my shyness."

"You were never shy with me."

"That's because you always got me, McKay. I never had to pretend with you." A strange look entered her eyes, as if she was embarrassed she'd admitted that.

"You always got me too, Aurora." He tucked a hank of hair behind her ear. "So yes, I'd love to spend the day with you. Even watching paint dry would be fun with you."

She smooched his mouth. "I swear, you say the most romantic things even when you're not trying to be romantic."

"But I do have one favor to ask."

"One night in the sack and he's already asking me for favors."

"My family is havin' a thing tonight and I'd like you to go with me."

"Like all the McKays? Or just your branch?"

"Just my branch."

"I'll think about it."

"Are you sure this is a good idea? Me crashing a family dinner?"

He kissed the back of her hand. "It's the best idea ever. I know what you're thinkin'. But I'm not bringing you along because I didn't want to go by myself. We are a couple. And next weekend, if you want, we can do the family thing with your mom and Gavin."

After all the remarks she'd made to her mom about the McKays—okay, one McKay in particular—how many times would her mother do the I-told-you-so dance if she said...*guess who's coming to dinner?*

About ten thousand.

"Besides, you've known my family forever," Dalton pointed out.

"I've known *you* forever. I've met your brothers. You talked about them. But that doesn't mean I know them. Or their wives."

"Jessie and Georgia are sweet. You'll get along with them just fine."

Why did men always say that? Since it was rarely the case?

Dalton turned on a rutted gravel road. Several ranch buildings came into view including an old wooden barn and a newer pole barn. The house looked different than she remembered.

"Do you know I was never in your house when we were kids?"

He turned off the ignition. "I never brought any of my friends home. Not that I was embarrassed by the house, but the thought of how Casper might act to my friends in the house."

"It looks nice."

"It's a helluva lot nicer now that Brandt and Jessie live here. Casper wouldn't spend the money to fix the place up."

Rory squinted at the license plate of the car in front of them. "Is your mother here too?"

"Yep. She probably brought Landon. I haven't seen him since he was the ring bearer."

As they walked up to the front door, Rory shivered.

Of course, Dalton caught it. He moved in front of her. His warm, callused hands cupped her face. "Hey. If you're not all right with this we just stop in for fifteen minutes and say we have other plans. That ain't a lie. I do have big plans for you tonight, Aurora."

He snared her mouth in a kiss. A perfect kiss.

A squeaking hinge sounded behind them.

"Seriously? Making out on the steps? Get in here."

Dalton's lips curved, ending the kiss. He faced Brandt. "You remember Rory."

Brandt rolled his eyes. "Of course I remember her. Glad you could join us. Come on in."

"Thanks." She tried to tug free of Dalton's hand but he held on firmly as he led her inside.

They were immediately surrounded by kids and adults.

Rory considered crawling into the coat closet until a small boy jumped out of it with a loud, "Rowr!" She screamed. Which caused the boys to laugh as they raced away.

"Sorry about that," Jessie said. "Scaring the bejeezus out of everyone is Tucker's latest thing. We hope he outgrows it. Soon."

"By then Wyatt will've learned to do it," Dalton said.

"Dalton McKay, bite your tongue," Jessie warned.

He merely grinned.

Tell exited the kitchen, in conversation with his mother. His gaze moved between Dalton and Rory. "Nice to see you, Rory. Glad you could make it."

"Where's Georgia?" Dalton asked.

"She's feelin' queasy so she laid down. I need to check on her."

Joan McKay threw her arms around Dalton. "Hello, son."

Dalton stepped back and grabbed Rory's hand. "You remember Rory?"

"Of course." Then Joan hugged her. "How are you?"

"Good."

"Dalton told me all about you. He was—is—thrilled you're living around here again."

Rather than demand to know what else Mr. Thrilled had said, Rory nodded.

They stared at each other. Awkward.

Then Joan smiled. "Landon, come and say hi to your Uncle Dalton and his girlfriend."

A lanky, dark-haired boy of about eight stood beside Joan.

"Wow, kid. You're like twice the size you were last time I saw you,"

Dalton said.

He smiled shyly.

"Do you remember me?"

"Uh-huh. I used to go to your house when I was little. We'd build stuff with Legos. We'd dig outside in the dirt and you let me play in the mud. You had a cool dog."

"Milo. He liked you too, except for the time you smacked him with a Tonka truck. Took quite a few dog treats for him to trust you again."

"I have a dog now. His name is Dixon."

"I'm currently without a dog, but Rory, here, has an awesome dog named Jingle."

Landon stared at her. Then his eyes—the same beautiful McKay blue as Dalton's—lit up. "Hey! I remember you."

"You do?"

"You were at Uncle Dalton's wedding."

"Good memory, kid."

"I was scared to walk down the aisle. You told me to pretend people were staring because they were trying to figure out my secret super power and to be very serious so as to not give it away."

Rory grinned. "It worked. You made it down the aisle without a hitch."

"Which is exactly what happened to Dalton. Ironic, huh?" Tell said.

"Hilarious." Dalton put his hand on Tell's chest and shoved him.

Tell shoved him back.

"Boys," Joan said. "No fighting in the house."

For the next hour as they chatted in the living room, Rory tried to discreetly watch the interactions between Dalton and his brothers. It looked seamless. Like he'd just slipped back into the family dynamic, but the set of Dalton's shoulders gave away his tension. Besides that, there seemed to be affection between them, although as grown men they showed it by ragging on each other endlessly.

The kids ran in and out, which drove Rory crazy, but everyone took it in stride. She realized her life growing up an only child and her life now as a single woman with unmarried, childless friends didn't allow for much experience with kids, let alone rambunctious boys.

Jessie and Joan headed to the kitchen to get supper ready and Rory followed them.

"Rory, dear, you don't have to help."

"I know my way around the kitchen better than I can sort through talk about cows, ranching and other McKay family members."

"I appreciate the help." Jessie handed her a stack of plates and a basket of silverware from the dishwasher. "Here you go. The placemats are on the sideboard."

Rory had just put the last fork in place when a little person wearing a helmet smacked into the back of her legs. "Ouch."

"Jackson McKay," a female voice said sharply. "You apologize to Rory right now."

A muffled, "Sorry," came from inside the helmet. Then he ran off.

"Sorry about that," Georgia said. "Terrible twos are not a myth."

"Are you feeling better?" Rory asked.

"Some. I get woozy at night for some reason instead of in the morning."

Rory's gaze briefly dropped to Georgia's belly. "When are you due?"

"About four months, so I've got a ways to go. How are you? I was surprised to hear you were back here, working for...?"

"The Wyoming Natural Resources Coalition."

"How's that going?"

Sucks ass most days wasn't a proper dinner party response. "It's okay."

"Your mom's gotta be happy you're back."

"She is. Although she's not around as much as she used to be. She's traveling with Gavin, which I'm happy to see."

"I imagine you hear from Sierra a lot more than we do."

"Not as much as I did before she turned twenty-one," Rory said dryly. "But we keep in touch."

"She was such a great cheerleader. I wish she would've cheered on the college level."

"Yeah, well, Sierra is out to make her mark in the business world. Like father like daughter."

"No doubt. Do you remember her BFF Marin?"

Rory nodded. "I always liked Marin. What's she up to?"

"After high school Marin got her CNA and kept working at the nursing home in Hulett. She saw the residents having problems with sore spots from their wheelchair armrests so she started making covers for them. Her demand got so high, from other nursing homes that she couldn't keep up with the orders. Sierra told Marin to quit her job and turn her sideline into a business." Georgia looked over her shoulder then back at Rory. "This isn't common knowledge, but Sierra became Marin's business partner. She fronted the money for more sewing machines, material, supplies and another fulltime employee. Within a year Marin had four employees and office space in Hulett. Now's she's got a catalog and gets orders from all over the world."

Seemed like her little sister had been keeping some pretty big secrets from her. "Sierra told you about it?"

"Only because I did some marketing for their company. I'm so proud of both those girls."

"Me too. Although I'll admit I didn't have a clue."

"I suspected you didn't. Sierra's got a lot going on, most of it on the down low. But she did mention to me at the last McKay gathering that she'd just bought a few rental properties here and there. Probably to prove something to her dad, the real estate mogul, but I don't know why she'd need to. She's definitely a chip off the old block."

It bothered her that Sierra had kept her in the dark about so many things in her life. Then again, Rory had been moping for the past few months and wasn't much fun to talk to anyway. She smiled at Georgia. "Is it possible to have step-sibling rivalry at my age? That girl is making me feel like a slacker."

Georgia laughed. "You're Rielle's kid. I'm pretty sure you've never been a slacker a day in your life."

"Supper's on," Joan trilled.

The guys wandered in from the living room.

Dalton's hands landed on her shoulders. He whispered, "Doin' all right?"

"Doing great." She turned and kissed his cheek, but the sneaky man turned it into a real kiss.

Landon said, "Eww, gross Uncle Dalton. We're just about to eat!"

He smiled at Rory before he looked at his mother. "Where do you want us to sit?"

"You? At the kids' table in the kitchen," Brandt said and ducked when Dalton tried to swat him on the back of the head.

"I oughta make you sit at the kids' table, Brandt, since half of the kids are yours," his mother pointed out.

Brandt put his hand on Jessie's stomach and kissed her cheek. "Soon to be more than half."

Holy crap. Jessie was pregnant too? Rory had considered ditching the condoms with Dalton since she was on the pill, but seeing these virile McKay males? Now she had half a mind to demand that Dalton double bag his dick—just to be safe.

"We're on the end," Dalton said, leading her to the chairs and pulling one out for her.

Jessie and Georgia exchanged an amused look.

Settled in, Rory tried to catch all the byplays between Dalton and his brothers, but she kept getting distracted. Dalton's hand on her thigh might've been part of it.

"So what did you guys do today?" Joan asked. "Anything fun?"

Well, it was fun when your son fucked me senseless first thing this morning. Then it was really fun after we finished painting and he fucked me in the shower.

Rory was saved from answering when Dalton launched into a lengthy explanation of how much prep work each room entailed.

When she looked up, Jessie's lips quirked in a knowing smile.

After supper Dalton asked, "Jess, is it okay if I give Rory a quick tour of the house?"

"Beware of opening the door to the laundry room. The pile of dirty clothes might cause an avalanche and bury you alive."

Dalton held her hand and towed her behind him. "After Casper gave Brandt and Jessie this place, they gutted part of it and added on. They took Mom's suggestions since she'd spent years in a small kitchen with a large family." They cut down a short hallway. "The back half of the kitchen, the laundry room, another main floor bathroom, the master bedroom and bath is all new."

She poked her head into the bedroom. "Nice. It's cool they have their own adult space. I loved that about my mom's house too. The little pockets of privacy."

He brought her back through the living room where Joan, Jessie and Georgia were in a hushed discussion that ended the instant they saw Dalton and Rory.

Another weird thing that Dalton didn't notice, or if he did, he didn't comment on.

They paused in the doorway that bisected the hallway.

Rory looked at the doors. "Which room was yours growing up?"

"Does it matter? It doesn't look the same."

"It's probably a lot cleaner," she teased.

"Doubtful. The place where I used to lay my head is now Brandt's office. He used to be such a slob." Dalton opened the door in the middle of the hallway. "This is it."

Rory shouldered past him and entered the room. "This is twice as big as my tiny bedroom growing up in the cabin."

"Tell and I shared this room."

"Did you have bunk beds?"

"For a while."

"What was it like, sharing a room?"

Dalton walked past her, toward the window. "I didn't know

different. I was the kid who never wanted to be by himself. I hated it when Tell got his own place. Probably why I moved out as soon as I could."

Rory slid her hands up his back as he stared out the window, lost in a memory.

"I'm glad this room isn't the same," he said after a bit. "It's like that part of my life never existed."

"You sure you never snuck girls in here?"

"Never. Fantasized about it." He laughed softly. "Went through a whole bunch of tissues during those wet-dream type of fantasies."

She kissed the base of his neck. "Would you've told me to get lost if I'd knocked on your window when I was sixteen?"

"Fuck no. I would've tempted Casper's wrath and let you in."

"So then we would've...what? Rolled around on top of the covers?"

Then Dalton spun around and pushed her against the door. "Oh yeah. I would've dry humped you at least twice."

Rory rested her wrists on his shoulders. "Then what?"

"Given my lack of sex ed at age eighteen? I would've wowed you with some sloppy kisses, groped your tits and tried to shove my hand down your pants." He paused. "Oh right. That sounds exactly like what happened between us in the truck. So sugarplum, you've already had the underwhelming teenage Dalton McKay experience—why would you ever wanna repeat it?"

"I have to admit I much prefer the recent Dalton McKay experience."

"That right?" He bent his head to kiss her neck. "Which one in particular?"

"Hard to choose because there are so many. But looking back to last night and how you teased me when you still had your jeans on, there was something very sexy about getting off—or almost getting off—when you're clothed."

"That's what I wanted," he murmured against her throat. "To get you off with hardly putting my hands on you. But someone—" he bit her earlobe, "—was impatient."

Her body tingled from that quick love bite. "So do it now," she said. "Pretend I climbed through your bedroom window and you're trying to convince me to roll around in the sheets with you."

"Rory—"

"Where's your sense of adventure, McKay? Someone could bust in on us at any time, just like in your misspent youth when you were constantly spanking the monkey all by your lonesome."

Dalton snorted. "You are such a damn romantic. *Not.* Fine. I'll get you off, but I draw the line at coming in my jeans at my age." He slipped a hard thigh between her legs and pulled her forward for a better angle as he moved against her. "Been there, done that too many times."

Him grinding that rigid quad against her clit didn't suck. Rory slid her body up and down his leg; the friction from the fabric made her pussy hot and wet. So when Dalton planted kisses across her collarbones and his tongue traced the upper swell of her breast, she was surprised at how close she was to blowing.

Two knocks on the door caused her to jump.

"Dalton? We wondered if you got lost," Tell said.

He froze. Then he lifted his head and quickly said, "We weren't doin' nothin' in here, just ah...talkin'."

"Guilty acting much, McKay?" she whispered.

"Hush," he hissed in her ear.

Tell said, "Thought you oughta know Mom's dishing up dessert."

"We'll be right there." Dalton covered Rory's mouth with his and kissed her hungrily. Between kisses he murmured, "Want you. So fucking much. Seems like days since I've touched you and I know it's only been hours. When I get you home...get you alone...it's gonna be fast, too damn fast but I won't be able to help myself."

Rory rested her cheek against his neck, holding onto him, wondering if he realized he was the one shaking. In that moment she knew why he'd insisted on going slow last night. To prove to himself—not to her—that he could. "You weren't kidding when you warned me you'd be fixated on this."

"On you," he corrected. His mouth—his hands never stopped moving on her. "Does that worry you?"

"Only that we'll run out of condoms. But I am on the pill."

"Aurora, please don't be flip. This kept me up last night."

That set off her warning bells. Her plan to enjoy the perks of Dalton McKay's sexpertise, while keeping some distance and perspective, was failing miserably, given the fact she'd barely left his side in the last twenty-four hours and she'd dined with his family. She needed to set boundaries from the start and this was the perfect opportunity to do it. "Really? I slept like the dead." She disentangled herself from him and smiled. "You'll be able to catch up on sleep tonight since I won't be there to distract you."

Dalton's eyes narrowed. "What are you talkin' about? Aren't you spending the night with me?"

"No." She playfully pecked him on the lips. "Oh, don't pout, McKay. I brought work home that I have to finish before Monday so I swear I won't be having fun without you."

"I will see you tomorrow."

Not a question. Rather than bristle at his assumption, or knuckle under because she really did like spending time with him, she poked him on the chest. "Only if I get my work done. Now let's go get some dessert so I can go home."

Chapter Fourteen

Sunday night...

"Oh my fucking god," she roared and came so hard her entire body bucked, vibrating like she was hooked up to a defibrillator.

Dalton's fingers tightened on her hips and he held on, never missing a stroke.

Her pussy throbbed from Dalton's cock plunging in and out of her like a battering ram. From her second orgasm in fifteen minutes.

The man was a sexual beast.

A half-shouted grunt echoed and then Dalton said, "Fuck," as his cock pumped inside her spasming channel.

She didn't rock back into him, but remained still, squeezing her inner muscles around that gloriously thick shaft.

"God I love fucking you," he growled against the back of her neck.

"Dalton. We've got to... Omigod, stop doing that thing with your hips right now."

"This?" He chuckled in her ear. "You don't really want me to stop."

"Yes, I do. We ah...need to..." What the hell word was she looking for? She couldn't think her brain was so scrambled. Oh right. "We need to talk. We can't keep going at it like this."

"Wrong." His hot breath drifted over her shoulder and she suppressed a shiver. "There's no goin' back. I will be all up in you—" Dalton's soft lips left a trail of kisses down her spine, "—all the time." He eased out of her body and pulled her upright. "At least once a day."

"Umm...yeah. But..." *Oh, hello, fingers on my nipples, I missed you in the last twenty minutes while you were on my hips.* When he put his hands on her like that, softly, sweetly, reverently...her mind became mush. Gluttonous mush that couldn't think beyond *more.*

"You were sayin'?" he murmured in that deep voice that dripped of sexually satisfied male.

"Oh. This is the third time today we've had rock-my-body, blow-my-hair-back sex."

"Really? Since you didn't mention scream-inducing sex, means I haven't been up to snuff the other two times, so sugarplum, I fully plan on goin' for four."

Monday evening...

"Seriously. We need to talk. We can't..." *Keep doing this*, her brain supplied lamely before it purred and went back into hibernation.

Rory's eyes rolled back in her head when Dalton switched to those butterfly licks with his tongue.

He lifted his head long enough to say, "I can't talk with my mouth full," and buried his face between her thighs again.

Between his fingers and his skillful mouth, Rory didn't stand a chance at holding back. The orgasm blasted through her like a grenade. No build up. Just *BOOM*.

Then Dalton was sliding into her. His teeth at her throat. His fingers twisted in her hair. "Put your hands on me, Aurora."

And she lost herself in him. In them. This was more than sex. This was Dalton imprinting her body with his. So she'd have no memory of any other man before him and want no other man after him.

She'd take advantage of his sexual obsession with her because she knew it wouldn't last.

Wednesday morning...

A warm mouth enclosed her nipple. Rough-tipped fingers skated across her belly, between her hipbones and back up to pluck at her other nipple.

In the pitch black of her bedroom, Rory had no idea what time it was. She stretched her arms above her head and turned to look at the clock.

"Keep your hands there," he rasped in that deep morning voice.

"Mmm-kay. But I did have pajamas on last night. What happened to them?"

"They were in my way this morning."

"By all means, just strip me when it suits you."

"I already did. And you, nekkid, warm and soft beneath me suits me just fine." Dalton's mouth reversed course, down the plane of her abdomen. "Spread your thighs and give me room."

As soon as she stretched her legs out, Dalton settled in the space she'd created. He opened the flesh hiding her clit with his thumbs and fastened his mouth to her sex. No teasing, just gentle coaxing as he kissed her soft tissues. He focused his flicking tongue and suction without pause until the first spasm pulsed against his lips.

She felt him swallow the juices pouring from her. Felt the male pride that he'd gotten her so wet that her essence coated his face. Then she felt the heat of his need blast over her like a shock wave.

His hands gripped her ass and he rolled to his knees, placing the backs of her legs against his chest. He leaned forward and slid into her pussy. His strokes began slowly but didn't stay that way for long.

Rory's arms were above her head and she braced herself. Dalton bent so far forward, getting so deep inside her that her hips were parallel to her shoulders. Keeping one arm strapped against her legs, he grabbed the headboard and hammered his cock into her. His eyes closed, his face tight, fucking her like a man possessed. The headboard slammed into the wall as he slammed into her.

Unbelievably hot, how strongly she affected this strong man.

He came in near silence.

But afterward, when he held her, the words came. Sweet words sometimes. Raunchy words others. Words that were a near confession and scared her as much as thrilled her.

Like now.

"You're mine, jungle girl," he whispered against her throat. "Only mine. I'm never walking away from you again." He sealed his mouth to hers, preventing a response.

But Rory didn't know what to say anyway. The more she held back, the more determined he became to hold onto her.

Dalton gradually broke the kiss. "It's early yet and I just...needed you."

Not wanted. Needed. She'd begun to understand the differences in those two words.

"Go back to sleep. I'll make coffee and let Jingle out."

After he left Rory's place on Wednesday morning, Dalton eyed the *No Hunting* signs hanging from the barbed wire fence on either side of the gate as he fiddled with the lock. Despite the rust and grime from constant Wyoming wind, the paddle lock opened easily. He unwound the four feet of chain and tossed it in the back of his truck.

After he pulled through, he pushed the gate shut. An open gate was an open invitation. Especially if the gate had remained closed the last three years. He needed time to sketch out his plans and he wasn't in the mood to explain them to his brothers or anyone else who might happen by.

In his truck he spread out the oversized copy of the land plat. Four years ago they'd bought two parcels of land totaling five hundred acres from neighbors whose marriage had hit the skids. Initially he and his brothers had intended to use the acres closest to the McKay ranch to run more cattle. Since a house and barn had been included with the property, Tell and Georgia had asked if they could move into it.

At the time, Dalton hadn't minded living in a trailer. But it had bugged him that he'd fronted every penny for the land purchase and it was just expected that all five hundred acres would be absorbed into the McKay ranching operation. He wouldn't have anything to show for all the money he'd put into it except joint ownership—split three ways.

So Dalton had consulted his cousin Gavin—beings he was a real estate guru—and Gavin suggested Dalton not give the entire section in a gesture of family largess, but personally retain a portion of the acreage, specifically the acreage that bordered Gavin's land.

Dalton had agreed even though it dragged out the official paperwork an additional two months. By then, he'd started dating Addie and his brothers assumed that he'd build a house on that section for his wife-to-be. Strange to think he hadn't even considered that option.

Once Brandt and Tell had taken possession of three hundred acres with creek access, they didn't ask what Dalton intended to do with his section, since it was less conducive to running cattle. And during the years Dalton was gone, they'd never asked permission to do anything with the land—neither had Gavin.

And now Dalton knew exactly what he'd do with it.

Two hundred acres wasn't much, but in this situation it'd be ideal because the elk herd could easily be contained by a combination of fencing and natural barriers. Much as ranchers lamented the lack of water in high plains desert, this was one instance where the lack of water would be a benefit. Hauling water meant he controlled placement of the tanks. It also meant animals wouldn't wander off in search of water because they'd know exactly where to find it.

Putting his truck in drive, he followed the tire tracks downhill, stopping every once in a while to mark off where the sections of fence would need to be higher.

The topography was a mix of rolling hills and deep crevasses. He'd have to get out at some point and study the raised ridge. But for now he stopped to add notes to his crude drawings and returned to inching across the landscape.

After traveling the last three years and living in the mountains for over a year of that, he'd forgotten the sparsity of the area. Several clumps of trees grew at the lowest points of the draws, providing more diversity in vegetation than he'd remembered. Also a point in his favor for an elk habitat.

136

Dalton spent hours traversing the land, checking the condition of the fences and possible problem access points. When he finished he understood how labor-intensive this project would be—work he'd be one hundred percent responsible for. But what else was he supposed to do with his time? Hang out in the hospital? No way. Or tag along opening fences for his brothers as they did chores? No way on that, either. He didn't have a burning desire to raise elk, but he did have a burning desire to convince Rory they were meant to be. That meant living here.

He flipped through the pages of regulations. No new surprises—he'd studied up on other states rules. There wasn't a huge difference between Montana stipulations and the proposed regulations in Wyoming.

As he headed back, he tried to take in anything he might've missed on the first pass. At the gate he installed the new paddle lock with the heavier, shorter chain and locked it up.

On the drive back into Sundance, his thoughts strayed to Rory. Sweet, sexy, funny insatiable Rory. They'd burned the sheets up and then some the last five days. As much as he loved that her desire, need, passion and obsession almost matched his, he realized he needed to slow things down. He had to show her this relationship was so much more than just hot sex.

Which reminded him that first lunch date he'd sworn to romance the hell out of her. And what had he done besides the candlelit seduction?

Not. A. Damn. Thing.

He needed to rectify that.

But how?

Then the perfect idea occurred to him.

She'll think it's lame. How can you even consider that romantic?

Better to try and fail than not try at all.

Dalton made a mental note for the additional items he'd need from the hardware store.

Four sharp knocks sounded on Dalton's door at three fifteen.

At least the kid was prompt. Dalton yelled, "Come in," and pulled his box cutter out of the yellow and brown linoleum before he rolled to his feet.

Kyler stood by the front door, ill at ease and Dalton couldn't fault him. Even before Dalton had left town, he and Cord's oldest kid hadn't spent time together besides attending McKay family gatherings. The odd thing? The age gap between him and Kyler was the same age gap between him and Cord.

"Hey, Kyler, what's up?"

"Not much." He looked around, hands jammed in the pockets of his jeans.

"How'd you get here?"

"I walked. My mom gets done around six so I gotta be at her massage studio then so she can give me a ride home."

"No problem. I'll leave it up to you if you want me to drop you off or if you wanna walk. We're workin' in the kitchen."

"Should I take my boots off?"

"Not unless they're covered in cow shit."

Kyler ditched his coat. "Wearing shit covered boots to school—not cool."

Dalton returned to the kitchen. "When I went to school some guys wore their barn boots to class, tryin' to prove they were real cowboys."

"Still got a few of them guys. It's worse when ranch kids try to be gangsta. Give me a freakin' break. Nothin' gangsta about livin' in Wyoming."

"You want a soda?"

"Sure. If it's no trouble."

So polite. But he didn't expect less from Cord's kid. Dalton passed him a can of Coke and cracked one open for himself. "So, I have to ask what you told your dad about why you're helping me out."

Kyler grinned. "A version of the truth. You gave my truck a jump and when I asked how I could repay you, you mentioned needin' a little help over here."

"Smart."

"Besides, Mom and Dad bust me every freakin' time I lie so it's not worth it. Most of the time."

"But this girl?"

He grinned again. "She is so totally worth a lie or two thousand."

Dalton laughed. "I remember them days. Hell, I remember them girls."

"That's the thing. I don't think my dad remembers what high school is like. He's got all these crap rules."

"I'd guess the crap rules are in place for you because Cord remembers *exactly* how he was in high school," Dalton said dryly.

"That's what Hayden thinks too. I swear my dad and Uncle Kane are way stricter than Uncle Cam is...and he's a cop."

"I imagine it doesn't do you any good to complain."

"Mouthing off just gets my phone and my truck keys taken away so I've learned to have all the arguments in my head. That way, I always win."

"I might've saved myself a lot of grief if I'd adopted that attitude at your age." Except Casper saw silence as an admission of guilt. He saw arguing as defending guilt. Dalton had been screwed either way. He noticed Kyler staring at him, waiting for further instructions. "We're stripping linoleum today. Don't know if we'll get to the point where we can move the appliances. I'll warn ya it's tedious stuff."

"Dang. I was hopin' we'd be bustin' cabinets with a sledgehammer or something."

The kitchen flooring had three layers of linoleum. The second layer had been glued on the first layer, which meant the flooring had to be removed in small sections, a layer at a time. Dalton showed Kyler how he wanted it done, handed him a box cutter and let him be.

After half an hour or so of zero conversation, Kyler sighed.

"Bored already?"

"Nope. But don't you listen to music while you're workin'?"

"Sometimes. Why?"

"It's kinda quiet in here. Music makes the time go faster." He shot Dalton a grin. "Might make us work faster."

Dalton pointed to the living room. "Sound system has an iPod dock. Or if you flip on the TV there are satellite music channels in the seven hundreds."

"I've got my iPod." He pushed to his feet. "But I don't wanna screw something up so maybe you'd better show me how to run the system."

Dalton needed to replace his blade anyway. He gave Kyler a basic rundown of the system, suspecting he was way more tech savvy than him. He watched Kyler dinking with buttons on the remote. Damn kid looked so much like Cord it was spooky. Even his mannerisms were the same.

No one had ever said that about you and Casper.

"Done. Now we can crank some tunes."

"I ask that you don't play any of that—"

"Rap?" Kyler supplied.

Dalton shook his head. "I don't mind rap. I'm not crazy about that hipster, emo, boy-band crap."

"Me neither."

Kyler left the tunes at a reasonable decibel. The music made him work faster and apparently loosened his vocal cords because he started asking questions. Lots of questions.

Thing was, Dalton had spent so much time by himself in the last

139

few years, he welcomed interest in where he'd been and what he'd done. Even his brothers hadn't taken much interest.

He hadn't seen Brandt or Tell since he'd stopped going to visit Casper every day, but he did talk to them. Dalton explained his absence from the daily hospital duty as he'd run into serious snags with the house remodel—not a total lie. But it was obvious they considered it bullshit. Neither of them had bothered to show up and offer a hand to fix those snags.

Might've been nice to have the company and the help, but Dalton reminded himself he didn't need it.

"Got big plans for the weekend?" Dalton asked.

"Football game Friday night. We're playing Gillette. They've got a bunch of big guys so I'm pretty sure I'll end up on my ass a lot."

"What position do you play?"

"Quarterback."

"Hello?" echoed from the front entry.

Rory.

Dalton stood and hoped it didn't look like he'd leapt to his feet. "In here."

"I heard music. Thought maybe you were having a party."

"Yep. With strippers and everything. Except we're the strippers." He kissed her. "Linoleum strippers."

Kyler snorted.

Rory smiled at him, then at Kyler. "Hey, Kyler. How'd you get roped into helping with this?"

Kyler gave Dalton an odd look.

"Let's just call it McKay community service," Dalton said with a straight face.

The kid snorted again.

Dalton reached out to run his hand down Rory's hair, but he caught a glimpse of his dirty fingers and dropped his hand by his side. "Kyler was telling me he's got a football game this weekend."

"I heard the people in the office talking about it," Rory said. "It's the big district playoff game. You ready to take the team to victory, superstar quarterback?"

Kyler blushed. "If we win, it'll be a team effort."

"He's so modest." Rory draped her arm over Dalton's neck. "What Kyler hasn't mentioned? He's been the starting quarterback since his freshman year and he's taken the Sundance football team to the state finals the last two years."

"We've made it to the finals but we haven't won," Kyler pointed out.

"He's also been named to the all-state team. The western U.S. all-conference team and he's in the top one hundred on the national who's who list of high school athletes. College scouts are sniffing around too."

Kyler blushed even harder and stood. "Where'd you hear all that?"

"Sierra. I talked to her last night. I'm pretty sure she was doing herkeys while she was bragging on your athletic prowess."

"Sierra exaggerates. Anyway, it's just high school football. Not like I'm a professional athlete like Chase. Or a professional poker player like Dalton, which is way cooler and takes a whole lotta skill and strategy."

Dalton tugged on Rory's hair. "See? Kyler knows Texas Hold'em requires skill more than luck."

Rory rolled her eyes.

Kyler looked appalled. "Dude. Seriously? She thinks it's a game of...luck?" He said *luck* as if it were a dirty word.

Dalton shrugged. "I've tried to explain it but she won't change her mind. Anyway, good luck with your football game this weekend."

"Thanks." He skirted the breakfast bar and snagged his iPod. "I'd probably better get walkin'."

"You don't want a ride?"

"Nah." Kyler slipped on his coat. "Since we didn't have football practice today I need some cardio. I'll get plenty of lifting exercise when I start chores."

Dalton moved in front of Kyler as he shouldered his backpack. He dug thirty bucks from his front pocket and held it out. "I appreciate your help today, Kyler."

"But...I didn't expect this."

"And I don't expect free labor. Now you've got a little extra to take your girl out and show her off." He grinned. "Or to put in a new battery in that truck of yours so you don't get busted again."

"Thanks, Dalton." He folded the bills and tucked them in his pocket. "You want me here next Wednesday?"

"If it doesn't interfere with football practice."

"It won't." He leaned in and said, "Maybe you oughta follow your own advice. Take Rory out and show her off, 'cause man, she is totally hot. You are so lucky to get with her." Kyler stepped aside, gifting Rory with a smile to rival the devil's. "See ya, Rory." He slipped out the door.

Rory sighed. "There's the first in another generation of devastatingly handsome and charming McKay males."

"He's a good kid. Sounds like Cord's got a tight leash on him. It'll be interesting to see what happens when Kyler breaks that leash, 'cause we all do at some point." Dalton turned around and Rory was right there. "Hey."

"Hey yourself, cowboy."

"I'm glad you're here." He kissed her sweetly, lazily, letting the simple pleasure of kissing her whenever the hell he wanted wash through him. He ended the kiss with soft brushes of his lips over hers.

"I liked that. Do it again."

"In a sec." He gazed into her beautiful eyes. "I need to clean myself up. Then what would you like to do tonight?"

"I'd like you to take me to bed."

"Besides that."

Rory's eyes turned thoughtful. "I don't know. What is there to do? Since I've been back in Sundance I either worked at the Twin Pines or I stayed home. I'm not in the mood to hang out in a bar, are you?"

"Not really."

"What would you be doing if you were in Montana?"

"If I'm bored I head out and shoot practice rounds. Not much else to do in the woods except improve my marksmanship." When she didn't respond, he said, "Sugarplum, why you lookin' at me like that?"

"It's just weird. I know you've hunted since you were a boy and you must be a good to be a professional guide. But in all the years I've known you, when we played Tarzan and Jane, pirates, and pioneers, we never played cowboys and Indians, or Bonnie and Clyde; I've never seen you holding a weapon—for real or pretend."

Dalton bristled. "It bothers you that I've held a gun and a bow and killed animals with these hands?"

Rory lifted his hands and traced the outside of his fingers. "No. I love your hands. I love your hands on me. You're so gentle, tender and thorough. You're also rough and exacting."

"But?"

"But nothing. My poorly made point is that there are things we don't know about each other. Like how we spend our free time."

"Aren't we past the testing phase? Where we each have to list our likes and dislikes?"

"You're missing my point, Dalton."

"You're missing mine, Rory. I want to fuck you twenty-four/seven. And we pretty much have been doin' that since Friday night. But that's not enough for either of us. We need to make sure we like each other out of bed, too. Which is why we're gonna do something else tonight besides fuck each other's brains out."

She wrinkled her nose. "Who are you again?"

He laughed and kissed her pouting mouth. "Won't take me long to clean up. You wanna head home, deal with your dog and I'll show up at your place in an hour?"

"Sounds good. Except for the waiting an hour part. Because I'm not waiting for what I want."

"Rory—"

"Aurora," she corrected as she herded him against the wall. "That's what you call me when we're getting busy, remember?" Her mouth started a southerly path from behind his ear as she unbuttoned his shirt.

"We're not getting busy, remember?"

"I disagree. And if I really think about your *we're not having sex tonight* edict, I might get pissed off. I have a say in when we have sex too, don't forget that."

He liked this aggressive side of her and she did have a point. "I need a shower. Been sweating outside and inside all day and—"

"I don't care." She licked his neck from the hollow of his throat to the bottom edge of his jaw and back down. "I like how your skin tastes." She dragged her fingers down his torso to the waistband of his jeans. "How your body feels beneath my hands."

By the time she palmed his cock through the denim he was completely erect. "Why're you doin' this now?"

"Remember on Monday night when I showed up here after my yoga class? You saw me in yoga pants and couldn't keep your greedy hands off me?" She rubbed her lips over the stubble on his jaw line.

"Ah. Yeah." Her lips were so soft on his face but her hand stroked his cock firmly through his jeans.

"Same thing hit me when I saw you in this sexy flannel shirt, looking all manly, holding tools and shit. I just wanna take a big bite outta you, Dalton McKay. So you're gonna let me."

And he was done for. Done for.

Rory had unbuckled his belt and undone his zipper before his brain and mouth connected. Then she was on her knees yanking down his jeans and boxers. That warm, wet mouth enveloped his cock and his brain ceased functioning entirely.

She did twisty things with her tongue that...damn. She did that sucking thing with her cheeks...Christ. Then she tried to deep throat him and he shouted, "Fuck."

"Yes. Fuck me." She brought his shaft into her mouth again and released him. "Fuck my mouth."

"No. I want to fuck your sweet pussy in my bed."

"No. Fuck my sweet pussy right here against the wall. Ditch the boots and jeans." She stood. Shucking off her pants and underwear, she watched him to make sure he did the same.

As soon as his legs were free, Rory's mouth was on his. She spun until her back was against the wall. She wrapped her arm around his neck and her leg around his hip.

He marveled at the strength in her thigh muscles for about three seconds. Then her hand gripped the base of his cock and she—holy shit—pulled him forward with it. Yeah. She was not messing around. Dalton knew she wasn't messing around when the head of his cock brushed the wetness of her pussy. She wanted this. She was ready for this.

Who was he to deny her?

He bent his knees and filled her in one thrust.

Her head fell back. "Like that again."

So he did it again. And again. And again.

No kissing, no touching. Just raw fucking.

Rory's hand landed on his butt in almost a slap and she urged his pelvis closer. "Grind on me. Yes. More. Feels so..."

"Feels so what?" he managed.

"Hot. I'm there already." Her nails dug into his ass. Into his neck. When her cunt pulsed around his shaft buried inside her, he had to grit his teeth to keep still.

When her grip loosened, he shuttled his cock in and out of her slick channel until that moment when pleasure blindsided him and he erupted. Wave after wave of heat shot out of his cock and he freakin' loved the slick feeling it added to her pussy since they'd stopped using condoms.

Once he could breathe, he kissed her neck. "Aurora."

"Say it again," she murmured.

"What?"

"My name. I love the way you say it after you come. It's so sexy."

"Aurora."

She shivered. Then she rubbed her bare leg up and down his. "Now what did you say you wanted to do tonight?"

"Hell if I remember."

Chapter Fifteen

Friday night after work Rory slid into the booth, grateful Mandie and Vanessa had ordered her a martini. She drained it in two big gulps and waved to the cocktail waitress for another round. "Ah. That's what I needed."

Mandie and Vanessa exchanged a look. "What is up with you? You're like thirty minutes late."

"I went over to Dalton's to change out of my uniform. Any time he sees me half-naked, he seizes the chance to get me completely naked and well, it's not like I resisted."

"So you just had sex," Mandie stated.

"Yep."

"And how was it?" Vanessa prompted.

"Let's put it this way, I'm lucky I'm only thirty minutes late. The man is a sex fiend. He's relentless." She grinned. "It is so very good to be me."

"I'm so freakin' jealous I could spit."

"I didn't spit when you were getting it on all the time with Thomas," Rory reminded Mandie.

"All the time," she scoffed. "He never lasted long enough to make me thirty minutes late for something."

"Is that why you broke up with him?"

Mandie shook her head. "I couldn't stand his family. I didn't see it going anywhere because of that."

The waitress brought a fresh round.

"Well I don't have to worry about Dalton's family because I'm just in it for the sex."

Even Vanessa looked skeptical. "Just sex? Nothing else? You're sure it's not becoming something more?"

No.

"Did he really last thirty minutes?" Mandie asked.

Why was her friend focused on that? "I don't know. I wasn't exactly looking at my watch while he was rocking my world. But probably. He does have incredible staying power. And recovery time."

She smirked. "And tenacity." And a possessive streak. He'd fucked her almost as a way to mark her before she went to a bar on a Friday night. Reminding her she'd never get it as good anywhere else as she was already getting with him. All. The. Freakin'. Time.

"How many times did you...?"

Rory sipped her drink with one hand and lifted two fingers in the air.

"Twice? You had two orgasms...in thirty minutes?"

Mandie groaned. "I hate you."

"Remember, we just started sleeping together. It'll probably burn out." Rory ignored her libido when it piped up and bet her willpower fifty bucks it'd never happen.

"How many times have you had sex this week?"

"Since Friday?" Rory thought about it and tossed out a random number. "Seventeen."

Her friends' mouths nearly hit the table.

"Seventeen?" Vanessa repeated. "After as long as you've gone without, I'm surprised you're not sore."

She was a little tender. But that disappeared when Dalton put his hands on her. Or his mouth on her. Or when he looked at her with that...gleam that made her go all hot and tingly and absolutely sopping wet.

"Well, even if she is sore she can't tell him she's sore," Mandie said.

"Why not?" Vanessa demanded.

"Because if she complains her lady part is chafed he'll just want anal instead," Mandie stated.

Rory choked on her drink.

"I wondered if part of the reason you're not sore after having sex seventeen freakin' times in a week is because you were taking it up the ass."

"Seriously, Mandie. What. The. Hell."

"What? No butt sex for you yet?"

"No!"

"He's gonna want it. Soon probably." Mandie's voice dropped to a whisper. "My advice? Lots of lube."

"I cannot believe we're having this conversation." She really couldn't. She and her mom had never discussed sex beyond the *you're going on the pill* conversation when Rory had left for college. She'd never wanted to hear about Addie and Dalton doing the nasty. Ditto for Addie and Truman. All the women in her office were much older and married. So she'd never swapped sex stories, tips, dos and don'ts, how tos with girlfriends until she'd started hanging out with these two. And up until last week, she'd had nothing to share. Her sex life with Dillon had been pathetic with a capital P. So she couldn't wait to share the juicy tidbits.

Dalton is a little touchy about his previous reputation as a horndog manwhore. He wouldn't like you blabbing to your friends about his studly moves in the sack.

The booze kicked in and the he-done-me-wrong girl inside her shouted *tough shit.* But when Rory opened her mouth to tell all about the size and shape and amazing tricks performed by Dalton's wonder dick...nothing came out.

Because you know it's wrong.

Tempting to drown her stupid conscience in half a dozen martinis and see if it still functioned properly.

"You got really quiet and then you looked like you were about to share something juicy," Vanessa said.

"No. I just wondered how Mandie knows so much about anal sex."

Mandie drained her martini and signaled for another. "I think Rory's right. We oughta talk about something else.

After Rory returned to Dalton's house from the bar, he dragged her back to bed and thoroughly fucked her in that slow and sweet way she craved because he did it so well.

So she was naked, sprawled on her stomach, the sheet twisted around her feet, basking in the afterglow. Happier than she could remember being in a long time.

Is that all it takes to make you happy? Sexual attention from a man who'd keep you tied to his bed all day and night until he gets tired of you?

Whoa. Where had that come from?

Dalton trailed his fingers up and down her spine. Then he'd randomly kiss spots on her body. The ball of her shoulder was the winner of that soft kiss. "I love bein' with you like this," he said.

"What? Naked, spent and sweaty?"

"Yes, but not just that." He brushed her hair away from her neck. "In our own little world."

Ooh. That was a sweet, melt-her-heart thing to say.

Sex-drunk and a little martini-drunk, you'd melt if he recited an ode to the pockmarks on your ass.

True.

"That was a heavy sigh. Something wrong?"

Yes. I'm pretty sure I left my backbone at home next to Jingle's rawhide treats. "No. Not really."

"That didn't sound very convincing, sugarplum. I don't want to pester you to talk to me, but I will."

"Pester," she said with a snort. "Nice way of saying you'll be a pushy bastard until I crack."

"So save me the trouble and tell me."

"Can we cool it on the sex for the rest of the night?"

His eyes darkened with concern. "Did I hurt you?"

"No. But I am a little sore from excessive use."

"That's because I can't get enough of you. But I will back off." Dalton kissed her shoulder again. "So, you had a good time with your friends tonight?"

"Mmm-hmm. They gave me shit for being late. And because of that our conversation turned to sex." She groaned. "That's actually a cliché, three single women in a bar, sipping martinis, dissing on sex."

"What'd you give as a reason for bein' late?"

"That you're an insatiable stud. Then Mandie went off on this tangent about anal sex. She pretty much guaranteed that if we were having sex this much you'd want that soon."

Dalton's fingers stopped moving.

"Is that true?"

He didn't respond right away. "Rory, I don't want you talkin' about our sex life to your friends."

She rolled away from him and pulled the sheet to her chest. "Excuse me. I thought I was doing you a favor by letting it slip that Dalton McKay is still a legendary cocksman."

"That's not who I am or ever wanna be again. I only give a damn about bein' a legendary cocksman in your eyes and in our bed. What happens between us is—"

"Special?" she said a little snottily.

"Yes. It is. It's intimacy on a level I've never had and I don't think you have either. So I don't want to share what's special between us with anyone else."

Rather than agreeing—Rory turned combative. "Maybe I didn't want you sharing the snatch-and-run job you did with my virginity with anyone else either, but that didn't seem to stop you."

"And...we're back to this. Fuckin' awesome." Dalton scooted to the edge of the bed. He yanked on his flannel pajama bottoms and a hoodie. Then he left the room without another word.

Way to go.

The thing that sucked? She knew tossing that in his face wasn't the real problem. The real problem was after totaling up the number of sexcapades for the last week, she realized she had been at Dalton's beck and call—and she'd sworn she wouldn't be. She had several job listings she should've applied for that she'd blown off to blow him. Her mom had returned from her latest trip and had asked several times when they could get together, but Dalton had Rory on her back too many times to even call her mother back.

Face it. Your inability to say no is not Dalton's problem; it's yours. And the only person who can fix that is you.

Lying in his bed, staring at the ceiling she understood his comment about their intimacy being special wasn't a bullshit line. Things were different this time around, maybe not in a good way because it seemed to be all-consuming for both of them.

That scared her. Mostly because it wasn't scaring him.

But that didn't alter the fact she needed to apologize. She hated that by reverting to the old Rory who lashed out, she'd forced him to walk away. They'd both grown past that behavior and this time it was up to her to prove it.

She slipped on his robe and wandered into the living room.

No TV. No music. Dalton wasn't staring aimlessly out the window like he sometimes did. He hadn't broken out the whiskey. In fact, she didn't see him at all.

Had he left like he'd done so many times before?

Then she heard *scrape scrape scrape*. She peered over the edge of the kitchen counter. Dalton was on his hands and knees scraping something from the floor. She stared at him a while without speaking because she was enjoying the view.

Get your eyes off his ass.

She cleared her throat. "Dalton?"

"What?"

"It was a childish thing to do, throwing our past history in your face. I don't even know if you did tell locker room stories back then. But it doesn't matter now." She took a breath. "So from here on out I won't brag about how awesome you are in bed to anyone. I'll just walk around with a smug smile on my face all the time because I get to experience that awesomeness firsthand. You can call me the Mona Rory. No one will know what my secret smile means."

He sighed. Then he stood and turned toward her. "I appreciate the apology and I'm sorry if it seems like I overreacted. What's between us *is* special. I don't ever want to lose sight of that or take it for granted,

Rory."

When Dalton didn't come forward and hug her after that sweet confession, she said, "That's it?"

"What's it?"

"We're not gonna kiss and make up or anything?"

A dangerous look flared in his eyes. "Sure we can. As long as I get to pick where to kiss you."

Her sex pulsed twice—the equivalent of yelling *pick me, pick me!*

Her cunt was such an attention whore sometimes.

She started to retreat. "I thought you agreed to take a break from *bom chicka wah wah.*"

"I did. But since your poor pussy is sore and that is my fault, I oughta kiss it all better." He stalked her. "Besides didn't you call yourself the Moanin' Rory? I'll make that happen and then some."

"The *Mona* Rory. A joke. From the *Mona Lisa.* Get it?"

"Yep. But you're gonna get it too."

"Dalton—"

"Aurora. Come here." His tone went from sexy and playful to sexy and demanding.

Shit. She never ever ever thought she'd be the woman who'd go all weak-kneed when a guy ordered her around. She never ever ever thought she'd be more focused on the inflections in his voice than the words.

"You should see your eyes. They're as dark as emeralds."

"That definitive tone of yours is a major fucking turn-on."

"I mean every word I say to you." Then Dalton was on his knees, urging her to lean against the counter, untying her robe, spreading her thighs apart.

Settling his mouth on her pussy, he undid her completely with sweetness. Gifting her with soft licks and gentle sucks. Using tenderness to soothe her tender tissues. Yet each pass of his mouth on her flesh made her hot, made her wet, made her dizzy, made her even more crazy for him.

The orgasm spun Rory completely out of orbit. Dalton's tongue didn't go wild when she started to come. He kept the easy cadence, alternating soft sucks of his lips with slow, long licks, drawing out the throbbing until her knees gave out.

Then he scooped her into his arms and carried her to the couch.

No man had ever just handled her like that. Whenever Dalton picked her up, like she was a normal sized girl and not a gigantic freak, she felt petite. Coddled. Protected. Something she'd never known she'd wanted. And he gave it to her without asking.

"How about if we take a break and watch some TV?"

"Okay." She curled into him. After thirty minutes of mind-numbing poker, Rory began to drift off. Half-sleepily she said, "You never answered my question."

"About what?"

"Anal sex."

His body stilled. "What about it?"

"Are you expecting it from me?"

"When it comes to sex I don't expect anything from you except honesty. If you don't like something we do, tell me. I can tell if you're into what we're doin' when I hear that sexy moan of yours." He stroked her hair. "You worried I'm gonna bend you over and ram my dick up your ass without warning?"

Rory blushed. Then felt stupid for it. She was twenty-eight years old. This man was her lover. It was natural to discuss all sides of sex. "No. Well, maybe. I don't know. I've never thought about it."

"No guy you've been with has tried to sweet-talk you into giving him a sample of this sweet ass?"

"Nope. And I've never been the adventurous type who'd just announce to a lover, *hey you know what would mix it up tonight? If we tried anal. I'll grab the lube and a corncob for a practice run.*"

Dalton laughed. "Well, don't kid yourself that you're not sexually adventurous if you're willing to stick a corncob up your butt."

"I have no idea where that came from."

"How about let's not dig too deeply into that."

"Deal."

"That said, any time you want to try a little back door lovin', I'm game."

"You've had experience with it?"

"Not with you and that's all that matters to me. If you're asking if I can make it good for you?" His mouth brushed her ear and he breathed, "Oh yeah, baby, I can make it *great* for you."

During a commercial break, Dalton said, "We probably better come up with something we can do together besides sex. Like a hobby."

Rory gasped dramatically. "So riding the hobbyhorse isn't a real hobby?"

"Shocking, I know," he said dryly. Then he pressed a kiss to her temple. "Stay with me tonight. I won't try and have my wicked way with you. I just sleep better when you're in my bed."

Say no. Retain your head, girl. Retain some control.

"I can't."

Dalton studied her patiently.

She could've said she needed to spend time with her mom, which wasn't a lie. By not giving him a concrete reason for saying no, she reiterated her position—their lives weren't completely intertwined.

He didn't argue; he couldn't when he'd told her he no longer offered justifications for his decisions to anyone, but she sensed his disappointment. And her supposed victory felt a little hollow.

Chapter Sixteen

Dalton had made progress updating the kitchen. He'd removed the melamine countertops and ordered marble laminate countertops that'd be delivered next week. He'd installed a deeper stainless steel sink. He'd painted the walls a khaki green, weird for a kitchen in his opinion, but it was what Sierra wanted. Good thing she'd color coordinated everything because he sure wouldn't have picked half the oddball colors.

He'd cracked a beer and was about to hang the refaced cabinet doors when someone knocked at his door.

His heart skipped a beat. His cock stirred—it had a mind of its own when it came to Rory—his brain roared *MINE*, and his body set out to prove it.

He opened the door with, "Baby, I've told you that you don't have knock." Except it wasn't Rory on the threshold but his cousin Ben. "Hey, Ben. Sorry, I thought you were someone else. Come on in."

"Just as long as you promise to never ever call me baby again."

"Deal." He stepped back to let him in. "Am I on the family's shit list and they sent the peacemaker to talk some sense into me?"

Ben shook his head and handed Dalton a paper bag that held a six-pack. He hung his black Carhartt on the coat tree Rory had bought for him earlier this week. "Are you telling me none of our other cousins have been over to see you?"

Dalton moved into the kitchen. "You're the first." He opened the bag and fished out two bottles of Moose Drool beer. "You joining me for a cold one?"

"Sure." He took the beer from Dalton but his gaze was taking in the kitchen. "You've got some major renovation goin' on here."

"Not too much actually. Person that owns this house is trading rent for my fixer-upper skills. She buys the materials and I follow the unending lists of what I need to do. Keeping me busy so far." Dalton pulled out a chair and sat.

Ben followed suit. "Looks good. You gonna be here long enough to do the whole house?"

"We'll see."

"I didn't know you were so handy."

"Neither did I." He shrugged. "Like most things I've had to learn on my own."

"So is it a new skill?"

"Some of it. But I gutted the trailer after I moved into it years ago. Learned more from screwing up than anything else."

"I hear ya." Ben frowned. "Don't remember if I've ever been inside your old trailer."

"Probably not. Didn't have drop by visits from anyone back then either."

Ben leaned back in his chair. "Fill me in on what's been goin' on in Dalton's life."

"That friend of yours, Boden? I kept in touch with him during my travels. When they lost their hunting guide last year before the opening of hunting season, I stepped in. Been in Montana ever since." Moping, as Sierra had pointed out.

"Whoa. How'd you and Boden get to be friends?"

Dalton looked Ben in the eye. "At the Rawhide Club."

That shocked his cousin. "Wait. Are you a member?"

"Guest." Dalton's face heated as it did every time he thought about how he'd reacted after seeing something he hadn't understood. "Look, Ben, that's the most humiliating thing I've ever done—calling your brothers and staging an intervention about your sex life. Not even walkin' out on my own wedding holds a candle to that boneheaded moment in my life."

"You gotta know that's been over and done with for a long time." He sipped his beer. "So the club must've made an impression on you if you're still goin' there...six years later?"

"The place—the whole situation opened my eyes. So a few months after you resigned from the club, I went in and ended up talkin' to Layla."

Ben's eyes narrowed. "What did she say?"

"Nothin' about you or Ainsley. That wasn't why I went in. I wanted to understand more about that lifestyle choice 'cause it was pretty fucking obvious I didn't have a clue."

"And? What'd you learn?"

"More than anything I learned different strokes for different folks."

Ben choked on his beer and Dalton laughed.

"Got ya there, cuz."

"Smart ass."

"Eventually I learned there ain't no one-size-fits-all sexual playbook. I stopped in and I took in scenes, figuring I'd try them out in the privacy of my own bed. I assumed once I had the right sex moves down I wouldn't have to try so hard with women. I'd be a killer lay." Dalton shook his head. "Jesus. This is really embarrassing to admit, so just tell me to shut the fuck up and we can go back to kitchen remodeling."

Ben shook his head. "Keep talkin'."

Dalton chugged most of his beer. "Without goin' into specifics, I've been in some pretty fucked up situations with women over the years. I never quite...got it. Hell, I even hooked up with a lesbian for a while so she could teach me about women. Didn't work. I think she knew less about what women wanted than I did."

Ben chuckled.

"I'm not qualifying this, but I never participated in any activities at the Rawhide. Not out of fear, or worry about bein' judged."

"Then why abstain? It is a sex club."

"Because when it came to sex I'd always acted first and didn't consider the results of my actions until it was too late."

"When did you come to that realization?"

"After Tell and Georgia got married in Vegas. Hot women were coming on to me only because they thought I had money. When I got back home, I realized women were coming on to me because my last name was McKay. Or some women were avoiding me because of my shitty reputation as a wannabe player." He felt like such a fucking pussy talking about this shit with his cousin Bennett, legendary Dominant.

Ben leaned forward. "I'm not judging you. Anything you tell me stays between us, okay? And it seems to me you need someone to talk to."

"Probably." Now that Rory was in the picture, he didn't want to screw this up with her. "So I needed to rethink my entire approach to women, to sex, and what I wanted out of it. That's why I went to the club a couple years later again."

"So what did you learn about yourself?"

"I'm more tolerant than I believed I could be. Watchin' some of those scenes just reinforced my stance that I'll never use a flogger on a woman, or a whip, or a strap." A shudder of revulsion rolled through him, though he tried like hell to repress it. "I doubt I'd even be interested in playful spanking."

"Why not?"

Dalton shrugged. "Just not my thing."

"That ain't all of it, Dalton." Then he pulled out the Dom voice.

"Tell me."

First time he'd heard that tone from Bennett. He sighed. "If I tell you, you gotta understand I'm not lookin' for pity."

"Now you've got me concerned."

Where in the hell did he even start this? Better to just barf it out upfront. "Casper...used to beat me with a strap. Started when I was seven and ended after I got bigger than him. He did it in private and embarrassment kept me from telling anyone. Every time Casper lit into me with that leather, he recounted all the things wrong with me and what I'd done wrong, so it was physical and verbal abuse."

Ben stayed quiet for several moments. "Christ, Dalton, is that why you freaked out when you saw me usin' the whip on a member in the club?"

Dalton couldn't meet Ben's eyes. "Yeah. The only experience I had with any type of beating was forced, so I didn't understand why someone would *want* to get whipped. Nor did I understand that not all people who wield the whip are sadistic bastards. I associated any hitting with shame and the strong preying on the weak."

"I need another goddamned beer," Ben said and took out two bottles, passing one to Dalton.

"I wondered if Uncle Charlie had used the 'spare the strap, spoil the child' philosophy on you or your brothers."

"Nope. But I can see why you'd think my former whip expertise stemmed from dealing with childhood trauma." He pointed his beer bottle at Dalton. "Kinda like you used to act out by getting into all them dust ups with any guy who looked at you crossways."

"I had a fucked up need to prove I could defend myself—probably why I instigated half of the fights."

"The only time I remember my dad raising his hand to one of us was when Chase was five. He ran out in front of the tractor when Dad was picking up hay bales. Dad jumped outta the cab so fast, grabbed Chase by one arm and spanked the living crap out of him. Me'n Quinn were shocked. Then Dad knelt in the dirt and got right in Chase's face. Talked to him, hugged the shit out of him and made him sit in the cab with him for the rest of the day. Which was the worst sort of punishment for Chase." Ben paused. "Your brothers didn't know when it was goin' on?"

Dalton picked at the label of his beer bottle. "One night after too many shots of Jagermeister I told Tell about Casper's random whippings when I was a kid. Shocked him because Casper used to smack me in front of them sometimes and Tell thought that's all there was to it. Sounds fun, don't it?"

"Not even remotely." Ben seemed to chug half his beer. "Your mom wasn't aware of what was goin' on in her own house?"

He looked at Ben. "It didn't go on in the house and it never happened when she was home. My fuckin' big-mouthed brother Tell spilled his guts about it to her after I told him." He drained his beer and twisted the cap on a new one. "The next day she tracked me down and..." That was one of the worst days of Dalton's life. Seeing his mother crumble. It'd crushed him knowing she'd carry guilt that wasn't her burden to bear. Especially seeing her broken after witnessing her transformation into a stronger, independent woman after she'd left Casper. Which was why Dalton wouldn't tell her about his conversation with Casper three years ago. It would shatter her all over again.

"Don't blame you for not bein' the forgive and forget type when it comes to him. Do your brothers expect that from you?"

"They're havin' a hard time forgiving me for bein' almost completely out of touch for three years. Now that I'm here...I don't wanna sit in Casper's room for hours on end while he glares at me and refuses doctor's orders."

"My dad said the same thing after he visited."

"And Casper wonders why he doesn't have hardly any visitors." He swigged his beer. "I assumed the cousins are still pissed off at me because they think I took off three years ago and left my brothers holding the bag."

"Holdin' the bag." Ben snorted. "I can't speak for anyone besides me'n Quinn, but we never saw it that way. No one blinked when Chase took off for different pastures. Or when Carter did. Or when Cam did. Brandt and Tell ain't been suffering from work overload bein's that Jessie and Georgia are sharing part of their daily work."

Dalton sighed. "How'd we get on this subject anyway? I thought we were talkin' about my life in Montana. You and Ainsley ever been up to Boden's hunting lodge?"

"Nope. He's invited us to visit but it's never fit into our schedule. Boden's not a cattle man so he doesn't understand calving." He stood. "Look, I'm glad you told me about this stuff even though it burns my ass that you went through it alone, say nothin' of when you were a little kid. Obviously in your time away you found a way to deal with it, or heal from it or whatever." Ben's eyes were somber. Conflicted. "Lemme know if you wanna talk. Or if you need an extra hand with the handyman stuff."

"Thanks."

He slipped on his coat. "Oh, heads up in two weeks we're playing poker at my place."

"Texas Hold'em?"

Ben snorted. "Regular poker. Not that made-for-TV game that relies on luck, not card skill."

If Dalton had a buck for every time he'd heard that. Wait. He did—from playing Texas Hold'em with guys who had that same attitude. He took their money and smiled. "Who's we?"

"Just the cousins. Been a while and I figured we could gauge if your public tournament loss changed the way you play."

It had changed him. Not only in the way he played cards, but how he could strip everything down to the basics. Cut and run if he needed to, or bluff his way into a better position if need be. "I'm in. But I don't wanna hear any bitching when I clean all you guys out."

"That's not fair! You're cheating."

"How is it cheating, Rory?"

She swung the Wii remote and smacked the onscreen tennis ball, sending it way out of bounds. Her avatar hung her head in shame when the scorekeeper announced Dalton's doubles team had won the match. She looked over at the man.

He grinned. "Another game? Or you wanna play something else? We haven't tried out that fantasy quest one yet."

"Let me think about it." Rory flopped on the couch. She never dreamed that playing virtual tennis would make her physically tired. She'd worked up a sweat. But so had Dalton so she didn't feel like an out of shape couch potato.

She'd been very resistant when Dalton had bought the Wii. Growing up, she'd never played video games. She'd secretly scoffed at those who did, thinking they oughta get a life. But Dalton had insisted she try a couple of the programs before passing judgment. And yeah, she'd gone into it expecting she'd hate it. But she hadn't. Not at all. The games were fun, a great way to blow off steam, get her body moving and spend time with Dalton doing something new and different—besides checking off sexual positions in the *Kama Sutra*.

He hadn't gloated and said I-told-you-so. He'd just reminded her they used to play games and make believe as kids. Then he'd picked up an extra unit for her place so they each had one.

So maybe Rory had been secretly practicing so she didn't get trounced every time, at every game.

Dalton had mad gaming skills, but not because he was one of those single men addicted to a virtual life. In college she'd dated a few guys who'd rather play online than play with her. Having a Wii hadn't cooled Dalton's libido at all—the man admitted he was addicted to her and proved it at least once a day. Had he ever proved it this morning before she'd gone to work. Just thinking about the heat and the intensity sent blood rushing to her face.

"I recognize that look," he said, sitting beside her.

Rory reached up and brushed the damp hair from his forehead. "The look where I'm thinking back to how you rocked my world in the predawn hours and started my day with a bang?" Her fingertips followed the contours of his sigh-worthy face. His smooth face. She loved the little things he did for her—like shaving later in the day so she didn't end up with beard burn when he kissed her, wherever he kissed her, because his mouth was on her a lot.

"Been reliving that a time or two hundred all day myself." Then he plucked her up and settled her across his lap, wrapping his arms around her. "So did whacking a tennis ball relieve your stress?"

"Some of it." She'd had a horrible day. Hannah had been a nightmare, barging in her office at least a dozen times, demanding explanations on reports Rory had filed months ago. Stupid, busywork questions that Hannah could've found the answers to herself if she'd bothered to look.

Even though Rory understood the disruptions were Hannah's bitchy reminders that she still retained dominion, it was annoying. Rory's tongue should've been bruised from biting it so many times. Plus, Hannah's continual interruptions had put Rory further behind on her current project—which Hannah also knew. After having autonomy with this project, Rory realized it'd be hell working with Hannah again.

Hopefully she'd get a callback from one of the other places she'd applied the past few weeks. Problem was, even if she got offered her dream job, she couldn't accept it until she finished this special project.

"You're awful quiet, sugarplum."

"Lost in bad workday thoughts. Thank you for coming over to try and chase them away."

He stroked her hair. "Nowhere I'd rather be than with you. If you're still needing a distraction, I have an idea on how to force them ugly work thoughts right outta your pretty head."

Rory straddled Dalton's thighs, tucking her knees by his hips as she faced him. "Force?"

"Coax," he corrected, placing a kiss on the center of her chest. "Damn. You always smell good."

"But I'm sweaty."

"I'm pretty sure my sodium intake is dangerously low today." He parted his lips and dragged his mouth across her collarbone. "You taste good too."

"Keep that up, McKay, and you know what'll happen next."

"Yeah. You'll be even sweatier wearing a big ol' smile."

Rory tipped his head back and ran her fingers though his hair. "Anything interesting happen in your world today? Did HGTV stop by and offer you a home improvement show?"

Dalton snorted. "No, but my cousin Ben did drop in."

Not that she'd ever say anything to him, but it bothered her that few of Dalton's McKay relatives had stopped by to see him. "What did he want?"

"To say hello and invite me to a family poker game a week from next Sunday."

"You going?"

"Hell yes. Gonna school them." He twisted a piece of her hair around his index finger. "So you know how we've been all social and stuff lately? I was lookin' in the paper to see what's goin' on this weekend and I saw that next weekend there's a poker tournament in Deadwood. Thought it might be fun if we rented a room Friday and Saturday night. I haven't played in a while so I figured I could brush up on my skills and we could make a weekend of it. Eat out. Hang out. Have lots of wild, kinky, loud hotel room sex."

Rory grinned. "I'm in as long as you're not expecting me to enter the tournament."

Dalton actually looked horrified at that prospect. "Ah. No."

"Cool. So if I'm arm candy for a high roller, should I plan on wearing my skankiest outfits? Wouldn't it be fun if people thought I was a hooker?"

"Jesus, Rory. That's not funny."

"Sure it is." She shifted her hips side to side across his groin. "We could even play the gambler and the whore." She rubbed her tits under his chin. "After all, it is Deadwood."

"I'll make reservations."

"Was Kyler there when Ben stopped by?"

Dalton shook his head. "He called to let me know he couldn't help out today. He has a big history project due. But he did say to pass along his thanks that we went to his game last weekend."

"It was really sweet that you wanted to go."

"Sweet. Right."

"I'm serious. You're such a sweet, thoughtful man."

His cheeks reddened. "Stop. You're about to get a demonstration of my not-so-sweet side."

"I'm game." Rory teased his lips with hers. "Want me to get out the handcuffs, blindfold and anal lube?"

Dalton's eyes lit up. "You bought anal lube?"

She smirked. "Nope. Just wanted to see your reaction."

"Oh, you're not gonna get the reaction you'd hoped for, jungle girl." Dalton pinned her to the couch and started tickling her.

"Dalton!"

He teased her and tickled her until she was laughing and yelling at him to stop. Just when she caught her breath, he'd start in again. The crazy man used to tickle her all the time when they were kids so he knew her most ticklish spots.

Jingle started barking and Rory seized Dalton's distraction to squirm away from him. "I swear I'm gonna pay you back for this when you least expect it."

But Dalton wasn't looking at her. Rory turned and saw her mother standing by the front door. She scooted upright and straightened her clothes. "Mom? What are you doing here?" What was up with people just barging into her private space without knocking today?

Her mom eyed Dalton before meeting Rory's gaze. "Sorry I just walked in. I didn't know you had company."

Bull. Dalton's truck was parked right outside.

Dalton said, "Hey Mrs. D.," and put his arm around Rory.

"So what's up?"

"I hadn't seen or heard from you for a couple of days so I wanted to make sure you were all right."

"I'm fine, besides my shitty workday. I ended up working late tonight and Dalton was sweet enough to bring me supper."

He leaned over and kissed her forehead. "I like takin' care of you."

Man. Could he act any more proprietary?

"I see that." Her mother pointed to the revamped doggie door. "Is that your doing too?"

"Yes. Isn't it awesome?" Rory answered. "Cold air poured in and Jingle had problems with it closing around her. Dalton fixed it for me, which was such a great surprise." Rory didn't tell her mom she nearly burst into tears after seeing Dalton's handiwork. He knew how much her dog meant to her and he couldn't have picked a more romantic gesture.

Her mom said, "That was really nice of you, Dalton."

"Wasn't a big thing. Just swapping out the seal and tweaking it here and there."

Silence.

"Anyway, I won't keep you. I brought you a loaf of pumpkin bread since it's your favorite."

Rory stood and walked over to her mom, giving her a hug. "Thanks. I've been bragging to Dalton how delicious your pumpkin bread is, so I might not get to eat the whole loaf myself this time."

She smiled. "I can always make more."

"Hey, before I forget, can you keep an eye on Jingle next weekend? Dalton is taking me away."

"Sure. Where are you going?"

"I haven't decided," Dalton inserted. "It'll be a romantic surprise for her."

Why had he said that?

"Sounds fun. Have a good night." Then her mom left.

After she left, Dalton said, "Good thing I hadn't gone with my first idea and stripped your pants off to tickle you with my mouth."

Rory set the bread on the counter. "Why didn't you tell her we're going to Deadwood?"

Dalton turned her to face him. "Because tellin' your mama that I'm takin' you to Deadwood, when she knows I've been a professional gambler doesn't sound near as romantic as it's gonna be." He kissed her. "It's late and I woke you up pretty early this morning, so I should go."

She cut the loaf of bread in half and handed it to him. "Here. For breakfast tomorrow."

"You're sharing your precious pumpkin bread with me?" He kissed her and grinned. "I think you're beginning to like me a little."

"Maybe just a little."

He chuckled. "Was that hard to admit?"

She gave a mock shudder. "Excruciating."

Dalton wasn't looking forward to his old friend Reggie's bachelor party. Maybe it made him pussy whipped, but he'd much rather be with Rory.

In the last week he and Rory had found common interests besides their sexual compatibility. They challenged each other at Wii games ranging from marksmanship to body balance to bowling. They'd also done more normal dating things—although they were well beyond mere dating in Dalton's mind. They'd sampled a few local restaurants. They'd gone grocery shopping, which they quickly learned they both hated. One night they'd gone out to listen to a band at the Twin Pines. They'd danced, had a few drinks and had run into a million people they both knew. No one seemed surprised he and Rory were together. His old pals were more surprised they hadn't seen him out and about in the month he'd been back.

After living in the Montana wilderness, where he'd purposely isolated himself, he realized he couldn't do that all the time in his hometown. Now that they'd seen him out with Rory, his former drinking buddies had been pestering him to hang out. Dalton knew he'd come across as a self-righteous reformed dick if he told them his barhopping, strip-club-visiting days were behind him. So he'd said yes when Reggie had asked him to stop by his bachelor party.

He plastered on a smile as he entered the private back room at the Golden Boot. He'd stay for an hour—max. Congratulate his buddy on his upcoming wedding, offer to buy him a shot and then bail.

He'd crashed bachelor and bachelorette parties over the years in this room. Odd to think the last one he'd attended here had been his own. Talk about tame. No strippers. No porn. No open bar. Dalton didn't recall much from that night—not because he'd drank to excess. He'd ended up sitting in the corner with Leif West—who'd tagged along to the party as Chet and Remy's guest—discussing Las Vegas gaming. Since Leif lived in Vegas, he had a completely different take on gambling, which Dalton had found fascinating.

So the big whoop-de-do for the last single McKay had fizzled out by eleven p.m.

"Dalton! Over here."

He turned to see Lee Anderson waving at him. As he crossed the room, he accepted a drink from the tiniest cocktail waitress he'd ever seen. She was the size of a twelve-year-old girl—the top of her head barely reached his sternum—and he wondered how in the hell she didn't tip over with her massive tits weighting her top half. Since she was scantily dressed in sparkly green, she reminded him of a slutty leprechaun. He heard his name again and looked up. When he looked down to excuse himself, she'd vanished.

Lee clapped him on the back. "Glad you could make it. Me'n Tick and Busby were beginning to think you didn't want nothin' to do with us no more, bein's you've been back in town for a while and we haven't heard from you."

Dalton knocked back a swallow of booze. "Aw, I didn't know you missed me so much. Didn't mean to butt hurt your poor wittle feewings."

"Fuck off." Lee grinned. "But I'm happy to see you ain't changed a whole lot in the past few years."

And there it was. The reason he hadn't wanted to come. That whole you-haven't-changed-a-bit bullshit. "Where is Busby?"

"Hell if I know. So whatcha been up to? We heard you were living on the streets in Vegas after you lost that poker game on TV," Tick said.

Dalton rolled his eyes. "Who'd you hear that from?"

"Don't remember now. But you ain't been back forever. You know how them rumors go if you ain't around to set 'em straight."

"I'll set the record straight now." He gave the bare bones version of his life. A few more guys from their graduating class joined their group, ragging on Dalton for missing their ten-year reunion. Busby showed up with two more "friends" both sporting tits the size of basketballs, collagen lips and vacant eyes. The room was getting crowded, yet Dalton's glass never dipped below the half-full mark.

The groom arrived and after being subjected to a speech about the horrors of marriage, he was dragged front and center for wedding night tips by Busby's friends.

All eyes were on the makeshift stage. As soon as the strippers had finished torturing Reggie, other guys pulled out their wallets to get in on the action.

Dalton didn't move.

Truman slipped in beside him and rested his elbows on the table. "I'm surprised you're not in line for a lap dance, McKay. Strippers used to be your thing."

"They used to be your thing too, Truman. So why aren't you in line?"

He shrugged. "Not my thing anymore."

"Not mine either." Dalton sipped his drink. "You think any of these married guys will tell their wives they paid a strange chick with monster tits to grind on them?"

"Hell no. We both know they're gonna go home and swear up and down there weren't strippers at this bachelor party." Truman shot him a sideways glance. "The only bachelor party that I've ever been to that didn't have strippers? Yours. And who'd believe that of stripper-loving Dalton McKay?"

Dalton laughed. "Point taken. So did you have strippers at your bachelor party?"

"Didn't have a party. Didn't do any of the normal wedding stuff with Addie after you..." He cleared his throat. "We opted for small."

The cocktail waitress, aka—the backup stripper, stood in front of Dalton and rested her enormous rack on the bar. Yeah, he looked— hard to miss those gigantic blobs of flesh when they were right in his fucking face.

She cooed, "Why the frown? You want a lap dance but don't

wanna wait in line?" She smiled and dragged a long red fingernail across her cleavage. "How about if I put a smile on that handsome face of yours, slick?"

"How much?" Dalton asked flatly.

"Twenty for a five-minute dance. Forty if you want me to face you and let you touch these." She cupped her breasts.

"Pass."

"You sure?" she purred. "What these hips can do puts these girls' lame moves to shame."

"Pass," he said again.

She might've muttered *cheap bastard* under her breath as she stomped away.

Truman laughed. "Well, you may not want them, but the strippers are still flocking to you."

"Flocking," he repeated with a laugh. "More like fleecing. Nothin' more attractive than a drunk man with an open wallet."

"Cynical."

"I prefer to think of it as mature."

Dalton had fun providing running commentary to Truman as they watched the strippers working the room. At one point they were laughing so hard a couple guys still in line gave them dirty looks.

After about an hour, Truman picked up his glass. "How can this be magically full again?"

Dalton squinted at the table in front of them after he saw a flash of green. Had that leprechaun chick been sneaking under the table and filling their glasses?

"What the fuck is in this drink?" Truman asked. "I swear I've had one and it feel like five. Shit. I'm buzzed."

"Me too."

Truman shoved the glass away. "Man. I gotta eat something and sober up. I'd never hear the end of it if I had to call my pregnant wife to haul my drunken ass home after a bachelor party." He clapped Dalton on the shoulder. "Great seein' you, McKay. I'm glad you're sticking around."

What? Wait. When had he said that?

Maybe he was drunker than he thought.

Used to be Dalton loved the happy buzz he got after several drinks. The happy place where he knew the people around him were his true friends. The happy place where he knew the women were laughing at his jokes because he was one damn funny man. The happy place where he knew he'd found his place.

But Dalton wasn't feeling any of that now.

This wasn't who he was anymore.

And he couldn't wait to get the hell out of here.

Dalton ducked out of the backroom and into the hallway. He had to close one eye because everything was so blurry. He slumped against the wall.

Fuck being drunk. He hated this. No fucking wonder he never did this stupid shit anymore.

He patted his pocket and found his cell phone. By holding his phone right up to his face he could sort of read the names. Selecting the one he wanted, he poked the Call button. "Hey. Sorry to do this to you but I'm at the Golden Boot and I'm really drunk and I need a ride so can you come and get me right now please? Thanks."

He hung up and stumbled outside to wait for his ride.

The caller ID on Rory's phone read *Sierra.* 'Bout damn time that little shit called her. Rory answered with, "Lemme guess; boy troubles."

"Fuck off," Sierra said by way of greeting. "I don't only call you when I've got guy problems."

"Do too."

"Do not. Anyway, it's not *my* guy that's giving me problems. It's yours."

"What's that supposed to mean?"

"I just got a phone call from Dalton. A very drunk Dalton. He's at the Golden Boot and needs a ride home."

Rory frowned. "Why would he call you in Arizona to give him a ride home in Wyoming?"

"He didn't. And he didn't let me speak. I'm thinking he meant to call you or Tell—since my name falls between yours and Tell's in his phone."

"Shit."

"So go get 'em, sis."

"I'm gonna kick his ass." Rory slipped on her coat. "Dalton swore he doesn't do this stuff anymore."

"He doesn't. So please don't ream him."

"I won't. Unless he's the drunken, belligerent Dalton I used to wanna punch in the face. Then all bets are off."

"Rory—"

"I'm kidding."

"If I remember correctly, you owe him a drunken ride home."

"Don't remind me."

Sierra laughed. "But to really even things up, you've gotta sleep with him when he's still slightly drunk and then be gone when he wakes up in the morning with a massive hangover."

Not a bad idea. In fact, that was a great idea.

"I was kidding." A pause. "No, you're not seriously thinking of doing that, Rory."

"Why not? He did it to me." Twice. "See if he likes being used for sex and then discarded?" she volleyed back.

"Sista, please. Even back then it was more than sex between you and Dalton and you know it." Sierra paused. "I think you both might've forgotten that there's *always* been more between you two. Anyway, you aren't a mean girl, a vindictive woman or a badass seeker of revenge."

Her inner bad girl flipped Sierra off with both fingers and cranked up the Joan Jett tunes.

"But you aren't a doormat either." Sierra belted out the first three lines of *I Will Survive* and laughed hysterically.

"Thanks for nothing, little sis. Your pep talk sucked as much as your singing. And you still owe me a phone call where I can properly grill you for hours on boys, boozing and the rumors about the mysterious businesses you're involved in."

"Goddamned gossipy McKay family," she grumbled. "Fine. I'll call you next week. Later." She hung up.

Rory had no idea what shape she'd find Dalton in when she reached the Golden Boot twenty minutes later. The parking lot was nearly full, forcing her to park at the far end of the lot.

The cold night air sliced through her as she walked around the corner to the front entrance. There he was, leaning against the building with his coat pulled up around his ears.

Dalton looked up at her approach. His smile...damn that smile of his. Even his drunken, lopsided grin was a sight to behold.

Kudos to herself for not morphing into a snarky bitch when she said, "Little too much liquid fun, McKay?" She jammed her hands in her pockets even when her fingers itched to smooth back his charmingly messy hair.

"My beautiful Rory. Thank you for comin' to get me. I'm, ah, a little drunk."

"I see that." When she got closer she smelled it too. "You okay to walk or should I bring the car around?"

"Probably need to walk it off." Dalton stepped away from the building and swayed.

"Whoa there, cowboy." She grabbed his arm and draped it over her shoulder. "Lemme help you."

His balance was way off so Rory half-pushed him and half-pulled him through the gravel parking lot to her Jeep. She propped him up on the passenger side wondering how she'd wrestle him in. But he climbed in as if he were perfectly sober.

"I'm sorry. Didn't intend to end up this way. I hate bein' drunk."

She backed out of her parking spot. "So what were you doing at the bar tonight?"

"Reggie's bachelor party."

"You must've had a good time."

"Nope. Saw a bunch of people I used to know. Most of 'em were getting drunk and acting stupid."

"What about you?"

"I didn't act stupid. Except for the leprechaun thing."

What the fuck? "Leprechaun?"

"Uh-huh. Leprechaun cocktail waitress. Think she was a stripper too."

"Guess they're hard up for chicks to strip in Wyoming if they're hiring leprechauns," she said dryly. Then she grinned. She was *so* going to lord this conversation over him. Maybe she'd even speak with a brogue. Dance an Irish jig while she served him Lucky Charms.

"They shoulda asked you to be a stripper," Dalton slurred. "You'd make a great stripper."

"Why would I want to be a stripper?"

"Because you're flexible. But mostly because you've got the body for it. Goddamn do I love your body. I just wanna put my hands all over it. Then my mouth. Right now."

"Not happening when I'm behind the wheel in a moving vehicle, bud."

"But I wouldn't want you stripping for anyone but me. No other man gets to see you nekkid. Ever. So no stripping."

"Shoot. Now my lap dancing skills will go to waste."

Dalton made that growling noise. "Where the fuck did you learn to lap dance?"

Not going there. "Did one of the strippers treat you to a lap dance tonight?"

He shook his head. "One tried, but when I told her I wasn't interested, she moved on to the next victim." He hiccupped. "Jesus, my head is spinning like a fucking washin' machine."

Rory snickered. "Maybe you shouldn't have been drinking so much."

"I didn't mean to. Know what sucks?"

"The shitty way you're gonna feel in the morning?" she said sweetly.

"That too. What sucks is that I don't do this kinda shit anymore. And by getting hammered in the most popular bar in town, everyone still thinks I'm the same drinkin' and fightin' and fuckin' around guy. But I'm not that guy anymore. And I didn't like that guy very much. So why the fuck did he show up tonight?"

"You sure that old Dalton was there tonight?"

He looked confused. "Huh?"

"Did you get into a bar fight?"

"Ah, no, I don't think so."

"Were you fucking around with women including magical leprechauns?"

"No. Fuck no. I'd never cheat on you, Rory. Never fucking ever. Been waiting a long goddamned time to have you. Now that you're mine, not gonna screw this up this time. I swear."

Not a combative drunk. A sweet drunk. And another sure sign he'd changed. Her inner romantic did a pirouette and blew her a kiss before yelling *told ya so, beyotch.* She sighed. "What sucks for me is you won't remember this conversation."

"The fuck I won't... Oh, hell. Stop the car."

Rory hit the brakes and pulled over.

"Gonna be sick. Shit." Dalton barely flung open the door before he started retching.

Awesome.

But at least he hadn't thrown up in the car.

Like you did that night with him.

Even more awesome to be reminded of that.

She considered turning up the radio so she didn't have to listen to him hurling, but she toughed up. He kept yakking.

Finally he swiveled back around, nestled his head in the headrest and slammed the door. "Sorry."

"You want to sit here a minute?"

"No. Pretty sure there's nothin' left since I threw up my stomach lining along with everything in it."

Rory shuddered. "No color commentary necessary."

"Sorry."

They were close to his place and she got him inside without much trouble.

He flopped on the bed in his room. Coat on, boots on, clothes on.

Lorelei James

Rory grabbed his wrist and pulled him upright. She lightly tapped his cheeks to get his attention. "Hey. Dalton. Gotta get your clothes off before you pass out."

Although his eyes were closed, he smiled. "I love that you always wanna take my clothes off."

"You have a bangin' body, McKay." First she peeled off his long black duster and he was zero help with that. Then she yanked off his left boot and then his right. She pulled the snaps on his shirt until it hung open. She couldn't help but run her palms down his pectorals. Warm. Firm. Rough. "Yes, you surely do have a bangin' body," she murmured. Her hands moved down his torso. She needed to undo his belt, but her fingers had another plan as they trailed across his ridged abdomen.

"I hold my breath when you touch me."

"Why?"

"Because I never want you to stop."

"Crazy man. If you don't breathe you'll pass out and not be able to feel anything anyway."

"The voice of reason."

"I'm not exactly the romantic type, Dalton." Rory unbuckled his belt, unzipped his jeans and pushed him back on the bed so she could strip him to his boxers.

"I am," he said softly.

"What?"

"The romantic type."

"I know."

"I don't show you very often, do I?"

"I don't expect it."

"You should. You deserve it. Especially from me." He sighed. "Thank you for picking up my drunken ass."

"You're welcome."

"Will you stay with me tonight?"

Yes. Then I'll get you hard, get myself off and leave you with your boxers around your ankles wondering what happened when you wake up alone tomorrow morning.

But she couldn't do it. She couldn't even say she'd stay and then just sneak out, which would be equally shitty.

Gazing into those vivid blue eyes, she brushed his hair from his cheek. "I'll stay."

Chapter Seventeen

"Where are we staying again?"

Dalton bit back a laugh. Rory hadn't stopped talking since he'd picked her up. He lifted their joined hands to kiss her knuckles. "At the Bullock."

"The one on Main Street?"

"The suite we're staying in is in a renovated building behind it."

"How far?"

"You've been to Deadwood. Everything is within walking distance."

"I know. But the fuck-me heels I'm wearing at your request—" she shot him an arch look, "—aren't exactly winter sidewalk friendly."

"Just hold on to me. I'll keep you upright." He grinned. "Unless I'm too busy keepin' you horizontal."

"I'm so looking forward to that," she purred.

"Me too."

Rory gave the questions a thirty-second rest before she started in again. "Is this a two-day poker tournament?"

"No. It's two one-night poker tournaments. Two different venues. Neither of which are at the Bullock. Which works out for us because I don't stay at the hotel where the events are held."

"That seems odd and inconvenient. Have you always had that superstition?"

Dalton shook his head. "Mostly it started when I traveled by myself and didn't want to pay the higher room cost. Didn't bother me when I split the hotel bill with Tell. So I found cheaper rooms close to the venue, because I wasn't actually in the room much. That's when I had much better luck. Don't know why that is, but I've done it that way for years."

"What are your odds of winning?"

"Better than most. Tomorrow's pot is bigger so we'll see if I have to throw tonight's game so I don't have people tryin' to knock me out in the first round tomorrow night."

"The strategy part of card playing boggles my mind."

Dalton laughed. "At least I've got you thinking there *is* strategy involved in Texas Hold'em and it ain't all luck of the draw."

Rory quit asking questions and gazed out the window.

The Black Hills were covered in snow so the drive up 385 to Deadwood was like a postcard. The setting sun reflected purple on the frosted trees and the sky. The roads were slick and the traffic was heavier than he expected.

This weekend marked the first time Dalton had brought a woman to a tournament. In years past he'd taken women back to his room when the games ended, but he'd never had a woman on the sidelines cheering him on. Winning or losing didn't matter to Rory—she'd be waiting for him regardless.

Deadwood didn't attract the big-league poker players, but the money was decent enough the mid-range players made it a destination. Those were the guys he worried about. The ones who considered Deadwood "their" town and banded together to defeat anyone new who dared to sit at the final table with them.

Rory waited in the truck while he retrieved the keys for their room. After he pulled up to the building he was glad for private parking. Deadwood appeared to be jam-packed. "Come on. Let's see the room. I'll come back for the luggage."

He unlocked the door and she stopped just inside the doorway. "Dalton. This place is awesome."

The suite of rooms wasn't decorated old west style, but modern. A living room filled with low-backed furniture that faced a gas fireplace. An eating area with a counter and barstools.

Rory disappeared around the corner and he followed her. "Look at this bathroom." It had a gigantic walk-in shower with a bench and two showerheads, and the room boasted an enormous sunken tub, surrounded by opaque glass bricks.

"Looks like we can have some fun in there, huh?" He took her hand. "Let's see the bedroom."

Rory squealed at seeing the king-sized four-poster bed and immediately jumped on it. "This has some give, which is lucky for us since you try to pound me into the mattress whenever possible."

"Is that a complaint?"

"Not at all, high roller." She kicked off her shoes and sighed.

Dalton wandered to the window and peeked out to see a view of the parking lot.

"What time do you have to check in for the tournament?" she asked.

"About forty-five minutes." He'd reached that antsy stage where he needed to expel his nervous energy before he started playing. He turned and Rory stood right in front of him.

She ran her hands down the lapels of his wool vest. "You look sexy as sin. With your black hat, jeans, boots and white shirt, now alls you need is a pocket watch with a gold chain, a thin cigar clamped between your teeth and you look every inch the mysterious rogue card sharp from Wild West days."

"Bit of a fanciful image from a woman who refuses to admit her romantic side."

"You have been showing me the benefits of a little romance in my life, McKay." Rory placed her hand on his cheek. "You okay?"

"Yep. Just ready to get goin' to the tourney. Why?"

"Would you be mad if I hung out here while you do your poker thing? You won't be there all night, right? I could just—" Rory pressed a kiss to the side of his neck, "—slip on something a little more comfortable and wait for you."

Her suggestion filled him with relief. He could get the feel for the people and the place without worrying about her. "That's a great idea. I'll get the luggage."

After he unloaded everything, Rory gave him a kiss for luck. Then she sang the chorus from "The Gambler" really loud.

"Thanks for getting that stuck in my head," he grumbled.

"You're welcome."

A few hours later Dalton brushed the snow off his shoulders and stamped the slush off his boots before he inserted the keycard into the door. Probably a good thing Rory had remained in the room. The weather sucked. Hopefully it'd be better tomorrow night.

The room was quiet. No TV, although she did have the fireplace burning.

He checked the bedroom before he tracked her to the bathroom.

The lights were dimmed, music drifted from her iPod. A sugary sweet scent perfumed the air. All nice enticements, but none as enticing as his Aurora, up to her chin in bubbles, all that glorious blond hair in a messy pile on top of her head. Her cheeks were flushed from the heat, and maybe from the half-empty margarita glass in her hand. Her lips were tilted into a sultry smile. "Hey, five-card stud. So did you win?"

"Eliminated in the third to last round."

"I'm sorry. Unless...that's what you wanted?"

He nodded.

"See anyone you know?"

"One guy acted like he didn't know me, which is fine because he's an asshole. Another wanted to take me out for a drink to brag about how well he's been doin'."

Rory sipped her drink. "Did you go?"

Dalton's hungry gaze roved over her, from her soft pink mouth to her pink toes peeking out of the bubbles on the opposite end of the tub. "When you're nekkid in a hotel room waitin' on me? Uh, no way in hell."

That curl to her lips got a whole lot sexier. "Why don't you come in and play?"

"Don't mind if I do." He shucked his clothes. His cock, already onboard with the bath idea, bounced against his belly as he started to climb over the wide ledge of the tub.

Rory said, "Wait. Grab some drinks first."

"Good thinking." He snagged a beer and a can of premixed margarita mix out of the fridge in the bar area. He noticed two dome-covered trays on the counter. Back in the bathroom, he refilled her glass and said, "Did you order room service?"

"I wasn't sure what time you'd get back and I doubted we'd want to go out for food, so I ordered in, figuring we could heat it up later."

Dalton grinned. "The only thing I wanna heat up right now is you." He threw his leg over the edge of the tub and immersed himself in sweet-scented water. He hissed. The water was hot.

"Feels good, doesn't it?"

Not as good as you're gonna feel. "Mmm-hmm." Sitting opposite her, he set his beer aside and wrapped his hand around her ankle. "How long have you been marinating in here?"

"About thirty minutes."

"What'd you do before that?"

"Wandered around. Watched the fire. I might've dozed off in that puffy bed, which is heavenly by the way."

"Which is ironic since we're gonna sin like motherfuckers in it."

Rory laughed.

He lifted her foot out of the water, pressed his mouth to her instep and lightly bit down.

"Got a foot fetish, McKay?"

"Only if the feet in question are attached to you." He kissed her anklebone. Her instep by the ball of her foot. Then he ran his tongue across the pads of her toes.

Rory groaned softly.

He set that foot down and picked up the other. He grazed his

Redneck Romeo

teeth across her instep and dropped kisses on the top of her foot. He
slipped his tongue between every toe.

Another soft groan.

Dalton slid his hands up her legs and floated toward her until
they were groin to groin. Keeping his eyes locked on hers, his hands
traveled up her body, over the curve of her hips, her belly, her ribcage,
over those beautifully full breasts, her collarbones, up the column of
her neck. He pulled her mouth to his, licking his way past her lips to
kiss her with heat and patience, which drove her crazy. Rory wanted
ferocious kisses. As much as he loved the passion that ignited in both
of them so quickly, he liked the seduction.

Then he pulled back, gazed into her eyes.

Rory's wet fingers traced the outline of his lips. "This mouth..."
She sighed. "I'm crazy for this mouth and all it can do."

He sucked her fingers and swirled his tongue around the tips.

She circled her legs around his hips and she canted her pelvis.
She caught him off guard when she spun them around so his back was
against the tub. "I'm pretty good with my mouth. So why don't you hop
on the edge and I'll prove it."

Dalton created a mini-wave he jumped up so fast.

Rory moved in, her fingers digging into the tops of his thighs. The
delicate way her breath drifted over the wet head of his cock, caused
him to shiver.

She fondled his balls and kissed the crease of his hip. Her lips
traveled from his left hipbone to his right, straight across his shaft. Her
hot little tongue licked away droplets of water on his skin as her lips
headed down.

Then her mouth engulfed him.

"Jesus."

He cursed again when she worked him in deeper and held him
there.

Rory released his cock an increment at a time until just the head
remained in that warm, wet sucking haven. She repeatedly flicked her
tongue over the sweet spot, her teeth holding his dick in place so he
couldn't push forward or pull back. She was in total control.

And he loved every second of it.

Dalton braced his hands on the ledge and let her have her way
with him. Wanting to close his eyes and lose himself in the sensations.
But watching her was a huge fucking turn-on. She seriously got off on
the power she had over him when his dick was in her mouth. He could
see it in the feminine tilt of her lips. The dark challenge in her eyes.
The little hums and moans told him that she loved winding him up

175

tighter and tighter until he begged for her to let him unravel completely.

She jacked his shaft slowly. Then quickly. Her tongue mapped every inch of his dick from root to tip. She sucked his nuts until they were hard and tight. Then she returned to deep throating him while her thumb swept over his anus. His thighs quivered. His abdominals were straining. His vision wavered.

Motherfucking hell, could she suck cock. This was epic.

Then her finger breached his asshole and she stroked the spot inside that sent a jolt of pleasure zipping through his entire body.

"Don't stop. So fucking close," he panted. His heart raced and he pumped his pelvis, trying to match her rhythm.

"Hold still."

"I'm tryin'... Oh, sweet lord, do that again."

Her hand stroked as rapidly on his shaft as her tongue flicked on the cockhead. Her mouth stopped long enough to say, "Watch me."

Dalton's eyes were starting to lose focus but he kept his gaze on her.

She rubbed that spot inside him; the *slap slap slap* sound of her hand working his cock bounced off the bathroom tile. When she used her teeth on the underside of the rim—that kicked him over.

"Fuck."

But Rory didn't hollow her cheeks and swallow that first spurt. It landed on her lips. Then she angled back and aimed the come shooting from his cock at her tits. Milky drop after milky drop hit her creamy flesh and clung before slowly sliding down the slope of her breast.

His body shook from her intimate touch, but also from the sexy way she closed her eyes and arched back. Biting her lip and softly moaning as if she were coming.

And she didn't let up. Her hand pulled every last twitch from his cock, her finger rubbed every last pulse in his ass, and those actions together milked every last bit of seed from his balls.

Even as he struggled to regain his sanity, he stared at the uninhibited woman who took as much pleasure out of giving it as she did receiving it.

Then Rory opened those stunning green eyes. She slid her finger from his ass as her tongue darted out to capture the pearly drop of come clinging to the edge of her lips.

Unfuckingbelievably hot.

Dalton practically leapt off the edge and on top of her. Fisting his hand in the messy topknot, he took possession of her mouth. Tasting himself, tasting the passion that exploded between them.

With his other hand he wiped his come from her chest. His fingers plucked her nipples. His palms smoothed over the heavy swells of her tits. He couldn't touch her enough. He ate at her mouth, sucked on her tongue, nibbled on her velvety lips. Then his hand followed the plane of her stomach, past the tight curls, straight down that juicy slit. He swirled his middle finger around the opening several times and pushed it inside that tight channel. The heat and slickness of her pussy already stirred his cock for round two. He fucked his finger in and out slowly, kissing her in the same purposeful way.

"More," she said against his lips. "Please."

"You are wet." His mouth slid to the tip of her chin. "Did you touch yourself while you were waitin' on me?"

"No. God that feels so good." Rory tipped her head back, allowing full access to her neck.

He slipped in another finger, pushing a little deeper, moving a little faster. His tongue lapped at the water beaded on her skin. He released her hair to toy with her nipples. Pinching and tugging the points—until her gasps became soft moans.

He swept his thumb over the edge of her pussy, stopping at her clit. "I wanna hear you when you come." Then Dalton slid the pad of his thumb over that bundle of nerves, his fingers inside her rubbed her pussy wall behind her pubic bone.

Rory tensed, knowing he hadn't put his mouth on her yet and whatever he did next would send her flying.

Dalton pinched her nipple hard and latched onto the pulse point in her throat; his tongue mimicked the cadence of his stroking thumb.

A husky wail drifted from her mouth—he felt the vibration on his lips as he sucked on her neck. Her body went rigid as her blood pulsed beneath his thumb and her pussy clamped down on his fingers.

Sexy as hell.

When Rory moved her head forward, Dalton backed off and slipped his fingers from her. Sliding his lips up the strong column of her neck, he rubbed his cheek along her jaw and swallowed her shallow breaths in a long kiss.

He finally released her lips and smiled. "Takin' a bath with you is some fun, jungle girl."

Rory smiled back. "You know it." She snagged her margarita. "Wanna stay in a little longer?"

"Yep. I hardly touched my beer." He reached for it and cranked on the hot water. Then he reached for her. "I love the feel of your wet body against mine."

She settled between his thighs, her back to his chest. She sighed and turned her head to kiss his jaw. "Thanks."

"For?"

"Bringing me here."

"Anytime. I just hope you're not too bored tomorrow."

"So I can't stand behind you while you're at the table and offer advice?"

Dalton snorted. "You already offered your advice in song form, remember?"

"But you have to admit the luck of the draw plays a part."

"Some. But card strategy and the ability to bluff are more key. There are two types of card players who win consistently."

Beneath the water she absentmindedly caressed his left thigh. "What types are they?"

"Methodical. The ability to gauge the worth of an opponent's cards by watching the betting strategy they use."

"Are you methodical?"

"I'm an instinctual player. I don't figure the odds in my head of winning or losing if X card is flipped. I don't go in with a plan. I just play my gut." He laughed softly. "I have had bouts of indigestion where my gut was totally off."

She laughed.

"Then there are the reckless players. They have some wins, but never consistent. They tend to play in local venues. So I'm hoping to be playin' against a lot of players like that tomorrow night."

"How often do you bluff?"

Dalton kissed the top of her head. "Whenever I have to."

"That's not an answer."

"It's an unanswerable question." He sipped his beer. "What kind of poker player would you be?"

"Boring. I wouldn't take any chances. I'd be too embarrassed that I'd get caught bluffing to actually try it. I'm not reckless. And I don't have the math skills to be methodical." She poked his leg. "I would've guessed you were the reckless type."

"Never when it comes to cards." Dalton put his lips on her ear. "And not when it comes to you."

They were quiet for a bit.

Then Rory said, "What do you see yourself doing in Sundance after you finish the house renovations?"

He'd wondered if she would bring this up. Like he needed to have a plan. Or another job lined up. But he didn't want to talk about the elk farm possibility specifically, so he hedged. "I've got an idea, something I've been working on. But it's out of my control, which makes me crazy."

She gasped dramatically. "No. You say you have a need for control? I never noticed it."

Dalton growled, "I got a couple of ways I can remind you if you like."

"Like what?"

"Both my ideas involve rope. And you bein' nekkid."

"What would you do?"

"Anything I want," he said silkily. "Because I'd have the ropes. But I'd make you come at least three times before I untied you."

Rory shivered and whispered, "Yes, please."

Setting aside his beer, he grabbed that mass of hair and angled her head to the side so his lips could barely skim the surface of her skin. "You want me to let that kinky and rougher side of myself out?"

"Have you been holding back with me?"

"Not at all. Why? Have I left you wanting more?"

"More hot sex with you? Absolutely. I'd just hate it if you think I'm some special butterfly that needs to be handled with kid gloves. When maybe...I'm the type that wants to get tangled up in the net." She slowly flipped around so they were chest to chest.

Dalton cupped her chin in his hand. "We can play all the sex games you want, Aurora, but what's goin' on between us is not a game to me." He pulled her closer, taking her mouth in a savage kiss. His cock swelled and she groaned softly as it pressed into her belly. He broke the kiss to command, "Outta the tub."

Rory pushed back and stood. Water and soap bubbles rolled down her lush body. She let him look his fill as she unpinned her hair and shook it free.

"Fucking gorgeous," he said in a low rasp.

She stepped over the edge and snagged a towel. She dried herself slowly, deliberately, her eyes held a hint of challenge. After wrapping the towel around her, she flounced out of the bathroom.

He sprang out of the water. He barely ran a towel over his body before he chased after her.

She'd nearly reached the bed when he tugged her towel free, leaving her naked. She whirled around and Dalton's mouth was on hers, with one hand fisted in her hair, the other clamped on her left butt cheek.

Rory's arms wreathed his neck and she kissed him with equal ferocity.

Dalton towed her to the living area and lowered her to the big couch.

"Aren't we making carpet angels in front of the fireplace?"

"I'm not feelin' angelic right now, Aurora."

Her gaze briefly dropped to his cock. In one long sinuous movement, she stretched her right arm along the plush sofa until it was artistically arranged above her head. "Bring in the devil."

When she put her feet up on the couch, Dalton said, "No. Keep your right foot on the floor. Like that. Press your left knee into the back of the couch so I can see every inch of your pussy." As soon as she complied his mouth dried up. "Jesus. You're a fucking goddess." Then he dropped to his knees and buried in face in her cunt.

Rory arched up and her hands automatically landed on his head.

Dalton lifted his mouth and looked at her. "No hands on me. Next time I have to tell you I will break out the ropes."

With her arms above her head, her body was a beautiful curve from her pelvis to the tips of her fingers.

He traced her slit down to her opening and slipped two digits inside. Then he tongued her clit relentlessly until her sex spasmed against his mouth and her juices coated his face.

While she came down from that fast orgasm, he kissed the inside of her thighs. Her bikini line. The curve of her knee.

Rory propped herself up on her elbow. "Crawl up here and fuck me."

Dalton scooted back, setting his left foot on the floor. Balanced on his right knee, he leaned forward and braced his left hand by Rory's head. Watching her eyes, he rolled his hips, gliding his cock along her pussy. Her wet, hot, wide-open pussy.

"You're good at that."

"What? This?" His shaft slid down her slick slit. He paused above the base of her pubic bone to drag the rim of his cockhead over her clit. Again and again and again.

Rory moaned. "Yes, that. Don't tease. Fuck me."

"Let's see how flexible you are, yogi." Dalton's fingers formed a circle around her left ankle and he pushed her leg up and up until her knee was parallel with her shoulder. "Very flexible." He angled his hips and pushed his cock into her to the hilt.

"Omigod. That feels..." She didn't finish her sentence when he started to move.

Dalton fucked her without pause. The position of her leg opened her completely, creating more skin contact when he bottomed out inside her. Every time. The slap of his body into hers, the harsh breathing, the creak of the couch surrounded him, adding to his urgency.

"Push into me right...there. Yes."

He kept his hand on Rory's leg as he pounded into her. She was so wet he had to pause before he thrust back in. "Arch your lower back. Yes. God that's so good."

Rory thought so too because she started to come. She threw her head back, her hair sliding off the couch; her hands balled into tight fists, her mouth went slack.

Beneath his palm, her thigh went stiff. He could feel her clenching her ass cheeks in time to the blood throbbing in her clit. The rhythmic pulls of her pussy muscles were like a silken vice around his cock, holding him in place.

He held on barely by the skin of his teeth as he rode out the storm with her.

When her limbs relaxed, he pumped into her so forcefully her body slid up the couch. His balls swung into her ass and he was done for.

He emptied himself into her, his mind blank.

But his heart? His heart was full.

Chapter Eighteen

The next night Rory showed up at the tournament ten minutes before it started.

After spending the day lounging around, goofing off, having sex on every piece of furniture in the hotel room, she thought she'd seen all of Dalton's faces.

Apparently not.

Dalton's poker face scared her a little.

She didn't always have a clear line of sight to him. People walked in front of her blocking her view. But she'd seen enough to notice that he defined impassive. No reaction if he won a big pile of chips. No reaction if he lost. The man was impossible to read, which was how he won the table and advanced to the next round.

During the break Rory hung back with the crowd of spectators and eliminated players, waiting to see if Dalton sought her out. He didn't.

He was a completely different person in this round than the previous round. He was friendly. Laughing. Trash talking. Very distracting. Acting as if winning was a surprise. He suckered them all in and handily walked away with that round too.

Rory paced, nerves getting the better of her during the next two rounds. If she was climbing out of her skin, how did Dalton remain so calm?

Because he's a master at masking his emotions.

No, that wasn't it. Was it?

One of the changes she'd noticed in him was Dalton's long stretches of silence. Any other man she'd call it brooding, but with him...she had no idea what was going through his head in those moments. Whenever she asked him, he smiled and deflected, just like he used to. Which made her think he hadn't changed as much as he'd insisted.

The announcement for the upcoming burlesque dinner show echoed through the casino and Rory refocused.

Dalton sat at the final table in the winner-take-all cash game with a payout of forty grand. If he won, he'd make more money in one night than she made in a year.

She'd wondered which Dalton would play in the final game. Impassive Dalton? Jovial Dalton? Nope. Neither. The Dalton seated fourth in on the left side of the dealer seemed antsy. Other players noticed and began to watch him for a specific nervous tic that could be construed as a tell.

Maybe they should've been paying more attention to their cards because it wasn't long before the table was down to three players.

Seeing how easily he slipped between three different personality types brought back her concerns. Did he treat her like a player to be managed in a card game? Could he gauge her mood and adjust his personality and responses accordingly? And if he was doing that, how much had he really changed?

Man, she had a crapload of doubt. And when they weren't rolling around in the sheets together, it made her wonder if they could overcome their tangled past.

Doesn't matter, remember? Hot sex, good times, when it's done it's done and there won't be any crying about what might've been.

Shouts and clapping brought her out of her reverie. A bunch of people were standing around the table but she couldn't see anything.

Who'd won?

Then everyone stepped away. Dalton's beaming grin was a sight to behold. No mistaking that for anything but a victorious smile.

Their eyes met. Rory recognized that look. Triumph and lust. A conquering hero hell bent on taking his prize.

So winning made him horny? Interesting.

If she was a betting woman, she'd drop a C-note that Dalton would drag her back to their room as soon as possible. He'd have her bent over the arm of the couch or pinned to the mattress within minutes of walking through the door.

But Rory didn't want that. Tonight she wanted to tease the beast. Sexually torment him to the point that he'd fuck her with that dangerously raw edge he tended to keep hidden.

Before she delved any deeper into that fantasy, the big, broad cowboy was in her face, lifting her, spinning her in a circle. "I won, I won, I won."

She laughed. "I see that. Remind me never to play strip poker with you. What happens now?"

"Gotta go to the cage, get my cash and give the tax man his due. Sign some papers." He stepped back and his hungry gaze took in her outfit. Cleavage-baring black bustier with a sheer pink blouse over the top. The stretchy black miniskirt clung to her ass and was about three inches shorter then she preferred. She hadn't worn hosiery, even though it was fucking freezing. She'd slipped on heeled black boots that reached her knees.

Dalton made that growling noise. "How long you been walkin' around wearing that outfit?"

"Some. Why?"

"Because you are smokin' hot. Jesus, woman. You're making me lose my train of thought."

"Maybe this will get it back on track." She placed an openmouthed kiss on his neck above his shirt collar. "Get your winnings so you can buy me dinner. I'm starved."

"I'll feed you. Then I'll fuck you."

Obviously Dalton didn't care that anyone within earshot could hear him.

Rory brushed the front of her body against his. "You're hard."

"Fuckin' right I'm hard. Winning always gets me hard. Add in the fact you're here with me? Lookin' like sex on legs? This hard-on ain't goin' away until I fuck you at least twice."

Pushing him to the edge wouldn't be a problem. The man was already there.

"Mr. McKay?" a staff member inquired behind him.

"Yeah. I know. Gotta get the paperwork done."

"I'm supposed to ask if you'd like to dine here. I can have a private table reserved for you."

Dalton looked at her. "How's that sound?"

"Good."

He kissed her cheek. "Hang out by the slot machines. I'll be back in ten."

Rory wandered on the main floor. She had more fun watching people shoving nickels in the slots than doing so herself. She didn't stop for long in one place; too much restless energy. She did pause to look at a display of Old West memorabilia.

She sensed his return. Feeling his hot gaze tracking her backside, from her heeled boots up her legs. Lingering on the curve of her ass. Her hips. Her fall of hair that brushed the bottom of her shoulder blades.

Then Dalton's hands landed on her hips. He swept aside her hair and placed a very possessive kiss on the side of her neck.

Gooseflesh broke out across her entire body and she released a soft moan.

"That moan drives me fucking insane. I wanna slip my hand

under your skirt and finger you until you come. Then I'd lick that sweet cream from my fingers."

Rory turned her head to nuzzle his jaw. "Then I'd suck it from your tongue." She actually felt his pulse jump.

"Jungle girl, we're gonna rip each other to pieces when we're alone." His mouth grazed her ear. "And. I. Can't. Fucking. Wait." He punctuated each word with a kiss.

Her entire body hummed with anticipation.

"But I promised to feed you first, so let's go."

Dalton clasped her hand and they climbed the stairs to the next level.

The host escorted them to a private table in the corner with windows on both sides.

She unrolled her silverware from her napkin and tried not to gawk. "This place is like...wow. Really upscale."

Dalton looked up from the menu. "Food looks good. Since this meal is on the house, have whatever you want."

The waiter delivered bottle of champagne and poured two flutes.

Rory raised her glass. "To Dalton McKay's poker face and his incredible luck at cards." When he growled, she laughed. "Kidding. To your winning strategy."

They drank. Dalton refilled their glasses.

As he contemplated the menu, Rory studied him. Candle glow looked amazing on him. He'd mussed up his hair during the games and she preferred that wild look. His full lips were pursed as if he was deep in thought. When he glanced up at her from beneath the brim of his black hat, she was struck anew by his rugged good looks. It'd taken him longer to grow into that handsome face, but man, was it worth the wait.

"Sugarplum, why're you lookin' at me like you've never seen me before?"

"Because you're gorgeous. Every woman in this restaurant is staring at you. They're wondering what you're like in bed."

"If there are women in here besides you, I didn't notice."

She bit back a sigh and refused to let her cynical side get a foothold and warn her it was just another line.

Dalton ordered the elk medallions with a wild mushroom and bourbon demi-glaze. Rory ordered the pumpkin ravioli in a sweet cream sauce.

After the waiter left, she glanced up at Dalton to see him staring at her with a decidedly predatory look. "What?"

"Think anyone would notice if you hiked up your skirt and

185

crawled onto my lap?"

"Pretty sure the entire restaurant would notice."

"I'm game."

"Well, I'm not. I don't want anyone to see how it is between us."

"Because it's special?" he prompted.

"Because it's so scorching hot between us that watching might make their eyeballs explode."

Dalton smiled the wolfish gleam that turned the delicious curl of want inside her into a raging inferno.

"Stop that," she hissed. "I am not gonna crawl on your cock and ride you like a pony."

"Shame. Do I have other options?" He drained the champagne and poured more.

"Such as?"

"Watching you masturbate."

"Right here, right now?"

"Yep."

"Are you drunk?" she demanded.

"Nope."

Rory cocked her head. "Suppose I did spread my legs and slip my fingers into my cunt to get myself off. You'd still be hard and horny. How would you benefit?"

Dalton plucked up her hand and rubbed the tips of his fingers on his lips. "The benefit for me is that you did what I told you. You have no idea how much I love watching you come. It's even better—" he kissed her fingertips, "—and hotter when you do it for me."

"Dalton, the list of things I won't do with you or to you or have you do to me is pretty short. But I draw the line at diddling myself between courses in a four-star restaurant."

That aw-shucks grin appeared. "Worth a try."

Tempting to chuck a dinner roll at him but she resisted. "Can you dial back the *I need to fuck your brains out* vibe, please? At least while we're enjoying this meal?" Her gaze took in every inch of his face. "It's a nice change for us, being out on the town, dressed up and eating fancy food."

His eyes softened. "Baby, I'll take you out for a nice dinner and show you off every night of the week if that's what you want."

"Not necessary. I want *this* night out with you. Celebrating you being the big money winner."

"Deal."

During dinner he entertained her with stories from his travels in

Europe.

Yet he didn't dial down the sexual intensity completely. It buzzed between them, making her hyperaware of his every movement. His every breath. His every uncompromising stare.

As Rory pondered dessert choices, she asked if he wanted to share. The molten look in his eyes when he murmured, "I'm havin' you for dessert," almost had her skipping the three layer chocolate cake with vanilla bean crème freche.

Almost.

Floating on champagne, an amazing meal and a cup of strong coffee, Rory faced Dalton when he placed his hand in the small of her back as they left the restaurant.

He lowered his head and she expected a gentle peck. But he consumed her mouth in a blistering kiss, revving that sexual need into overdrive. When he finally released her lips, she knew the buzz she felt was all from him.

The elevator dinged and the doors slid open. As soon as the doors closed, Dalton shoved a keycard into the slot and they descended to the lowest level—which she remembered was not street level.

"Dalton—"

Then that avid mouth was on hers again. He'd crowded her into the corner with one hand gripping her hair and the other hand squeezing her hip.

By the time the elevator stopped, her head spun, her heart raced, and the inside of her thighs were damp and sticky. He could get her hot and bothered in the span of two floors.

After the doors opened he hit the button sending it back up. The space was dark. The only illumination came from the glow of the exit signs.

"Where are we?"

"The extra gaming room in the basement. The casino only uses it when they run a big tournament. No cameras down here," he said against her throat. His big body pushed her backward. "Jesus. I want you so fuckin' bad I can't even walk a straight line."

"But how..." Rory moaned when his teeth skimmed the tendons straining in her neck.

"The head of hotel security owed me a favor."

Her ass bumped into something solid and she stopped.

Dalton said, "Hold on to me and hop up."

Once she was seated, she glanced down to see what she was seated on.

A table covered in green felt.

He created space for himself between her thighs. "So fuckin' hot in this skirt," he hissed in her ear as he rolled it up to her hips. "Need to get under it, get in you, before I explode."

Seeing Dalton this crazed to have her, feeling that pure sexual energy pulsing off him, made her wet, made her burn, made her brave. For him she could be the kinky girl who got fucked on a gaming table in the basement of a casino. In his eyes she was the red-hot lover that her lover couldn't get enough of. She could prove she was the reckless woman who got off on getting her man off any time, any place.

His lips danced across her skin, soft and wet and perfect. "I want you." A soft pass. "But first I'm gonna eat my dessert."

"How did you—" was all she managed before she found herself flat on her back—on a poker table!—with Dalton yanking her thong aside.

Then she didn't give a rip where she was. Dalton's mouth was licking her pussy, sucking every bit of juice from her swollen tissues. His growling moans vibrated against her flesh until that teasing tingle started behind her tailbone.

But that wasn't what she wanted or what he needed.

She clapped her hands on his cheeks and pulled that skillful mouth off her. "I'm wet, you're hard. Fuck me. Now."

His eyes glittered and he undid his belt. His jeans and boxers hit the tops of his boots. He gripped the insides of her thighs and shoved them wider apart.

Then he crammed his cock into her so fast and hard she arched off the table.

"Hold on," he panted as he worked his cock in and out with long strokes. "Pull your shirt down so I can watch your tits bounce as I fuck you like this."

Rather than rip the buttons to do his bidding, Rory undid the buttons one at a time. "You like these?" She cupped her breasts and pushed them up, creating a deep line of cleavage.

"Yes," he gritted out. His hips began doing that twisty thing as he pumped inside her. "Show me."

"Huh-uh high roller. You wanna see 'em, free 'em yourself."

Dalton's palms moved up her hips. Wearing the depraved grin that made her belly swoop, Dalton unhooked the first two hooks on the bustier before he tugged it down. Then her breasts were free, bouncing with abandon. "Fuck that's hot." He watched with a gleam in his eye, bottoming out on every thrust to make the flesh shake.

"I love the way you fuck me."

"And what way is that?"

"However you want."

Keeping his eyes on hers, Dalton bent forward and licked her nipple. Just one lash of his wet tongue. "Brace your hands above your head on the rail."

As soon as she did, his hand slid between her legs and he traced her slit from where his cock filled her to the fleshy folds of her pussy lips. He bit down on her nipple—the shock of pain immediately gave way to pleasure as the heat and wetness of his mouth surrounded the rock hard tip. He lifted his head, dark hair falling across his forehead in that untamed manner and his teeth hovered over her nipple. But the same time he bit down, he pinched her clit.

Rory gasped as the orgasm came out of nowhere. Her clit throbbed beneath his pinching fingers; his sucking mouth was firmly latched onto her nipple as he fucked her into that white void of bliss.

Soft kisses on the upper swells of her breasts brought her back to reality.

"Need you from behind." He pulled out and rolled her over, yanking her body down the table. Her hips were against the outside edge and the tips of her shoes could almost touch the floor. Almost. In this position Rory was completely at Dalton's mercy.

Good thing she didn't need to use any brain cells; hers were still buzzing from that outstanding orgasm.

Dalton lifted her ass cheeks and shoved back into her pussy. His hands pushed against her butt to keep her hips from slamming into the edge as he hammered into her.

"So fucking perfect how this hot cunt grips me. It owns me."

Rory squeezed his cock on his next pass and he yelled, "Fuck."

His fingertips tightened on her flesh a split second before he released a long shuddering groan as he came.

And came.

Dalton's legs shook. So did his voice. "So fucking... Jesus. I can't even come up with a word to describe that."

Then his hand was in her hair, cranking her head so he could destroy her with a searing kiss that managed to be sexy as shit and sweet as honey. When he finally released her mouth, she sighed again.

He lightly rubbed his lips back and forth across the shell of her ear. "You rocked my universe this time, jungle girl."

"I'm feeling a little spun out of orbit myself."

Then in typical Dalton fashion, he tended to her. Gently lowering her to her feet. Straightening her thong and tugging her skirt back into place. Kissing her with an erotic tease as he adjusted her bustier and buttoned her blouse.

Clasping her hand in his, he headed for the elevator, but she pulled him back.

"What?"

"Does your key card work for the stairs? Because I don't wanna parade through the lobby with sex hair."

Dalton kissed her forehead. "Of course. Let's go back to the room. But first..." He pushed her against the door to the stairs and planted a kiss on the side of her neck. "Thank you for tonight, Aurora. It's been one of the best nights of my life."

He'd rocked her to the core. But she also feared it wasn't her specifically who'd starred in his fucking-on-a-poker-table fantasy—she was just the woman who'd helped him fulfill it. So to keep things between them light and sexy, she cooed, "Of course it's one of the best nights of your life. You won a shit ton of cash, ate a fancy meal for free and got your rocks off."

His entire body stiffened at her flip response.

But Rory refused to feel guilty for reminding him—and herself— that this was all fun and games.

Chapter Nineteen

In years past, Dalton had arrived at McKay family poker games with Tell. Then after they'd lost—always on purpose—they'd hit a bar, or a party, or a strip club.

Trucks lined the driveway. It appeared he was the last to arrive. Stupid to have a bout of nerves. He'd known these people all his life.

Ben answered the door before Dalton could knock. "Hey, come in. You're just in time—we're drawing names." He held out a cowboy hat. "Pick a slip of paper."

"For what?"

"Which table you start at. There's too many of us so we're setting up two tables. Top three winners from each table will get to the final round. Now that you're here and there are thirteen of us..." Ben frowned. "That don't divide evenly."

Once again Dalton felt like the odd man out. Last to arrive, last one picked for the team, the one everyone else had to move to make room for.

Ben clapped him on the back and looked at the number on the paper. "No matter, we'll go seven and six."

With the exception of Ben and Keely, Dalton hadn't seen any of his McKay cousins since he'd returned. They all seemed friendly enough, but it wasn't like it used to be. *Maybe because you're not who you used to be.* He declined a beer from Quinn, who played bartender, and opted for soda.

Keely sidled up to him for a hug. "You're keeping yourself mighty scarce, Dalton."

"I've got some stuff goin' on."

"Like Rory? Family gossip says you're seeing her all official and like."

"How in the hell do you have time to keep tabs on me when you've got four kids?"

"No clue. Some days are a blur. JJ and Liam have hit the terrible twos and are absolute hellions. Hellions," she repeated. "Luckily Piper loves to tattle so I hear everything those boys try when I don't have my eye on them."

"What goes around, comes around, little sis," Colt said.

"I was never that bad. Even Mom says so." She smirked. "But it oughta be fun hearing how Jack's afternoon went, since he's taking all the kids to grocery store today. Even I'm not brave enough to do that."

"That's why it's great to have a built-in babysitter," Cord said. "Although Kyler don't appreciate havin' to stay home and watch his little brothers and sister when he'd rather be out tearin' around." Cord crossed his arms over his chest. "Find it odd he volunteered to help you when he's got plenty of chores to do at home."

"Kyler is a good kid. I'm glad to have his help. He mentioned you and AJ had another boy. Belated congrats. How old is he now?"

"Vaughn is two and a half. We keep our angel away from Keely and Jack's twin devil boys so as to not give him any ideas," Cord said, ducking Keely's swat.

"Looks like the McKay ranch will be goin' strong for another generation with all the ranch hands in training," Dalton said.

None of them suggested that he get on the stick, get married and add to the fray, since that hadn't exactly worked out last time.

"We've the table assignments, so listen up," Kade said. "Table one will be, me, Keely, Quinn, Tell, Gavin and Colby. Table two will be Ben, Colt, Cam, Brandt, Cord, Dalton and Kane." He pointed to Ainsley at the end of the bar. "Ainsley has volunteered to be the banker."

"I didn't volunteer; I was volunteered by my husband."

"Handling money is a natural state for you, darlin'."

Dalton wondered if Ben saw her stick her tongue out at him.

"So head over and get your chips if you haven't yet. Buy-in is fifty bucks."

Dalton stood in line next to Tell. He leaned in to whisper, "You playing it safe today, bro?"

"Not on your life."

"Me neither. Get ready for the showdown between you and me in the championship round."

"Wanna bet who comes out on top?"

"I ain't makin' a side wager with you, Tell." Dalton grinned. "Be like takin' food outta your kid's mouth."

"A hundred bucks says I win it all."

Sucker. Dalton stuck out his hand. "You're on."

As soon as he took his seat at the table, he said, "Who's dealing?"

"This ain't no fancy casino game. We take turns dealing," Kane said. "Ainsley keeps an eye on things so there's no cheating."

"Who would ever cheat at cards?" Cam said with a mock gasp.

"You. Which is sad considering you are an officer, sworn to uphold the law," Colt said.

"I ain't wearing my gun or badge now so alls fair," Cam retorted. He rubbed his hands together with anticipation. "Let the bloodbath begin."

A lot of trash talking happened during the game. If anyone noticed Dalton didn't join in it wasn't mentioned. He just played until he ran Brandt out of chips. Cam took out both Cord and Colt. Kane eliminated Ben.

They took a break to grab snacks and more drinks, although they seemed to be drinking a lot less booze than they used to.

Gavin caught Dalton by the chips and dip. "Have you heard from my daughter lately? She told me you two have been in contact over the years. And yes, she confessed she owns the house you're living in."

"Now why would she do that?"

"A couple of my business associates contacted me and asked, if Sierra was my heir, then why she wasn't buying property through Daniels Development. So I did a little research and found out she owns six properties. One here, one in Casper, one in Cheyenne and three in Arizona."

"Girl's got ambition," Dalton admitted.

"She's also got a financial backer. I'm sure she used some of her inheritance from her grandparents to fund this...venture. But she'd need someone older to partner with. Someone with solid credit. I'm assuming that's you?"

He shot a look over his shoulder and lowered his voice. "Look, Sierra is a savvy young woman. Her ideas are sound. She's grown up in the real estate business so she's not some wet-behind-the-ears kid earning a business degree with no practical experience. My gut instinct was to back her and it hasn't proven to be a bad investment. Return on investments are slow at this point, but I didn't give her any capital I couldn't afford."

Gavin's eyes remained skeptical. "Your brothers—no one in the McKay family has any idea how well-funded you are, do they?"

"Nope. And I'd like to keep it that way. You should be proud of Sierra. The whole reason she's been doin' this is to prove to you she's a self-starter and she's qualified to run the business with you."

"Thank you for saying that. I'm damn proud of that girl and she's a good judge of character."

"What're you two whispering about over here?" Tell asked.

"Issues I had fixing Rory's doggie door. Gavin installed it six months ago and we're brainstorming on how we can repair the broken seal," Dalton lied with a straight face. "Why? What'd you think we were talkin' about?"

"The two of you ganging up on me in the final round because I'm the real threat in this contest."

Dalton and Gavin looked at each other and laughed. "Nice try, bro. See ya at the table."

Keely, Gavin, Tell, Cam, Dalton and Kane made it to the final table. Ben offered to act as the dealer.

"So, we have any side bets goin'?" Kade asked.

"If I stay in longer than Cam, he's taking all of our kids so me'n Jack can have a night out. If a miracle happens and he stays in longer than me, I have to take his girls and mine fishing. No men allowed, which means I'll be baiting hooks and removing hooks." She shuddered.

Laughter.

"No one else?"

Dalton and Tell smirked at each other but said nothing.

"Well, I ain't gonna say who the odds on favorite is—Gavin *cough cough*—because he gambles with so much money every day. But if you're feelin' lucky, Ainsley is takin' bets on who'll take home the cash pot." Ben shuffled the cards. "Here we go."

At first everyone played conservatively. Then Tell bluffed his way to a win, which kicked in Kane and Cam's competitive sides. Unfortunately for them, they were suckered in by Tell's manipulation and they went out. Keely lasted a few more hands before she was down to zero chips. Gavin went all in with a full house eights high. But it wasn't enough to beat Dalton's full houses nines high over sevens.

So it came down to Dalton and Tell. Dalton let Tell think they were evenly matched as he kept dinging him for a few bucks here and there until Tell was down to two hundred bucks.

Dalton bluffed, knowing Tell would see through it. Tell won the hand and got a little overconfident. Dalton bluffed a few more times and lost several hands, but not in a row.

When Dalton was sitting on three aces and a pair of queens, he glanced over to see a hard set to Tell's jaw, which meant he was trying his damndest not to grin.

Gotcha.

Odds were Dalton had Tell's hand beat. Tell most likely didn't have a royal flush since Dalton held an ace and a queen from two suits. So unless Tell was holding onto four kings or four jacks...

Dalton said, "Check."

Tell looked at his chips and pushed them into the center. "All in."

A chorus of oohs rang out.

Dalton looked as his cards, unfanned them into a single pile and set them on the table.

"To you, Dalton," Ben reminded him.

He shoved his chips into the middle of the table. "All in."

Tell spread his cards out and grinned. "Read 'em and weep, bro. Hate to hand you another public loss, but there it is." Tell had a spade flush queen high.

"As purty as that little flush is? It don't beat this, does it?" Dalton flipped over his cards one at a time...and his family alternately cheered and booed.

"Thank you." Dalton scooped all the chips to his side of the table.

"But..." Tell said, completely shocked. "I know all your tells."

"You *knew* all my tells. Been a long time since we've played cards."

Everyone surrounded Dalton, congratulating him. Someone said, "Speech," and Dalton knew the time had come.

"Thanks for inviting me to the poker game and handing over all your money."

Boos rang out.

Kane drawled, "Whatcha been up to since you've been back besides practicing polishing your poker hand?"

"Usin' my handyman skills renovating my friend's house. And another opportunity has come along and I've already started to pursue it."

He watched his brothers exchange a confused look.

"Which is what?" Cam asked.

"Remember that section of land I bought from the Fox family? The two hundred acres between Tell's place, and where the upper half borders Quinn and Ben's section, and the lower half borders Gavin's land?"

"Yeah? What about it? You gonna put a casino on there?" Colt teased.

"No. I've applied for a permit for the state's pilot program for commercial elk farming."

Laughter broke out.

"Good one, Dalton, you almost had us there," Cord said.

"I'm not kidding. I already filed all the appropriate paperwork with the state."

"Please tell me you're doin' this so if you do get picked you can let it sit there fallow to show the state they can't mess in our livelihood,"

Lorelei James

Quinn demanded.

Dalton shook his head. "I'm dead serious. That chunk of land is perfect. It's rugged and hilly. I've got the means to build the required fence. I've got game supplier contacts in Montana."

"Is that why you put a new paddle lock on the gate?" Tell asked.

"One of the reasons. I hauled some fencing down there that I didn't want anyone messin' with."

"Do you have any idea how much damage a herd of elk can do to grazing land? Not to mention how freakin' much feed it takes to sustain them. And if they can't find that feed in the fenced-in area, well, where the hell do you think they're gonna go lookin' for it?" Ben demanded.

Colby, Cord and Colt jumped in to back Quinn and Ben. All talking at once, yelling at him about what a big mess he was making of everything.

Brandt and Tell stared at him, clearly unhappy that he'd brought this up in front of the entire family.

The words selfish and irresponsible and childish, vindictive and troublemaker were tossed around, hitting him center mass just like goddamned daggers.

He needed to get the fuck out of here now.

The noise escalated to the point the only thing that cut it was Keely's shrill whistle.

"Enough!" Keely shouted. "Hurling accusations isn't helping."

"Don't see why the hell you're even getting involved," Cord snapped at Keely. "You don't have a stake in the ranch and it ain't gonna affect your life at all."

Colby and Colt backed him. Then Quinn and Ben joined in and Cam had to break it up.

"Knock it the hell off! Jesus. I'da stayed home if I wanted to referee pointless bickering."

"Then stay out of it, little brother. Because you don't have a stake in the ranch anymore either," Colt said hotly.

"Take a deep breath, Colt," Kane said.

"The hell I will. And why are you and Kade sitting on the sidelines? This'll affect you too."

"It's not like we could get a word in edgewise," Kade said, "Which is par for the course lately. You, Colby and Cord just talk over the rest of us anyway, because your opinion is the only one that matters, right?"

Fuck. This was getting ugly and it was just the beginning.

Gavin stepped forward. "Let me speak."

196

Dalton waited for someone to point out he didn't have a stake in the ranch, and he wasn't even technically a McKay. But no one chimed in.

That's because they respect him.

"I'm not a rancher. But I do think you guys are getting all bent out of shape about something that might never happen. Dalton applied for the permit. That's it. That doesn't mean he'll get it. So the time to hold the discussions about elk escaping and affecting grazing land and hay stores is not now."

A few grumbles, but everyone quieted down.

But Quinn wouldn't let it go. "So where do you stand, Gavin?"

It appeared Gavin would hedge and Dalton didn't blame him. He didn't want to get into it with his brothers either. So Gavin's response shocked the shit out of him.

"If we're making these lines or whatever purely on border issues, then this elk farm would affect almost my entire acreage. And to be honest, the land I own has been a point of contention in this family for a number of years. Everyone has approached me on how to improve it, how to make it cattle friendly. I listened. But no one actually stepped up and gave me a solid plan on why I ought to draw up an official lease agreement. Except for Dalton."

Dalton felt all eyes on him while his remained on the floor.

"He drew up a workable, sustainable plan. Timetables for the clearing process, a growth chart of the number of head in the herd year by year, even when portions of it would remain fallow so it wouldn't be overgrazed. He asked for a five-year lease, which would go into effect after the improvements were made on the land—improvements which were promised to be made on his dime."

A moment of quiet. "Dalton. When did you do all that?" Brandt asked.

"Four years ago," Gavin answered. "At the time Dalton was confident with the addition of Georgia and Jessie into the McKay workforce all the brush could be cleared and improvements made within six months."

"Why didn't we know any of this?" Ben asked.

"Because the contract was between me and Dalton, since technically he was the sole owner of the chunk of land that bordered mine."

"Is that why you asked me if we had any plans for it?" Quinn asked.

"Yes. And you told me neither you nor Ben had the time nor the inclination to do what needed to be done to make that piece of land useable for your operation." Gavin rubbed the skin between his eyes. "When a full year rolled around and no improvements had been made because Dalton couldn't do it by himself and didn't have the help he'd counted on, he approached me, requesting that we void the contract. He didn't want me to be beholden to it and lose out on an opportunity to lease the land to someone else in case it came up.

"I'm sorry, that is not the action of a selfish man. Or a childish man. Or a vindictive man. Or a goddamned troublemaker. I don't know who tossed out that accusation because that's one thing Dalton isn't. Maybe he was wild as a kid—I can't say because I didn't know him then. But I know him now, and in case you haven't been paying attention, he's not a kid anymore. He's a man trying to make a living like all of you. Takes a lot of guts to show up here, after being gone from the family fold for a number of years, and share his plans. He didn't have to. He did it out of courtesy and respect for all of you and you've shown him none in return. None."

Maybe no one would notice if he dropped to the floor and crawled away.

"So if you're truly asking me to pick a side?" His eyes met Ben's and then Quinn's. "I vote yes for the elk farm. I'd even re-up my lease agreement and give him a bigger acreage to work with because I know Dalton will make sure everything is done right." Gavin set his hand on Dalton's shoulder. Then he grabbed his coat and walked out.

To say the McKay family was stunned into silence was an understatement.

Before the arguing started again, Dalton snagged his coat and left.

Wasn't until he was halfway home that he realized he'd left his poker winnings on the table.

Chapter Twenty

It was especially hard to go to work on Monday morning after her fun weekend in Deadwood.

When the stack of elk farm applications arrived from the Cheyenne office, Rory was tempted to crawl under her desk and hide. She hadn't reached the land inspection part of her job yet—she was still mired in the permit process. But the cutoff date loomed. Hopefully she'd get out in the field soon.

No morning staff meeting meant Rory could dig right in and get to work. She'd cleared five applications—checking with the register of deeds that the applicant was the actual property owner, adding to her map which sections of land in which areas had applied and grouping the applicants by county.

Since it was almost lunchtime, she put everything aside and retrieved her sandwich and salad from the break room fridge. Most days she didn't mind eating with her coworkers, but Hannah's presence had Rory returning to her office. No need to end up with Hannah-induced indigestion.

Rory checked her phone. No missed calls or texts from Dalton. Very strange. He hadn't contacted her last night after his McKay poker game. She'd fully expected to hear how he'd cleaned them out.

She and her mom were supposed to have an early supper since Gavin had also been at the poker game, but she'd called around five begging off. Left to her own devices, Rory snuggled up with her dog and watched a marathon of *What Not To Wear*.

After lunch she dug back in to work. No issues with the next two applications on the stack. But the third application? Rory had a big, big problem with it. Because the applicant's name was Dalton McKay.

A thousand questions jumped into her head.

But the biggest question was why hadn't Rory known Dalton intended to apply for an elk farm permit? Surely that would've come up in all the times they'd spent together. Then again, whenever she asked about his day, or what he'd been doing, he gave the same response: working on a few projects here and there. Which she'd always taken to assume meant remodeling projects.

That's what she got for assuming.

First she checked the land deed. Dalton had owned that piece for four years. Then she looked at the proposed plat of land for the feeding grounds. It was wedged between the McKay Ranch on the left side, more McKay land on the right side and at the bottom, a small section owned by Gavin Daniels. Aka, the land her mother used to own; aka, the elk farm would be close not only to the house Gavin and Rielle owned, but to the cabin on the property where she lived.

She checked the application date. Dalton had applied the week after he'd returned to Wyoming.

The week she'd started the special project.

Well. Wasn't *that* a coincidence?

Not.

Rory hadn't talked specifics of her job with him, keeping the details of her special project under wraps. She'd mentioned she had paperwork to sort through before she got into the fieldwork portion of the assignment.

So how had Dalton found out vetting elk farm applications was her project?

Easy. The man sauntered into the office frequently. That dimpled smile worked wonders—even horrible Hannah hadn't been immune to his sexy cowboy charm. Since he usually cooled his boots in the reception area, he could've overheard the project info from any number of sources. Or someone—a female someone—could've told him just to get an up close look at his amazing blue eyes.

Which begged the question: why had Dalton applied?

To screw with his family after they'd screwed with him?

Nah. He wasn't that kind of guy.

Or maybe it was the opposite. Maybe this application was a sleight of hand orchestrated by his family? The McKays were one of the most vocal opponents to the program. Had they figured since Rory was in charge of the project, if Dalton applied, she'd choose him? Then the McKays would let the project molder and die.

Rory pawed through the rest of the applications but didn't see any with the last name McKay. Wasn't a surprise that the ranchers with land bordering the McKays hadn't applied for the temporary permit. No one wanted to tangle with the McKays. They'd chew you up and spit you out like an old wad of tobacco. Then they'd grind you into nothing beneath their boot heel as they walked away.

No more. She'd had her fill of being walked on.

Since she had autonomy with this project, she backed up her files, made a copy of Dalton's application and shoved it in her purse.

Then she locked everything else in her filing cabinet and left the office.

By the time she arrived at Dalton's house, she'd worked herself into a lather.

Dalton answered the door but his smile dried up immediately. "What's wrong?"

"Like you don't know."

"I don't. That's why I asked."

"Let me in and I'll tell you." Rory practically shoved him aside.

She started for the kitchen, only to wheel back around so fast Dalton ran right into her.

"Whoa. You wanna tell me what put that murderous look on your face? And why I get the feeling I shoulda slipped on a cup before I answered the door today?"

"This." She slapped the paper in the center of his chest.

He snatched it and stepped back. Straightened it out and scanned the text.

His expression didn't change.

Stupid professional poker player face.

Dalton said, "Where'd you get this?" without looking up.

But before she could answer he crowded her, his eyes flashing fire. "Did my brothers bring this to you first thing this morning? Or my cousins? Which ones? And why the fuck did they drag you into it? To embarrass me? I knew they were seriously pissed off yesterday, but I didn't think they'd put some McKay muscle behind it. What am I saying? That's exactly what they do. They don't like something, they pull some strings and try to get it changed."

This was not going at all like she expected.

"How did you get ahold of this application, Rory?"

"It was delivered to my office today."

"By who?"

"By the State of Wyoming. It was in a box with all the other applications I'm processing."

"Other applications you're processing?" He frowned. "What are you saying?"

"You know damn well what I'm saying. The special project I was assigned at the WNRC? This is it. I'm in charge of vetting applicants for this test program. I'm the one who sends the recommendations to the state board on who gets awarded permits."

No change in his expression.

"So when you were hanging around the WNRC offices waiting for me, who told you it was my project? Someone had to spill the beans because the information sure as hell didn't come from me. And I find it really...coincidental that the date on the application is the week I officially started working on it. You'd been in Sundance a week before you filed. One week."

"What does that have to do with anything? The permit process was listed in the paper that week. That's how I found out about it."

"Really?"

"Really. Why is that an issue?"

"Because you know exactly how to manipulate me, Dalton McKay, you always have. Alls you had to do was charm me, bed me and convince me you've changed. Then act all crazy about me while you followed your own goddamned agenda. Just like usual. Nothing ever changes with you." She briefly closed her eyes. "I'm such an idiot. You're using me again."

Then he said two words that chilled her to the bone. "Get. Out."

"What?"

"You heard me. I don't need this shit from you on top of everything else that's come down on me in the last day."

Rory's jaw dropped. "The hell I will. I deserve an explanation."

"Why? You've got it all figured out. You'll argue with anything I tell you. And you're so worried that I'm gonna fuck you over again that you can't even see the truth when it's right in front of you." He threw the paper at her. "Now get out."

Stung, she snapped, "Oh, I'll go. But guaranteed I won't even consider your piece of land for the program given your manipulative behavior."

Dalton got right in her face. "You will give me a fair shake in all of this or the next place I go is to the state board to file a grievance with them. About you. You don't get to be judge, jury and executioner on this, Rory. I will fight you and the WNRC to make sure my application is given as much consideration as the other applicants'."

"You'd do that?"

"You're leaving me no choice! You storm into my house, accuse me of all kinds of underhanded shit—none of which is true. You know how I feel about you. Goddammit, you know that I'm not fucking playing you, Aurora."

She watched his jaw flexing as he ground his teeth together.

"But I'll never be able to convince you, will I? You'll never trust me or trust in this. That it's real. And that goddamn sucks."

His voice had dropped to that quietly resigned tone that scared her far worse than if he'd yelled at her.

Dalton stepped back and opened the door but he wouldn't look at her. "You need to leave before one of us says something we'll regret and ruins everything that we've—or maybe I should say that *I've*—been trying to build with you."

Did Dalton really believe that she didn't give a damn about him?

This was about fun times and sex games—didn't you remind yourself of that fact every time things became serious? Self-preservation, remember? This isn't only about your relationship; this is about your livelihood. And now he's fucking with you on both levels. Why are you surprised?

Because there was more to it than that. And she wanted—she deserved—some answers.

Maybe you should've thought of that before you barged in here spewing accusations.

Before she cleared the doorjamb completely, Dalton said in a hoarse voice, "I'll be out of town for the next two days. We can talk about this when I get back."

Rory spun around. "What? Why are you just telling me this now?"

Those hurt blue eyes hooked hers. "I'd planned to tell you tonight over dinner. But now... Anyway, I didn't want you to think I was running away again."

Then Dalton shut the door in her face.

He'd given her no choice but to back off and process everything that'd just happened. Dammit. She wanted to beat on the door and resolve this now. She hated fighting with a lover. *Hated it.*

As Rory drove home, the reality of the situation hit her. What did it mean that she was more upset about what this meant for their relationship than how this might affect her job performance?

Dalton figured his brothers would need a day or two to cool off so he was surprised to see them on his doorstep Monday evening.

"Can we come in?" Tell asked.

"Depends on if this is an ass-chewing session or a rational discussion. I've had enough shit flung at me today that I'm feelin' like a monkey."

They both looked at him blankly.

Guess his sense of humor sucked too. "Yeah, come in."

"Nice place," Tell said after they'd trooped into the kitchen.

"It's getting there." He gestured to the table. They sat and he rested his back against the countertop. "I'd offer you guys a beer but I'm out. You want coffee or something?"

"Nah. Just wanted to come over and clear the air after the bullshit that happened yesterday. You took off pretty damn fast," Brandt said.

"Not that we blame you," Tell added. "It's just...the whole elk farm thing caught us off guard."

"And you wonder why I didn't tell you about my plan before I blabbed to the whole family?"

Brandt and Tell looked at each other and nodded.

"The reaction from the family yesterday was what I expected." He frowned. "With the exception of Gavin's comments. But I needed to make sure you guys were surprised by it too, so our cousins couldn't accuse either of you of not tellin' them about something that affects the ranch. Or could possibly affect it. Nothin' is guaranteed except the State of Wyoming cashed my five hundred dollar check for the permit application."

"Gavin was the only one makin' sense. And I hated how fast Cord, Colby and Colt turned on anyone who didn't agree with them." Brandt scrubbed his hands over his face. "Been goin' on a while and we've sorta let it slide, but seein' that Kade and Kane feel the same way, I reckon it's time to take Uncle Carson's kids to task."

"About this?"

"Not only this," Tell said. "But they oughta know that we're supporting you no matter what happens."

Dalton tried not to let his shock show.

But it must have, because Tell said, "Why in the hell does that surprise you?"

"Maybe because you haven't always thrown in behind me."

Brandt snorted. "If you're talkin' about the years you spent getting in bar fights, I'll remind you that me'n Tell backed you plenty of times."

"Any time we had a problem with you or what you were doin' or what you weren't doin', little bro, we told you. And if you really think about it, us getting in your face about shit didn't happen all that often."

He couldn't argue with that.

"Besides, the last couple years you were here workin' on the ranch, after Dad got sober and Mom left, we had no idea what you were doin' with yourself in your off-the-ranch hours. You slammed that door in our faces whenever we asked. So we stopped askin'."

Dalton couldn't argue with that either.

"We might've gotten concerned you had a gambling problem if we'd known how often you were playing poker during that time. But when you told us that you paid cash for the Fox family's land...well, we couldn't exactly chew your ass for bein' a successful card player, now could we?" Tell complained.

"So we think it's bullshit, whatever stick you've got up your ass about this. About us." Brandt's jaw tightened. "One thing we've always been able to count on is the three of us stick together. No matter what. That ain't changed just because you have."

At least they recognized he had changed. But he hadn't found the balls to give them the real reason for his fear that *they'd* change toward *him*. So he deflected. "You're both on board with my plans?"

"It's your land, Dalton. You can do whatever the hell you want with it. You get that permit, well, then we'll talk."

"All of this might be a moot point anyway. I found out the hard way that not only is the Crook County branch office of the WNRC in charge of processing applications, they also determine who's granted the permits."

Tell's eyes widened. "Oh shit."

"Yeah. I knew Rory had been assigned a special project at the WNRC, but she wasn't allowed to talk specifics. And I kept my application on the down low for obvious reasons. So guess whose application came across Rory's desk today?"

"Yours."

"Yeah." Dalton ran his hand through his hair. "She showed up here a few hours ago and lost her mind on me. Rory and I have a tangled history, some of it not pretty. Needless to say, she thinks history is repeating itself and that I was just usin' her to get a fuckin' permit. Jesus. That burns my ass because she knows better. I'm not fuckin' around with her this time."

Brandt looked skeptical. "You two are involved, seriously involved from what I've seen, and neither of you had any idea what the other one is doin' outside of the hours that you spend together?"

When Brandt put it that way...it sounded unbelievable.

"Maybe it's because you two ain't doin' a whole lotta talkin'?" Tell wiggled his eyebrows. "I remember them days."

"That could be part of it. She's pissed and I'm pissed and we're cooling things off for a few days."

Tell pointed at the duffel bag against the wall. "Is that why you're goin' somewhere?"

"No. I talked to my buddy Boden last night. I left some stuff undone since I wasn't sure how long I'd be gone when I left. So I'm leavin' for Montana in the morning." Or maybe he'd just take off tonight.

"When're you comin' back?"

"Thursday."

"Don't suppose you're gonna stop by the rehab hospital on your way outta town?" Brandt asked.

Dalton shook his head.

"Been a while since you've been there."

"Has he made any improvements?"

"No. But that don't mean—"

He held up his hand. "I don't want to talk about Casper." Ever. "If you need me to check cattle or fix fence or babysit your kids while you're visiting him, I'm more than willing to help out. But it is not helpin' out sitting in Casper's room and letting him glare at me. I'm done with that."

Neither of his brothers responded. They weren't happy, but at least now maybe they'd stop bugging him about it.

Brandt stood. "Well, drive safe. Let us know you made it up there okay."

"Will do."

Tell clapped him on the back. "Fair warning. I'm totally takin' you up on the free babysitting offer." He dug in his jacket pocket. "Before I forget..." He handed Dalton a wad of bills. "You forgot the jackpot, so me'n Brandt picked up for you."

"Thanks." Dalton pretended to count it.

"You don't think it's all there?" Tell demanded. "You are one suspicious motherfucker."

"Nope. Just checking to see if you added the hundred you owed me for the side bet." He smiled. "Is it included in here?"

"No."

Dalton held out his hand. "Pay up, bro. Fair's fair."

Brandt laughed and said, "Told ya he'd remember."

Chapter Twenty-One

Rory yelled, "Come in," after two knocks sounded on her office door Thursday morning.

"Hey, Rory."

Her jaw might've actually hit the desk when she saw Dillon Doland, her ex-fiancé, in the doorway. "Dillon? What are you doing here?"

"I'm in the area for business. Thought I'd stop by and say hello."

Remembering her manners, she gestured to the chair in front of the desk. "Please. Sit down."

"Thanks." He pinched the crease of his khaki pants after he sat.

At their first meeting, Dillon's fussiness with his clothes made her wonder if he was gay. After their less than spectacular sex life when they dated, she still wondered that.

Not nice, Rory.

Dillon bestowed his movie-star bright smile. "You look great."

"Same goes for you."

"You still part-time here?"

"Technically? Yes. But I'm on special assignment so I'm fulltime until that ends."

"What's the special assignment?"

She winked. "Super duper secret." She'd been so mad at Dalton she'd just blurted out that information and she shouldn't have. Wouldn't it be her bad luck if he blabbed to everyone...just like he used to? What would happen if the director found out?

Then the worst kept secret in the office would be out. Big deal. The permit application cut off date is tomorrow anyway.

"While I applaud your loyalty... You know you can trust me. Keeping secrets is an official part of my job." Dillon raised an eyebrow. "Or I can guess if you'd like. I've got a good idea what you've been tasked to do, given your field of study."

"Was I assigned this job because of your recommendation?" she asked sharply.

"No. So why don't you tell me what it is?"

She sighed. "I'm processing applications and then screening applicants' land for the elk farm test program."

"Really? Congrats on landing a big project because it's an important program to the state. How's it going so far?"

"Busy. I didn't think we'd get so many applicants."

"With the drought, ranchers have been forced to cut down their herds. Everyone is looking for replacement income. I imagine you're getting applications from ranchers whose land fits the criteria, but have no intention of turning it into an elk farm."

"The director mentioned that to me. I'm hoping he's wrong and all these applications are legit." After she'd calmed down following the confrontation with Dalton, she wished she'd had the presence of mind to ask if his application was legit. Yes, she'd shown up at his place loaded for bear, but she stood by everything she'd said—on a professional level. On a personal level? Well, she'd have to wait and see.

She tuned back in to Dillon's commentary. He hadn't noticed her momentary blip in concentration. "...it's been interesting seeing it from a different angle. Any chance this temporary position could roll over into fulltime?"

"Doubtful. This WNRC office is fully staffed. I'll return to my previous part-time position once I'm finished."

Dillon looked thoughtful. "Did you take this job because it's in your hometown?"

Tempting to lie, but she admitted, "No. It was the only job available." On such short notice.

"Except for the job you already had at the Wyoming State Parks."

"That wasn't a permanent position."

"I had the pull to make it permanent," Dillon reminded her.

Didn't he understand that's why she'd left? She'd be stuck there with him? At least working here part-time she had options. "It was best if we didn't work together after..."

Silence ensued.

Dillon sighed. "You broke it off with me without really much of a reason why."

Rory's eyes narrowed. "Is that why you're here? To get answers?"

"Maybe. Things were going great between us and the next thing I knew, you returned the engagement ring and left town."

Going great. Right. "Look, this isn't the time or the place—"

"Then have dinner with me tonight so we can discuss it."

Crap. She'd fallen right into that one.

Redneck Romeo

"You owe me that much, Rory. I also wanted to mention new career opportunities for you, but it wouldn't be prudent to discuss them in your current place of business."

He knew that would intrigue her.

"Is there a quiet place we can have dinner and a conversation?"

"The Twin Pines is a supper club outside of Sundance."

"Sounds good to me. Will six o'clock work?"

"Yes, that'll give me time to change."

"You'd look beautiful wearing a flour sack."

Dillon's compliment, while sincere, didn't affect her the same way Dalton's compliments did. "Thank you."

He smiled and stood. "Looking forward to seeing you at six. I'll let you get back to work." He left her office.

Rory didn't waste time dwelling on how their discussion would play out tonight. She had plenty to accomplish before then.

Three raps on her door and Glennis poked her head in. "Rory? Can I come in?"

"Sure. What do you need?"

"Just checking on whether..." She sighed. "Okay, I'm a snoopy busybody and I'm dying to know if that man really was your ex-fiancé."

That startled her. "That's how Dillon introduced himself?"

"He said he was Dillon Doland, assistant director for the Wyoming State Parks and he used to work with you. Then he chuckled and mentioned he'd been engaged to you."

"I find it weird he'd say that."

Glennis's gaze sharpened behind her glasses. "Know what I find weird? That Dillon has more than a passing similarity to Dalton. Tall, dark-haired, blue eyes. Charming."

"Which describes half the men in the world," she retorted.

Glennis shook her finger. "Maybe you didn't realize at the time you'd started something with Dillon because he reminded you of Dalton."

"Bullshit."

"I know you and Dalton have a history, Rory."

"How?" she demanded.

"Because of your familiarity the first day he sauntered in here. And sweetie, I am a Sundance native. I've got a grasp of geography and I know you grew up practically next door to his family's ranch." She crossed her arms over her chest. "Does Dalton have any idea that you almost married a man who looks like him?"

"No."

"What do you think he'll do when he finds out?"

Rory stared at the door after Glennis left. She was wrong. Her attraction to Dillon had nothing to do with his looks and that he had some of the same physical characteristics as Dalton.

Did it?

And besides, didn't all women have a type that appealed to them? Tall, dark-haired, blue-eyed men did it for her.

Putting it out of her mind, she got back to work.

Dillon was waiting by the hostess stand at the Twin Pines when Rory arrived.

He pulled her in for a hug and brushed a kiss on her cheek. "Rory. You look beautiful."

She'd put extra effort into her appearance, wearing a form-fitting dress in dark pink, topping it with an iridescent shawl she'd crocheted herself and finishing her bohemian look with bone-colored riding boots.

"You look stylish, as usual." He'd worn a navy suit jacket, blue and white striped shirt, jeans and loafers. One thing about Dillon; he was always impeccably put together. Even after spending all day out inspecting parks land on horseback, he'd return to the office in the same condition he'd left.

"Hey, Rory." Naomi the manager looked between her and Dillon with a frown. As if she'd expected to see her with Dalton.

Rory bristled. She could have a business dinner with whoever she wanted. And the only reason she was here was because Dillon might have a lead on a job or two for her.

Naomi led them to a table in the middle of the restaurant. "I know you prefer a booth, but this is all I've got at last minute. As you can see we're swamped tonight."

Dillon pulled out her chair. "Thanks." To Naomi she said, "What's going on?"

"The Wyoming Wildfire band is playing on the club side. That gets people out on a Thursday night. Enjoy."

"I take it that's a popular band around here?" Dillon asked.

"Hugely popular. They only do one-night gigs, so they always play to packed houses."

"Makes good business sense. The band I played in in college should've done that."

"You were in a band?"

210

"Cover tunes only. I played bass."

"You never mentioned that."

"There's a lot you don't know about me. If you don't mind, I'd like to head over after dinner and listen."

Rory agreed only because Dillon didn't dance. She checked to see who was bartending before deciding on a cosmopolitan.

After they ordered and the drinks were delivered, Rory got right to the point. "I call bullshit on you just being in the neighborhood, Dil."

"I am on WSP business. Headed to Buffalo and Sheridan to discuss a more detailed operating plan for the summer season. Part of the plan is to integrate the new with the old since two positions will be opening up. Fulltime positions. Habitat management in Sheridan and assistant park services manager in Buffalo."

"Are they new positions? Or vacancies?"

"New position in Sheridan. In Buffalo the park services manager is retiring, his assistant is moving up to fill the position so we're hiring outside the office for a replacement." Dillon sipped his drink. "Do either of those sound like something you'd be interested in?"

"Both, actually. When will the openings be listed?"

"Now. Final selection in roughly six weeks."

That would work out perfectly. She'd be done with the special project. "What else?"

"What do you mean?"

Rory poked his forearm. "There's something you're not telling me. So spill it."

"You're right, but it's not about either of those jobs. Strictly between us, there will be an opening in the Cody BLM office. Fulltime in Ag management."

BLM usually hired and promoted from within the organization before they opened up outside applications. "Why?"

"The guy is retiring. The only catch...this position is pretty much universally hated by everyone in the community."

"Is that why the guy is getting out?"

"No, but it is why no one in that branch office has applied for the job and why the BLM is listing the position on the job boards next week."

Rory drummed her fingers on the table. "Think the locals' attitudes would be worse if a woman took over the BLM job?"

"Any woman besides you? Yes. But I've seen you in action, Rory. You can be coy and forceful. Most people don't realize they've given you exactly what you want until they walk away."

"That's not always a good thing."

"It'll make those good old boys believe they can 'manage' you right from the start. We both know better. Bob Buckman who heads that office can really use your skills."

"Starting salary?"

"Fifteen grand higher than the standard because of the extra bullshit with the position. Possible yearly bonus."

"I'm very interested in that one."

He smiled. "Thought you might be. I already sent the paperwork to your home address with all the pertinent information for the Wyoming Parks jobs. Along with three letters of recommendation from me."

"That's...above and beyond, Dil. Thanks." Rory should've left it at that, but she didn't. "But I have to know what's in it for you to share all the info about available positions?"

"As assistant Wyoming State Parks director, I want the best people for the jobs. You are a perfect candidate, Rory."

"And you came to Moorcroft to tell me you mailed me some paperwork?"

Dillon studied her for a moment before answering. "I'm here because of you and our unfinished business so don't pretend that's a big surprise."

"Not pretending when I say your visit today caught me off guard."

"Didn't think you'd ever see me again? As soon as Cheyenne reflected in your rearview mirror you left all the memories behind?"

Pretty much, but it'd hurt Dillon if she admitted she rarely thought of him. "I have memories. We'll both always have them, but it's in the past."

"That's what I don't get. It's not that far in the past. What did I do to make you turn away from me?" He paused. "Or maybe it's what I didn't do?"

Rory knocked back a healthy swig of her drink. "I know it sounds like a line, but I'm being honest when I say it wasn't you—not at all. It was one hundred percent me."

Dillon shook his head. "I loved you. I wanted to spend my life with you. Doesn't—*didn't*—that mean something to you?"

"Why did you want to marry me in the first place?" she demanded. "What did we have in common besides that we worked together?"

"We're both invested in our careers. We liked to watch movies. We liked to cook together. We both came from single-parent homes." He frowned. "Doesn't that seem like a lot to you?"

"It didn't seem like enough."

212

That surprised him.

In for a penny. "You were nice to me when I didn't know anyone in the office. You took me under your wing and our relationship sprouted from there. We were comfortable together."

"And again, there's something wrong with that?" he asked tartly.

"Yes. I realized I wanted more out of a marriage than just companionship." She leaned closer. "If you'll remember, we didn't have sex all that often. There was no intimacy between us. No passion." Rory held up her hand when he started to interrupt. "Please don't tell me that passion fades and a steady partnership is what really matters."

Dillon flushed.

"I like you as a friend. And I mistook that friendship for something deeper. That's why I said yes to your proposal. But it's also the reason I broke it off."

The food arrived and they both dug in.

When Dillon said, "There wasn't someone else?" out of the blue, Rory choked on her asparagus.

Once she'd quit coughing, she assured him, "No, there wasn't anyone else. I think the break up would've been easier for you to understand if there *had* been another man."

He sighed. "Easier to stomach than the *you lack passion and I foresaw a life of boredom with you* answer I just got."

"Dillon. I didn't say *you* lacked passion. I said there wasn't passion between us—*us*—which means the blame falls squarely on my shoulders too."

"Would it've made a difference if we would've talked about this?"

Rory shook her head.

"So it's not fixable?"

"Why would you want to fix it?"

"You find it hard to believe that I'd want to try again?" Dillon took her hand. "You're a beautiful woman. Smart and funny. You're a great person, and I just let you walk out of my life without a fight."

There wasn't anything to fight for. What didn't he understand about that?

"I can change, Rory."

She froze. What was with men always spouting off that *I can change* bullshit line? And why did most women believe it?

Don't you? Don't you want to when it comes to Dalton?

"I'm sorry. I can tell this is upsetting you." Dillon pointed to her steak. "Enjoy your dinner. We can talk about this after we're done eating."

As soon as she finished her meal, she felt like she'd swallowed a bowl of Mexican jumping beans. She needed to pace, move, do something besides sit here politely and eat food she couldn't enjoy. She said, "Excuse me," and fled from the table.

She cut through the restaurant to the bathrooms and leaned against the hallway leading to the kitchen, taking a second to just breathe.

Why in the world would Dillon want to try again? She'd just laid out all the reasons why they hadn't worked.

Wait. Was she some sort of...self-challenge? To see if he could win her back? Men were stupidly egotistical about things like that.

As she walked past the men's room, a short guy barreled right into her.

"Shit, I wasn't watching where I was goin'." He looked up. A wide grin spread across his face. "Rory! Hey, are you working tonight?"

"No, Busby, I quit, remember?"

"No wonder I ain't seen ya. So you here with Dalton?"

Busby and Dalton were old friends and they'd run into him when they'd gone out. "No. I'm with someone else."

That comment piqued Busby's interest, rather than ending it. "Male or female? 'Cause if it's a female friend, you could introduce me to her and then the four of us could go out on a double date."

Damn nosy man. "Not a woman. An old friend of mine from Cheyenne."

"Huh. You guys goin' next door?"

"Probably."

"Save me a dance. It don't bother me none that you're taller than me."

The pervert just wanted to bury his face in her chest.

"See ya." He bustled away.

But after she returned to the dining room, she noticed Busby hadn't gone far. He eyed her from the bar as she sat next to Dillon.

"You all right?" he asked.

"Fine. I ran into someone I knew."

"The band must be ready to start because everyone's cleared out."

"I'm ready to go whenever you are." She hoped he took that as she wanted to go home.

Dillon signaled the waitress for the check. "It'll be fun to dance together since we didn't get the chance during our brief engagement."

She met his gaze. "You dance?"

"Yes. See? You don't know everything about me."

I know enough. I know when you reached out to grab my hand I felt nothing. I know when I look in your eyes I don't see burning desire that consumes you. I don't feel a sense of urgency...

"Thanks for dinner," she said as they waited in line.

"My pleasure. I think we broke new ground tonight by talking this out."

What the hell? How had their discussion encouraged him? "Since I work tomorrow I'll have to leave after the first set."

Dillon paid the cover charge and they squeezed together at a tiny table in the back. "You want another drink?"

"I'm good. But go ahead if you want one."

"Okay. Be right back."

Not likely. They'd only staffed the bar with two bartenders. And this crowd liked to drink. She'd made three hundred bucks last time she'd worked this gig.

By the time Dillon returned, the band had started, making it hard to hold a conversation. That didn't deter Dillon. He kept trying to talk to her and she kept saying, "What?"

He did give up beyond commenting on a song or to point out a dancing couple. After he drained his drink, he took her hand. "Let's dance."

Luckily the first two songs were fast. Then the band announced the next song would end the first set.

Dillon pulled her closer and she winced when he tromped on her foot. "Sorry."

Rory caught herself trying to dance faster, like she could get this over with sooner.

"I've been thinking about you a lot lately," Dillon said.

"Because of the job openings?"

"No. I miss you."

"Why? We weren't together that long and I'm not that cool."

Dillon laughed. "I forgot that you're so funny. Would it be so bad, giving me another shot?"

"Stop talking, Dillon. This isn't going to happen."

"Let me convince you another way." He clamped his hands over her ears and mashed their faces together, laying a kiss on her.

No. Dammit, no! She didn't want this. She tried to twist her mouth free from his, but he held fast, his tongue pushing between her lips.

Then he was ripped away from her and Dalton was in Dillon's

face. "What the fuck do you think you're doin' with her?"

Dillon blinked with confusion then demanded, "What does it matter to you?"

Rory tried to step between them, but Dalton was immoveable.

"Answer the question."

"What is your problem, buddy?"

"My problem is you, fuckface."

"Back off."

"Or what?"

"Or I'll make you back off," Dillon snapped.

Dalton loomed even more. "Gonna hafta grow a bit before that happens."

People were starting to take notice. Rory said, "Stop it. Both of you."

"Rory, who is this redneck asshole?" Dillon demanded.

"He's my..." Boyfriend seemed too tepid a term. Lover was too intimate.

"Why you havin' trouble explaining who I am to you?" Dalton said without looking away from his opponent.

"Dalton, this is Dillon. My ex-fiancé."

Then Dalton did turn and look at her. "Are you fuckin' serious? What the hell is Dildo doin' here? Dancing with you? Goddamn *kissing* you."

"I wasn't kissing him back," she said quickly.

"Jesus, I know that. It's why I'm so pissed off."

"Dalton—"

"I take it you're the new boyfriend," Dillon said.

"I am one helluva lot more to her than some simple goddamned boyfriend."

"If that's true, then isn't it funny she never *once* mentioned your name during our dinner?"

Dalton made a low, snarling noise.

"A dinner in which she and I talked about getting back together?" Dillon taunted. "You must not mean as much to her as you think you do, redneck."

Dalton didn't punch Dillon; he jumped him, knocking him to the floor.

Then he punched him.

Dillon rolled away and slammed his fist into the side of Dalton's head. He tried to hit Dalton in the throat, but Dalton blocked it and delivered an uppercut. Dillon looked dazed for an instant before he leveled a punch to Dalton's gut.

Unfazed, Dalton lunged for Dillon again and they both crashed to the floor. Dillon dodging Dalton's fists, bucking his hips to throw Dalton backward. Then Dillon was on top, whaling on Dalton.

Rory watched the fight, a dull roar whooshing in her head. All she could hear was the sound of her own breathing and the rapid thump of her heart.

She couldn't move.

Both men on the ground were bleeding.

A crowd gathered, but no one stepped in to stop them.

Then they were on their feet again. Swinging at each other. Dalton picked Dillon up by his shirtfront and threw him. Dillon crashed into a table and hit the floor.

Now that the men were separated, the bouncers stepped in.

Shit, not just the bouncers. Dalton's cousin Cam McKay had one hand fisted in Dalton's shirt. Cam wasn't in his deputy's uniform but he might as well have been, the way the crowd scattered.

Rory glanced over at Dillon and saw the bouncers had helped him to his feet. A cocktail waitress handed him a wad of napkins to mop up the blood on his face.

Dillon was listening to the bouncers, not paying attention to her.

When she returned her focus to Dalton, he continued to glare at Dillon while Cam dressed him down. A spike of fear went through her when Cam beckoned her over.

"Yes, deputy?"

Cam scowled. "I'm not on duty. I'm here on a rare night out with my wife, so dealing with this hothead wasn't part of my plan. Goddammit, Dalton, when are you gonna learn fighting ain't the answer?"

"Already learned it. I don't do this anymore."

"Then what was this tonight?"

"A warning. That fucker doesn't get to put his hands on her, or his mouth on her. Ever."

Dalton still didn't look at her.

"If I let go of you, you'll go after him again?" Cam asked.

"Most likely."

"Fuck that. I'm taking you outside to cool you off."

Dalton shook his head. "I'm not leavin' Rory in here with him."

"Dalton. I can take care of myself. It was all a misunderstanding—
"

Then he was in her face. "Don't defend him. I don't give a shit

217

what he was to you once; he's not that to you anymore. He has no rights to you. All those rights belong to me now."

"Omigod. Like I'm a piece of fucking property?"

Cam grabbed Dalton's arm. "Not kiddin'. Outside. Now." To Rory he said, "We'll be waiting for you."

Dalton snarled something but Cam got him moving.

Rory didn't move toward Dillon until she knew Dalton was out the door. The bouncers left them alone.

Dillon was still mopping blood from beneath his nose. His right eye had swelled. Knuckle-shaped marks dotted the left side of his jaw. He'd bruise, most likely. His shirt was untucked and ripped. Yeah, he didn't look so put together anymore.

He spoke first. "You could've mentioned you were seeing a fucking psycho."

"He was supposed to be out of town."

"Like that's an excuse. Next you'll tell me the two of you had a big fight."

Her life was one big cliché. "Yeah, we did. He's the jealous type."

"How long have you been with him?"

"I've known him since I was six. He almost married my best friend and we lost track of each other after that."

"Now you're both living back here," he stated flatly.

"So it appears."

"Don't give me that coyness. I'm bleeding, beat up and really pissed off at myself for coming here. So at least tell me if you've always been in love with him."

Rory stared at him like he'd just said the most idiotic thing on the planet.

Dillon pressed his point. "I get it. Star-crossed lovers or something. Been in love with him since you were six. He broke your heart, or you broke his. You couldn't have him so you settled for me, a guy who kind of looks like him."

After seeing them together the only similarity between them was they were both men.

"Psycho-cowboy and I have more than a passing resemblance to each other, Rory. And don't think he didn't notice it too as he was punching me in the face."

"I don't know what you want me to say, Dil."

"How about goodbye? Because I finally understand that we're done. I also finally understand why you're willing to stay in a shitty-paying, low-level state job."

"Dalton has nothing to do with that. I didn't even know where he lived when I took the job with the WNRC."

Dillon squinted at her. "One thing I did learn by coming here? You're right. We didn't know each other. Because the Rory I thought I knew? She would've already filled out the applications for the positions with the Wyoming State Parks and she'd be the first in line to apply for the BLM position. The Rory I knew was ambitious, planning for a career and not just settling for a job. Your skills are being wasted at the WNRC. We both know it. So I hope he's worth it."

Rory lifted her chin. "I guess we'll see if he thinks *I'm* worth it, because I am applying for those jobs, Dillon. All of them."

A calculating smile stretched across his face. "Good. Now get away from me before he comes looking for you and finds you talking to me."

She grabbed her purse and coat and exited through the employee entrance.

Coming around the corner, she saw Dalton pacing and Cam resting against the side of the pickup. Air puffed out of Dalton's mouth with every step. He reminded her of one of those cartoon bulls—not that she'd voice the comparison.

The soles of her shoes scuffed on the gravel and they both turned around.

Then Dalton was on her, his big hands gripping her biceps. "What the fuck is goin' on, Rory? I'm out of town two fucking days and I get a phone call from Busby, who says you're out with another guy? A guy who I find out just happens to be your former fiancé?"

"He asked me to dinner. I accepted. We have a history, Dalton, whether or not you like it."

"I don't like it. Not at fucking all. Why didn't you tell him about us?"

How was she supposed to answer that?

Dalton's hands fell away.

The hurt on his face sliced through her like an ax.

"I can't...do this right now." Without another word he climbed in his truck and burned rubber getting away from her.

Cam stood beside her. "It's best to let him cool off."

"Says you. I'm giving him a five-minute head start, then I'm going after him. I caused this, I will cowgirl up and deal with it and with him."

Cam said nothing.

"Thank you for stepping in. It would've been easier to ignore it."

"He's my cousin, Rory. I'd never ignore him and turn my back on him when he's hurtin'. I know what that's like."

"Then you understand that I won't leave him alone when he's hurting and caught in my mess."

Cam sighed. "I've broken up more of his fights than I care to admit to. I've seen him drunk, belligerent, broken and pissed off. I've never seen him on edge like this. So I gotta ask if you're sure you can handle him?"

"Dalton won't hurt me." He'd been hurt in anger too many times in his life to do it to someone else. "Go in and enjoy the rest of the night with your wife."

Rory got in her car and drove to his house to face the music.

Chapter Twenty-Two

If Dalton needed to replace the Sheetrock in the living room, he might've put his fist through the wall. Instead, he paced. Beyond angry with himself. With Rory. With the whole fucking situation.

Since he'd left Wyoming, he avoided barroom brawling. Yet, after seeing that cocksucker kissing Rory, there he was, fists leading the way. He rubbed his jaw. Guaranteed he'd feel the aches and pains come morning.

He'd hear about the stupidity of his public display from his brothers too. They'd railed on him about his fighting ways the last two years he lived in Sundance. He hadn't been trying to prove anything; but there'd been a whole slew of guys angling for bragging rights for kicking the shit out of a McKay.

So yeah, he'd lost more fights than he'd won, simply because he'd been in more fights than his brothers and cousins.

And of course one of his cousins had to be around when he lost control—and of course that cousin had to be Cam. Then again, Dalton had expected more grief from the deputy. The usual, *pull your head out of your ass and quit being a little shit* lecture he'd gotten umpteen times.

But Cam had removed him from the situation and that was it.

Dalton hated he wouldn't have known about the situation if not for Busby's drunken phone call warning him that Rory was out with another guy.

Come to find out it wasn't just any guy. But her ex-fiancé.

He stalked to the fridge and grabbed the orange juice, drinking straight from the carton. Whenever he wanted whiskey, or felt he needed whiskey, he thought of how Casper acted under the influence. That immediately cut the craving for booze.

He stared out the dining room window, wishing he had a pile of logs to split and stack. Every muscle in his body straining as he swung the ax. Feeling the physical vibration racing up his arms as the blade connected with the wood. Hearing the satisfying *crack* as force altered a solid object into pieces. Nothing was more satisfying.

Well, nothing except for raw, down-and-dirty sex.

That's when three loud raps sounded on his door.

Go the fuck away.

"Dammit, Dalton. I know you're in there. I'm not leaving so you may as well open the door."

He didn't rush over; he prepped himself for the best way to send Rory on her merry way.

"I know you don't lock your door so you either let me in or I'll barge in."

He opened the door.

Rory stared at him for several long seconds before she said, "Let me in."

"What do you want?"

"To talk."

"Not in the mood." He rested his forearm above his head on the doorjamb, essentially blocking her. "Go home, Rory."

Her gaze moved to his throat. "Is that a bruise?"

"Probably."

She lifted her hand to touch his face and he flinched. "Not kidding. Go home. You don't wanna be around me now."

"Or is it that you don't wanna be around me?" she countered. "Because tough shit. I'm not leaving."

Dalton leaned forward until they were nose to nose. "Don't fucking push me."

"Don't fucking push me away."

"Oh, that's rich, coming from you."

"Let me in, Dalton."

"You tough enough to walk through this door?" he taunted. "Because if you do, I'm not letting you leave until we work this out. And we'll work it out my way."

Rory turned her face from his; he half-expected she'd take the out he'd offered. But she pressed her warm mouth to the bruised spot on his throat. Then she whispered, "Yes, I'm tough enough. But you already know that, don't you?"

God. He was so fucking insanely in love with this woman. Curling his left hand around her nape, he consumed her mouth. No sweet start that gradually morphed into passion. Dalton took her mouth like he wanted to take her. Hard and fast, with an almost brutal possession.

She wrapped herself around him, kissing him with hunger.

When the kiss grew even more intense, he jerked her inside and kicked the door shut. He stripped off her coat and herded her toward the bedroom.

What are you doing? Sex is not the solution. She'll fuck you and walk away and nothing will get resolved.

Dalton released her and stepped back. "No."

Rory looked confused. "No what?"

"No we're not doin' this. You wanted to talk. So talk."

"But..."

He brushed past her and skirted the breakfast bar. He stopped in the kitchen and grabbed the orange juice carton. "Talk."

"Dil showed up at my office today on state business."

"Bullshit. He either lied to you or you're lyin' to me, so which is it?"

She flipped her hair over her shoulder. "He said it was personal so no one in the office would know he wanted to talk business with me over dinner."

Dalton laughed snidely. "So when Dildo had his hands on you and his tongue down your throat—that was part of the plan to fool your boss? Give me a fucking break."

Rory slammed her hands on the countertop. "Will you let me explain? Or do you have it all worked out?"

"Just like you had it all worked out when you stormed in here and laid out your theories as facts that I used you and lied to you? Not only about the application for the elk farm permit but about my real reasons for starting a goddamned relationship with you?"

That shut her down for a second. But she rallied back with, "Fine, I was an idiot, all right? Is that what you wanna hear?"

"I wanna hear why the fuck you spent all this time talkin' to your ex-fiancé and he knew nothin' about me. Or us. Because I'm nothin' to you, is that it?"

"No. That's not true, Dalton and you know it."

"That's the thing Rory, I *don't* know it."

She stared at him with guilt, shock and embarrassment.

Dalton hated he was still on such shaky ground with her. Would she ever believe he'd changed? What else could he do to convince her?

Rory blurted, "After our business discussion ended, he started saying all this ridiculous stuff about our broken engagement, regretting that he let me walk away without a fight. He said he wanted to try and win me back."

Dalton couldn't stop the snarl that accompanied, "The hell that's ever happening."

"By that time, I wanted to leave but I told him we'd listen to the band. He asked me to dance and then he kissed me." Her gaze scrutinized his face. "You were there. You know I wasn't kissing him back."

"Alls I know is that I saw his hands on you and I wanted to rip them clean off his body."

"You nearly succeeded."

"Apparently not, because that motherfucker got in his licks." Dalton took a long drink of juice.

"I know something else is eating at you. So just say it."

"I also noticed that he and I..." He paused and watched her eyes. Even after all his attempts at showing her that he was around for the long haul, she still acted so wary. "We look alike." He started toward her and she immediately retreated. "He's tall. He's got dark hair. Probably has blue eyes. And he's totally fucking in love with you. Willing to fight for you. Remind you of someone else you might know?"

"This isn't—"

"Answer. Me."

"I don't know what you want me to say. Just stop. Please."

No way. He'd come this far. "So is it a coincidence that I look like the man you almost married? Be hard to tell us apart in a dark bar, wouldn't it?"

"No."

"What about in a dark room, Rory? When you were with me could you pretend I was—"

"Stop it. I haven't been with you because you reminded me of Dillon."

"Are you sure?"

"Yes, I'm sure, all right? I was with him because at first, on the surface, he reminded me of you. But there's no comparison, Dalton. None. You're ten times the man he is."

A few beats of stunned silence passed as he waited for her to elaborate or to confess she felt something more for him than she ever had for Dildo. But her mouth remained stubbornly closed.

So Dalton kissed her.

Passion, desire, need exploded—a melee of hungry mouths, frantic hands, avid bodies, harsh breathing and harsher kisses.

Dalton wanted to pin her down and fuck the memory of every other man out of her brain and out her body. Imprint himself on her, in her so she'd feel him as part of her even when he wasn't around. Mark her with his mouth, his teeth, his goddamn hands so she'd see those marks and remember only him.

Rory dug her nails into the back of his neck. Then her hands moved down his chest, over his ribcage, across his belly, stopping at the waistband of his jeans. She nuzzled him, scattering kisses, nips and tiny licks on the cords straining in his neck. "Let me show you. Any way you want. Tell me what you want."

"This." Dalton pushed on her shoulders and she dropped to her knees. Her hands unbuckling his belt, unzipping his fly and opening his jeans. Then she yanked his boxers and jeans down, freeing his cock.

Her mouth, her goddamned mouth, so hot and wet and perfect; she destroyed him every time she sucked his cock like she was starving for it.

Well she was gonna get it all and then some tonight.

Rory worked him fast. Driving him to the point where his balls tightened, where he was more animal than man, teetering in that moment when he was so fucking close to coming he could taste it.

He yanked harder on her hair. He squeezed his fingers against the side of her face, digging his thumb deeper into her neck, holding her in place as he fucked her mouth exactly as hard and deep as he wanted.

*Almost, almost...*he glanced down at her face and saw his hand fisting her hair so strongly it pulled her scalp. Saw the red mark on her cheek from his palm. Then he saw how she squeezed her eyes—in pain?—every time his dick hit the back of her throat.

You're hurting her. You're punishina her with sex.

Is that how you treat the woman you love—as a vessel to pour your anger and frustration into?

No. Goddammit no.

Horrified, Dalton abruptly pulled her off his cock and held her head in his hands. "Stop."

"What's wrong?"

"This."

"Dalton—"

"Not like this. Never like this." He shaped her beautiful face with his fingers. "I never want to touch you when I'm angry, Aurora. Never."

She looked confused. "I don't understand you."

"I don't understand myself sometimes. But this...isn't right." Dalton helped her to her feet and yanked up his clothing.

Then he took her hand and led her to his bedroom.

She was still breathing hard. Wariness darkened her eyes.

He stripped first. As he stood naked before her, his rush of masculine power had vanished, leaving him feeling vulnerable.

"Dalton," she whispered, trapping his face in her hands, "Talk to me."

"I love you."

Rory blinked at him.

"I love you and the thought of losing you, of you walking away from me because I'm not the man you want...makes me crazy. It keeps me up at night. I've changed. But have I changed enough so you believe—"

She kissed him. "You are the man I want. Just you. I'm here with you and there's no place I'd rather be."

He traced her swollen lips with the pad of his thumb. "I was rough. I'm sorry."

"Then you'd better kiss it and make it better, huh?"

Dalton kissed her. Touched her. Showed her.

She responded in that sweet melting way she always did, giving herself over to him completely.

After he'd removed her clothes and they were stretched out on his bed, skin to skin, heart to heart, he said, "You're mine, jungle girl. Only ever mine. I'm never letting you get away from me again."

Her satisfied moans rang in his ears as he showed her twice just how much he loved her.

"I'm still mad at you."

Dalton's gaze moved over her naked body. Lingered on her sex-mussed hair. Then he lifted that one dark eyebrow. "I can tell."

Rory shoved him.

He laughed. "You can be mad at me more often if that's how we work out our differences." He leaned forward and placed a tender kiss on the cup of her shoulder. "That was...mmm."

"Mmm? What's mmm?"

"The sexual hum of a satisfied man. Mmm. I make that sound a lot around you. Thought you'd recognize it." He propped himself up on his elbow and traced her nipple with his fingertip. "I don't have a bunch of smooth words. What's between us defies description. I never knew it could be like that. And it's like that between us every damn time."

Don't know any smooth words, my ass.

"So why don't you go on and get your mad worked out. I can take it."

She sighed. "Why didn't you tell me you applied for a permit?"

"Why didn't you tell me you were processing the applications?" he countered.

"Because it was supposed to be kept under wraps. But the people in the office knew what I was working on—I blame Hannah for trying to sabotage me. And the way I told you..." She shuddered. "I wasn't supposed to tell you at all. Not only because I thought it'd cause problems between us. I know most ranchers—especially the McKays—are against this program."

"True." He stroked the upper swell of her breast with the back of his knuckles. "But somehow you forgot that I'm not a rancher anymore."

"Also true."

"And we don't talk about our jobs. Me, mostly because I don't have one. So can we have a rational discussion about what happened?"

"While we're naked?"

"Yep."

"Fine. When I showed up on Monday, why did you assume your family had something to do with me learning about your application?"

"Because I had a big goddamned fight with them about it on Sunday after the poker game."

As Dalton told her what'd happened with the McKays, she felt even worse for how she'd handled it with him. "I'm sorry. I was way less than professional."

He tipped her chin up and looked into her eyes. "Wasn't your lack of professionalism that bothered me. I thought things had changed between us. That you understood I'd changed. But you believed the worst of me from the get-go, and I ain't gonna lie. Pissed me off more than it hurt me. At first."

Rory curled into him, resting her head on his chest and trying to wrap herself around him. "I'm sorry. This isn't an excuse for the way I behaved, but seeing your application caught me off guard. I figured your family would apply in the hopes of getting selected so they could tank the program. But you're serious about this."

"Completely. Since I've been gone for three years I had no idea what'd been goin' on with the laws until I saw it in the newspaper. I was really shocked to read the elk farm pilot program had made it through the Wyoming legislature and the lawmakers hadn't bowed to the livestock producers' demands and killed it in committee again."

"Took them long enough. You should see the book of regulations just for the temporary permit."

"I'm sure the regulations are brutal—I don't envy you that—I'm just happy this trial might end the stranglehold that Yellowstone and The Tetons have had on the feeding grounds."

She drew circles on his chest. "So this application isn't a whim for you? And right now, I'm not asking as a WNRC employee, but as your..." Lover? Girlfriend?

"As my what, Rory?"

"As the woman who has humbly asked your forgiveness."

Her response didn't make him happy, especially in light of the fact he'd confessed his love for her.

"I didn't plan on staying here when I first left Montana. Then my priorities changed and the elk farm opportunity caught my eye. I've done the research. It'd give me something to do here instead of returning to ranching." Dalton's palm skated down her arm. "My brothers are on board with my idea. One hundred percent. Even though the rest of the McKays are not."

"I'm surprised they're giving you full support."

"I'm not. If I get awarded the permit, it'd give me a reason to stay and be part of the family again."

Rory tried not to freeze up. She tried to keep her breathing steady. She tried not to think about what that statement meant. An ugly, horrible thought occurred to her. For once in their relationship, she had all the power. Her decision would determine whether or not he stayed.

Dalton's hand cupped her face and he tilted her head back so he could look at her. "I've gotta know that you're gonna give me a fair shot."

She kissed the base of his thumb. "It's good that this is out in the open. But it can't all be out in the open. There are things I can't talk about, Dalton."

"You mean things about your job that you can't talk about, right?"

"Ah, right."

Dalton knew she was hedging but he allowed it. "Are we done talkin' for now?"

"Sure. Why?"

"'Cause we've still got a lot of kissin' and makin' up to do."

In the past ten days since their big blow up, Dalton and Rory had stuck to the parameters of not discussing specifics of her job. But he wondered if she had anyone to talk to about work-related stuff, because she was really stressed. She'd barely touched her lunch. "You gonna finish them fries?"

Rory slid the plate at him. "I told you not to order a salad because you'd be hungry."

"I ordered a salad because you never finish all your food and I hate to see it go to waste."

She didn't say anything funny or cute in response, which wasn't like her. She tapped her fingers on the table and stared into space.

"Something wrong?"

"Not looking forward to my next inspection."

Dalton picked up her restless hand. "Want me to come with you? I'll knock the guy around if he disrespects you."

"Bizarrely sweet offer, so thank you, but I have to fight my own battles. I just wish there weren't so damn many of them."

"That's all it's been this week?"

She nodded. "And last week."

"I promise you no battles when you inspect my land." He kissed her knuckles. "But the offer stands if you need a bodyguard when you're makin' your rounds. 'Cause sugarplum, you know how much I love your body."

"Same goes." A naughty smile curled her lips. "But anytime you wanna dress like a bodyguard in a tight black T-shirt, black camo pants, a leather jacket and badass don't-fuck-with-me sunglasses...well, cowboy, you just go right ahead."

Dalton laughed.

A shadow fell across them and they both looked up.

His cousins Cord and Colt stood at the end of the table.

Awesome. Dalton hadn't seen them since the poker game and didn't know what he'd say to them.

Cord smiled at Rory. "Hey, Rory. Haven't seen you in a while. How've you been?"

"Good. How're things with you?"

"Can't complain." Cord looked at Dalton. "Dalton."

"Cord."

"We didn't mean to interrupt your lunch," Colt said.

Like hell.

"I need to get to work so you can have my spot and keep Dalton company while he eats that piece of bread pudding he's been eyeing." Rory paused. "Unless you're here to gang up on him? I'll stick around in case it gets heated."

Dalton loved that she had his back.

"We ain't gonna gang up on him," Cord said.

"Good." She leaned across the table and mock whispered, "Lucky for them that I don't have to break out my kung fu moves in defense of you, huh?"

He couldn't help but laugh; she cracked his ass up.

When Rory slipped out of the booth, Dalton stood and tugged her into his arms. After kissing her soundly he said, "Be careful out there."

"I will."

"Let me know if you're up for doin' anything tonight."

"Always." Rory gave him another quick peck. She reached for her coat. "Later, McKays."

"See ya, Rory." Then Cord looked at Dalton. "Got a minute to talk?"

"I guess." He signaled to the waitress. He'd been in here enough times the past few weeks that she knew what he wanted. She slid a plate of warm bread pudding in front of Dalton and poured Cord and Colt each a cup of coffee.

"So what's up?"

"We owe you an apology."

That'd come out quick. But his cousins weren't the type to beat around the bush. Dalton sliced off a chunk of dessert and popped it in his mouth.

Colt said, "Neither of us handled the news about your plans in the best way. I'd blame my reaction on booze except I don't drink."

Dalton snorted.

"So bein' an asshole is all on me, cuz, and I am sorry for that," Colt said.

"While I still don't agree with what you're doin' as far as applying for an elk farm permit for land that borders our ranch land, it don't excuse me bein' a dick to you."

"It happens."

"Happens a lot, according to my son," Cord grumbled.

"Kyler said that?"

"Yeah." Cord pushed his hat up and looked at him. "Kid's got a case of hero worship since he's been helpin' you. So when he overheard me'n AJ talkin' about what'd happened after the poker game, he lit into me. Jesus. Said I was a hypocrite and if I took issue when someone tried to tell me what I could do on my land, then I had no right to tell you what to do with yours."

Dalton bit back a smile.

"And rather than waitin' to see if he'd made his point with me, he kept goin'. So in addition to bein' a hypocrite, I'm a controlling asshole who doesn't remember what it's like to be young. Or what it's like to want to do something besides bein' a rancher."

"Ouch. How'd you handle that?"

Cord sighed. "Not well. But that's pretty much par for the course between me'n Ky these days. Half the time I wanna throttle him."

"And the rest of the time?"

"I want to make the most of the two years we've got left before he heads off to college because it doesn't seem that long ago he was five and he hero worshipped me."

"He's a good kid, Cord. At least he ain't afraid to voice his opinion to you."

Colt nudged Cord. "Getting off the subject."

Dalton shrugged. "It's probably a more productive subject for us anyway. Not that I'm one to offer up any advice about father-son relations."

"No change with Casper?" Cord asked.

The man is incapable of change. "Nope."

"That's gotta be hard on you guys. But I know Brandt and Tell are glad to have you back." Colt sipped his coffee. "Man, did they lay into us. Between them and Kane and Kade tossing in their two cents' worth I felt about an inch high by the time they finished with me."

"Me too," Cord added. "Though I'm pretty sure Tell was jokin' when he suggested we write our apology in blood."

"Is that why you're here?" Dalton asked suspiciously. "Because my brothers demanded it?"

Colt laughed. "Take it down a notch. We're apologizing because we said a buncha shit to you that was wrong. Colby would've come too but he got waylaid."

"Letting something fester ain't good. Best to get this out in the open, deal with it and move on," Cord said.

"Along those lines, Ben said to tell you that the two of you are squared up now. Something about you both bein' dumbasses that overreact?" Colt looked at him. "Does that make any sense to you?"

"Yeah, it does."

Cord raised an eyebrow but didn't ask specifics. "So on certain points of this issue, we'll agree to disagree for the time bein'."

"Agreed. I appreciate the olive branch."

"So we're cool then?" Colt asked.

Dalton grinned. "At least until the next poker game and you guys are pissed off that I cleaned you out again."

Chapter Twenty-Three

Seething, Rory sat in the WNRC truck and beat her hands on the steering wheel, punctuating each, "sonuvabitching, motherfucking, cocksucking, goddamned asshole" with another smack of her hands. When she missed and hit the horn, she scared herself so bad she screamed.

Okay. Enough. Breathe. Focus on deep cleansing breath in, negative energy out.

Rory closed her eyes. Inhale one, two, three...hold. Exhale one, two, three. Again. Three more cycles and she should've been calmer. She shouldn't have been thinking, *fucking know-it-all asswipe douchebag* and imagining clipping him with the four-wheeler so hard he tumbled into the ravine.

She really, really, really fucking hated her job today.

Up at the crack of dawn, hauling an ATV on back roads two hours away. Only to be confronted by a foul-tempered, big-mouthed, sexist, ageist, government-hating rancher who spewed vitriol from the moment she'd opened the pickup door until three hours later when she'd finished the survey of his land for the proposed elk farm permit.

And to top it off, the smug man had only applied for the permit to fuck with the "useless, liberal-leaning, pseudo-regulatory agency" that she worked for.

The trip was an entire waste of her day. She could've checked out three other proposed landowner sites, but no, she had to give each permit equal consideration. Even those who openly professed they were dicking with her.

Rory had half a mind to report the jerk-off to the brand board for improper tagging or to the Wyoming Livestock Board, aka—the Wyoming CDC-cow disease control—for possible foot and mouth disease.

Sucked that she was too...honest to do it. Sometimes she wished she could just be a devious, coldhearted, vengeful bitch.

Who was she kidding? She couldn't even be honest with herself. What happened to her plan of indulging in the most amazing sex in the history of mankind with sex god Dalton McKay and not falling for him?

She was so so so screwed.

Berating herself wasn't helping. She needed a physical activity that'd burn off this negativity. Too bad she couldn't chop wood. That always worked off a good mad. But her mom had replaced the wood stove in the cabin with electric heat.

Not enough snow to shovel.

She could take Jingle for a run. Except Rory didn't run—*ever*— and Jingle preferred to sit on the couch like a pampered pooch.

Yoga...for being a great workout, her mind needed stimulation, not serenity.

Rory could tag Vanessa and see if she was up for booty-shaking at the Back Porch, the college dance bar in Spearfish. But then she'd be tempted to drink and she had to get up early tomorrow and face another angry rancher or three.

Wait. Wasn't a Zumba class offered at the community center tonight? The body-pumping, sweating action with loud music blocking out all her crappy, crabby thoughts was exactly what she needed.

She parked the truck and trailer in the fenced-in lot at the WNRC and hopped in her Jeep. Since she had her gym bag with her workout clothes she drove straight to the community center.

The class was jammed with women of all ages. The mood in the big gymnasium buzzed with high energy even before the class started.

Rory wasn't familiar with the routines so she picked a spot in the very back of the room. When Heather, the class leader, bounded in, headset on, hands clapping in the air, the room went wild.

Huh. She never got that kind of reaction at the start of yoga class. Then again, Heather was one of those itty bitty pocket-sized women— five foot one, ninety pounds of solid muscle, gleaming red hair, alabaster skin, infectious smile. Rory could hate high-energy Heather if she wasn't the most genuinely sweet person she'd ever met.

"All right, ladies! Let's get this party started. And pay attention because I'm gonna sneak in some new dance moves."

The music blared from the speakers and bodies started gyrating to the beat.

Forty-five minutes later, Rory was sweaty, gasping for breath and much happier. As she waited in line at the drinking fountain, laughing with other class members, her yoga student Ricki nudged her. "Don't turn around, but that guy who came to your yoga class that one time is here."

"Dalton?"

"Uh-huh. And if his eyes could talk they'd be yelling at you to strip and get on all fours."

"Ricki!"

"I'm serious. He hasn't taken his eyes off you—I mean off your butt—since the moment I saw him. With the way some of the women were looking at the doorway the last ten minutes of class, he must've been standing there watching you then."

"Why were women turning around?"

"Duh. Because the man is sex on legs. And he's wearing a skintight wife beater and my *god*, have you seen his freakin' chest and arm muscles? What does he do for a living? Lift cars?"

"No, he lifts logs, actually."

Ricki's eyes widened. "You know him?"

Rory mopped her face with her towel. "Yep. I'm sleeping with him."

"I kinda hate you a little bit right now."

She laughed. She took several long drinks of water before she walked over to where she'd left her gym bag. Knowing Dalton's gaze was on her, she twisted her shoulders as if working out some kinks in her neck. Then she set her hands on her hips and slowly leaned forward, until the top of her head touched the floor. Hanging upside down, Rory sent him a look that said, *baby, I'd love to work out some kinks with you.*

The depraved man grinned at her and crooked his finger.

So, yeah, maybe she added an extra sway of her hips as she sauntered over to him. And maybe she hooked her arm around his neck and gave him a big smacking kiss in front of everybody, her *he's mine* vibe readily apparent.

Dalton's blue eyes shone with male amusement. "Kiss me again. I don't think those two women in the corner quite got the message that you'n me are a couple."

"Gladly." This time she hooked the towel around his neck and tugged him closer, her mouth snaring his in a steamy kiss.

When Dalton emitted that sexy rumble in the back of his throat, she broke the kiss with a quick laugh.

"You feelin' ornery, Aurora?" he whispered in her ear. "'Cause I've got a cure for that."

"So do I, but it'll cost ya."

He leaned back and raised an eyebrow. "Whatcha got in mind?"

"How long were you skulking in the back watching me dance?"

"Skulking," he snorted. "The damn door was open. And sugarplum, your ass is like a goddamned beacon for me. I started watching it and couldn't look away."

"Aw, such a sweet-talker." Rory slid her hands up his chest. "You like the way I dance, cowboy?"

"Yes ma'am."

She twisted her fingers in the damp tendrils on the back of his neck. "Remember that night I picked you up after the bachelor party and you asked if I'd give you a lap dance?"

"Vaguely. Why?"

"Then when we were in Deadwood and you were Mr. High Roller, begging me to give you a lap dance, peeling twenty dollar bills off the stack of cash saying, 'I make it rain, I make it rain, I make it rain'?"

Dalton grinned. "All in good fun."

"I know." Rory pressed her body to his. "Well, I'm in the mood to give you that lap dance tonight. But like I said, it's gonna cost ya."

"I'll pay it."

She cocked her head. "Just like that? Without asking the price or the parameters?"

"Parameters?" His eyes narrowed. "Lap dances don't have parameters except for no touching."

"My lap dance has parameters 'cause it's not your money I'm after, McKay."

"Then what do you want?"

"Your soul." Rory laughed at his skeptical look. "Kidding."

He clamped his hand on her ass and pulled her closer yet. He angled his head and placed one soft kiss below her ear. "You want my soul? It's yours. Since you've already got my heart."

Oh, you suck, Dalton McKay, with your sweetness and fire and always knowing the perfect thing to say, and how the hell was I ever supposed to resist falling for you?

"You were saying," he murmured against her throat. "What parameters were you talkin' about?"

"You have to be naked."

"Ah, Rory darlin', that ain't how lap dances work."

"My parameters, remember? If I can get you off during the lap dance, without using my hands on your...pole, then you'll agree to be my sex slave for two hours."

"What if you can't get me off? What's *my* reward?"

Uh, yeah, Dalton wouldn't be able to hold off. No way, no how. Rory fought a cocky smile. "Then you get to do anything you want to me. Except for demanding a threesome. Not into that. Ever."

"Never happening, because no one—" he got right in her face, "—and I mean *no one*, ever gets to put their fucking hands on you but me. Understand?"

Holy balls. Talk about intense. Talk about possessive.

Talk about hot.

"Do you understand?" he repeated.

"Yes, sir."

"Good." He relaxed. "There's gotta be a time limit to this lap dance."

"Shoot. Thought you might not remember to ask about that. Five songs."

Dalton shook his head. "Two songs."

"Four songs."

"Nope. Two songs."

"Three songs."

"Three songs no more than nine minutes total."

She smiled. "Deal." She kissed him. "I'll follow you home."

"Lemme grab a quick shower here first—"

"No. I'm not gonna shower either. I like your scent after you've been working out." She turned her head and let her tongue follow the ridge of his biceps, licking the salt from his skin. "I like how you taste after you've been working out."

Dalton made that growling noise again.

"On second thought...I'll race ya." She pecked him on the mouth and practically skipped out of the gym.

But somehow, Rory still didn't beat him to his place.

Inside, Dalton leaned against the breakfast bar separating the living room and kitchen, his arms crossed over his chest.

Poor man wore a scowl. She dropped her coat, kicked off her shoes and moved to stand in front of him. "You're supposed to be looking forward to this, Dalton, not like you're about to face a firing squad."

That brought out his sexy wicked grin. "Trust me, baby, I'm all about this lap dance. Just thinking about what I'm gonna demand from you."

"Putting the cart before the horse, ain't ya, cowboy?"

He laughed and smooched her nose.

"You get the chair and I'll plug in my iPod."

"Where's the chair gonna go?"

"Living room. You might wanna move the coffee table."

Rory scrolled through her song list and selected her seductive tunes. Then she plugged her iPod into the audio system and turned around.

The straight-backed dining room chair sat where the coffee table usually did. Dalton curled his hands over the top of it. "Now what?"

"I'd tell you to strip, but I wanna help you do that."

His eyes turned suspicious.

"Relax. If you don't like something I do...tell me to stop."

He snorted. "You have *got* to be kiddin' me."

"No sir."

"Start the music."

"This doesn't count as part of the lap dance. Stand still so I can strip you." Rory slipped her fingers beneath the bottom edge of his tank top and began to pull it up. When the material cleared his nipples, she gave each flat disk a kiss. Then a lick. Then a suck.

"Rory."

"What?"

"You know what."

She jerked the shirt over his head and tossed it aside. She planted kisses down the center of his torso as she lowered herself to her knees. Hooking his gaze, she mouthed his cock, which was already hard—big surprise—through the material.

"Rory!"

"What?"

"Stop."

She sighed. "All right." Hooking her fingers in the stretchy waistband, she slowly tugged the shorts down, watching as the tip of his cock bounced against his lower belly. He hadn't worn a jockstrap.

"Word of advice, sugarplum? You frowning at my dick ain't instilling any confidence in me."

Her eyes met his. "Sorry. Just wondering if you ever wear a jockstrap or a cup when you're working out?"

"Jesus. Really?"

"Yeah, why? Is that a weird question? Because I seriously don't know about these man things—no dad growing up, remember? And since your body is so buff, that means you work out a lot, so I just wondered."

"Such a curious kitty. Yeah, sometimes I wear a jock. Depends on what I'm doin' in the gym and what workout shorts I'm wearing." He ran his knuckles down the side of her face. "Satisfied?"

"Yep. But sometime, I wanna see you model them. I'd probably really love how the straps frame this tight little ass of yours." Rory yanked his shorts to his ankles and licked his shaft from root to tip before opening her lips and swallowing him.

And releasing him.

And swallowing him.

She did that about five times before his big head overruled his little head.

Dalton clamped his hand on her jaw and pulled her off.

Very, very slowly she might add, but hey, who was keeping track?

She was, heh heh heh. Rory ahead by giving head, one to zero.

"Back. Away. From. My. Cock."

"Never thought I'd hear you say that, big guy."

He groaned.

Rory rolled to her feet and pointed to the chair. "Get comfy."

Dalton grabbed a throw pillow off the couch and plopped it on the seat before he sat. "What?" he said defensively at her questioning look. "The seat is wood, you're gonna be bouncing on my lap and I don't want my balls to get pinched."

"Poor balls. I could kiss 'em and make 'em better?" she cooed.

"You're gonna be doin' that anyway when I win this lap dance off." He threw his arms wide. "Bring it on, baby."

"Hands by your sides, *baby*, and no touching, remember?" Rory pulled the elastic band, freeing her hair from the ponytail. Shaking it loose so the soft strands swished across his face. Then she peeled off her T-shirt and ditched her sports bra. She kicked her feet out and stretched, keeping her ass right in front of him, knowing he could see her tits swaying as she loosened her muscles.

He cleared his throat. "Topless ain't fair, Rory."

"Aw, it's so cute how you think that'll matter. Because you're goin' down." She looked over her shoulder at him and smirked. "Literally. You're gonna go down on me for two hours straight after I win this lap dance."

"Be a little hard for me to have my mouth on your pussy when my dick is gonna be buried in your sweet ass when I win."

She laughed and leaned over to turn on her iPod.

The first strains of Santana's "Smooth" drifted through the speakers and Rory started out with her back to him. Arms above her head. Ass swishing over his crotch, the end of her hair teasing his chest. She ground down on him a little harder each time. Feeling that hard cock twitching and jerking against the lower curve of her butt cheeks.

Dalton's heavy breathing echoed to her even over the sounds of the music.

A wave of want rolled through her. Yes, she wanted to win this contest, but mostly because she wanted to know that she—the way she moved, the way she teased him—turned him on as much as her mouth or her hand on his cock. She loved the byplay between them. The tension in his body. The heat in his eyes. All for her.

He groaned when she cupped her own breasts. And arched her back against his chest.

Then Rory sat on his right thigh and placed her hands flat on the floor, dragging her pussy up and down that rigid muscle. The cant of her hips showcased her ass. She arched and rolled like a cat, each pass making her pussy wet and her nipples harder. She stood and pressed her butt against his chest as she leaned into a forward bend with her hands around his shins.

"Holy hell, you're flexible."

"All the better to use my body to twist *you* into knots." Rory mounted his other leg and rolled and shimmied. Her hair swinging, her booty bouncing, sweat started to bead on her skin.

His deep voice cut through her concentration. "I can feel how hot and wet your cunt is. Let me touch you and bring you off."

"Tempting, cowboy, but I've only just started. I'm gonna get a lot wetter and a lot hotter in the next two songs."

The music ended.

Rory spun around and pressed her pussy against his shaft when the next song started. The chair's low proximity to the ground allowed her to raise and lower herself easily, so she kept constant pressure on Dalton's cock as she moved up and down. And the extra bonus? With her hands on those broad shoulders of his for balance, her tits were in his face. Right in his face.

The sneaky man tried to move his head back, out of range, but she just moved her hands to the back of his neck and held him in place.

"You're killin' me."

"That's the plan." She slowed and shifted her hips side to side instead of up and down.

His belly muscles quivered. His arms were stiff by his side, probably because he was clenching his fists.

Then a wet, warm tongue lashed the side of her breast and circled her nipple.

Rory stopped mid-grind. "Hey. Keep your mouth to yourself, buddy."

"No. God, I love your tits." Dalton kept his eyes locked to hers as he enclosed her nipple in his hot mouth and sucked hard.

"Dalton! What are you doing? You oughta lose by default."

Dalton licked and sucked and growled against her flesh. "So indignant and bossy. And yet, you're not getting these hard nipples outta my face."

Of course he'd noticed that. She slid her palms to his cheeks and tipped his head back. "Stop."

"No. You said no touching with my hands. You didn't say a damn thing about not usin' my mouth."

"That was assumed."

"Not by me. But whatever. Unless you're—" his eyes gleamed and he flashed his pearly whites, "—*afraid* that my mouth on you is too big a distraction?"

Cocky man. Rory brought her nipple right up to his lips and said, "Have at."

Someplace in the foggy haze of being face to face, chest to chest and groin to groin with him, so close she could smell his skin, feel his heartbeat, she realized she'd sort of lost control of the situation.

But if she retreated now, forcing him to stop the delicious assault on her breasts, Dalton would think she was backing off because she was losing.

Hell. No.

Rory writhed against him more forcefully. Faster. Pumping her pelvis in time to the crescendo of the music. If she kept up this pace much longer, she'd be coming, not Dalton. Especially if he used his teeth on her neck. Right. There.

Not fair. The sneaky man had abandoned her nipples for her neck, completely aware that made her lose any coherent train of thought.

Needing a breather, she stopped and slid back until she balanced on his knees.

The music changed again.

Dammit. She had three minutes left to make him come. She wanted this victory.

But as Rory stared into Dalton's gorgeous face, seeing those beautifully expressive eyes and the secret way he was smiling at her, she understood they'd both won.

The sultry sounds of Faith Hill singing "Breathe" flowed through the room.

Dalton's eyes were on her as he reached up to curl his hand on her neck. He stroked her jawline with the edge of his thumb. "I remember this song."

"You do?"

"We danced to this at Keely's wedding. The way you wrapped yourself around me, and how your head just seemed to fit perfectly on my shoulder, I never wanted that song to end."

"It was one of those moments," she said softly. A perfect moment.

"Aurora, you're beautiful, you're sexy, you just gave me the best goddamned lap dance I've ever had, but can we be done with this now, please?"

"Call it a draw?"

"Yes."

"Okay, yes."

Dalton picked her up, took her down to the floor, stripped her yoga pants off and impaled her.

The sweetness of their conversation didn't translate to sweet lovemaking. He pounded into her. Hot, sweaty and hard. Demanding. Clasping her right hand in his left, he pinned it above their heads. Pulling her left leg up high, around his hip, opening her fully so every time he thrust, his pelvis connected with her clit.

She gasped. Instead of waiting for that gradual buildup and the explosion, she felt as if this connection was one long body-shuddering orgasm.

"That's it. I love seein' you like this."

"Dalton, I... It's too much."

"No. It's perfect. So close, baby. Bring me with you."

Rory arched up and tightened her cunt muscles around his pistoning shaft. One long hot kiss later and they hit the detonation point together.

Chapter Twenty-Four

Brandt and Tell were sitting in Tell's favorite booth when Dalton dragged himself into the Golden Boot.

"Hey." He shucked his duster and hung it on the wall hook before taking his spot on Brandt's right side. He noticed they'd ordered beer for themselves but not for him. "You got another round comin'? Or am I buying my own beer tonight?"

"We weren't sure what you were drinkin' these days."

"Cheap beer, same as always." Dalton gestured to the bartender for a round. Then his gaze moved from Brandt to Tell. They'd both cleaned up and wore nonworking clothes. The old Dalton would've made a sneering remark about them dressing up to please their wives, but he let it lie. "So what's up?"

"What makes you think something's up?" Brandt asked evenly.

"It's a Thursday night. You guys are both getting kids to bed and stuff during the week. I usually see you on the weekends."

"Not lately, bro. You've been spending all your weekends with Rory."

"And most weeknights," Tell added. "We asked you out last week, but you had plans."

"Rielle invited us over for supper. First time she's acknowledged me'n Rory are involved, so it was kind of a big deal." He didn't know why Rory's mom intimidated the hell out of him; she just did, which was ridiculous because the woman was the same size as a garden sprite. But her love for Rory—holy shit, talk about fierce. No doubt if Dalton somehow wronged her baby girl, she'd just bury him in her garden and no one would ever know the difference.

"So you're not avoiding us?"

"No."

"Just certain family members?" Brandt asked.

Meaning Casper. Maybe he oughta just buck up and tell them the truth so they could be done with this.

Lettie brought the beer to the table, mostly so she could flirt with Tell. Tell gave it right back to her in a way that had both Dalton and Brandt laughing.

Dalton took a drink of beer and settled into the booth. "How long's it been since you guys hung out here?"

"Me'n Georgia used to come here all the time. No surprise Jackson's arrival into our lives cut our bar time short. But we meet up with the gang at least once a month."

"Hitting the bars never was me'n Jess's thing, so it's been a while for me." Brandt looked around. "Nothin' ever changes in here, does it?"

"Yeah, well, not all change is good," Tell said.

Dalton decided to tackle that statement head on. "Hard not to feel that was directed at me, Tell."

"And if it was?"

"Then I'd ask how far into this family shit you're willing to wade. 'Cause it goes a helluva lot deeper than what you're seein' on the surface."

That response jarred them into silence for a bit.

But Tell wasn't a back-down kind of guy. "And that right there just proves my theory."

"Tell, don't," Brandt warned.

"It's all good, Brandt. I wanna hear his theory."

Tell leaned forward. "You didn't cut and run only because of Addie. And you knew that day you said goodbye to us that you wouldn't be comin' back anytime soon. So I gotta ask if staying away had to do with something me or Brandt had done to you."

This was it. Dalton spun his bottle on his cocktail napkin. "You guys hadn't considered that might be part of my issue until I pointed it out to you the day I left. Did any of it resonate? Or was the problem—aka me—solved when I bailed?"

"To be honest, it seriously fucked us both up," Brandt said hotly. "You laid that on us, took off, and left us with such goddamned...guilt and no way to make it right with you. If your intent was to force us to stew in our own juices, then it worked."

Dalton shook his head. "What I said to you that day, I said without malice or without an ulterior motive. Do you wish I'da just left without giving you any idea on why?"

"Some days, yeah. Those days that Brandt and I spent drivin' around doin' chores together, when we couldn't talk about it because there was just another big hole in our lives, that no amount of talkin' would ever fill. You think your leavin' didn't affect us? Fuck you. We'd already lost one brother and then poof, you were gone too. And we had to live with the fact that we played a part in driving you away." Tell drained his beer. "Fuck. I don't wanna do this. There's part of me that believes talkin' about this shit is actually gonna make it worse."

You have no idea.

"But you're here, we're here, and it's time, little bro," Brandt said in that don't argue tone.

"Order another round. We're gonna need it." Dalton headed for the bathroom, but ended up pacing in the hallway. He had a bout of motherfucking nerves that just about had him bolting out the door.

He pressed his shoulders against the wall and closed his eyes, his last conversation with Casper three years ago pushed front and center just like it'd happened yesterday.

He'd been sitting outside his trailer, nursing a whiskey when Casper had shown up. As soon as the man had climbed out of his pickup, and Dalton had seen the mean set to his mouth, he slammed the booze, knowing he'd need it.

"I'm surprised you're out of hiding. You always have run away instead of bein' a man and facing up to your mistakes."

Dalton said nothing. His dad was on a tear and he'd stay on it until he'd had his full say.

"You're a fool for leaving that sweet Addie at the altar. Don't know how you ever convinced that nice Christian girl to marry you anyway with your reputation for drinkin', gamblin', whorin' and brawlin'."

He shoved his ball cap back and looked right into those cruel blue eyes. "How's a church-going, recovering alcoholic, who don't even live in this town anymore, who don't have nothin' to do with his sons, know so much about my supposed reputation?"

"Such a smart mouth," Casper sneered. "Don't think this scandal is gonna go away anytime soon. You really screwed the pooch on this one."

Dalton laughed. "Thought you cut out all vulgar language."

"What I said ain't as vulgar as what you done." His gaze scrutinized Dalton's every facial injury. "See some of it's already caught up with you."

"Nothin' I can't handle."

"I'd love to be around the next time someone knocks that smug look off your face."

Dalton flashed his teeth. "Or you're welcome to try and do it yourself, right now, old man."

Casper snorted. "Says a lot about your character that you'd get off on beating me up."

"You only have yourself to blame since that's a trait I inherited from you."

"You inherited nothin' from me," he spat. "'Bout time you knew the truth. So after this last stunt you pulled, I prayed for divine assistance, needing His direction. He gave me the sign I needed."

"And what did God tell you to do? Ride out here and berate your son until he begged for forgiveness for adding another black mark to the McKay name?" Dalton demanded.

That malicious glint in his face showed again. "Your mama oughta be asking for forgiveness for the lies she told. Lies everyone has always believed. But I knew. The sign is as plain as the nose on your face."

Was Casper going senile? "You ain't makin' a lick of sense. What's my nose and a sign got to do with anything?"

"What's your nose got to do with it? Look at that nose. That face of yours. Have you ever taken a good long look at yourself in the mirror, boy? When you ain't been preening yourself like a peacock? If you ever had, you'd realize that you don't look nothin' like your brothers and you sure don't look nothin' like me."

He had dark hair and blue eyes, just like the rest of the McKays. He was bigger than his brothers—bigger than all the McKays except for Cam. "Cam and Carter favor the West side so that don't mean nothin'."

"It sure does mean something. It means you ain't my kid."

Dalton laughed.

"I'm not joking. Your mom screwed around on me and I had to look at and deal with the ugly result of that since the day you were born."

"Wow. So I get a two-fer? You're showing that nasty-ass mean streak you're so goddamned proud of while you're telling a bald-faced lie?"

"Watch your words. God is lookin' down on you."

No, you're the one who's always looked down on me.

"This ain't a lie. Because blood types don't lie. And you don't have the same blood type as Luke, Brandt and Tell."

That didn't prove anything...did it? Fuck, he'd slept through that part of biology. How was he supposed to remember his brothers' blood types? When he couldn't remember his own?

"And if you want real proof that you ain't mine? I'd even take a paternity test."

A niggling feeling of unease started at the back of his neck. What if he was telling the truth?

"Why do you think your mom coddled you? Protected you? She knew I knew that you weren't my flesh and blood."

"She didn't coddle me and she sure as fuck didn't protect me from you or else I wouldn't have been on the receiving end of your strap so many times." Or maybe...that's why he'd been singled out.

Don't fall for this.

"Ask her," Casper challenged. "Look her in the eye and demand to know what man she was with when she left me for a week. Oh, roundabout nine months before your birth."

"I won't because you're a fucking liar."

"You won't ask her because you know it's the truth. Part of you has always known you don't belong."

There's no way that bastard could've known that Dalton had always felt that way. "Why are you doin' this?"

"It's past time you knew the truth."

"Just me? Or everyone? You're gonna make an announcement to the world that your ex-wife fucked around on you? That'll be seen for exactly what it is: an old man's bitterness."

"I don't give a hoot about sharing that info with the world at large. I just thought you oughta know."

"Why? So you can hang this over my head? Threatening to spew this supposed secret to my brothers, thinking it'll keep me in line?"

"Brandt and Tell won't hear the truth from me. They'll hate the messenger and ignore the message, as usual." His lips twisted in a parody of a smile. "Besides, you're still their brother even if you ain't my kid."

Dalton couldn't think straight. So much of who he was, was about being a McKay—and all it meant to be part of that family.

Who was he if he didn't have that?

And was it really a surprise that Casper had held onto this crucial, critical information until the lowest point in Dalton's life?

No.

Casper could kick a man who was down and smile while doing it.

Dalton tried to make his voice hard and cold. "What exactly am I supposed to do with this information, Casper?"

"Use it to find some direction," Casper snapped. "You've been content floating through life, letting your brothers do all the ranch work while you're spreading your sins across the five state area."

"You have nothin' to do with the ranch so how would you know what Brandt and Tell are doin'?"

"Don't think your brothers haven't mentioned it to me a time or two, how little you're involved. It's obvious Brandt and Tell don't need your help running the ranch. And you've got no claim on it anyway."

"Beings that I'm not a McKay," Dalton said dully.

Casper kept his arms crossed over his chest and gave him a patronizing look. "Yep. Don't you be putting your burdens on folks that don't need them. When you're the real burden."

That's when Dalton had known he had to leave Sundance right away.

He opened his eyes, surprised to find himself in the hallway of a bar and not sitting on the steps in front of his trailer watching Casper's taillights disappear.

Dalton still didn't want to tell his brothers what had gone down. But he'd given this secret way too much power to wreck the brother bond he had with Brandt and Tell. He headed back to the table, his heart pounding like he'd run the mile.

Brandt and Tell weren't talking. They looked up at his approach.

He knocked back his beer to wet his suddenly dry mouth. "Tell was partially right. I wasn't honest with you guys about why I left so fast. I made the decision after Casper showed up at my place."

Tell said, "Fuck, that must've been fun."

"I'll put it this way: it left its mark."

"What'd he say?" Brandt asked.

Now that the moment was here, Dalton couldn't even look his brothers in the eye. He focused on his beer bottle, his fingernail edging the soggy label as he tried to peel it off in one piece.

No one uttered a word for an excruciatingly long time.

Finally Tell said, "Shit. This is gonna be bad, isn't it?"

Dalton nodded.

Brandt gently pried the bottle out of Dalton's hand. When Dalton looked up at him, Brandt said, "No more stalling."

"Casper said I'm not his son."

Tell and Brandt exchanged a look. The *why'd you let him get under your skin and make you believe bullshit like that that's obviously not true* look.

Then Brandt nudged another beer at him. "You're gonna have to walk us through it, so we can understand why you—"

"Believed him?" His embarrassment turned into anger. "Fuck you both if you don't remember what a master manipulator Casper is. I know you've forgiven him or something. Fine, that's your choice. I won't judge you for what you've decided works for you and what you can live with when it comes to him."

Both his brothers squirmed—as he'd meant them to. Dalton didn't judge them. He deserved the same courtesy.

"Take it down a notch," Tell said evenly. "We don't have some touchy-feely, all-is-forgiven attitude when it comes to Dad."

Brandt's face had gone the mottled red that indicated he was a hair away from exploding. "How'd the conversation where Dad told you all this come about?"

"He came to the trailer. Spewing his usual bullshit about me. You two only put up with me because you didn't have a choice. He baited me and like I'd done way too many fucking times in my life, I took the bait." He upended his beer. "He leveled the boom that I wasn't a McKay. Mom had an affair and tried to pass me off as his kid, but he'd always known I wasn't."

"Bullshit," Brandt spat. "How is that even possible?"

"Did you know that Mom actually nutted up and left Casper one time?"

"No. Where'd you hear that? From him?"

"Yep. But Mom mentioned it in another conversation. Here's the kicker. It happened nine months before I was born."

Both Brandt and Tell's faces went white from shock.

Dalton should've taken a breath, given them a chance to absorb it, but he kept going. "That would've been enough to give anyone doubt, so when you add in the fact he's called me Mama's boy, a mutant, a freak and waste of space my whole life, it cements that doubt."

"Dalton—"

"And let's not forget he secretly beat the fuck outta me for years, like I was a redheaded stepchild," he said, ignoring Tell's interruption. "Yes, I've got blue eyes and dark hair, but I don't have the same blood type as you guys."

Brandt paled further.

"Casper hammered away at me. And I fucking hated I stood there and let him do it. I was at the lowest point of my life—other than when Luke died—and he went out of his way to make it worse. To make me doubt everything I thought I knew about myself and who I was."

"Did he tell you to leave?" Tell asked.

"Nope. He suggested no one would notice if I did go. Especially not you guys."

"Fuck."

"And after that conversation, nothin' could've made me stay in Sundance. Nothin'."

Silence fell between them.

Finally Brandt said, "It doesn't matter."

"That's where you're wrong. It mattered to me. It changed me in a fuckin' instant. I had to face the fact that so much of my identity for twenty-seven years was based on havin' the McKay last name. If I wasn't a McKay, who was I? Up until that point my life was predetermined. Grow up, get married, be part of the McKay ranch. I knew that life was no longer an option for me."

"Why didn't you come to us? Talk to us?" Tell asked.

"Probably because that's what Casper expected me to do."

"Did you talk to Mom about it?"

"I couldn't make myself ask her. Afraid to know either way, I guess. But within a month of my conversation with Casper, within a month of bein' gone from here, I felt freed. I didn't have the fear I'd turn into a raging asshole for no reason. I stopped letting Casper's influence be an excuse for everything shitty I did in my life. For fightin', for drinkin', for usin' and discarding women."

"Do you believe it? That he's not...?" Brandt asked.

"He offered to take me in for a paternity test, which also went a long way in convincing me that I wasn't his kid. It's a moot point to me now whether or not we share DNA. Whatever definition I needed about who I am I found on my own." He released an embarrassed laugh. "I swear I haven't become some philosophical hippie-type, yammering on about finding myself. But I had to go."

"Jesus, Dalton. I don't even know what the fuck to say to this."

Dalton looked at Tell. "Which is why I didn't share this shit with you guys."

"It's also why you didn't wanna come back here, isn't it?" Brandt asked.

"Yeah."

"What are we supposed to do with this?"

Dalton leaned forward. "I'm asking for one thing. I don't want you to bring this up with him. Period."

Tell shook his head. "The mean motherfucker can't—won't—speak so it's the perfect time to give him a piece of my mind about the absolute fucking wrongness of what he done to you. 'Cause he can't say shit back and he'll have to sit there and take it like we did for so many years."

"Damn straight," Brandt agreed.

"To what end? He's in the hospital. You really gonna be able to forgive yourselves if by layin' into him he has another stroke or something? No sir. I won't have that on my conscience or yours. So promise me you'll leave it be. Both of you. You'll never bring it up with him."

"Dalton, be reasonable—"

"Promise me," he bit off.

"Fine, fuck, I promise," Tell snapped.

Dalton looked at Brandt. "You too. I need your word."

"You've got it." He crossed his arms over his chest. "So nothin' changes."

"With Casper? If I had a quarter for every time I hoped he'd change, I'd be a rich man. The whole freakin' point of this conversation was to clear the air between *us*."

"Has it?"

"Other than the smoke comin' outta your ears? As far as I'm concerned? Yes. The topic is done. Now can we talk about something else?"

They tried. But by the thirty-minute mark Dalton knew it was a lost cause. Although it was still early, they called it a night.

Brandt texted Jessie to let her know he was on his way home, but he had things to do in the barn so not to wait up.

He'd managed to keep it together at the bar. But the instant he stepped into the barn, stripped off his shirt and slipped on boxing gloves, every bit of rage exploded.

He didn't think. He just started hitting.

He didn't fucking care if Dalton was Casper's kid. Dalton was his fucking brother. And the fact Dalton had been hurting for three long goddamn years, with no support from either of his brothers, with him believing they thought the worst of him, that they were no different in their opinions than their dad, just kicked his rage, sorrow and sadness to another level.

And he kept hitting the bag harder.

No wonder Dalton had left. It was a wonder he'd opted to return.

Fuck, fuck, fuck.

He punched until he couldn't punch any more.

Once Brandt had stopped moving he felt the chill in the air. His lungs burned. His face was wet. Sweat for sure. Maybe some tears. His arms ached. As did his shoulders and his jaw. But not as much as his heart ached. The weight of it had him clinging to the heavy bag.

"Brandt?"

Her sweet voice roused him from the darkness as it always did.

"Yeah," he said hoarsely.

"Come inside and let me patch you up."

"How long you been standing there?"

"Long enough."

"Go back inside, Jess. I'll be there in a sec."

"I'll wait."

"The boys—"

"Are sound asleep." He heard her footsteps on the gravel getting closer. "You gonna tell me what happened tonight?"

I don't know if I can.

Jessie approached him slowly. The beat-the-fuck-out-of-the-heavy-bag sessions were rare these days, but he didn't try and hide the fact he needed them. Jessie accepted everything about him. Even this.

"Brandt?"

"I didn't know. I didn't fucking know."

Her arms came around him. "Come on. I've got you. I've always got you."

She led him into the house. In the bathroom she cleaned his hands, spreading antibiotic ointment on his bleeding and bruised knuckles. As she fixed him up, Brandt started to talk.

When he finished speaking and looked at his wife's tear-stained face, he realized something was missing. Somehow she'd known at least part of the story.

"Jess. This doesn't come as a shock to you?"

"The part where Casper convinces Dalton he's not his kid? Yes. Then again, I shouldn't be shocked by anything that twisted fucker says or does." Jessie met his gaze. "But yes, I knew that Casper had physically abused Dalton."

Brandt fought a surge of anger. "How?"

"From Luke."

"Why the fuck didn't you tell me you knew?"

"Because I wasn't sure if you knew about it."

"Not until after Dalton left. Tell finally told me. Just how long have you known?" Brandt saw the guilt in her eyes. She'd known longer than he had. "Why didn't you tell me?"

"For the same reason you kept it to yourself after you learned the truth from Tell." Jessie placed her hands on his cheeks. "Brandt. I love you. You know that. I was married to Luke and although we had issues, one thing I'd never do is break a confidence."

"Even after he's dead?"

"Even then." Her eyes searched his and Brandt felt his guts twist up all over again. "Up until now. I didn't tell you because I saw what it did to Luke; it ate at him like a damn cancer. He didn't know about the abuse until the day Dalton finally stood up to Casper when Dalton was fourteen years old. Luke was in the machine shed that day, sleeping off a hangover, so neither Casper nor Dalton knew he was there. When he heard the voices and Casper demanded that Dalton drop his pants..." Jessie looked away.

Brandt had to clench his jaw to keep the bile from spilling out.

"Luke thought Casper might've been...sexually abusing Dalton.

Evidently Luke grabbed a shovel and was ready to beat Casper to death. Then he heard Dalton go ballistic and tell Casper he wasn't taking any more beatings—seven years was enough. Then Dalton punched him or something, I really don't know the specifics. I just know that after Dalton took off, Casper was shocked to see Luke. And really shocked when Luke told him if he ever laid a hand on Dalton again, he'd kill him.

"Their relationship wasn't great before that, but it got worse afterward. Luke had so much self-loathing for not protecting Dalton. He knew it'd further crush Dalton if he realized his older brother knew about the abuse. And since Dalton had stood up to Casper that day, in Dalton's mind, he'd finally put a stop to it himself. Luke figured Dalton deserved to think he was strong enough to fight back, so he couldn't ever bring it up with him or anyone else."

"But Luke told you?"

"Yes. And he made me promise that it stayed just between us. Luke always felt it was his job to look out for you guys. To make sure Casper couldn't destroy the love you had for each other and the solidarity Luke had tried so hard to build between the four of you."

Brandt rested his forehead on Jessie's shoulder and fell apart.

When he could breathe without it hurting, when he didn't have any tears left, she kissed him, touched him and stayed strong enough for both of them.

"I'm so fucking tired of all this, Jess."

"I know, baby. Come on. Let's get you in bed."

Once they were in their bedroom, Brandt pulled her into his arms and her body fit against his like it was meant to. "I love you. You're the best thing in my world. And I'm glad that Luke didn't have to shoulder that burden alone. I'm grateful he had you to talk to about it. Thank you."

After a few moments, she said, "You don't talk about Luke with me and that's fine. I just hope you are talking about him with your brothers. He deserves to be remembered and missed."

"Yes, he does."

"You and Tell and Dalton...you will get through this."

Meanwhile, just up the road, Tell sat in the driveway in front of his house for a long time before he climbed out of his truck.

Although Georgia had left the light on in the living room, he expected she'd gone to bed. Which was probably good because he planned to drink a helluva lot of whiskey. Then he could blame the sick feeling on booze.

He shucked his coat and kicked off his boots. He headed directly to the liquor cabinet, pulling out the bottle of Koltiska that Brandt had given him to celebrate Jackson's birth. He remembered missing his baby brother that day. Dalton had been a part of damn near every milestone in Tell's life so it'd seemed...wrong somehow for him to miss that one.

Tell didn't even bother with a shot glass; he just chugged straight from the bottle.

How the fuck could Tell ever look at his father again with anything except disgust? With this...Casper had gone beyond alcoholic asshole unhappy with his lot in life and taking it out on everyone around him. The man was a fucking psychopath. An evil manipulator. A fucking puppet master. An evil sonuvabitch.

Casper McKay had pitted his sons against each other. He wreaked havoc with his own brothers and caused a rift in the family that'd taken years to repair. He verbally abused his wife. All of those things were bad by themselves.

They should've washed their hands of him years ago. Fuck that forgive and forget mindset. Fuck that honor thy father tenet.

There was no doubt in Tell's mind that Dalton was Casper's kid. No doubt. If Dalton had spoken to their mother, he would've learned firsthand that Joan McKay hadn't been unfaithful. Yes, she'd left Casper once. She'd gone to stay with her family in Nebraska. But her aunt and uncle had convinced her that marriage was a lifelong commitment in the eyes of God and advised her to return to her husband and work it out. So she had.

Tell had accidentally overheard that conversation between his mother and mother-in-law one night last year when he'd been up feeding Jackson. They'd talked about their struggles with being more afraid to leave a bad marriage than to stay in it. How long it'd taken to muster up the guts to leave for good.

He thought of Jackson and got that warm surge of love. How could a father do to his own child what Casper had done to Dalton? Plant the seeds that his son wasn't really his son and watch that kid cut himself off from his entire family?

Because he could. Because Casper knew Dalton wouldn't tell anyone. Just like he hadn't told anyone about the years of physical abuse he'd suffered at the hands of their father.

Fury boiled through Tell like hot lava.

What a fucked up mess.

The booze hit him hard. He shoved the bottle out of reach and cradled his head in his hands. If he felt this lost and miserable for

Dalton, how had Dalton felt the last three years?

After Dalton had first left, Tell had reached out to him, but when Dalton's response times got longer, it'd gotten easier to put off making that phone call. If he had any guilt, he'd quickly squashed it with the self-righteous reminder that the phone lines ran both ways.

Dalton had shut himself off and they'd let him. They'd fucking let him.

He'd never felt more like a miserable fucking excuse of a human being as he did in that moment.

The floorboard creaked behind him. "Tell?"

He was too choked up to respond.

"Sweetheart, are you okay?"

He shook his head.

"What's wrong?"

"Everything," he said hoarsely.

A pause. "Talk to me."

"I don't know if I can."

Georgia draped her arms over his shoulders, hugging him from behind. "I'll be right here, holding on to you until you're ready."

Tell took the strength and comfort she offered and began to talk.

After he finished, his beautiful, sweet wife rested her damp cheek against his. No surprise his tenderhearted love had shed tears for Dalton. "I'm sorry. What else can I do for you?"

"You're doin' it. Every day you do it for me. I've got so much...because of him. He's the one who kicked me in the ass to tell you how I felt about you. He all but gave us this house. It's fuckin' killin' me that he's been dealin' with this shit alone." Tell didn't bother to hide his tears. He just closed his eyes, held onto her and let them fall.

"You can be there for him now. You guys can get past this."

"Why would he want to?"

"If he didn't want to, he wouldn't have come back."

"He came back because me'n Brandt didn't give him a choice. He's staying here because of Rory."

"Will Dalton go to her?"

"No. I'm pretty sure he hasn't told her about any of this."

"Tell. Baby. Rory deserves to know."

"That's not my call."

"Then I'm making it mine." Georgia retreated and unplugged her phone from the wall charger. She scrolled through her contact list and held the phone to her ear, sliding a notepad on the counter within reach.

"Georgia. What are you doin'?"

She held up her hand. "Hey, Rielle, it's Georgia McKay. Look, I'm sorry to be calling so late, but I need to get in touch with Rory. No, it's not an emergency. All I can say is it has to do with Dalton. Okay. I'm ready." Georgia scrawled the numbers on the notepad. "Thanks, I appreciate it. I'm sure nothing is wrong, but I wanted to check in with her. Good-night."

Georgia immediately dialed the number.

"Rory? Hey. It's Georgia McKay. Your mom gave me your number. Have you heard from Dalton tonight? He went out with his brothers and Tell just got home. I wondered if Dalton drove to your place afterward." Pause. "Don't worry; they didn't end up in a fistfight. And Tell...he's a bit wrecked after what went down and he says Brandt is the same way. I don't know how Dalton is faring, or if he planned to call you, but I figured you'd want to know. Uh-huh. As far as I know. I'd start there first. If Dalton needs anything, please call us right away—no matter what time it is. Thanks, Rory." She hung up.

"Why'd you do that?"

Georgia set down the phone. "Whether or not Dalton tells her is his choice. But if they're involved on the level I believe they are, it's also Rory's right to know if he needs her. It's her right to be there for him."

He closed his eyes when she wrapped herself around him.

"Come to bed."

"In a bit. I should call my mom. She needs to know—"

"And you need some time to process this. Besides, didn't you promise Dalton you wouldn't bring it up with her?"

"No. We said we wouldn't bring it up with Dad. I'll honor that. But I won't keep this from her."

"You shouldn't. But Joan will have plenty of sleepless nights after you talk to her. So let her have the rest of tonight."

Chapter Twenty-Five

The porch light was off so Rory knew Dalton wasn't expecting her.

She'd gotten a little freaked out by Georgia's phone call. Whatever happened must've been bad.

Why hadn't he reached out to her?

Because he's always dealt with family stuff on his own. Rory wondered if he'd ever told his brothers or even his mother how often their dad had taken a strap to him.

She remembered the first time she'd found him after Casper had finished with him. Dalton had tried to blame his red-rimmed eyes and wet face on hayfield dust, but she'd known he'd been crying. She'd never seen the marks, he'd never talked about it, but she had seen how Dalton winced sometimes when he sat down.

Except the summer he'd grown several inches. They'd met by the creek and she'd been shocked by Dalton's giddiness. Now that he was bigger than his dad, the man no longer had the advantage and the beatings were over. Rory had hidden her horror at hearing the abuse Dalton had endured for years—she wondered if he remembered the rapid-fire way he'd blurted the whole thing out, almost like he was in shock.

She recalled crawling into her bed and crying herself to sleep. When her mom had asked her what was wrong, she couldn't tell her.

What if Dalton didn't want her here?

Tough shit.

Rory marched up to the door and banged on it.

No response.

She banged louder. "I know you're in there."

The door opened. "Rory? What're you doin' here?"

She ducked under the arm blocking the doorway before he could shut her out. "I didn't hear from you today."

"Yeah, well, sorry. I had shit goin' on."

"Since I'm here, let's swap 'how was your day, dear?' stories." Rory kicked off her boots and dropped her outerwear into a pile before she headed for the kitchen.

"You can't just show up at someone's house at ten-thirty at night without warning."

She whirled around. "Why not? You do it to me all the time."

Dalton stared at her.

Sweet Lord. His eyes were so...haunted. She automatically curled her arms around his waist and pressed herself against him. "I missed you, okay? Is that so wrong?"

Then Dalton squeezed her so tightly tears rushed to her eyes. "Not wrong at all. I was needing...missing you too."

The fact he admitted he needed her, yet he hadn't reached out to her, cut a little. She tipped her head back to look at him. "You know you can just call me up to chat about stuff any old time."

Dalton pushed her hair back from her face. "Who called you and said I might need to chat about...stuff?"

Rory considered lying, but Dalton should know his family was worried about him. "Georgia."

His eyes turned wary. "What'd she say?"

"Just that you had a meeting with your brothers and maybe you'd need someone to talk to. Which I took as the secret McKay code that you really needed sex. And you know I'm all over that and all over you whenever possible because you're a beast in the sack."

He smiled. But it was a sad smile. "Will you believe me if I admit I'm not in the mood?"

"I can see that. So what were you doing before I got here?"

"Spacing out." He brushed his lips across hers. "I'm fine. You don't gotta hang around like I'm on suicide watch."

"Shoot. I was really looking forward to being all heroic by saving your life and shit. Way to wreck my night, cowboy."

Dalton chuckled. "I see you're in one of them moods."

"So you gonna let me stick around?"

"You gonna be a pain in the ass while I'm tryin' to watch my show?" he volleyed back.

"Probably. Are we watching porn?"

"You wish. I DVR'd the Universal Poker Tour."

"Hate to point it out, McKay, but that *is* porn for you."

"Busted." He led her to the couch.

When she sat next to him, he grabbed her legs and draped them across his lap. He wrapped his arm around her and pulled her close. "I am glad you're here, jungle girl."

For the next hour Dalton gave running commentary on every hand. Pointing out what he felt were mistakes and how he would've played it differently.

"You know...have you ever told me why you quit the poker circuit?"

"Most people assume I quit because I lost my ass."

"I'm not most people, Dalton. But that's not the case, is it? You let people think that."

"Yep."

"Why?"

"It's easier than tellin' them the truth."

"Which is what?"

He paused. "I made a fuck ton of money and quit while I was ahead."

Rory shifted to straddle his lap. She held his face in her hands, forcing him to look at her. "A fuck ton? Is that an official financial term?"

"It is according to my accountant."

"I'm not asking this because I want a detailed financial spreadsheet, but there's one thing we haven't talked about. The fact you don't have an official job. You said in the last couple of years you were a logger, and a hunting guide. Now you've applied for the elk farm. None of which will make you rich, and yet you don't seem to be struggling to make ends meet while you're waiting for that decision to be handed down."

He closed his eyes. "Do we really have to do this now?"

"Yes. And I'm not asking in an official capacity."

Dalton remained quiet for a minute or so. "The truth is, I've got enough cash and investments that I don't need a job."

"For how long?"

Then those blue, blue eyes hooked hers. "Forever. Since I played my cards right."

Rory groaned. "I'm ignoring your puntastic-ness to ask if you're serious?"

"Yep. I can pick and choose what I want to do because the job interests me. Granted, I can't buy a mansion in Beverly Hills or a fleet of sports cars or a yacht, but I'm comfortable."

"Why didn't I know this?"

"Talkin' about it smacks too much of bragging. I got to this point by havin' a successful run at poker for about four years prior to leaving here. I didn't blow the money on booze and broads—well, not all of it." He smirked. "Even though I was winning, I had a budget and I stuck to it." He shrugged. "Getting paid once a year when I was ranching meant

I was already used to stretching out my money. Early on Jack Donohue gave me good financial advice. Then Chase recommended an investment guy and he's diversified my initial investments. Now I'm able to live off the income."

"Who knows this?"

"My banker. My accountant. My investment guys." He twirled a section of her hair around his finger. "And now you."

"But... Why don't you—"

"Tell people that I'm not a lazy drifter, picking up odd jobs here and there and shirking my ranching responsibilities, but I'm independently...comfortable?"

"Yes!"

Dalton tugged her closer by her hair and brushed those full lips over hers. "Because I don't care what people think of me, Rory. I spent way too many years tryin' to live up to family reputations and expectations. Now the only expectations I live up to are my own."

Here was her opening. "Is that what happened with your brothers tonight?"

"I don't wanna talk about it, especially not when I have a gorgeous woman on my lap who offered to take my mind off my troubles with hot sex."

"You turned me down, remember?"

"That was then. Now I'm thinkin' a nekkid dose of sexy you is exactly what I need." He cupped her ass and warned, "Hang on," before he stood. He set her on her feet and kissed her in the sweetly seductive way guaranteed to melt her resistance.

Rory threaded her fingers through his and followed him into his bedroom.

He reached for the bedside lamp but she stayed his hand. "I think the darkness fits tonight."

"But I love lookin' at you when you come."

She pushed his T-shirt up and he yanked it off. Then her mouth and hands were all over his warm chest. Her fingers mapping every ridge of his abdomen. Her mouth following the curve of his pectorals. She loved his chest hair. The feel of it on her face. The scent. She rubbed against it like a cat, filling her senses with him.

And while she licked and tasted and nibbled, he ran his hands through her hair. From scalp to tip. Dalton could be so gentle or he could grab a fistful and be forceful. When she used her teeth, that forceful side appeared.

He held her head in place and said, "I love your mouth on my nipples."

Rory tortured him and those sexy male grunts and groans told her he enjoyed every second. While her mouth focused on his incredible chest, her hands roamed everywhere else. Over his beefy biceps and strong forearms, broad shoulders and muscular back. His masculine form wasn't only powerful, it was beautiful.

His hands cradled her head and tipped it back. "Aurora, did you just growl at me?"

"Probably." She twisted out of his hold and sank her teeth into the meaty slab of his pectorals. "Because I love, love, love this body of yours."

"Good to know—sweet Jesus, you're killin' me with that hot little tongue."

Rory's fingers inched to the waistband of his sweatpants. One tug of the string and they were down around his ankles. His cock bounced against his belly. She cupped his balls, playing with them before her fingers enclosed the shaft.

Dalton hissed.

She moved her hand up and down, adding the slight twist at the head that made him crazy. Her tongue traced his collarbone from the hollow of his throat to the ball of his shoulder.

Then his hands were in her hair, his mouth taking control as he kissed her.

His passion could be overwhelming at times. But this was sweet heat. A need for tenderness. Rory fell into the kiss so completely her hand stopped moving on his cock.

Dalton finally released her lips. He whispered, "I need your skin beneath my hands, Aurora."

She managed to disentangle from him and stepped back. In less than thirty seconds she was naked.

Immediately those work-roughened hands were on her.

Her body became a mass of gooseflesh, quivering from his touch. "As long as it's dark and I can't see your face, hands and knees on the center of the bed, beautiful."

"While I love how you think you've got a say in this, you don't." Rory put her hands on his chest and shoved with all her might.

Dalton hit the mattress and laughed. "Okay."

"Now how about *you* make yourself comfy in the center of the bed."

"Are you sure you don't want me to turn the light on?"

"No lights." Rory crawled up his body. She bent her head and licked his cock from bottom to top.

His entire body jerked.

She laughed and tongued the tip, precisely on the sweet spot. Then she slipped that hot hard shaft into her mouth and held it there.

"That wasn't what I was expecting, but damn do I love your mouth on my dick."

She hummed around the thick meatiness of him and he jackknifed.

Rory eased back, an inch at a time until the wide crown rested on her bottom teeth. She suckled the tip and released him. Once again she placed her hands on his chest and shoved him back. "Behave, McKay, or I'll spank you."

That comment caused his entire body to go rigid.

She scooted up, hanging above him, hoping to see his face. But the blackness was absolute. "Hey, I'm sorry. I was kidding." She found his mouth and kissed him until he relaxed and kissed her back. Then she scattered kisses along his jawline, stopping at his ear. "You know I'd never do that without your consent."

"I know." His hands skated up and down her back. "It just caught me off-guard after the stuff I talked about with my brothers tonight."

"Do you want me to stop?"

"No, baby, I want you to make me forget."

That broke her heart a little. "I'll take that challenge." Rory planted kisses straight down his body from his chin to his cock. She jacked his shaft while she sucked his balls. Then she licked that stiff pole up one side and down the other. She swept her thumb across his anus as her head bobbed.

"Stop. I love that but I can't take much more before I blow."

"What if I want you to blow?" Rory nuzzled his groin, the musky scent familiar and it always made her wet.

"Then you'll swing that ass of yours around and sit on my face so I can blow your mind while you're blowing mine."

She pushed up onto all fours and zigzagged her tongue from his left hipbone to his right. "I want you in me, Dalton." She poised herself above his pelvis and impaled herself on his cock.

Her head fell back and she released a long groan. "I'll never get used to how amazing this feels." She rode him a few more strokes and then Dalton reached for her.

He palmed her breasts. Caressed her nipples. Followed the contour of her belly with deliberate sensual strokes until he reached where their bodies were joined. He pressed his thumb into the creamy center of her, swirling over her clit.

"More."

"I like that word." Dalton pushed up on one arm and latched onto her nipple while working her into a writhing mass.

Rory kept a slow and steady rhythm as she braced her hands on Dalton's thighs.

"You got me so riled up I'm hanging on by a thread," he said. "What do you need to get there?"

"Your mouth on my nipple." She groaned when his hot mouth enclosed the tip. "Move faster on my clit. Yes."

He thrust his pelvis up, thumb flickering madly on the exact spot. His tongue performed the identical rhythm on her nipple.

There wasn't a long build-up. Rory was lost in his mouth and his hands and then zing, there it was. The sweet throb that sent her body rocketing. Her hands squeezed his quads. She gasped when Dalton's teeth scored the stiff peak of her nipple.

Then his hands were on her hips, pushing her higher and pulling her back down. "Squeeze me," he panted.

Rory angled forward to hold onto his shoulders.

"Right. Like. That." He slammed into her hard one last time and his body shuddered with his release.

After a bit, Dalton fell back onto the mattress and he dragged Rory down with him. Maybe it made her a sap, but she liked that he didn't pull out right away. He kept their bodies joined as long as possible.

She connected their mouths in a deep soul kiss. She loved kissing him, but he needed extra kisses and touches tonight and it was such a joy to give them to him.

He swept her hair aside and placed his lips on the pulse pounding in her throat. "You are sexy as fuck and I'm lucky you're here with me tonight."

Rory felt that melting sensation.

His callused hands floated over her naked back. He kissed her temple. "Told you a dose of your sexy ways was the perfect antidote to my crappy night."

"I'm sorry you had to deal with crappy family stuff."

"They wanted an explanation on why I've stayed away. So I gave them one."

"What did you say?"

His fingers stilled for a moment before resuming again. "I told them about Casper tracking me down five days after the wedding fiasco."

"Five days? You saw him the same day we talked?"

"It was a few hours after that. And in that thirty minute conversation with him, my life changed."

Rory lifted her head to look into his eyes, but he'd turned his face away from her.

This wasn't good.

"Was that why you were—"

"Gone the next day? Yep. Had I planned on leavin' before that conversation? No."

"And you never told anyone what happened?"

"Not until tonight."

She disconnected their bodies and covered them with the comforter. "Sorry. I was getting cold." She snuggled into him. "If you want to tell me, fine. But if you'd rather not discuss it, I'm fine with that too."

"You probably oughta know."

With her cheek on his chest, Rory felt his heart rate pick up.

Then he began to talk. Relaying the conversation in a tone so dead and flat her stomach hurt.

And when he finished talking, her heart ached.

"Shocked you into silence. That's gotta be a first."

Don't be flip. I can't imagine the level of hurt you're feeling. How isolated and alone you must've felt.

"Rory?" he murmured.

"Sorry. I'm stunned. I don't even know what to say."

Dalton kissed her forehead. "It's okay."

But it wasn't okay.

The longer she lay there, the more upset she became. When she couldn't hold back her anger and sorrow, she untangled herself from his arms and rolled across the bed, setting her feet on the floor.

Then the tears came full force. She had to clap her hand over her mouth to keep from crying out. But she couldn't stop her body from shaking.

"Rory? What's wrong?" Dalton flipped on the light. Then he was crouched in front of her. "What... Are you crying?"

"Yes I'm crying."

He waited for her to explain.

"You can't tell me something that fucking heartbreaking and just expect me to roll over and go to sleep." She covered her face with her hands. It was so wrong and she hurt for him so bad.

"This is exactly why I didn't tell you. This is the reason I didn't tell anyone."

"No wonder Georgia said Tell wasn't all right when he got home from talking to you."

"That's me. Mary fucking sunshine. Spreading love all over the goddamned place. My brothers couldn't even look me in the eyes when they left the bar. And now you're bawling in my bed." He stood abruptly. "Just stop. I can't stand to have your pity."

She leapt to her feet. "My pity? That's why you think I'm crying? Because I feel sorry for you? That's not it. Not even fucking close."

"Then why?"

"It's because of guilt! From the time we were kids I knew that your dad was hurting you."

Dalton winced.

"I did nothing, Dalton. *Nothing.* I could've told my mom or one of your brothers or even your mom but I didn't. And to find out he's still fucking with you? He's still bent on reducing you to that scared little kid? It kills me. It kills me and enrages me and if that man were in this room right now I'd tear him to pieces. So I'm back to crying. That's all I've been able to do for you is to weep like some helpless little girl. Then and now."

"Baby. Please. Stop."

"I can't. You've deserved better from everyone around you including me. How you can even look at me..."

Dalton's hands framed her face. "I look at you because I love you. That you're crying for me shreds me inside. To know that crazy wild friend, a tough girl who refused to cry after you sliced open your knee, cried for me all those years ago? That grabs me by the throat and makes it hard to breathe."

"You were always so tough, McKay. I didn't want you to think I was a wussy girl so you'd stop coming around."

"Nothin' would've stopped me from coming around. I acted tough. A front I kept up for years. Probably why I picked so goddamn many fights. I had to prove I was tough enough to win. And if I couldn't win, then I showed them I was tough enough to take whatever was dished out.

"Nothin' you would've done back then could've changed anything. Do you hear me? I stood there every single time he brought out the strap. Until the day I didn't." His thumbs wicked away her tears. "You were there that day. I was so damn proud of myself."

"The beatings stopped. But that mean mouth of his didn't, did it?"

"No. And it'll always be like that with him."

"So are you done with him? Has sharing the truth with your brothers about what an unforgiveable asshole Casper McKay is freed you to walk away from him?"

"It freed me years ago. But knowing that past history between him and me, can you see why it was so easy for me to believe his claim that I wasn't his son?"

Rory's eyes searched his. "That's the question, isn't it? Do you think you're his son?"

"Either way, I don't care. I spent the last three years comin' to terms with who I am. Not as a McKay, not as a rancher, not as a gambler, but as a man on my own. Once I liked that guy staring back at me in the mirror every morning, I knew it didn't matter."

Dalton took a step back.

That's when she noticed a half-packed suitcase behind him. "Dalton? Why is your suitcase out?"

A guilty look crossed his face. "I was heading to Montana this weekend. There's some stuff I need to get."

"And you also want to avoid your brothers, don't you?"

He jammed his hand through his hair. "Yeah, that was part of it."

Rory marched up to him. "You dropped this on them tonight and then you run off the next day? How is that fair? Maybe you've had years to come to terms with the idea you're not Casper's son, but they haven't."

"Which means it'll take them more than a few hours to process it, Rory. Me goin' away for a couple of days ain't gonna matter."

"You don't know that. You're assuming a lot."

"So are you."

"Are you telling me to butt out?"

Dalton touched her face. "No, baby, I'm not. I'd never do that. This affects you too. It affects us."

"Then when did you plan to tell me you were leaving?" When he looked away from her, she knew. "On your way out of town." Despite her fury, she kept her tone icy. "You say you've changed? Bullshit. You're still running away."

"I'm not!"

"Yes, you are."

"Goddammit, I'm not."

Was he trying to convince her? Or himself?

Rory got right in his face. "Don't do this. Stay here and deal with it. Stay here with me and let me help you deal with it."

"Rory—"

"You say you love me? Prove it. Don't go." She wrapped herself around him. "Stay. Please. Grab that suitcase and come home with me. Let me take care of you."

He hugged her so tight she couldn't breathe. "Okay."

Chapter Twenty-Six

Dalton hadn't seen much of his brothers in the week that'd passed since his...confession or whatever the hell it was. He'd talked to them both on the phone. That'd been easier than a face-to-face meeting, especially since Brandt and Tell were still in shock. He understood it wasn't that his brothers didn't believe him; they just didn't want to believe it.

Those conversations were the first in the past two months they hadn't asked if he'd be visiting the rehab hospital.

His sweet, wonderful, thoughtful sisters-in-law had each stopped by in the guise of dropping off a decent home cooked meal for the lone McKay bachelor. He hadn't minded that Jessie hugged him a lot. He'd held it together when she'd broken down about Brandt's reaction after he'd left the bar. While part of him was relieved to hear Brandt's reaction in front of him had been more about saving face until he could unleash his anger in private, another part hated that his brother was dealing with any guilt.

And Rory...after she'd begged him not to go to Montana, something had shifted in their relationship. But he hated to think the change was because she felt sorry for him. And asking why she wanted to spend all their free time together when she'd been so insistent on showing him she had a full life without him, smacked of desperation.

So this official business meeting with Rory gave Dalton a case of nerves. He needed this elk permit. After all he'd been through with his brothers, he knew that he'd never return to ranching with them. As much as he'd harped on honesty between them, Dalton couldn't tell Rory that the only reason he'd applied for the permit was because of her. If she wasn't living here he wouldn't have bothered.

There were a number of ways she could take that—none of his explanations sounded good in his head so he'd be better off not giving voice to them.

And he had to take care today to separate the Rory in his bed from Rory the WNRC employee who was evaluating him. Her evaluation wasn't as a person. She wasn't judging him as a lover, or a lifelong mate, but an acceptable risk for the test program.

He'd left the gate open and parked off to the side where she could see his vehicle. He hadn't unloaded the ATV he'd borrowed from Tell. Rory would need to unload hers and he figured he'd seem overeager if he was ready and helped her without asking. Rory was independent that way.

The wind began to blow. He checked his cell phone to see if he'd missed a call. Might seem like Rory was late, but he'd been twenty minutes early.

The government vehicle bounced into view and pulled up beside him.

There was a moment of awkwardness when they faced each other. But then Rory said, "This is ridiculous," and leaned in, giving him a quick peck on the mouth. "We're adults. We can be professional about this."

"Agreed. So at the risk of offending your professional status, do you need help unloading?"

"No. I've got it."

"Cool."

They were ready to go at the same time.

"Do you have a preference what I show you first?" Dalton asked.

"Natural boundaries. Then where you'd supplement with fencing. Proposed feed and water sites. And if there's a section not covered in snow, I'd like to look at the native grass and vegetation, although I realize it's not an accurate representation this time of year."

"All right. Since I know the terrain I'll lead, but if you have any questions or need me to stop or slow down, just honk."

"Will do. But a slower pace is better for me."

After adjusting their clothing, heading into the wind, Dalton started down the easiest path. He tried to catalogue the area as Rory might. It did appear a little desolate in this section. No cover at all. Rocky. There was enough vegetation in the summer to run maybe twenty head of cattle but he wasn't sure what that translated to as far as head of elk. But this wasn't the area where he'd concentrate the feeding grounds.

As if she'd read his mind, Rory honked. He stopped and she pulled up alongside of him.

"In your application, you didn't plan to utilize this area for anything?"

"No," he shouted over the engines. "Too close to the road. I'd add higher fencing, but where I envision the habitat starting is down a little farther."

"Thanks. Let's go there."

When they arrived at the first section, about halfway into the piece of land, with the natural boundaries, they left the ATVs and walked.

Rory didn't say much. She took out a small notebook and wrote in it. She'd ask a question or two. Do the silent survey thing and they'd move on. Seemed they walked most of the bottom half of the property. She was very thorough—he'd give her that.

The wind kicked up and snow started coming down harder. Pretty snow—huge flakes that swirled like a white tornado in the gusts of wind.

She moved closer to him. She'd worn coveralls and a heavy jacket, just like he had, but even three layers wasn't much protection. "Getting nasty out here. Let's head back."

The trek back to the ATVs was uphill and straight into the wind, making conversation impossible. By the time they reached the vehicles they needed to catch their breath.

Dalton faced away from the wind, resting his backside on the back end. He tugged Rory against him. "Lemme be your windbreak until we're ready to go."

"Thanks."

Maybe it made him a sap, or stupid, but it felt right in that moment. Holding Rory while the snow blew around them. She anchored him in a way he'd never imagined.

She stepped back. "Okay, my lungs stopped burning."

"Mine too. I'll lead the way."

Even with all the stops on the way down, it still took them longer to get back up to the flat land.

After they'd loaded their respective four-wheelers, he said, "Wanna sit in my truck while your vehicle warms up before you head back?"

"That'd be great. I have some more questions anyway."

Rory ditched the hat and the hood before she loosened the scarf and pulled off her gloves. "Man. I didn't know we were supposed to get a snowstorm today."

"We're not." He removed his gloves and grabbed the thermos from the bench seat. He twisted the cup off the top and unscrewed the lid.

"Is that...hot coffee?"

"Yes ma'am. Don't know how hot it is anymore." Dalton poured the steaming liquid in the cup and passed it to her. "Have the first sip. We'll share."

Rory tipped the cup and drank. Then she moaned. "Still hot enough. God. This is heaven."

"Few things are better than a cup of hot coffee after you've been out workin' in the cold."

"True." She gulped the remainder and passed the empty cup back. "Your turn."

He poured himself a cup and couldn't help but sigh after the first sip. He reached over and cranked the heat higher. "You said you had more questions?"

"Biggest one is why do you think you can keep elk within the boundaries?"

"Because they're dumb. Give 'em food and water in the same place and they'll stick around. No different than cattle really."

"What about when the male elk are in the rut? Think the bulls will go looking across other pastures for more cows to breed?"

"I don't think so. The way to keep that from happening is limiting the number of bulls. Given the size of the farm, I'd say between forty and fifty elk is the maximum number for the herd. Then cycle the bulls out after two years. Let someone else grow bulls for size and horns. I'm more interested in keeping a healthy herd and that means calves. Isn't the survival rate of an elk calf in the wild under ten percent, given the number of predators?"

Rory nodded. "The whole let-nature-run-its-course argument isn't valid. Especially not in Wyoming. The state has been supplementing feed for the Yellowstone and Teton herds since the 1930s."

"You know a lot about this." He held up his hand. "Don't take that the wrong way. I know you've got a master's degree, but to be honest, I wasn't exactly sure what your degrees were in. Now I understand why your boss selected you for the project. But you oughta be workin' in Yellowstone or the Tetons. Hell, you oughta be running those programs."

She looked at him strangely. Fidgeted. "Can I have another cup of coffee?"

Why had she hedged? "Sure." He poured and handed it over.

"Thanks." After she took a drink, she asked, "So what will you do if another section of land is selected for this program?"

"I've been lookin' at land in Montana. My buddy Boden is one of those naturalists. He doesn't stock elk on his hunting preserve, which is just a backwards way of thinking when he already feeds the damn animals. It'd be better for his business if he could guarantee an elk to the guys who pay the astronomical out of state hunting fees."

"You'd have an outlet to peddle your elk flesh?" she asked with a grin.

"Yep." Dalton grabbed her hand. "So it's all on your shoulders whether or not I make this venture work here. If it's a no go..."

"What?"

He shrugged and hated himself for the lie that was about to come out. "Then maybe I'll have to go."

Rory didn't get indignant and warn him she hated ultimatums. A shrewd look entered her eyes and vanished. "Well. Then let's hope your land measures up in the end."

"Any chance you can tell me who I'm competing against?"

"No chance. But I will say I'm at the tail end of these inspections."

"Saved the best for last, huh?"

She laughed.

"Are you comin' over tonight?"

"I hadn't planned on it. Why?"

"Because I didn't see you last night and I'm missin' you."

"Dalton—"

"It's fine, sugarplum, if you've got other plans. Your loss that you won't get to see the romantic surprise I had for you."

"What kind of romantic surprise?"

"The usual kind. I tell you I've got a surprise and refuse to tell you what it is."

Rory laid her hand on his cheek. "You are a horrible tease. But I'll be there."

He pressed kisses up the inside of her wrist. "Drive safe."

Dalton followed her vehicle out the gate and locked it behind him, wondering what he'd been thinking, promising her a surprise.

He had a few hours to figure it out.

Rory had just finished her last inspection of the day and was finishing up notes, when her phone rang with an unfamiliar number. "May I please speak to Aurora Wetzler?"

"This is Rory."

"Ah, so I see you did list that as your preferred name. This is Lonna Davis, administrative coordinator from the Cooperative Ecosystem Studies Unit in Missoula. We received your application for the opening in the Ag management division. We wondered when would be a good time to set up a phone interview with the CESU director?"

Holy. Shit. Stay calm. She'd sent in that application four months ago. Since she hadn't heard anything, she'd assumed the position had been filled. "I imagine the director is busy, so what would work best with his schedule?"

"He's free Thursday afternoon. Around three o'clock?"

"That would work."

"Excellent. Is this the best number to reach you?"

"Yes."

"If anything changes I'll be sure to let you know."

"Thank you so much."

"You're welcome."

After Rory hung up she had to recheck the caller ID to make sure she hadn't been dreaming. Yep. Montana area code.

A phone interview was huge. She hadn't made it past the application status with any of the jobs she'd applied for in the last six months.

And now she had two possibilities.

She'd gotten a callback from the BLM in Cody, which she hadn't expected. She had an in-person there next week—barring any road-closing snowstorms. So Dalton bringing up her qualifications for a job in Yellowstone would've been the perfect time to tell him about the interview. But then he'd made that crack about leaving Sundance if he didn't get awarded a permit, and she was glad she'd kept her mouth shut.

Chances were slim she'd get the Yellowstone job anyway.

She'd looked at the job description for the assistant's position in Buffalo and decided not to apply. Although the fulltime job paid well, it was close to what she faced every day at the WNRC—busywork that had nothing to do with her degrees.

As much as she appreciated that Dillon had put in a good word for her with the Wyoming State Parks in Sheridan, even if she got a callback from them she'd wonder how much of that was due to Dillon's influence.

But this CESU job...she'd applied for that one on her own. So if she made it past the phone interview she might have a chance at scoring her dream job.

Rory couldn't help but squeal with excitement. But it would be nice to have someone to share her excitement with.

"No offense, Dalton, but this is not what I'd call a romantic surprise."

"What? A few games of ping pong will get your blood pumping." He bounced back and forth at the end of the ping pong table like a professional tennis player awaiting a serve. "It sure does mine."

Rory lobbed the ball at him. "You don't need any additional stimulus in the blood pumping department, Mr. McKay."

Dalton grinned. "Come on baby. Show me whatcha got."

"I suck at this."

"No, you don't. You did great when we played it on the Wii."

"Not the same. It's like believing I can be a rock star because I shredded on Guitar Hero."

He lifted a brow. "Shredded? Woman, I totally wiped the floor with you. High score, remember?"

Rory shook her paddle at him. "That's what I mean. You are so competitive!"

"Winning competitions is the best way to prove my manliness. To show you that I can protect you and provide for you." He grinned. "And rock your world with a bitchin' power ballad that makes you wanna get nekkid with me."

"Oh. My. God."

He laughed. "So we playin' this or what?" He crouched and spun his paddle. "I'll even let you serve."

"Since I'm pretty sure I'm gonna lose, I'll only play if I get to pick our next activity." When she saw the glimmer in his eyes, she amended, "An activity with our clothes on."

"Shoot, sugarplum, that ain't no fun. Winner should get to choose."

"Fine. Winner's choice. Let's get this over with."

Dalton pitched Rory the ball. "Serve it up."

The first game didn't last long; Dalton won by four points.

He said, "Best two out of three?"

The second game...Rory won by two points. She acted surprised. "Wow. We're tied up. How'd that happen?"

That's when Dalton got suspicious.

And his suspicions were justified when Rory creamed him in the third game by thirteen points.

Her victory dance was short-lived. She had six feet three inches of bested cowboy in her face.

"What the hell was that?"

Rory smirked. "Think you're the only one who can bluff, McKay?"

The muscle in his jaw worked as he stared at her.

She hadn't thought this new improved Dalton would be a sore loser. "What's wrong?"

"Didn't expect that kind of sneaky-assed behavior from you, Rory." The hard line of his mouth softened when he grinned. "Which is why it's so awesome!" He picked her up and spun her around. "You totally had me snowed. I might make a poker player out of you yet."

She snorted.

"So tell me how you're so damn good at ping pong."

"The bar I worked at in Laramie had a ping pong table. And since I bartended there for four years...I got pretty good. Used to have guys demand to play me for free shots."

"How many free shots did you give away?"

"One. But the guy was a tourist and had been a championship ping pong player in China or something. So I gave him a whole bunch of shots, got him drunk and challenged him to a rematch." She buffed her nails on her shirt. "I beat him. Not the most stellar example of fairness, but hey, I won and that's all that mattered to me."

Dalton laughed. Then he kissed her. "I love that you constantly surprise me."

"Speaking of surprises...how did you come up with playing ping pong as a romantic surprise for me?"

"Lucky guess?"

Rory poked him in the chest. "Try again."

"An odd whim?"

Another two pokes to his chest as she shook her head. "Tell me."

"Here's the truth. I'd intended to take you out for a nice dinner at Field's. Renting a private room, hiring one of them fiddle players that walks around."

"You mean a strolling violinist?"

"Yeah. Whatever. Anyway, I thought it'd be romantic, sharing a candlelight four course meal, champagne, roses, chocolate..."

"But?"

His gaze hooked hers. "But since you inspected my land today, I worried all that hearts-and-flowers shit might look like a bribe. Not only to you but to others in the community and I'd never put your professionalism at risk." He blushed but didn't look away. "So I brought you to the community center for a game of table tennis, an activity which ain't romantic and you'd never mistake as a bribe. Especially since you whupped my ass."

The man was an idiot. A sweet idiot, but an idiot nonetheless. And she was so insanely in love with him it scared her.

"So since you won our battle, you choose what happens next."

Rory ran her palms down his shoulders, his biceps, his forearms. On the way back up her fingers traced the cut muscles and well defined bulk. She loved seeing him in sleeveless black T-shirts, the tighter the better. He worked hard on this body, he oughta show it off. She curled her hands around the back of his neck and leaned in to rub her mouth across his pectoral. And she got that rush of want from his scent—laundry soap, sweat, deodorant and his underlying musk.

"Rory, you keep doin' that and I won't be able to walk out of here."

"I can't help it. Sometimes I just look at all this—" her hands slowly cruised down his chest, stopping on his abdomen above his pelvis, "—and I'm blown away that it's all mine."

Dalton's fingers on her chin lifted her face to look into her eyes. "Are you admitting you own me every bit as much as I own you?"

Her this-is-just-sex side didn't even bother to speak up anymore. Nor did it lodge a protest when she said, "Yes."

"Need to get you home. Now," he said in that low, dangerously sexy growl.

She swept her lips over his in a fleeting kiss. "Hold that thought. I won so I get to pick the next activity." Took every ounce of restraint to step back instead of closer.

"I hope it's wrestling."

She laughed. "Nope. But it does begin with a W."

"There ain't a pool in there so it doesn't have to do with water."

"It's weight lifting. You lift; I get to watch."

"Why in the hell would you wanna watch me lift weights? Lots of grunting, straining, sweating." His eyes narrowed. "Get that look off your face, jungle girl. It's not even close to sex and it sure ain't sexy."

"I'll be the judge of that, won't I? It'll be interesting to see you pump something besides me for a change."

So she'd never actually watched a lover working out with weights before. Oh, sure, she'd seen guys lifting weights in the gym. Quite a few of them had amazingly hot bodies, but it hadn't affected her beyond her appreciation for the strength and beauty of a buffed up masculine form.

But watching Dalton pumping iron? Whole. Different. Story. Seeing his biceps and triceps flexing and glistening with sweat. Taking in every inch of his bulky forearms. Seeing the strain across his shoulders beneath his T-shirt as he pulled on the weight and pulley thing. Watching the V ripple in his quads as he performed squats and that also caused the thick bulge in his calf to contract.

Wasn't like Dalton paid attention to her attentiveness to him. He remained focused on each exercise and when it ended he'd move to the next one. He didn't watch his weightlifting form in the mirror like she'd seen so many other gym rats do. No admiring smug glances as he stared at himself.

She knew he'd started working out in hotel fitness facilities as a way to stave off boredom before poker tournaments. It wasn't like

Dalton was overly muscular with biceps bigger than her waist or his own neck. He needed that strength in his logging job. He didn't work out to impress anyone, although that cut, ripped and toned body was an impressive benefit. For her.

"Christ, Rory, stop doin' that."

Her gaze moved from his butt to his eyes. "Stop doing what?"

"Licking your lips."

"Uh, I wouldn't be licking my chops, cowboy, if you didn't have the very finest chops I've ever seen."

"And all the times we've been nekkid together, what? You weren't lookin' at me?" He set down the dumbbells and perched on the edge of the weight bench.

"I look at you plenty. Touch you plenty." She sauntered forward.

"I still don't get the point of this. You've been watchin' me lifting for half an hour."

Rory straddled his legs and lowered herself onto his lap.

Dalton's hands circled her hips to steady her. "Whoa, sugarplum, what are you doin'?"

She licked a rivulet of sweat from the hollow of his throat up to the edge of his jaw. "Having a little taste of you."

"So does that mean we're done here?"

"No." She sucked on his earlobe before she blew in his ear. "It's late. We're probably the only ones left in the whole place."

"Which means it's time for us to go home."

"I can feel you getting hard," she breathed against his damp skin. She inhaled a lungful of him and sighed. "You smell delicious. Your muscles are so pumped up right now. I bet you could lift a small truck, couldn't you?"

"Uh...yeah. I guess."

She slipped her hand between them and lightly stroked his nipple as she strung kisses down the column of his throat. "Just looking at you gets me hot. I suspected it'd be sexy watching you pumping iron, but I had no idea it'd make me so wet." Rory sank her teeth into the warm, salty section of skin where shoulder curved into neck. "So very, very wet and ready."

"Woman, unless you want me to pin you to this weight bench and fuck you, you'd better take it down a notch."

Rory pulled his hair, yanking his head back when he attempted to nudge her away from his neck. "I was thinking more of you fucking me in the storage closet. But this weight bench will work." She nibbled the edge of his jaw up to his ear. "Or even the ping pong table."

He groaned when her lips hit the spot that made him shiver. "You are—"

"A master at great ideas. I know." She flicked her tongue across the spot just to feel him shudder again. "So where's it gonna be, power lifter?"

"Closet." With his hands on her ass, he pushed upright and carried her to the far corner of the room. He set her on the floor and she turned to open the door. Once they were crammed into the tiny space, she didn't bother to turn on the light.

The storage closet held the usual cleaning supplies and stacks of folded towels on the shelving.

"How'd you know about this place?" Dalton asked against the back of her neck.

"Found it when I was looking for something for my yoga class. God, do that again."

"This?" He used his teeth on her nape.

"Yes... Wait."

"No waiting. Jeans off. Panties off."

So much for being in control.

No, you do have control. "Your shirt comes off too."

She only managed to get naked from the waist down before Dalton's hard, damp muscle-bound body was crowding her.

"I'm fucking you against the wall, baby."

His deep voice vibrated from her ear straight to her clit.

"But first, since you've been teasing me about how wet you are—" his big hand cupped her mound and two fingers slid down her pussy to her opening, "—I'd better make sure." Then he plunged his fingers inside her. In and out. Twice. "Fuck yeah. You are dripping wet for me."

Rory drifted into that floaty space, where her body was primed, her senses were attuned to the heat and scent of his body.

He removed his fingers and she held her breath, waiting for that first hard thrust.

But his fingers touched her lips. "Open your mouth."

She parted her lips and he slipped those slick digits onto her tongue. She tasted the muskiness of her sex and the salt on Dalton's fingers.

His sexy, raspy voice exploded in her ear. "Suck like you were sucking my cock."

Rory hollowed her cheeks. With his fingers all but vacuum-sealed, she sucked hard.

"That's it." Dalton dragged openmouthed kisses down her throat as she sucked and swallowed. "Fucking love that you're a dirty girl. Sucking your come from my fingers. So crazy to fuck me that you drag me into a damn storage closet." He wiggled his fingers free from her mouth and smashed their lips together in a mind-bending, orgasm-inducing kiss.

He broke free long enough to demand, "Jump up and hold on."

One leg up, both legs up and then her thighs were circling his waist.

Dalton pressed her against the cold cement wall with the sheer strength in his body. Holding her ass cheeks in his hands, he tilted her pelvis and plowed in to the hilt.

Her nails dug into his shoulders. Each powerful snap of his hips had her clinging to him more tightly, gasping more loudly.

The only noises coming out of his mouth were grunts and labored breaths. The heat from his chest seeped through her shirt making her wish for better skin on skin contact. Then his hips started the side-to-side grinding motion.

"This'll get you there. Move on me. Take it. I'm so close I won't last much longer."

"Know what'll get me there?"

"What?"

"Whisper dirty things in my ear."

"You like that?" he asked, slamming into her. "When I tell you this hot, wet cunt is sucking on my cock like you do when you deep throat me? My cock is so slippery with your juices they're running down my leg." He let his tongue trace the shell of her ear. "Hottest fucking thing in the world would be to see you on your knees lapping up that sweet juice on the inside of my thigh and then that wicked tongue of yours licking my dick clean."

"Oh God. Faster."

"You'd do that for me, wouldn't you, dirty girl?"

"Yes. Please just..." Rory threw her head back as the throbbing in her groin started, pulsing around Dalton's shaft from her clit rubbing against the hard ridge of his pubic bone.

"Fuck, I'm done." Dalton drove in one last time.

Her tissues were so sensitive, still tingling from her climax, that she felt every hot spurt shooting from his cock.

He shuddered in her arms. This man gave her his all every time, in so many ways.

Dalton leaned back and locked his gaze to hers. "I guess a date playing ping pong is more romantic than I gave it credit for."

Chapter Twenty-Seven

Dalton was finishing his second cup of coffee at seven a.m. when he heard the knock on the door. He half-expected to see Rory standing on the steps. Holding a box of doughnuts and wearing that I-want-to-bang-you smile. But the grin he had in place vanished at seeing Brandt and Tell on the other side of the door.

"What?"

They pushed past him and they faced each other in the entryway. Both his brothers looked like hell.

His gut tightened and he repeated, "What happened?"

"Dad had another stroke sometime last night. And..." Brandt closed his eyes.

And Dalton knew before Tell said, "He didn't make it."

The words hung between them.

Did he feel sad? Guilty? Angry? Relieved?

No. He felt fucking numb. Like this was some sort of trick and they'd go to the rehab hospital and Casper would be sitting there, glaring at them, with his fooled-you-boys-again look on his face. So Dalton didn't say anything, lest he say the wrong thing.

"The hospital called me on my cell about five-thirty this morning when I was out feeding cattle." Brandt scrubbed his hand over his razor-stubble jaw. "They found him in bed and it, ah, appeared he'd died a few hours earlier."

Dead dead dead dead dead, kept echoing in Dalton's brain.

"Brandt caught me right after I finished chores and we thought we'd better tell you in person."

He nodded. *Say something.* "I've got coffee on." He led them into the kitchen and poured two cups. "So what now?"

"We gotta call the uncles. Three of us, three of them."

Dalton didn't want to do that. Why couldn't Brandt do it? He was the oldest.

"I figured we'd talk about who's calling Mom. I guess I'd better call Barbara Jean too."

Silence.

Dead dead dead dead dead.

Stop. It.

"Dalton? Did you say something?"

His head snapped up. "Nope."

Brandt drained his coffee. "Ain't gonna get any easier if we put it off. I'll call Carson, Tell, you call Cal, and Dalton call Charlie." Then Brandt pulled out his cell phone.

"Wait a second. What are we supposed to stay? That Casper is dead and we'll be in touch?" Dalton asked.

"He has a point, Brandt."

"Let them know that's all the information we have for now, we haven't even been to the funeral home yet."

Dead dead dead dead dead.

"I don't have Uncle Charlie's number," Dalton said.

Tell read off the number and Dalton punched it in. Brandt had wandered into the living room, so Dalton headed to his bedroom.

His Uncle Charlie picked up on the fourth ring. "Yeah, who's this?"

"It's Dalton, Uncle Charlie."

A beat passed.

"I apologize for calling so early, but we got word this morning that Casper had another stroke."

"Is he okay?"

"No. He's uh..." *Dead dead dead dead dead.*

"He...passed on?"

"Yep. The hospital called Brandt so we're letting everyone know."

"Ah hell, Dalton, I'm sorry for you boys. I truly am."

Dalton figured he'd better get used to accepting condolences. "Thanks, Uncle Charlie. I'll pass that along to my brothers."

"You do that. So Carson and Cal...?"

"Brandt and Tell are letting them know as we speak."

"Good. Is there anything we can do?"

"Not right now. We'll be in touch soon, okay?"

"Sure. Don't hesitate to call on any of us, if you need us."

"Thank you."

He sat on the edge of the bed. Talk about feeling disjointed. None of it seemed real. And he knew it'd get a lot more surreal in the upcoming days. He needed to be grounded. Almost without conscious thought he called Rory.

Resting his elbows on his knees, he waited for her to pick up.

"Hey, handsome. A phone call from you is a great way to start my day."

Dalton had such a sense of relief just from hearing her voice that a lump clogged his throat.

"I missed you last night. I wish we were kissing each other goodbye at the door right now."

Me too.

His nonresponse tipped her off. "Omigod. What's wrong?"

He cleared his throat. "Casper had a fatal stroke last night."

"Dalton. I'm sorry. When did you hear?"

"Brandt and Tell are here."

"So you're not alone?"

"Nope."

"Oh, baby, I know you're in shock. And I wish I could be there with you—"

"Don't worry about it. You have a ton goin' on at work right now and I'm not sure what all we'll be doin' today anyway. I just needed..."
You.

"I can get an emergency day—"

"I appreciate it, Rory. I don't want you to waste your time when I don't know what'll happen."

"But you will keep in contact with me today? Promise."

"I promise. And, uh, thanks."

"Don't mention it." She paused. "I'm glad you called me."

"You're the first person I thought of."

"Sweetheart. Take care of yourself today until I can come and take care of you later."

"Okay."

Dalton hung up. He looked at the rumpled sheets. He wanted to crawl back in bed and yank the covers over his head. Dealing with this shit was gonna suck.

But he returned to the kitchen to make plans with his brothers.

Four hours later they were in Casper's room at the rehab hospital. No time for grieving as far as the hospital was concerned; they needed the room. They provided boxes and asked if Brandt, Tell and Dalton needed help packing up. But there wasn't much of anything. Some clothes, a Bible, a few notepads, toiletries and the bedding.

After they loaded the stuff in Brandt's truck, they drove to Casper's apartment. At some point Brandt had called Casper's pastor and he agreed to meet them there.

Dalton hadn't ever stepped foot in the place and he really didn't want to be here now. When Brandt and Tell asked his opinion on what should be done with the furnishings, he suggested donating it all to the church. He knew his brothers thought he was being sarcastic, but he wasn't and was forced to explain. Someone needed this stuff a lot more than any of them did, it didn't hold sentimental value and Casper would've preferred that anyway.

Pastor Joneki arrived. He immediately prayed for God to give them strength in their time of grieving.

Then they sat at the kitchen table and the pastor opened a folder. "I have your father's funeral plans here as well as how he'd like his belongings distributed."

Dalton exchanged a look with Brandt and Tell.

Brandt spoke. "When did he make those arrangements?"

"Last year. After he had a mild stroke."

"When did that happen?" Tell demanded. "Because we didn't hear nothin' about it."

"As was Casper's preference. He spent two days in the hospital and was released. As his spiritual counselor I wasn't allowed to divulge that information." He smiled benevolently.

Dalton bit back a nasty question about how much having a spiritual counselor cost Casper each week in the collection plate. But Pastor Joneki didn't look like the conman religious type. An aura of...comfort surrounded him.

"We'd appreciate anything you can tell us now," Brandt said.

"The stroke scared him. From my understanding, his stake in his family ranch had already been dealt with. I've not seen a copy of his will, so I've no idea what that entails."

At least Casper hadn't been able to give his stake to the church because no doubt the man would've done it just to spite his brothers and his sons.

"And so you know I'm on the up and up and didn't in any way coerce Casper into his generosity, he had this list notarized before he brought it to me and then we had it notarized afterward." He smiled again. "It's in everyone's best interests to make sure everything is official. So let's deal with the items he's donating to the church." The pastor set the list in the center of the table and they all leaned closer to look at it.

Bottom line: he'd left everything to the church. So Dalton had gotten his wish in not having to deal with rummaging through his dad's stuff.

Next he'd bequeathed all the cash in his bank accounts to the church.

Tell looked at Brandt. "Any idea how much that is? We talking five hundred bucks? Or half a million?"

"Guess we'll have to talk to the lawyer and see what we're legally allowed to know."

"Like you, I have no idea of the amount of money either. Next, on to the funeral plans. The funeral will be held at Our Lord and Savior Christian church. No visitation. Closed casket. A casket that he's already chosen through the funeral home. Hymns to be chosen at my discretion."

Dalton had the fleeting thought, *Please don't pick "How Great Thou Art".*

"Private burial will be in the McKay family cemetery, next to his firstborn son Luke."

"Did he denote pallbearers?" Brandt asked.

The pastor looked at his notes and frowned. "His three sons and each of his brothers' oldest sons. Six total."

So, the bastard wasn't spiting him from the grave and leaving him off as a pallbearer.

"I know it's only been a few hours, but with so many things already taken care of, have you considered a day for the funeral?"

"Friday," Dalton said. "With all the family livin' here three days is plenty of time." He looked at his brothers. "Unless you want to try and do it Thursday?"

"Friday is fine," Brandt said and Tell nodded.

The pastor stood and they all followed suit. "If you need anything at all, please don't hesitate to call me."

"Thank you, Pastor Joneki, we appreciate it."

"I'll be in touch on Thursday just to make sure we're all on the same page. Are any of you going to speak on your father's behalf?"

Silence.

"No," Brandt said at last. "We'll keep it a simple ceremony."

"I will tell you that the congregation will want to host a light meal directly after the service."

"Why?"

"Casper was very well-liked with the members of the congregation. They'll want to share their condolences with you."

None of Casper's sons knew what to say to that.

The pastor left, and Brandt, Tell and Dalton stared at one another. Tell looked around and rubbed the back of his neck as if spooked by something. "Do you ever get the feeling you're in a parallel universe?"

"Yeah. And on that note, let's get outta here."

Rory showed up at Dalton's house right after work. She didn't mention the half-empty bottle of Laphroaig on the coffee table in his living room. Nor did she mention the fact he stared blankly at the TV that wasn't on. She just crawled into his lap and wrapped herself around him.

Despite him dosing himself with scotch, his body was nowhere near relaxed. She ran her hands through his hair. "Hey."

Dalton came out of his haze enough to say, "Hey," and kiss the top of her head.

She was at a loss for what to say, so she just stayed close. Whether he needed or appreciated her gentle touches wasn't the point; she just wanted him to know she was there.

After a bit he sighed. "Did you want a drink?"

"No." She got in his face. "Maybe I'll just get a little taste from you." She pressed her lips to his. Licking and teasing until his mouth opened and her tongue snuck inside.

Rory moaned softly at the smoky mix of scotch and Dalton. She sought out every taste, keeping the kiss easy.

His hands slid up her back and curled over her shoulders, pulling her closer so they were chest to chest. Then those wonderfully rough-skinned, highly skilled hands were in her hair.

The man had such a thing for her hair.

The kiss didn't catch fire; it stayed on the sweet side, the comforting side. The I-love-you-and-I-don't-know-how-to-help-you side.

Dalton moved his lips to her ear. "I'm glad you're here, Rory."

She angled back to look into his eyes. "Is there anything I can do?"

"I'd ask you to get drunk with me, but I hit it a little hard earlier so I'm done for the night."

"Are you hungry? I could make you something to eat."

He smoothed the strands of hair he'd tangled up. "Come to think of it, I haven't eaten all day."

"Let me fix you a quick sandwich."

"I'd like that." He didn't loosen his hold on her so she waited. "Can you stick around a little longer after that?"

"Of course." She left a lingering kiss on his lips before she retreated to the kitchen.

Her stomach growled so she made an extra grilled cheese sandwich for herself. She heated up a can of tomato soup, found the crackers and set everything on the table.

She draped her arms around his neck from behind and kissed his temple. "Soup's on."

Dalton ate most of the meal. He didn't speak besides to tell her thanks for cooking for him a couple of times.

Rory couldn't remember the last time she'd felt so helpless. But she wouldn't push him to talk even when she wanted to know everything running through his brain. Every weight on his heart.

He stood. "I'm gonna hit the shower." His gaze swept over the stove and returned to her. "Don't even think about doin' them dishes."

"Quit bossing me around and take your shower."

As soon as she heard the water kick on, she loaded the dishwasher and cleaned up the kitchen. She poured him a glass of iced tea and left it on the coffee table next to the scotch.

She didn't have a change of clothes and she'd worn her uniform long enough, so she grabbed a pair of Dalton's athletic shorts, a sleeveless T-shirt and a pair of socks. She was in her bra and panties when he walked into the bedroom, holding a towel around his waist.

A little drool might've slipped out the corner of her mouth. As many times as she'd seen his sculpted body, as many times as she'd had her hands and mouth all over those cut muscles and pressed herself that warm male skin, she should be used to the rolling wave of lust whenever she caught sight of him nude.

But she hoped she'd never get used to it. Never take for granted this sexy hunk of man was with her. And if he had his way, he'd be with her for the long haul. Rory had started to believe that might actually be possible for them.

Then he dropped the towel and that tight round butt was within reach.

Under normal circumstances she'd play grab ass with him. Scrape her nails down his back while her mouth attacked the back of his neck. Or she'd drop to her knees.

Rory did none of those things. "I borrowed some clothes if that's okay."

Dalton spared her a glance. "Anything I have is yours, so no worries." He slipped on a pair of flannel pants—he'd gone commando, no surprise—and a white T-shirt.

The man rocked a plain white tee like no one's business. She could see the muscles in back ripple. The flex of his arms showed off those biceps, triceps and forearms. Not to mention his shoulders seemed nearly as wide as the doorframe.

"While I love how you're lookin' at me, sugarplum, I don't think I'm up to takin' you for a tumble."

She saw he'd been watching her in the mirror. "I was just admiring you." She walked to him and wrapped her arms around his middle, resting her chin on his shoulder. "No pressure to get naked with me. But I won't hide my lustful thoughts from you either."

Dalton lightly brushed his lips over hers, and said, "I love you. It's there. All the time. Like your lust. And I won't hide it from you or anyone else either." He planted a chaste kiss on her forehead and grabbed her hand. "Watch some mindless TV with me?"

"Sure."

In the living room he flipped on the TV and stretched out on the couch. He patted the cushion and she stretched out in front of him so their bodies touched from head to toe.

He wasn't the guy who clicked through channels. He picked a channel and stayed there. Some sitcom was on but Rory had no idea which one and she doubted Dalton would know either.

Talk to me. Please.

Rory felt his lips on her crown. The random kisses and constant caresses were the only sign of normalcy in him. She had no idea how much time had passed and she'd started to drift off when he spoke.

"The funeral is Friday."

Her tongue seemed frozen.

"Will you come with me?" he asked softly.

"Of course."

"Did that just sound like I asked you on a date to my father's funeral?"

"No." Rory rolled over and looked into his eyes, repeating, "No. We're beyond dating anyway." She placed her hand on his heart and snuggled into him.

A moment later he said, "It was seriously fuckin' bizarre today. Even now I can't believe it's happening." He talked in a monotone, detailing the events. She remained still, tucked against him, her thumb sweeping back and forth over his pectoral.

"After the meeting with the pastor at the apartment we went to the funeral home." A shudder worked through him. "Creepy fuckin' place. Since my dad had made arrangements beforehand, it was just some weird formality. Like if there were additional charges who'd pay for them and all that bullshit. I mean, what kind of charges can a dead guy rack up?"

She barely stopped herself from flinching at his flip response.

"So then this mortician asks if we want to see him, since there wouldn't be visitation."

"What'd you say?"

"Brandt turned green like he was gonna pass out. Tell shook his head. But I..." He swallowed hard. "I said yes."

Oh, baby, no.

"Sounds fuckin' horrible, but I had to see him for myself. That he really was dead, not just playin' some big goddamned joke on us, to see if we'd mourn him when he was gone. And how fuckin' pathetic is it that's even a possibility? That he's such a mean bastard he might actually do something like that?" He took a breath and exhaled with frustration. "So I followed the guy back to the viewing room or whatever the fuck it was. And it smelled..." Dalton shuddered again. "I don't even wanna talk about or think about that. Anyway, there he was, on a steel table, just like on TV, with a sheet covering him. Only part of him I could see was his head. And even though I felt like I was gonna throw the fuck up, I got close enough to look at him. Really look at his face. His skin was this pasty gray, but it was him. The only thing I could think of was he carried that goddamned sneer of his into death. So I got the hell outta there. I don't even remember what I said to Brandt and Tell. I just know when they dropped me off the first thing I did was crack open the scotch."

"I think it's good you got a final look at him. You'll never have to wonder."

"Except wonder what the fuck is wrong with me."

"Dalton—"

"I felt nothin' when I looked at him, Rory. Nothin'. Not sadness or anger or even relief. What kind of cold bastard does that make me?"

Her heart was breaking for him but she managed to keep her voice from cracking. "Sweetheart, you're in shock, okay? Give yourself a break. It's only been about twelve hours since you found out."

"So this next stage. Am I supposed to cry?"

Tread lightly. "I think so. Why?"

"What if I don't? Does that make me an unfeeling bastard? Especially when after Luke died and all that shit went down I swore the man would never make me cry again."

"Everyone grieves in a different way. You won't grieve for him like you did your brother. And your brothers won't grieve the same way you do either."

He remained quiet, but tense. The way he rubbed her back fluctuated too between lazy and fast. Then he quit touching her entirely.

"I didn't expect my mom to be upset," he said after a bit. "Brandt called her and he said she started crying so hard he couldn't understand her. I guess Dad's girlfriend had a hard time too. Then she asked if she could sit with the family during the service and how the hell are we supposed to make that decision? My mom was married to him for forty years. By all rights she should get the goddamn sympathy from people, not some do-gooder chick Casper picked up in church. So see? I hear myself say shit like that and I feel like an asshole."

"Dalton. It doesn't make you an asshole if that's how you feel."

"And I really don't wanna talk about this. I don't. Knocking back the scotch did shut off the goddamned voices in my brain. I just wanted to pass out. Wake up hung-over as shit tomorrow because then at least I'd feel something."

Rory placed her fingers over his lips and tilted her head back to look at him.

But his eyes were squeezed shut.

"Maybe we should down that bottle of scotch."

He smiled slightly and her hand fell away.

Then those blue eyes were open, open in so many ways.

"Screw the scotch. I've got you. You're more potent than a barrel of any booze." Dalton pushed her hair behind her ear. "And when I drink you down, you fill me up. You don't leave me feeling empty."

A weird booze analogy but she'd take it. He kept staring at her. "What?"

"I need you."

"I know. That's why I'm here."

"No. That's not what I meant. I need you to take me to the place where it's only us. Where no one else can get in. Where nothin' exists but you and me."

"I can do that. I'd love to do that. But I have to be sure you won't use the fact we made love on the day your dad died as another mark against yourself today."

"I won't."

"Promise?"

"Promise."

She touched his face. Outlining his jaw. The wide-set cheekbones. The pillow of his lips. "Okay." Rory turned her head so his mouth connected with her cheek. She didn't have to say anything, he just seemed to know that she needed the connection of his lips on her skin.

He trailed soft kisses down the side of her jaw, adjusting the angle on the way back up so he was kissing her neck. Then he retreated and his fingers were tugging and twisting her hair. "Bedroom."

They undressed quietly, separately.

Dalton wrapped his arms around her and lowered them onto the bed. He held onto her for the longest time. She wondered what he was thinking about, if he was already regretting this, but she didn't want to break the moment. Then he stretched his body on top of hers. "I love you. So fucking much."

Rory ran her fingers though his hair. "I know. So please let me be what you need."

His stormy blue eyes bored into hers. "You are everything I need."

Then Dalton kissed her so sweetly, with such surety that Rory finally believed him.

Chapter Twenty-Eight

Dalton decided it'd been smart for Aunt Carolyn and Uncle Carson to hold the family get together after the burial at their place. That way he, Brandt and Tell and their families could leave when everything got to be too much.

He was wound as tight as a top. Shocking to see so many people at the service. Although Dalton suspected the funeral attendees were there to support the living and not pay respect to the dead.

He'd kept his hand in Rory's throughout the service. When the pastor went on for ten solid minutes about the good Christian man Casper had become. How he'd turned his life over to serving God. How he'd proven no one is ever too old to change. And the whole time, Dalton's resentment built. His father hadn't apologized or asked for forgiveness from the family he'd wronged over the years. He'd added to his list of horrors he'd inflicted on his sons after getting sober and finding Jesus.

Just when he decided he couldn't sit through another minute, the sermon ended. The final hymn was sung. He did his duty alongside his brothers and cousins as a pallbearer. He suffered through the endless parade of parishioners who expressed condolences and spoke highly of Casper to the point Dalton wondered if he'd somehow ended up at the wrong funeral.

And even when he knew how wrong it was, he couldn't keep the thoughts from taking over his head.

So needing a minute or ten, Dalton practically sprinted outside. He stared across the pasture, wondering what happened now. Knowing the numbness he felt wasn't from the cold.

Rory wouldn't chase him down to chat. His brothers might. But they were busy wrangling kids and talking to various family members.

So color him surprised when he heard footsteps. He turned to see his Uncle Charlie ambling toward him. "So this is where you wandered off to."

"I needed some air."

"Can't say as I blame you. Hard to hold a conversation in there."

"That many people makes me a little on edge...not that I don't appreciate the family's support." Dalton sighed. "Been livin' alone in the woods too long I guess."

"I'd rather have it loud like that than if everyone was sitting around staring at each other not sayin' a word."

"True." He figured his uncle had a specific reason for tracking him down.

"Any word on the elk farm permit?"

"Nope. Rory's got a couple places left to inspect. And just because we're together don't mean she's gonna pick my land for it."

"I don't envy her, havin' to make that decision. Even if you are the best candidate folks around here will believe you were picked because of that relationship."

"Other people's opinions ain't something either of us can control."

"True. So much stuff in our lives is out of our control, ain't it?"

"Yep."

"Look, there's something I hafta say to you."

Dalton's gut tightened. "About?"

"What Casper done to you. And I don't want you getting pissed off at Ben."

Shit. "When did he tell you?"

"A while back. He needed a couple of days to cool off before he brought it up with me. And lemme tell you, I don't know if I've ever seen my even-tempered son that upset."

Dalton said nothing.

"Suppressed rage ain't really something me'n Vi have had to deal with when it comes to our sons, either when they were younger or now. Don't know if that comes from me bein' a lot more laid back than Carson, Cal or Casper. Or if it's just plain dumb luck. Alls I know is if I'd heard a whisper of the beatings my brother doled out to you, I would've dealt with it."

"Which is why I never told anyone."

"Your mom never knew?"

Dalton shook his head. "Casper always knew exactly what to say to get me to fall in line. He said if I told her, he'd turn the strap on her, since it was her fault that I'd become a lazy mama's boy."

"How old were you when it started?"

"Seven. Old enough to take the punishment and old enough to keep quiet about it." He shifted, leaning over the fence—not like he was trying to jump it and get away or anything, but it was damn tempting. "Mom had to go to work around that time, remember? Luke had gotten sick with pneumonia and the hospital bills were bad and we didn't have health insurance. I know Dad got pissed off at Luke like it was his fault. Anyway, with Mom workin' at the nursing home and Luke, Brandt and Tell doin' most of the chores after school, it was just me'n Dad at home. Most the time he yelled at me. Or ignored me. It wasn't like he beat me every week or every month. That'd be too predictable. He liked the element of surprise. His punishment tool of choice was a thin black strap. He never put the marks where anyone could see them."

"Might've been better if he had because then maybe your mom or brothers or someone at school would've seen 'em. Maybe one of us would've seen them." Charlie fiddled with his hat, a sure sign of nerves. "We shouldn't have let you be. None of you boys. No excuses. No matter if we couldn't stand Casper, we should've done more to protect you from him."

"My brothers didn't need protection. And there's no way you could've known. My own mother lived in the house with me for years while it was goin' on and she didn't know. If someone had seen the strap marks, we both know Casper would've said it wasn't your business on how he disciplined his sons and that would've been the end of it."

The silence that followed probably meant Charlie understood but was frustrated by the truth of the long ago situation. Dalton hadn't told him that to alleviate Charlie's guilt—his uncle's guilt wasn't his problem.

"So you've just accepted that your dad beat the shit outta you on a regular basis?" Charlie demanded. "Christ, Dalton, you don't think you somehow deserved it, do you?"

"Back then? He had me convinced I did. Now? I know he was an abusive asshole who got off on a mindfuck. One thing I'll never do is make excuses for him for what he did to me. The past is the past. But I'll be damned if I'll let the memory of that consume me. Ruin me. Ruin my future. Make me into a bitter motherfucker who uses verbal and physical abuse on the people in my life. That means letting this go. I'll never be like him. Never," he repeated hotly. "I've had a lot of years to come to terms with this, Charlie. While I appreciate your concern, I'm dealing with enough shit right now without havin' to revisit this."

"Sorry. It might be old news to you, but it ain't to me."

"Did you tell Uncle Carson and Uncle Cal?"

Charlie shook his head. "Not Vi either. Ben told me in confidence. But I refused to promise him that I wouldn't bring it up with you." He paused. "Or with Casper. And I did talk to Casper about it."

Not what Dalton had expected. "When?"

"Last week. I needed time to cool off too. Even now that he's dead

I don't regret what I said to him."

"Can I ask what you said to him?"

"Just that there'd been lots of times over the years he'd pissed me off. That he'd done shitty things, and selfish things, and stupid things. But all them paled in comparison to him abusing his son. I told him he was the worst kind of coward and I was ashamed of him, more so than I'd ever been in my life. That if I'd known what he'd done to you, I'da taken a strap to him myself. Then I'da turned him over to Carson and Cal who'd take their pound of his damn hide too. Our dad, for all his faults, never whipped us. He might've been a gruff man with a short fuse and had no time to bear fools, but he'd never done nothin' like that to any of us. So what the fuck? Where had Casper picked up that abusive behavior?

"Then I warned him he couldn't blame his actions on booze, because it wasn't the goddamned bottle that'd been hittin' you. I said if he thought what he was doin' to you wasn't wrong, then he wouldn't have hidden it from his wife and his sons and everyone else. I asked him how he intended to explain his actions toward a child—his child—when he stood in judgment before God. That he oughta hope God had a more forgiving heart than me because I'd never forgive him."

Charlie looked at him. "I also said he should've spent more time begging for forgiveness from you than sitting in church pretending to be the good Christian man decent folks would shun if they knew what he'd done. If they knew how black and cold his heart and soul really were they wouldn't welcome him with open arms."

Holy. Shit.

"I know there are some people who'd rip me to pieces for acting that way toward a man who couldn't speak to defend himself, but I stand by my actions. I did it because it was time someone took him to task. So I'm hoping you ain't upset that I was the one who done it."

"I'm...shocked. But I'd never judge you on doin' what you felt you needed to, Uncle Charlie."

"Good. I understand you'd moved on from all that childhood bullshit, Dalton. I knew you'd avoided goin' to the hospital to see him and maybe I'd chalked it up to you bein' a selfish kid who needed to grow up. But I finally saw your avoidance for what it really is. Self-preservation. I admire the hell out of you for bein' the bigger man. For walking away. For not letting him define you."

Good thing Dalton was holding onto the fence or he might've fallen down. "Thank you."

"I don't deserve your thanks for doin' what was right for a change. And even when it was the last time I spoke to my brother, I don't have any regrets about what I said. I just thought you oughta know."

"Thanks."

Charlie clapped him on the back and walked away.

The chill was getting to him. He'd almost reached the house when he saw his brothers, sisters in law and their boys walking down the steps. Carson stood on the porch steps, watching them go.

When he saw Dalton, he motioned him over. "You okay? You've been out here a while."

"Yeah, well wasn't like I was hiding out here so no one would see me cry."

"Don't think anyone's shedding a tear that he's gone." Carson scrubbed his hand over his jaw. "Sweet Jesus. And ain't that a fine thing for me to say about my brother on the day we planted him in the ground."

Dalton kept his eyes on his uncle. "Him bein' dead don't change who he was when he was alive. And I'm more than ready to put this day behind me." *I'm more than ready to put him behind me.*

"Me too. Anything you need?"

His gaze moved to the front door. "Is Rory still inside?"

"I believe so. Want me to get her for you?"

"Nah. But would you tell her I went home and I'll see her tomorrow?"

Carson frowned. "Son, you sure you don't wanna come in and tell her yourself?"

"I'm sure. Tell Aunt Caro, Aunt Kimi and Aunt Vi I said thanks for everything."

"You got it. Night, Dalton. Take care."

"See ya."

Dalton didn't remember much from the drive home. He could barely keep his eyes open. Once inside his house he plugged in his nearly dead cell, stripped and crawled between the sheets.

His mother showed up at his door two hours later.

Dalton wished he would've stayed in bed. But then they'd be having a conversation in his bedroom instead of the living room since she'd just barged in.

"By all means, Ma, come in."

"You left Carson and Carolyn's without saying goodbye."

"I don't think anyone noticed."

"I noticed."

"Is that why you're here? To chew my ass about some post-funeral breach of etiquette? Don't care."

His mother waltzed into his kitchen and opened cupboards until she found what she was looking for.

Booze.

She snagged two plastic cups and pointed to the couch. "Sit.

"Why are you—"

"Son, you had to be expecting this."

And don't you want to know the truth?

No. He'd already come to terms with this.

Dalton sat in the recliner.

His mother perched on the end of the couch closest to him.

And he noticed her hand shook when she dumped scotch in the cups.

Fuck. Why was she nervous?

Yeah, you've really come to terms with this.

He didn't look at her when he picked up his cup. "Who told you?"

"Tell. Don't be mad at him."

"I'm not. We called him Tattle-Tell for a reason growing up."

She barked out a laugh. "I'd forgotten about that."

Dalton sipped his drink. "Was it hard for you today?"

"Harder than I thought it'd be, if you want to know the truth." She lifted her glass. "Some asshole at the senior center asked me if the only reason I was going to the funeral was to make sure my ex was really dead."

"Jesus."

"Yeah, well, like my mother always said, consider the source. Which leads to why I'm here."

"Ma. Don't. Okay? It doesn't matter."

"I'll have my say, Dalton, whether you like it or not. So could you look at me please?"

He counted to ten before he raised his head and met her eyes. Kind eyes. Eyes spilling over with tears.

"After everything I went through with that man over the years. Some of it pretty awful stuff...I didn't think I could hate him any more than I did. I was wrong. After what he told you..."

Don't say it. Please don't say it.

"I almost didn't come here tonight to tell you this. But I want all this shit done and buried now that your father is gone."

Dalton didn't move. He didn't breathe.

"Casper McKay was your father, Dalton. Period. I never cheated on him when we were married. The time in question, when I left him? Unlike your father's claim he didn't know where I'd run off to and I'd shacked up with some guy, I stayed with my aunt and uncle—my elderly aunt and uncle. And you can imagine how miserable that must've been if I returned to my husband after a week."

"Why didn't you want to tell me?"

"Because I think you secretly hoped he wasn't your father. And that hope...changed you." She poured another splash of scotch in their cups. "I'm not excusing what he said to you. But not knowing if he was or wasn't your father allowed you to cut ties with everything that'd always defined you, which you needed. Probably more than you knew. And I understand why you believed him without question. I suspect he'd been laying the groundwork for something like that for years."

Dalton swirled the scotch in his cup. "Did he believe I wasn't his kid? That'd explain the beatings and the ridicule he leveled on me."

"Oh, that bastard knew very well that I never screwed around on him. He never doubted you were his kid, but he made you doubt it and that's where he got that sense of power. After all the shit you'd been through the week you called off the wedding, Casper knew he could say whatever the hell he wanted to you and you wouldn't tell anyone, just like you'd kept quiet on the abuse." She knocked back a slug of scotch. "I confronted him about that, you know."

"No, I didn't know," he said evenly. "When?"

She stared into her cup. "A few months after I started seeing a counselor. She told me I needed to face him head on so I could deal with my guilt and place the blame where it belonged; on him. So I showed up at his church one Sunday morning. Hoo-boy was he shocked to see me. More flustered than I'd ever seen him. He did not want me hanging around chatting up his new churchy friends."

He couldn't even smile.

"I asked him out for coffee. I think he would've agreed to anything to get me out of his little religious sanctuary. In the restaurant I let fly with everything I had. My disgust for him, for everything he'd done to you. And do you wanna know what that sonuvabitch said to me?" Her haunted eyes met her son's. "If I'd been a better mother I would've known. He knew exactly what'd cut me the deepest and he did it without blinking."

"I hope you punched him."

His mom reached out and squeezed his knee. "No, but I did lose my temper. He laughed and claimed you hadn't told anyone about it until you were an adult because then you could exaggerate the past events to make people feel sorry for you and hate him." She squeezed his knee again. "That's when I realized he was afraid people would believe you. Imagine his shock when I told him since he'd spoken so highly of his minister, I intended to ask for his help in learning to find forgiveness."

Now that made Dalton smile. "You didn't."

"I did. He lost his mind and the restaurant manager had to intervene. I left. I let Casper stew on that for a few weeks. Petty thing to do, but it gave me a sense of satisfaction and I was able to overcome a few blocks I had with the situation. I did show up at his church a couple times a year, just to be ornery, just to watch him squirm."

"God, Ma. I love you."

She smiled. "Good to hear. So you might think after Tell told me this last bullshit manipulative lie your father spewed I would've confronted him. But this time I didn't."

"Why not?"

"Because that's what the man wanted and I wouldn't give him the pleasure. You didn't give it to him either. Isn't it pathetic he's been waiting over three years for the fallout to begin? He died disappointed and alone and maybe it makes me a horrible human being to say this, but I can't think of any man who deserves it more."

Dalton watched her chin tremble and he picked up her hand. "But?"

"But as much as I hate him and what he's done, if not for him...I wouldn't have my sons. My wonderful sons. You boys are the light in my life and living proof that genes don't matter. You're all fine examples of good men, and that's a miracle to me because you didn't have that example growing up. You became who you are in spite of your genes and I couldn't be prouder." She sniffled. "And today, I couldn't be sadder that your father died without really knowing any of you. Really sad because that was his choice."

They stayed like that for a while. Not speaking, just holding hands, lost in their own thoughts.

Finally Dalton said, "Were you with Brandt and Tell tonight?"

"For a little while."

"How are they?"

"Surrounded by their wives and kids."

"They're lucky." He shook his head and drained his booze, shoving the glass aside. "Not lucky. They worked to have the lives they've got. I'm happy for them."

"There's room for you in all their lives. In mine too. We missed you, but we're all very glad you're back home." She stood. Wobbled. Laughed and sat back down. "I think I've had a little too much."

"Probably. You oughten be drivin'. Where are you staying

tonight?"

His mom looked confused. "Hadn't really thought about it."

"So crash here. I'd like the company."

Tears swam in her eyes. "I'd like that too."

Dalton picked up the bottle of booze. "But we're putting a lid on the truth serum."

She stretched out on the couch.

"Ma. I don't expect you to sleep on the couch. You can have my bed."

"I'm fine here. I prefer it actually. That way when I can't sleep I'll have more room to pace."

He probably wouldn't sleep much either.

After he'd brought her a pillow and a blanket, she asked, "Did the truth set you free?"

"No. But it hasn't weighed me down, either."

"I can live with that."

He could too.

Jingle barked like crazy and jumped off the bed, growling as she raced to the front door.

Rory sat up and squinted at the clock. Midnight. Sometimes turkey or deer would trip Jingle offline, but the barks were a sharp warning, which meant a person, not an animal was outside the house.

Just as Rory reached for her handgun in the nightstand drawer, Jingle's barks turned into happy yips and she knew her late night caller was Dalton.

He'd left Carson and Carolyn's house without a word to her. As helpless as she'd felt, as much as she'd ached to comfort him, she had no idea how to go about it, so she'd left him alone. The last thing Rory wanted was to intrude on his grief.

She hadn't heard from him yesterday at all.

She remained in bed, listening to his deep voice as he talked to Jingle. The cupboard door squeaked. The man was such a sucker, spoiling the dog with treats. In the small entryway she heard the *thump thump* of Dalton's boots hitting the floor. The faucet turning on and off. The gnawing sound of Jingle attacking her rawhide chew.

Footsteps moved closer, stopping at the edge of the bed. The rustle of clothes being removed. The mattress dipped and that warm, hard male body spooned in behind her, pulling her close.

He sighed.

"You know, you're ruining Jingle's killer instincts. She was ready to tear your leg off to protect me."

"Which is why I rewarded her with a treat for bein' your badass protector when I'm not around." He kissed the back of her head. "Sorry if I woke you. I just..."

"Dalton. It's okay."

After a long while, he said, "I couldn't sleep."

"That's understandable."

"I thought I wanted to be alone."

"Also understandable. I imagine it's been rough."

That's when he pulled away from her. He rolled over and sat on the edge of the bed.

Rory saw him hunched over, his head in his hands. Was Dalton...crying? She pushed to her knees and moved in behind him, pressing her face into the back of his neck and wrapping her arms around him.

But he wasn't crying.

"I don't know how to do this, Rory."

"Do what?"

"Grieve him," he said softly.

Her chest tightened. Her throat constricted.

"I don't know if I can. That makes me a cold goddamn bastard. Even after all the shit he did I never wished for him to die. But now that he's dead and buried, I still don't feel anything. No relief, no remorse, not even a tiny kernel of happiness that I'll never have to deal with him again. Makes me sound fucking heartless. But at least if I was gloating or angry that nothin' ever got resolved between us I'd feel *something*."

She squeezed her eyes shut. Hurting for this man on more levels than she could possibly fathom.

"The worst part is I never held out hope there'd be reconciliation. I wouldn't have believed him if he'd tried to make amends with me. How fucking sad is that?" He shoved his hand through his hair. "That movie mindset is fucking with my head in a bad way. Where there's some kind of deathbed apology, confession, whatever, where all the past issues are resolved, where forgiveness is offered and accepted, where everyone has a good cry and the person who wronged you your whole life drifts off, finally at peace. Real life ain't so tidy. People die and shit doesn't get resolved. And the person who doesn't deserve the peace is the person who's dead. The living are the ones who need it."

Rory tilted her head and wiped her tears on the sleeve of her nightgown. Dalton didn't need her tears. He needed her strength.

He shivered. Then he tried to shake her off. "Sorry. You don't need me showing up at midnight and laying all this bullshit on you."

"Stop apologizing." She tried to tug him back into bed but he wouldn't budge. She tugged harder. "Come here."

"Rory—"

"Get under the covers with me. You're freezing."

"I should go."

"No. You should stay with me. I've missed you." She squeezed him hard. "Please."

After a few beats, he said, "Okay."

Rather than snuggling into him like she usually did, she propped herself up on the pillows and brought his head against her chest.

When Dalton curled into her completely, she briefly squeezed her eyes shut to stem the tears.

She sifted her fingers through his hair. Petting him. Soothing him. Trying to comfort him.

Dalton pressed a soft kiss on the top of her breast. "Thank you." Finally his big body relaxed. His breathing turned slow and steady.

Rory couldn't get to sleep. She'd been tossing and turning before he'd showed up. Wondering how she'd tell him she'd be gone all this week.

What kind of woman left her lover alone to deal with his grief just a few days after he'd buried his father?

She'd debated on postponing the in-person interviews she'd scheduled, but she'd opted to keep the appointments. She'd waited for nine months for these opportunities so no way could she afford to pass them up.

Chapter Twenty-Nine

The call from Tell the following week asking Dalton to come over wasn't posed as a request. Or maybe he'd misunderstood. Seemed he'd been doing that a lot these days.

The weather was crappy. Blowing snow that cut visibility to a few feet out on the road. Took him fifteen minutes longer to reach Tell and Georgia's place than it should have.

He entered the screened entryway and brushed the snow pellets off his outerwear before he hung up his duster. He automatically kicked off his boots. He glanced up to see Georgia standing in front of the glass door that connected the house and the entryway.

She smiled and opened the door, standing back so her baby bump wasn't in the way. "Glad you made it. Looks like it's getting worse."

"It is. I left Sundance forty minutes ago."

"The good news is we've got food, drink and an extra bed if you get stuck here." She playfully pushed him. "Oh, don't look so horrified. Might be fun."

They walked through the kitchen into the living room.

Brandt and Tell sat on opposite ends of the sofa watching TV. "Hey, bro. Come check this out. It's so bad out there we made the national news."

"Uh, yeah, I know. I was just out in it."

"They're advising no travel," Brandt said.

He stared hard at his brothers. "And yet you insisted I haul ass over here right away, in a freakin' blizzard?"

"Yep. Cause we're supposed to get ten more inches," Tell said. "Checkin' cattle is gonna suck. Good thing we've got an extra pair of hands."

Then both Brandt and Tell looked at him.

"Forcing me to do cattle checks with you? Is this your way of makin' me feel included in the family business?"

"Yep." Brandt grinned. "Won't it be fun? All of us bein' snowed in together?"

"You have got to be fucking kidding me."

"Nope. And watch the F-bombs, little bro. Little pitchers have big ears and all that."

"Where are the boys?"

"Watching a DVD in the family room. Jessie's not feelin' well so she's lying down upstairs."

"Jessie is here too?"

"Wouldn't be fun if she and the boys were snowed in at home and I was snowed in here."

Dalton sat on the recliner. "You guys planned this?"

"Not the snow, but we figured we could take advantage of it. Spend time together when none of us can hop in our trucks and drive away."

"Besides, don't you remember when we were kids how much fun it was havin' a couple of snow days?" Tell asked. "We gotta take these opportunities when they come. Who knows if they'll ever come again."

Any anger Dalton might've had about his brothers' manipulation...disappeared. He flopped back in the recliner. "I remember that one snowstorm; I must've been eight or so. Luke taught us how to play poker. Guess we didn't understand that strip poker is something you're supposed to play with girls, not your brothers."

Brandt grinned. "Was that the time you had to run outside in your underwear and make snow angels?"

"Yes and the snow was hip deep. Luke and his stupid effed up games. More like truth or dare than poker." Dalton looked at Tell. "Didn't you have to eat something weird?"

"A raw egg mixed with a can of sardines." Tell shuddered. "Nastiest thing I've ever put in my mouth. It tasted a whole lot worse comin' up two hours later than it did goin' down."

"I didn't know you barfed," Brandt said.

"Like I was gonna confess that," Tell shot back. "Luke would've made me eat another batch because he would've claimed it didn't count."

"No lie. After I lost the final poker hand, he made me do one-handed pushups until I collapsed." A few seconds of silence passed. Then Brandt said, "Why'd we let Luke boss us around like that? He never let anyone else be in charge."

"Because Luke always had the best ideas. And his ideas were usually fun. Plus, he included all of us. He was always like that—from the time Dalton was old enough to toddle along." Tell stared into his coffee cup. "Even when Luke was in his early twenties and out tearing it up with his buddies, he still made time for us."

"Might sound stupid, but Luke was more a father to me than

Casper ever was," Dalton said softly. "I ain't sayin' Luke was perfect, although as time passes I think we tend to overlook the faults of the dead." That wouldn't ever happen with Casper's memory; Dalton could guarantee it. "Along with teaching us all the ranching shit Dad didn't know or wouldn't pass on to us, Luke made sure we had fun. We never would've gone huntin', fishing or camping if not for him."

The conversation had taken a turn toward melancholy and Dalton wondered what Brandt was thinking. Had to be a Catch-22 for him; he wouldn't have the life with Jessie and his kids if Luke was still alive. So when Brandt opened his mouth to speak, Dalton braced himself.

"I reckon Luke would expect us to stick together and take advantage of this time to have some fun." He leaned over and lightly punched Tell in the arm. "Since you're the most fun lovin' of the three of us, and I'm the oldest, I'm makin' that your job. Bein' the ambassador of fun."

"Ambassador." Tell snorted. "I expect you both to salute me from now on."

Dalton and Brandt flipped him off at the same time.

"Nice, guys. Real nice."

Brandt turned off the TV. "Let's get the cattle check done."

They traversed the shitty roads to feed cattle. Luckily the herd was in a pasture between Brandt's and Tell's places, so they didn't have to venture far into the blowing snow and frigid conditions to roll out bales of hay. Since the feed truck would've gotten stuck in the snow banks, they had to fill buckets with cake by hand and then scatter it close to the line of hay.

For as cold as the outside temperature was, by the time they'd finished checking and feeding three hours later, Dalton was soaked with sweat.

Back at Tell's house he showered and called Rory. "Hey, sugarplum, how you doin'? You hunkered down all nice and toasty in your cabin?"

"No. My power went out first thing this morning so I'm at mom and Gavin's. Are you sitting in your living room watching endless hours of Universal Poker Tour?"

"Actually, I'm snowed in at Tell and Georgia's with Brandt and Jessie and all their kids. And dogs."

"Really? How'd that happen?"

"I was suckered into it, but it's all good. Really good. Might sound stupid but now I remember why I liked to hang out with them. Not just because they're my brothers but they're genuinely good guys. I feel like I've got my family back."

"I'm glad."

He stretched out on the air mattress. "Wish you were here."

"Me too. I hope it clears up by tomorrow. I'm scheduled to hit the road for some work stuff."

He frowned. "How come I didn't know that?"

"Sorry. It's a last-minute thing."

That sucked. "How long will you be gone?"

"Four days. Possibly more." Rory sighed. "And I've been warned by the office the cell phone service is spotty at best."

"No cell phone reception in Wyoming? I'm shocked."

"I wanted to warn you if you don't hear from me not to worry that I've been eaten by bears."

"I appreciate you letting me know." He dropped his voice to a growl. "The only one who's allowed to eat you is me."

"Dalton."

"Aurora."

The door swung open and all three of his nephews jumped on him. Whoa. The little buggers could bounce pretty high on an air mattress.

"Uncle Dalton, come on, you promised."

"I gotta go. Please call me while you still have phone service, okay? Wyatt, dude, this is not the WWE."

Rory laughed. "Have fun, you deserve play time."

"I will. Bye." Dalton clicked the phone off and tossed it aside. "All right boys, you asked for it."

But he let them dog pile him anyway.

Later that night, Dalton, Brandt and Tell were sitting at the dining room table, drinking beer and playing dice. Jessie and Georgia were in the den watching an *Iron Chef* marathon, the boys were in bed and the dogs were snoozing by the door.

It seemed like old times, but better than old times.

Brandt said, "You're wearing a goofy grin, Dalton. We ain't playin' poker so that's not your bluffing face."

"I'm just thinkin' this is fun."

"You glad we gotcha snowed in with us?" Tell asked.

"Yeah, I am." The only way it would be better was if Rory was here.

Tell got up from the table.

Dalton looked at Brandt. "Was it something I said?"

"Nah. He probably had to take a leak. We've been hard on the beer tonight."

"No lie. I don't drink like I used to."

"None of us do."

"But we're gonna change that tonight," Tell said, plopping a bottle of booze in the middle of the table along with three lowball glasses.

"Holy shit. That's high-end Redbreast whiskey," Dalton said.

"Yep."

"That's like over a hundred bucks a bottle."

"Figured we deserved a few belts of the best Irish." Tell looked at Dalton. "After all the years you dealt with the worst sort of Irish belts."

Silence.

Then Brandt said, "Jesus, Tell, really?"

"What? Too soon?"

Dalton started laughing.

His brothers looked at him like he'd lost his marbles, so he managed to stop laughing, but his grin stayed in place. "No, Tell, it's not too soon. In fact, this shit has been doggin' me for a long damn time. I'm more than ready to kick it in the ass and give it a final send off."

"Let's crack the seal then and give that motherfucking shit a sendoff we'll all remember." Brandt grinned. "Or maybe we won't remember."

Tell twisted the cap and sniffed the bottle. "Aye, it smells like the peat bogs of me youth. I can almost taste the salty brine of the ocean and see the heather blowing in the meadow breeze, me laddies."

"Dude, that's the best 'frosted Lucky Charms they're magically delicious' impression I've ever heard."

"Fuck off, Dalton."

"Gimme a whiff of that." He waved the bottle under his nose. "Oh yeah, that's the good stuff."

Dalton passed out the glasses. "Pour it, 'cause you gotta let it breathe for little bit."

"How long?"

"Half an hour."

"Bullshite," Brandt growled. "Pour the bloody stuff. And I'm talkin' more than a wee dram, boy-o."

Tell's mouth dropped open. "Brandt is speaking in tongues. It's a miracle."

"Hallelujah and pass the whiskey," Dalton said.

"What about letting it rest?"

Dalton grinned. "Total bull. You still don't know when I'm bluffing, do ya?"

"You suck."

Tell filled the glasses only to the quarter mark. He raised his glass. "To snow days."

They clinked glasses and downed the whiskey.

A sweet, slow burn warmed Dalton from the inside out.

"That is the best stuff I've ever tasted," Brandt said. "Damn. Who knew I had expensive taste?" He nudged his glass over. "Hit me again, barkeep, but this one's a sipper."

"Ditto."

Once their glasses were half-full, Dalton told them about his experience at an Irish bar in London.

After he finished, Tell asked, "Do you plan on traveling anymore?"

"Don't know."

Brandt rested his elbows on the table and looked at Dalton. "Me'n Tell got something to say about that."

"Really? You have to do this now? When we've been havin' such a good time?"

"That's exactly why we need to do it now," Tell said.

Rather than waiting, Brandt launched right into it. "We know why you left and why you stayed away. I'm just sorry we didn't know the why of it when it happened. But that's neither here nor there. Dad was an obstacle to you coming back here and to you sticking around."

Tell sipped his drink, then said, "No need to sugarcoat this. He's gone; obstacle gone."

"But," Brandt inserted, "we know Dad wasn't the only reason you left. We've accepted our role in it, and I speak for both of us when I say we're sorry."

"Really fuckin' sorry," Tell added.

"There ain't nothin' we can do to undo what's been done to you. But we can do a couple of things to change how we handle stuff from here on out."

"Like what?"

"Like making sure Dad doesn't have a voice even though he's dead. He wrecked a lot of things in our lives. You leavin' meant he took that time you were gone away from us too. So he finally accomplished what he'd been tryin' to do for years; he drove a wedge between us. And I say fuck that shit. No more. He don't have that power."

"Amen, brother."

Dalton didn't get where this was headed.

"Bottom line is we want you here, man. With you back it's like it's supposed to be. So we've come up with a plan. 'Course it's a contingency plan, but hear us out."

Brandt said, "With all the crap that's gone down in the last month, we've realized we don't give a shit if you're raising elk or wildebeests or owls as long as you're doin' it here close to us. And if by some miracle your elk integration plan isn't accepted by the state, we'll help you turn that chunk of dirt into another enterprise. Raising buffalo or turtles or unicorns. Whatever you want."

"If that don't work for you, we'll put in that feedlot like we talked about," Tell said. "I've got the updated regs and what we don't understand I thought Rory could help us figure out, since she's fluent in the government's language. But the truth is we'll support you in whatever you decide. We want you to be part of lives, Dalton. A permanent part. That's why we wanted to talk about it now. While—"

"We're a little drunk?" Dalton supplied.

Brandt shook his head. "While we're reminded that we got a responsibility to each other. All three of us. No one gets left behind in this family. No one gets forgotten in this family. Not ever again."

Tell leaned closer. "We just thought you oughta know."

"Thanks, guys. It means a lot." He wouldn't get choked up. Would not.

So it was a belated wake of sorts, for Casper McKay. But they didn't toast him. They didn't curse him. They didn't talk about him much at all.

They let him go.

Rory was updating her latest files in the guest bedroom when her mom knocked once and poked her head in.

"Am I interrupting?"

"No. It's a good time to take a break." She patted the bed and Jingle jumped off. "Come on in."

Her mom waggled two bottles of Mike's Hard Lemonade. "I brought refreshments."

"You're such a bad influence on me, Mom."

"Right. I was a teetotaler until you started bartending. Now look at me. I'm a cocktail connoisseur."

"Sorry, that stuff is low end. Surprised you can drink it after Gavin's spoiled you with expensive hooch." Rory gave her a one-armed hug. "You look great, as always. A little too High Pro glowy—if you get my drift."

Her mother rolled her eyes. "No comment."

"So Gavin rocked your world before he kicked you out of bed and turned on ESPN?"

"I didn't come down here because my husband ditched me. It's late and I came to check on you to see if you fell asleep doing your homework like you used to."

"Ha. Ha. I've got a few hours left. I have to get it all done and turned in by next Friday. I'll lose the rest of this week and the weekend to travel—provided I can actually leave tomorrow."

"Where all are you going?"

"Cody first."

"Is Dalton going with you since he doesn't have a job?"

It was on the tip of her tongue to toss out Dalton didn't have to work—ever—but she refrained. "He has a job. Finishing the house remodel, remember? And he's awaiting my decision on the elk farm."

Her mother swigged from the bottle. "Does he have a better shot than most at you choosing his land?"

"No. I can be completely unbiased when it comes to doing my job." Her personal life when it came to Dalton? Whole different manner.

"Of course you can. That wasn't an accusation."

"Sorry. I'm a little sensitive about that. Part of me fears if I do choose Dalton, people will accuse me of nepotism. And if I don't choose him, he'll think my decision was based on avoiding charges of nepotism."

"As long as you don't regret your decision, it was the right decision at the time." Her mom crossed her legs. "Things going all right between you and Dalton?"

"Yes. Why?"

"Just curious. The last time I saw him was after..."

"He's in a better place. In fact, he's snowed in with his brothers right now. Sounds like they're having a good time."

"Which is great to hear. But I still get the feeling something isn't right."

The boozy lemonade hit her stomach like battery acid and she set the bottle aside. "Everything is right between me and Dalton for a change. He's a better version of the guy I used to be so crazy about. This time it's not bullshit. He doesn't want anything from me...but me. I know he's in love with me, which is why it's so hard for me to keep my distance until I get a few things sorted out."

"What kind of things?"

"Career decisions."

Her mom frowned. "Is that why you're going to Cody? I didn't think that area was part of your district."

"It's not." Rory snatched the bottle and swallowed a mouthful of booze to bolster her courage. "This isn't a WNRC business trip. The office believes I'm taking personal time. Which I am, but not for a vacation. I'll be there for a job interview. Three job interviews in fact. One is in Cody, one is in Sheridan and one is in Missoula."

That startled her mother. "Montana? I didn't know you were looking for work elsewhere."

"Really? Since you've kept mentioning I've been in a funk since I moved back here."

"You were in a funk. And I didn't know it was your job making you so unhappy," she said a little snippily. "It's not like you talk to me about this stuff anymore. There were plenty of other things that happened to you around that time to put you off your game."

She winced. "I'm sorry. Breaking off my engagement with Dillon didn't cause this funk. I've been unhappy with this job from day one. I settle. That's my pattern. I settled for the first guy I met in a new town and I was so eager to end that relationship, I settled for the first job that came along. Dalton coming into my life shook it all up—but for once I didn't make decisions based on anything besides what I wanted. So I've applied for jobs with other organizations. This is my second interview with CESU in Missoula. I'm really excited about that one. I'd get to utilize my degrees and it could chart the course of my career."

"And? Or should I say...but?"

"I haven't told Dalton about any of the job applications. I'll admit I had an ulterior motive at first for keeping it to myself. But after handling this special project, I've regained some of the confidence I lost after feeling unemployable for months." She laughed. "When it rains, it pours, huh? I have three interviews in three days and in the past nine months I couldn't even get one place I applied to call me back."

"I have faith in you in finding the right career path—even if that path leads you away from here." Her mom touched her knee. "I never expected you'd settle in Sundance permanently."

"But?" Rory prompted.

"But what will you do if you don't get any of those positions? They'd be a fool not to hire you. Granted, as your mother I'm a little biased."

Rory shoved aside the papers. "It's hard not to get my hopes up. So the answer is...I don't know." And she couldn't share the other problem dogging her; if she picked Dalton for the permit, he'd be stuck in Sundance another two years.

Problem was, she loved Dalton—not that she'd told him. After everything that'd gone on with his family, Rory didn't see Dalton leaving here. He'd been killing time in Montana, waiting for the right time to return home to Wyoming.

So even if she didn't choose his land for the elk program, he'd find another use for it because he had his brothers' full support. And it would be the ultimate test on whether he'd choose her. Whether he really had changed and meant everything he'd said about them belonging together.

"Rory?"

She glanced at her mom. "Sorry I'm a little spacey."

"It's okay. I want you to do what makes you happy, sweetheart. Wherever that may be and whoever you might be with."

"Meaning...you don't think Dalton—"

"What matters is what you think. But more importantly, it matters what you do." Her mom grabbed the empty bottles and stood. "One thing's for sure, you'll have plenty of time to think about it with all the time you'll spend in the car the next few days."

"Thanks Mom."

"Anytime."

Chapter Thirty

Rory showed up on Dalton's doorstep a week later. Although they'd kept in touch, it'd been two long weeks since she'd seen him.

She knocked on the door.

Dalton opened it and stared at her like she was an apparition. He said, "You're here," and crushed her against his chest. His mouth found hers, and he kissed her with surety and tenderness. With love. With passion. This kiss was perfect. So perfect how he knew exactly what she needed. A girly rush of emotions pushed front and center and she just about blurted out that she loved him when he broke the kiss. Just to be safe, Rory kept her face tucked in his neck.

"I wasn't expecting you."

"I like to keep you on your toes."

"And I like to keep you on your back."

She lightly punched him in the stomach and he laughed.

Then he nuzzled her ear. "I missed you like crazy, Rory."

As much as Rory took comfort in that, her belly fluttered with nerves. "I missed you too, McKay. I just finished up the last of the paperwork for the special project. I thought I'd swing by. So we could talk."

"Is this a coffee conversation? Or a whiskey conversation?"

"Got the makings for an Irish coffee conversation."

"Compromise. I like that about you." Dalton took her hand and pulled out a chair at the breakfast bar. "Sit. I'll start the coffee."

She dropped her satchel on the chair next to her. "Tell me about your day."

"Not much to tell. I spent the day doin' my Cinderella imitation cleaning this place now that all the remodeling is done."

"Looks great. I love that you're comfortable enough in your masculinity that you don't see cleaning as demeaning." She groaned. "Unintentional rhyme, I swear."

Dalton grinned. "Glad to hear it. I worried maybe you'd secretly been penning poetry."

"Dealing with government regulations has sucked every ounce of verbal creativity out of my soul."

"I imagine." He grabbed two coffee mugs. Poured a generous slug of whiskey in each one.

"It smells clean in here. Sometimes I wonder if my house smells like dog." *Way to babble. Maybe you could ask him what product he used that left behind the lemony fresh scent.*

"Not that I've noticed." His gaze pinned hers. "Why you acting so nervous?"

"Because I am. I have something to tell you."

Dalton crossed his arms over his chest. "I'm not gonna like this, am I?"

"Depends."

"So this paperwork you finished up... That means you've made your final decisions on who gets awarded the permits?"

She nodded.

"Is that why you're here?"

"Partially." *Stop stalling.* Rory dug in her satchel and pulled out two pieces of paper.

"What's that?"

"Your future." She placed the identical documents on the counter. "I did all the research on this, but the final decision is up to you." She tapped the closest document. "This one recommends your land for the elk farm permit." Then she tapped the next. "This one denies it."

"I'm confused."

She shoved both papers at him. "You get to choose. Whether you stay here and run it. Or whether you don't. I'll back you on either decision."

He stared at the papers in silence. Then he poured coffee.

"I know it'd mean a lot to you, finally getting to utilize the land you own for something you want. And I wouldn't recommend it if I didn't believe the habitat was more than adequate."

"So why are you givin' me the option?"

"There's something else you need to know first." Rory swallowed a mouthful of coffee. The burn of the whiskey and the hot liquid sent her into a coughing fit.

Dalton was right there, rubbing her back, asking if she was all right, asking how he could help her.

"I'm okay. Maybe some water."

"Be right back."

Maybe his concern was a stupid little thing, but it just reinforced her feelings for him. Dalton McKay was a capable caretaker, something she wouldn't have believed if he hadn't proven it to her time and time again over the past few months. No one had ever believed Dalton capable of taking care of himself, let alone anyone else. The fact he showed her that side of himself meant she had a part of him that no one else did. He didn't only act sweet and loving when he wanted something from her in return.

He handed her the glass of water and watched as she drank. "Better?"

"Much. Thank you."

"Will you please tell me what's goin' on?"

"I haven't been happy in my job, prior to this special assignment. I've been dreading going back to being a part-time lackey."

"I thought you said they might reward you for a good job and move you up the ladder?"

Rory forced herself to maintain eye contact. "That was a lie. I've been applying for jobs with other agencies for months. I never intended on staying in Sundance permanently."

"Why didn't you tell me that?"

"Because you're you. Or I thought you were the same love 'em and leave 'em guy you'd always been. Showing up here after three years and swearing we were meant to be together. I didn't believe it. I didn't trust it. I didn't trust you. I suspected you had an agenda—even before the permit issue arose between us." As much as she wanted to hide her face, she looked him dead in the eye. "I decided I'd hang out with you to cure my loneliness, gorge myself on hot sex with you until I had a great new job and I'd move on."

The strong muscle in his jaw worked but he said nothing.

"But something happened. I fell in love with you. The Dalton I knew now. Not the asshole from years ago, not even the sweet, bossy Dalton I used to antagonize when we played in the woods."

"Rory—"

"Just hear me out. Inasmuch as I realized that assholish side of you didn't exist anymore, I understood I haven't been that wronged girl for a number of years. I may talk tough, may act tough sometimes, but I'm not cruel. I've never been a cruel person and I won't start being that way now—especially to you. You've dealt with enough cruelty in your life, Dalton. You don't deserve that from someone who loves you."

"You really love me?"

"Really. Truly." She fought tears. "Which is why this is so hard."

"Aurora. Love makes everything easier," he said softly.

Such a vulnerability to this man. That just made her love him more. "But I'm not the only one who loves you. Your family loves you and they've got you back. You finally came clean with them about what had kept you away. You just lost your father and you're dealing with some pretty mixed emotions about that. You've stopped running from your problems so it's not fair to ask you to run away with me. Seems like we both have horrible timing with the *run away with me* thing, huh?"

That startled him. "What are you talkin' about?"

"Last week I got offered a permanent fulltime position with Cooperative Ecosystems Studies Unit in Missoula."

"So you're takin' it?"

"Yes."

"For sure."

"For sure. I interviewed there in person last week and they offered me the job on the spot. I also interviewed with the BLM in Cody but didn't make the final cut because they were looking for someone with more experience. Anyway, I gave notice at WNRC. Next week is my last week." She stared into those compelling blue eyes. "So I'm leaving Sundance. But I don't want this to end. I'm asking you to come with me to Missoula."

Stunned silence.

"I want to be with you. But I realize the timing for this couldn't possibly come at a worse time for you."

"Rory, that doesn't—"

She put her fingers over his mouth. "Don't. Even if you're convinced you've made up your mind and know what you want, I'm asking you to take a little time and really think it through. Talk to your brothers. Talk to your mom. Make a rational decision, not an emotional one."

Dalton was so shocked or deep in thought that he couldn't speak.

Rory shouldered her satchel and walked out.

She made it to her Jeep before she heard the screen door slam. She whirled around and Dalton was in her face.

"Don't make an emotional decision?" he demanded, crowding her against her car. "That's the only kind of decision that's worth anything." He snapped the paper in her face. Then he crumpled it into a ball and threw it over his shoulder. "Deny me the elk farm permit. The only reason I applied for it is because I thought you'd be livin' here and I'd need something to do."

"What?"

"I wasn't completely honest with you. I don't have a burning desire to raise elk. I saw an opportunity, a reason to stay in Sundance. Yes, I have family here and I've dealt with some issues that will keep my brothers and their families part of my life. But Rory, I was here for you. I stayed for you. If you're not here, there's no reason for me to stay."

She blinked at him. Maybe the inability to speak was contagious because she couldn't make her lips move.

"I love you. I thought I lost you once and that's never happening again. Never. I don't even need five seconds to make a decision. You go, I go. We belong together. Not just while you're killin' time waiting for a killer job, or I'm killin' time hoping to heaven that you'll fall in love with me. We are forever." Dalton curled his hands around her face. "So yes, I'll run away with you to Missoula. But when we go, you'll be wearing my ring."

"Are you asking me to marry you?"

"No. I'm telling you that we *will* be married. I'm willing to wait until you're settled in your new job, but I want you as my wife, Rory. I want everyone to know that you're mine. That we're building a life together."

Over the past few months when Dalton looked at her a certain way, or placed a kiss below her ear, or ran his finger down the inside of her arm, she sensed his satisfaction. His possession. She'd chalked it up to sex. Now she saw it for what it really was. Love that went beyond anything she'd ever thought any man could feel for her, let alone this man who owned her heart, body and soul.

It was past time she let him know she felt the same.

She ran her hands through his hair. "I love you."

He quit breathing entirely. Then he said, "Say it again."

"I love you." Before she could repeat it for a third time, because she knew that's what he'd ask for, his mouth was on hers. Not consuming her with a fierce kiss, but leveling her with tenderness and gratitude. And hope. There was so much hope in him, in this kiss, that her eyes grew wet.

The kiss went on and on. Gentle and hot, packed with the type of sweet need that caused her to cling to him tighter.

When he finally released her mouth, he murmured, "You really mean it?"

"Yes, I do. I love you, McKay."

"This is the best day of my life. Right now, in this moment with you."

"Mine too."

314

Epilogue

Six months later

"Do you, Dalton Patrick McKay, take Aurora Rose Wetzler to be your lawfully wedded wife? To have and to hold, for better or for worse, for richer, for poorer, in sickness and in health, to love and to cherish, from this day forward, until death do you part?"

Dalton froze.

This was it. The next step would tie him to this woman permanently and the judge's final words would pronounce them husband and wife.

Dalton McKay, husband.

That sounded...perfect. Really fucking perfect actually.

"I do." He lifted Rory's hand to his mouth for a kiss. "I do, I do, I do. I cannot wait for this woman to be my wife."

"You sorta went off-script," Rory whispered.

"I'm an off-script kinda guy."

The judge cleared his throat. "May I continue?"

"Ah, yeah, sure, go for it."

"Do you, Aurora Rose Wetzler, take Dalton Patrick McKay to be your lawfully wedded husband? To have and to hold, for better or for worse, for richer, for poorer, in sickness and in health, to love and to cherish, from this day forward, until death do you part?"

"I do."

They exchanged rings.

Then the judge said the magic words. "By the power vested in me by the State of Wyoming, I now pronounce you husband and wife. Kiss your bride. Kiss your groom. This union is official."

Dalton curled his hands around her face, the beautiful face of this woman whose eyes were shining with love for him. "I love you." He kissed her with sweetness and devotion. And he had to laugh softly when he finally pulled back. "Sugarplum lip gloss. Nice touch."

Loud clapping behind them echoed through the trees.

They turned together and faced their family.

Hugs and claps on the back and even more hugs were exchanged.

Then everyone backed off, giving them time alone.

They'd kept the ceremony for immediate family only. His brothers had stood up for him. Rory's mom and Sierra had stood up for her.

Now they stood before each other, husband and wife, in the exact same place where they'd met for the first time.

"What are you thinking about?" she asked.

"Us. How perfect this is. But also in all those years we hung out here and all the games we played, we never once played house." He kissed her again. "Why?"

"Because playing house isn't a game for us. It's for real. For keeps."

And she swore she didn't have a romantic streak. The fact she'd insisted they get married here and she carried a bouquet of plum blossoms and her lip gloss spoke volumes to him.

"I recognize that look, McKay. You were thinking of a way to get me up onto that rock just so you could push me off."

"No way. It wouldn't be the same because the six-year-old Rory I remember wouldn't be caught dead wearing a princess dress. She would've jumped into the creek before I could shove her off, just to save face."

She grinned at him. "You're right."

"But you look spectacular." The white satin dress clung to her every curve from the waist down. From the waist up it was all fancy beading, lace and poufy stuff. Rory had let her hair hang loose rather than putting it up, knowing the second Dalton got her alone, all the pins would come out and he'd take it down anyway.

"Thank you. You look pretty spectacular yourself."

He'd chosen a western-cut black suit with a plaid vest and no tie. Not once during the brief ceremony had he felt like he was choking.

"Sweetheart," Rielle said to Rory, "Gavin and I are heading up to the house to make sure everything is set for the party."

Rory kissed her mom's cheeks. "Go on. We'll be up in a minute." As soon as her mother was out of earshot, Rory murmured, "I cannot believe she's hosting the wedding reception at her house. I know it's just a family reception, but that means all those McKays. And all their kids."

"Hey, you're one of them too now, Mrs. McKay."

Tell and Georgia's little girl, Carly, started to fuss. As Dalton's first niece she was the official flower girl even when she didn't do anything but look cute as a button in her beribboned dress. Tucker had done better than expected as ring bearer, but he'd lit out for the creek with Landon, Wyatt and Jackson as soon as possible.

Brandt and Jessie's baby girl, Bethany, let out a loud wail.

"I think we'll grab the kids and head up to the house too," Brandt said and yelled for the boys.

Dalton's mom gave him another hug. "I'll ride up with the judge."

"Well I'm not staying here by myself to watch the newlyweds suck face," Sierra announced. Yanking up the skirt of her bridesmaid's dress, she whistled for Jingle and shouted, "Hey Dad, wait up."

And then they were alone.

Dalton faced Rory with a grin. "You know, we could..."

"Absolutely not, Dalton McKay. I am not having sex with you on that rock... Omigod please, stop doing that. Right now. Seriously..."

"In a minute," he murmured against her throat.

Rory grabbed a handful of his hair and yanked so they were looking at each other. "Save it for the honeymoon."

"You mean tonight, right? And not waiting to have my wicked way with my wife until we're in Spain?" Having Rory to himself for two weeks in Europe was gonna be some fun.

"Of course I mean tonight. You do have a room reserved for us someplace?"

"Don't need reservations in the great outdoors."

"You are *not* expecting me to spend my freakin' wedding night in a sleeping bag out in the woods, are you?"

He laughed. "Nope. You get enough of the great outdoors in your job." Their transition to living together in a new state, as a couple, had gone much smoother than they'd imagined. They'd bought a house, a small fixer-upper to give him something to do. He'd found a logging company that needed part-time seasonal help and he planned to serve as a hunting guide in the fall for Boden. But for the most part, he was content being in their home, taking care of Rory, supporting her in the career she loved.

She swept his hair from his forehead. "I love you. Promise me we won't get separated for too long at the reception?"

"I promise." Then he kissed her. The kiss caught fire, like it always did between them. His mouth wandered, as did his hands. He'd just about had her talked into a quickie, when he heard motors gunning behind them and a series of annoying beeps.

Dalton stepped in front of Rory so she could straighten the top of her dress.

Kyler pulled into view in a side by side ATV that'd been decorated with white streamers and graffiti and had tin cans tied to the back end. A big sign said, *Just Hitched.*

More loud beeps sounded and he saw Sierra riding another ATV.

She pulled in behind Kyler.

"Please tell me she's not wearing her bridesmaid's dress on that muddy ATV."

Sierra waved at them with the bottle of champagne and yelled, "Wahoo! We started the party without you, suckas."

"And...she's drinking."

Dalton laughed.

Kyler bounded over. "Your wedding party got back to the house and realized they hadn't left you a way to get back." He tossed Dalton the keys and pointed to the ATV. "Your chariot awaits."

"Thanks Ky. Could you—"

"Drive Sierra back to the house? I'd planned on it." He propped his hands on his hips. "Not sure an open bar was the best choice for the reception. Anyway, I'll keep an eye on her tonight."

"Thanks, I appreciate it," Rory said.

"Don't mention it. Seriously. Don't say nothin' to my parents." He frowned. "If they think I'm havin' any kind of fun they'll make me stay with the little kids."

Kyler looked at Sierra when she honked the horn ten times in a row and yelled, "Come *on*, little cuz. Time's a wastin' to get wasted!"

Kyler looked back at Dalton and Rory and grinned. "Hey, someone's gotta teach me how to be a wild McKay now that the last single man's been married off."

They watched as he climbed in the driver's seat. At the top of the hill he spun the tires and threw mud everywhere as Sierra loudly egged him on.

"You know, this is really starting to seem like an episode of *My Big Fat Redneck Wedding*," Rory said.

Dalton laughed. "Then I guess that makes me...your Redneck Romeo, huh, jungle girl?" He swooped her into his arms and carried her to the four-wheeler, the happiest man in the world.

About the Author

Lorelei James is the *New York Times* and *USA TODAY* bestselling author of contemporary erotic western romances set in the modern day Wild West and also contemporary erotic romances. Lorelei's books have been nominated for and won the *RT Book Reviews* Reviewer's Choice Award as well as the CAPA Award. Lorelei lives in western South Dakota with her family...and a whole closet full of cowgirl boots.

Connect with Lorelei James:

on Facebook: www.facebook.com/LoreleiJamesAuthor

on Twitter: @loreleijames

email: lorelei@loreleijames.com

website: www.loreleijames.com

It's all about the story...

Romance

HORROR

www.samhainpublishing.com

CPSIA information can be obtained at www.ICGtesting.com
Printed in the USA
LVOW07s2330250414

383252LV00001B/100/P